Books by

STAR FORCE SERIES
Swarm
Extinction
Rebellion
Conquest
Battle Station
Empire
Annihilation
Storm Assault
The Dead Sun
Outcast

IMPERIUM SERIES
Mech Zero: The Dominant
Mech 1: The Parent
Mech 2: The Savant
Mech 3: The Empress
Five By Five (Mech Novella)

OTHER SF BOOKS
Technomancer
The Bone Triangle
Z-World
Velocity

Visit BVLarson.com for more information.

Tech World

(Undying Mercenaries #3)

by

B. V. Larson

UNDYING MERCENARIES

Copyright © 2014 by the author.

This book is a work of fiction. Names, characters, places and incidents are either products of the author's imagination or used fictitiously. Any resemblance to actual events, locales or persons, living or dead, is entirely coincidental. All rights reserved. No part of this publication can be reproduced or transmitted in any form or by any means, without permission in writing from the author.

ISBN-13: 978-1500756291
ISBN-10: 1500756296
BISAC: Fiction / Science Fiction / Military

Definitions from the only Hegemony-approved civics textbook:

The Galactic Empire – The greatest governmental system ever conceived. The Empire encompasses sixty-one percent of the star systems in our Milky Way Galaxy and lays valid claim to the rest. The Empire is an achievement all civilized species admire and it has persisted for many millennia. Every man, woman and child on Earth is proud to be a member of this immense society.

The Core Systems – At the center of our Galaxy is a supermassive black hole. Orbiting this dense mass are the oldest of suns, clusters of stars in close proximity. Known as the Core Systems, all the elder races rose to power in this brilliantly lit region of space.

The Galactics – The Core Systems are inhabited by an unknown number of superior species known as "Galactics." Ancient and wise, these benevolent beings guide thousands of lesser civilizations in unimportant star systems. One of these minor civilizations developed upon *Earth* and calls itself *Humanity*.

Earth's Government – Humanity's modern government is called *Hegemony*, with Sector, District and Local sub-governments. Earth is managed locally by a political collective.

Independent nations no longer exist on our world—and as everyone knows, that is a very good thing.

Earth's Monetary System – Due to Imperial benevolence, every world in the Empire is self-governing. Only interstellar interactions are Imperially governed—as they should be! Earth's monetary system was established to promote commerce. Two-tiers of credit units exist: Hegemony credits and Galactic credits. Hegemony credits are valid for any interaction between humans in our star systems, while Galactic credits are valued for trade anywhere within the Empire. Typical exchange rates place the value of a single Galactic credit at well over a thousand Hegemony credits. Galactic credits are required to purchase alien-made trade goods.

The Nairbs – The Nairbs are alien bureaucrats who serve the Galactics with unswerving loyalty. Their bulbous bodies are deceptive; there's no escape from their relentless pursuit of justice.

All potential wrong-doers are hereby forewarned: The faithful Nairbs exercise the will of the distant Galactics with zealotry. For them, no ruling is too unjust, no technicality too arcane. They prosecute the smallest infractions, following the letter of every law precisely as it was written.

Frontier 921 – Our star system drifts within the boundaries of Frontier 921, an outlying province. It's an unimportant backwater of the Empire located in the Orion Spur of the Perseus Arm of the Milky Way Galaxy. Despite our insignificance, Humanity must strive to serve our betters with enthusiasm.

Battle Fleet 921 – Our local Battle Fleet is perhaps the most amazing of the many gifts our beloved Empire has bestowed upon us. Consisting of a thousand vast ships, the fleet has only visited Earth once—to our good fortune. On that thrilling day in the year 2051, the fleet silvered our skies as they do any planet they visit.

Provincial Battle Fleets are normally tasked with delivering ultimatums of annexation to newly discovered civilizations—or charged with punishing those that fail to obey the Galactics. Both missions are necessary tasks to maintain order and expand the rule of law. Battle Fleet 921 possesses the weaponry to reduce any world in the province to ash, but to obedient beings, it represents a comforting, protective strength.

Recent Addendum: Unfortunately, Battle Fleet 921 has been recalled to the Core Systems to help resolve unspecified disturbances.

Humanity's Faithful Service – As a level-two civilization within the glorious Empire, we've recently been awarded the title of "Local Enforcers" and tasked with maintaining order inside the borders of Frontier 921. The local Battle Fleet may no longer be available to support our efforts, but we will soldier on determinedly!

Earth's Legions – Maintaining a century-old tradition, Earth's spacefaring legions still march to the stars serving the highest bidder.

Legion Varus – The most notorious of all Earth's legions, Varus is often maligned by the press and the rest of our military. It's unknown exactly what purpose they serve, but it is understood that they perform missions no other legion would care to undertake.

"I love honor more than I fear death."
– Julius Caesar, 51 BC

-1-

I was born on Earth, a craptastic planet in the middle of Frontier 921. We were about as far from the Core Systems at the center of our galaxy as you could get—and therefore we were about as unimportant as a civilization could be within the Galactic Empire.

When Galactics visited us—which they rarely did—they invariably complained about how cold and dark it was out here along the Perseus Arm. Our solitary sun was dim and dull to them as they were creatures accustomed to the nearness of a thousand ancient stars. As far as they were concerned, we lived in a desert, lightyears from the next stellar source of heat and life.

I didn't care what the Galactics thought about Earth. It was my home, and I loved her. The Imperial types always made a point of sneering at our relative poverty and pathetic tech as well, but that didn't bother me. Throughout my short lifespan, my family and I had been carving out a low-wage living on our backwater world. It was only over the last year or so that we'd gathered enough hard-won credits to begin enjoying ourselves. From my point of view, things were looking up.

My parents had managed to get real jobs again and new hope. As soon as they could manage it they took their scraped-together fortune and left Atlanta. They moved to the Georgia countryside, down around Waycross. They couldn't afford much land but managed to find a free-standing place with a few overgrown acres around it. The house was more than a century old, and the scrubland looked like no one had farmed or even trimmed it for nearly that long.

What surprised me the most was the structure itself which was built with actual *wood*. I didn't believe it until I went down into the basement and ran my hands over the bare splintery stuff myself.

The best part of moving out of the city and into the sticks was that I got my own room out of the deal. It wasn't a bedroom—not exactly. It was more like a free-standing shed which had been converted into a living space at some point in the distant past.

It wasn't a palace, mind you. Curling, faded, polymer strips were tacked to the walls as decorations and the floorboards creaked enough to wake the dead—but I really liked it. I moved in and made myself right at home.

Now, don't get me wrong. I'm not a freeloading bandit. I'd chipped in plenty of my own cash, and my folks were glad to have me staying on with them. Like most enlisted legionnaires I didn't want to be bothered with permanent housing on Earth. So far, I'd been deployed something like nine months out of every year on average, and when I was left dirt-side by the legion for an extended shore leave with one-third pay, I didn't have the credits or the gumption to set up a permanent residence of my own.

I knew that at any time the legion might muster out again and take me to the stars to work a new contract. We legionnaires never knew how long we had with our feet on the ground, so we didn't bother to play house unless we had a family—and as of yet, I didn't.

So, in late spring I lived with my folks and whiled away my free time. For me, vid games were now a thing of the past. I'd been spoiled by real life, real beer, and real women. Games couldn't hold my attention like they used to.

In June, I became obsessed with constructing an unlicensed floater in my room. When the damn thing worked right, the floater was a lot of fun. It wasn't much, just a surfboard with a simple gravity-repelling unit attached. The secondhand repeller had about a three hundred kilo lift-rating which was enough to get me almost a half-meter up off the ground. Repeller units were easy to come by these days as Earth had credits, and alien traders now visited our planet with regularity. They no longer treated us like third-rate losers. In the eyes of the traders, we'd risen to the status of first-class hicks.

I hugely enjoyed cruising around the back lot on my floater, taking it out over the local Satilla River with a drink in one hand and a steering wire in the other. It was fun, and the summer passed quickly.

Now and then I was even lucky enough to coax a few lady-friends into accompanying me back to my tiny shack. They always crossed my threshold diffidently, like housecats that suspected you were taking them to the vet. After a couple of strong drinks and a ride or two on my makeshift floater, they usually spent the night.

After three months of wasting time and money, I had to admit I was becoming a little bored. It was August, and anyone who's spent much time in Georgia can tell you that hanging around in a converted garage in the last days of summer can get to be a little extreme.

I'd gotten into the habit of leaving the cooling unit blowing at night, but it had begun overheating and throwing breakers. I didn't want to waste credits on a new one as it might be years before I'd use it again after this shore leave was over. Left with nothing better than a whirring fan, I made the best of it. I kept the windows open, the lights dim, and the fan aimed so it blew directly on my sweating skin. It was comfortable enough once you got used to it.

One Thursday night in August, a tapping sound began as someone rapped on my door. I was dozing, and it must have been around midnight. I startled awake, spilling fresh beer on my heavily stained carpet.

"Shit," I muttered, hauling myself up. I shook my head and padded on bare feet to the door. I automatically assumed it was my mom, coming out to ask me something that could easily wait until morning—like whether or not I thought we needed more milk for breakfast.

Lifting a hand to the door, I paused. I could see through my half-assed window screens, and I noted with surprise that the tiny light over my parent's backdoor was out. That wasn't surprising in and of itself as lights in the country attracted more bugs than anything else. But if it *was* my mom on the other side of my door, tapping insistently, wouldn't she have flipped on her porch light to guide her on her way across the yard?

Frowning, I put my hand on the rattling, worn-out doorknob—yeah, my shed had real, honest-to-god doorknobs, they must have been a century or more old—but I hesitated.

The tapping sound repeated itself. I considered ignoring it.

Tap, tap, tap.

I shrugged and threw open the door. In the same sudden motion I flicked on the light. I don't know who I'd expected to see standing outside, but I was surprised it was Natasha.

"Hi," she said, looking nervous. She tried to smile, but it flickered out.

I'm not very good when I'm surprised. I don't have an automatic, happy-time grin on my face when the unexpected happens. Maybe that's because I've been killed a lot, I don't know. The Legion psychs gave us a course on that kind of stuff before every deployment, droning on about the long-term effects of our chosen occupation—but I'd never listened to any of it.

Natasha took in the blank look on my face and my lack of a greeting and reacted in the worst possible way. Her smile vanished, and she did a U-turn.

"Sorry," she snapped, "I shouldn't have crashed your party."

Head held high, she marched away into the dark. She took about three quick steps back toward the main road. I could see the dark hulk of her car out there, skids-down on the pavement.

"Hey, come back!" I called, half laughing. "You surprised me, that's all."

She looked over her shoulder, and paused. "You've got someone in there, don't you?"

"Nope. Not even that damned tomcat that keeps coming around."

7

Frowning slightly, she came back to my door and craned her neck to look past me.

"It's awfully dark in there. Don't you have any lights?"

"The cooler is broken," I said. "Lights make heat—and besides, I was just falling asleep."

She looked into my eyes again. "Maybe I should come back in the morning."

I reached out and touched her arm. I didn't *grab* her, I just rested my hand on her elbow.

Beckoning with my other hand, I gestured toward my couch. "Come on in."

Natasha stood still, but her eyes were running over me and everything else. I was a mess, and so was my place. I'm the kind of guy who shoves everything into the closet when a girl comes over, but I hadn't expected one tonight.

I let go of her arm, heaved a deep breath and walked to my crappy little box-fridge. I'd gotten it from a Legion surplus shop for cheap. I grabbed out a beer and cracked it open. I didn't even bother to look at Natasha. Maybe it was the heat or the time of night, but I was done feeding this park squirrel peanuts. She could come in or go.

She finally came in. I handed her a fresh brew, and found her a place on my couch to sit down. The first thing she did was notice my floater which I was using for a coffee table.

"There aren't any legs on your table," she said.

"Yeah. Cool, isn't it?"

"You spent money on repellers just to build a *table*?"

I laughed. "No. It's a vehicle. I fly it everywhere. It's great fun. If you're around tomorrow, I'll give you a ride to the lake."

Natasha gave me a reproachful glance at the mention of her being around in the morning, but I pretended not to notice. She and I had had a thing going for years now. We'd never been in a really tight relationship, but we'd enjoyed a number of fine nights.

"You're place smells a little moldy," she commented.

"Sorry. Hey, you want to tell me why you came all the way out here to see me?"

"I wanted to know how you're going to vote."

I frowned, having no idea what she was talking about. "I'm not much into politics. Is there a District election I should know about?"

She laughed. I liked her best when she laughed. Her face lost all caution and worries during those few seconds, and that made me smile.

"I'm talking about the Legion vote," she said. "You must have made your decision by now."

"Uh…"

"You're kidding me!" she exclaimed, setting aside her beer. "You turned off your tapper again, didn't you? What if they summon us to the Hall?"

I lifted my arm so she could see the tapper embedded there. I poked at it, and it came reluctantly to life, making my skin glow with organic subcutaneous molecular shifts.

"I did some mods," I admitted. "You're the tech. Check it out."

I showed her my custom settings. I'd blocked out all non-critical spam from the Legion—and from everyone else.

"That's against regulations," she complained.

"It's *my* shore leave," I said. "You techs should appreciate that. If the Legion really wants me, they can get me with a priority message. In the meantime, anything non-critical gets dumped."

Natasha shook her head and made clucking noises with her tongue as she tapped at my arm.

"Hey," I complained, "don't mess up my settings."

"I didn't touch your settings," she said. "I just brought up today's report. Check it out, top of the list."

I sighed and grumbled as I scrolled around with my index finger on the inside of my forearm. I tapped at a legion-wide announcement and read what it said aloud. "Friday night, eight pm, is the deadline for voting. As a Specialist, you're allowed two votes as per Legion bylaws. If you've abdicated your—"

I frowned and stopped reading. I looked at Natasha. "What the hell are we voting on?"

"To join Hegemony," she said in exasperation.

"All of us?"

9

"Yeah," she said. "All of us. All the Legions have been given the option. We can either stay independent, or we can sign on with Earth's Central Command."

"What brought this on?"

She laughed, but this time I thought her laugh was tinged with bitterness. "If I had to guess, I'd say *you* brought it on, James McGill. You talked the Nairbs into making us Enforcers, remember?"

"Yeah sure," I said. "But what's that got to do with folding Legion Varus into Hegemony?"

She shrugged. "I guess as Enforcers Earth has a new source of credits, a new service we provide to the Empire. We don't all have to play mercenaries to the stars anymore. And Hegemony expects to be called upon to do some 'enforcing' at some point by the Nairbs or maybe even by the Core Systems. Hegemony needs experienced troops."

"Experienced troops..." I echoed. "That's us. The independent legions. There's no one else who's been out there."

"Exactly."

I thought about the situation for a time. The more I thought about it, the less happy I was. I didn't want to join up with Hegemony. Those guys were self-important pukes.

"What if we say no?" I asked her.

"I don't know," she admitted. "No one does. They might disband us. Or they might hire us and send us out anyway. No one really knows how this is all going to go down."

"One thing's for sure," I said, beginning to work my tapper. "Earth isn't getting all these credits from the Galactics for us to sit on our hands. They'll want us to do something soon."

Natasha nodded then frowned as I kept working my tapper steadily. She scooted her butt over the couch to see what I was doing, and I let her.

I'd gone into my settings first and done a full reset. When it booted back up, I tapped in a message and selected the send-all option. It questioned my sanity, and I confirmed the choice—twice. I hit the final acknowledgement before she could stop me.

10

Her tapper beeped, and she opened the message I'd just sent to her—and everyone else in the legion. Her jaw sagged.

"You're crazy," she whispered. "You can't do that. You can't spam the entire legion at midnight!"

"I just did."

Natasha read my message on her own arm while I downed the rest of my beer and got out two new ones. When I returned to the couch, she waved me away at first, but after a few seconds of reading, she took the second beer and guzzled it.

She shook her head and laughed. Then she began reading the note again, out loud this time. "'As one of only two individuals in this legion who was personally involved in negotiating Earth's new status, I urge my fellow Legionnaires to reject Hegemony's offer. Let's stay independent and free rather than chained up by sanctimonious dirt-siders who think they know the stars better than we do. Specialist James McGill, Legion Varus.'"

"It's just one man's opinion," I said, shrugging.

Natasha laughed again and drank. I joined her.

"I didn't have to come all the way down here to know your answer, did I?" she asked. "All I had to do was think about you, and I would've known how you were voting."

Somehow, my arm had snaked its way around her shoulders. She sat up close to me, and I could feel her warmth. Usually, I avoided warmth of any kind in August—but this was different.

"You're going to get into trouble," she said.

I scoffed. "What are they going to do? Kill me?"

It was a favorite joke of all Legionnaires, and it never failed to garner a bitter chuckle from our fellows. We often died in the field, but we almost always were returned to life. That sounded great—until after you went through the agony and helpless terror of dying a few times.

Natasha and I ended up making love on that grungy couch. We fell asleep immediately afterward. Outside, the katydids buzzed and the fireflies floated on warm humid air between mossy trees.

11

-2-

The Georgia dawn pinked the skies several hours later. I was startled awake when a fist hammered on my shack's door, rattling the windows.

Natasha and I were entangled. We separated and stood up. Natasha grabbed a shirt and pressed it over her bare breasts. It wasn't smart cloth, so it didn't cover her very well.

"Who's there?" I said gruffly, stepping to the door. Automatically, I stood to one side. Natasha hadn't moved or said anything, she was just watching me.

"Open up, McGill. Military Police."

Frowning, I threw open the door. Natasha pulled more clothes on quickly, but I stood there in boxers, uncaring.

Outside, there were three men. The two in front were beefy—one well-built and the other one with a gut that overflowed his belt buckle. In the rear was a thin man with only a few wisps of curly hair around his balding head. He had eyes like a possum.

It was the thin man in the back who spoke up first.

"What kind of a shithole is this, McGill?" he asked me. His eyes cruised around my humble home. "We were led to believe you were a specialist, but I'm seeing an inbred knuckle-dragger in a stinking shack. I'll have to report back that we visited the wrong damned man."

I nodded to him. "That's right," I said. "You came to the wrong house." I began to swing the door closed into their faces.

A hand shot out and stopped it.

"You're under arrest, funny man," the fat one said.

I took a second to take in their uniforms and ranks. They were Hegemony. The patches on their shoulders depicting blue-green globes told me that. Judging by their other insignia the front two were regulars—probably reservists called up for active duty. Since Earth had been announced as an Enforcement branch for the Empire, Hegemony had panicked and mobilized every reservist they had.

The thin guy in back was older and wore a specialist's markings. They were all security detail—MPs.

"Arrest?" I asked. "What's the charge?"

"You'll be briefed at the station in Atlanta," the thin specialist snapped. "Come with us—wait, who's that with you?"

"A friend," I said, glancing back at Natasha. She still hadn't spoken.

All three men leered for a moment at Natasha. This annoyed me. Her legs were bare and my tee-shirt didn't cover everything else.

It was the first thing in the morning, and I hadn't been arrested for months—especially without good cause and paperwork. The situation struck me as wrong, somehow.

"This is about the message I sent last night, isn't it?" I asked. "Who signed the arrest order?"

"Are you coming willingly, or are you coming in manacles?"

"I'm not Hegemony," I told them. "I'm Varus. We're independent. Send some MPs from my Legion, and I'll go wherever they take me."

"I think you fail to grasp the situation," the leader said, shaking his head with mock sadness. "This is a priority arrest, and I have my orders."

"Screw your orders," I said, becoming angry. "They're illegal. You don't have any jurisdiction here. Get District cops or my own MPs. You can't come here and demand I submit to arrest without any authority to back you up."

The skinny guy finally stopped ogling Natasha and glared at me.

13

"You off-world types always think you're hot shit, don't you?" he asked. "Well, all that's over with now. It's time you became accustomed to new masters. Gentlemen, arrest this—"

I slammed my door in their faces and threw my shoulder into it. I'm a large man, easily larger and stronger than any of these dirt-siders—but there were three of them. The door bucked against my shoulder and daylight flashed through the crack a moment later. I heard cursing, and one of them shoved a truncheon through the opening.

"What the hell are you doing?" Natasha hissed at me.

"Climb out one of the back windows. I don't like this, and I'm not letting these jokers arrest you too."

"You're holding them off for me?" she asked, surprised.

The door bucked harder than ever, and I was jostled backward. I almost lost my stance, but managed to get myself set again. The truncheon sticking into my shed crackled with energy. The bastard holding it had switched it on.

I looked at Natasha. "Go on, will you?"

She shook her head and stood behind the door. "You're going to need a witness."

I growled in frustration. Timing my next move with their next shove, I threw the door open again. The fat guy fell onto his face at my feet, and his sidekick staggered in surprise. The thin leader in the back was breathing hard and baring his teeth. They hadn't been in a great mood at the start, and now they were truly pissed.

I took a step or two backward, and they rushed me.

Forever afterward, I'll never be sure why I decided to resist them. I guess it's because I knew they were in the wrong and abusing their authority. Sometimes that happened with cops of any kind. I understood they didn't have easy jobs, but these guys had rubbed me the wrong way. I wasn't thinking anymore at this point, I was reacting. Violently.

There's something different in the way a starman faces a fight after he's died a dozen times—or a hundred. It starts with an odd expression Legionnaires call the "dead man's stare." Maybe the look comes to legionnaires because we've been gifted with an unnatural knowledge of death. I've had many

14

bitter experiences that should've been forbidden to the living, but which to a man like me had become almost familiar.

"Don't do it, James!" Natasha said, reading my state of mind accurately. "I'll be fine."

I didn't even look at her. I didn't really hear her, either. My eyes were wide with the shining whites revealed all around. My face was otherwise strangely blank—only my staring orbs revealed the intensity of my mood.

Now, don't get me wrong—I was pissed. But it was a different kind of pissed. I was in a cold state, with full certainty of mind. I had a confidence in battle that these others couldn't possess.

The fat guy climbed to his feet and stepped forward, his face sweating and his eyes blazing. He lifted his truncheon, and it sizzled with energy. One touch would numb a limb and daze the mind, but I ignored the weapon, concentrating instead on the man who held it.

The start of the fight wasn't fair, not really. But then fighting isn't usually about fairness—not to my kind, the brethren of the walking dead.

As fat-boy took his first steps in my direction with his sizzling shock-stick in hand, my foot snapped out kicking the floater I used as a coffee table. Gliding through the air with great force, the floater caught the MP in the side of the knee—a bad spot. There was a double-crack, and he went down on his face, keening.

"Crazy redneck!" he moaned from the floor.

The second guy at least looked like he worked out. I stepped to meet him as he dropped his truncheon and reached to his belt to drag his sidearm free.

A gun—that raised the stakes. I knew they might well kill me now, but I hardly cared at that moment. If I killed just one of them, that man was going to endure his first death with all the associated terror and pain. As Hegemony men, the MPs had been copied and stored the same as I was, but their first death experience would linger with them for the rest of their lives. To me, a death was like a bad day in the dentist's chair. Nothing to look forward to, but hardly life-changing. The way I looked at it, as long as I killed at least one of them, I'd won this fight.

15

"Shit, James, *shit!*" Natasha said. But she joined the fight when she saw the guy reaching for his gun. She stepped to the thin Specialist and kicked the guy while he lingered in the doorway. She missed his balls, but nailed his narrow gut.

The specialist reached for her and the two struggled. She tried to trip him and almost managed it. I had to admire her pluck. She was a Tech Specialist, not really a line combatant. He finally straight-armed her, and she flew right into my toolbox which crashed to the floor.

Her attack hadn't been spectacular, but she'd managed to briefly distract them. The muscular goon glanced back to see what was going on with the group's commander, and I took the opportunity to arm myself.

Another behavioral trait that's often shared by men like myself was a tendency to hide weapons around our residences. We typically collected guns, knives—just about anything that could be used to perform a violent act. I've read that people who've experienced starvation are forever afterward fascinated by food and tended to hoard it. I was like them in my own way.

I reached into the couch cushions and drew a machete from underneath them.

When I'd bought that blade, I'd told myself it was to chop down the brush on my parents' back lot—but part of me had known better. I'd bought it and never used it until this very day. I'd oiled it and slid it under the couch cushions—but I'd never swung it at a bush or anything else.

The muscular man's hand didn't come off, but it was missing two fingers about a half-second later. It's hard to handle a gun with a thumb and two fingers—just try it sometime. He lost his grip on the weapon and it clattered to the floor.

I scooped it up and straightened. The thin man at the door finally had his weapon out and held it with shaking hands. He still stood in the doorway framed by the pink light of dawn.

"This has gone far enough, McGill!" he shouted. "There's no reason for any of this bullshit. Drop that gun and come in with us."

"There are plenty of reasons for this," I said calmly.

16

I held the gun, but didn't level it at the man in doorway. He had the drop on me after all, and I didn't want to take the first bullet.

Instead, I held the gun out to my side. Crawling at my feet was the man with the missing fingers. He'd picked the digits up and was trying to wrap them in a tissue he'd pulled out of his pocket. I could have told him it wasn't worth the effort.

The man with the broken knee seemed to be in the most pain. He had gone white from shock and slid himself over to lean back against my box-shaped fridge. His breathing came in hitches and gasps, but at least he wasn't screeching anymore.

"Put the gun down, Specialist," the man standing in my doorway said. "This is insane. You're under arrest, and you'll come with us, dead or alive."

"You had no warrant," I said. "You had no cause. You came in kicking and pushing. You can't treat a Legion man like that. Don't they treat you hogs anything?"

"Hogs" was an especially rude term some Legionnaires applied to Hegemony people. The man's face purpled slightly. I would have thought he was too freaked out to care much about insults—but I would have thought wrong.

"All right," he said, anger taking over again. "We're supposed to bring you in alive. That's a firm order. But no one said anything about her."

He turned his gun on Natasha, who glared and winced away.

The second the thin man's gun was off me, I shot the man with the bad knee—the guy whose was resting against my fridge. I'd chosen him first because the gun in my hand was aimed in his direction to start with.

I aimed low—mostly because I didn't want to wreck my fridge. His chest popped red, and he sagged down in surprise. I was annoyed to see the shot had gone right through him and ruined my fridge after all. Damn.

The man in the doorway forgot about Natasha and swung his weapon back in my direction. That was a good move, because my gun was swinging toward him.

We both fired and staggered back. He fell out into the yard and lay there coughing. He might pull through, but I hoped not.

I was on my back now, and I knew from experience I'd been hurt bad. When you're bleeding out, it's a funny feeling— by funny, I mean a *sick* feeling. Your vision really does go black, strobing in and out with your heartbeat, dimming more each beat.

The man with two missing fingers got to his knees and loomed over me staring into my face.

"Why the hell did you do this?" he demanded.

"You ask yourself that," I wheezed, "when the revival machine is crapping you out in about an hour. Maybe you'll figure it out then."

Then I shot him in the head, and we both died.

There are a few funny things that people have to understand about revival machines and how they operate in order to understand what happened later that same hot Friday in Georgia. Our bodies are only backed up occasionally, starting with the day you're recruited. When you're brought back to life, you usually came back as you were on the day your cells were copied—at least physically.

There are exceptions to this however. If you needed corrective surgery of some kind or if you improved your physique with exercise and training, you might back up your body's cellular scans afterward to ensure you returned to life later in the best possible condition.

The mind of a Legionnaire is recorded separately. It's done with incremental backups, transcribing only the changes to our neural nets. This process is done far more regularly so that we can remember our training and life events. Usually, our tappers do the job of transcription. If they're within range of a transceiver relay unit, they'll upload the data concerning our neural networks quite often, every minute or so. That's how we can recall the circumstances of our own deaths.

The only living witness to the debacle that had occurred in my little shack was Tech Specialist Natasha Elkin. She knew me, and I thought sometimes she might even love me a little. Whatever her true feelings were, she covered for me that morning.

Natasha was a tech and a good one. She hacked all three of the dead Hegemony pricks' tappers, dumping their last uploads. The exact circumstances of their deaths were therefore recorded in her mind and restored in mine, but the Hegemony pukes had forgotten the dramatic finish. They knew they'd come to my place. They knew they'd pushed their way in and argued. But they had no idea how they'd died, or who had been at fault.

When an alien machine in downtown Atlanta gave birth to me once again, there was already a Hegemony squad waiting on site to arrest me. Fortunately, I wasn't taken by surprise. Stumbling and naked, I had just long enough to read a private message from Natasha on my tapper before they hauled me away to a holding cell.

"Stay cool, stay dumb, no memories," her message read.

I swiped my numb fingers over the text, and the words erased themselves, lost in the mysteries of the net. I allowed myself a small smile.

Playing dumb comes easily to me—some say it's my only natural skill. The Hegemony MPs held me, and they grilled me, but they eventually gave up.

As far as they could determine, I didn't remember a damned thing. At least, no more than the other three dead men did. Only Natasha's story of three amateur-hour MPs pawing her and abusing her boyfriend was left behind to fill in the gaps. The memory loss was blamed on bad net service in the region—a believable enough excuse. Even I could testify to that much of the cover-story.

By the end of a very long day, I had a uniform issued to me and I was told Natasha had driven up from Waycross to pick me up. There were mumbled curses from the Hegemony people at the Atlanta Station as I was discharged from custody. I accepted their irritable behavior magnanimously and left in high spirits.

Natasha and I left the building as soon as we could get away. But at the exit door—which was powered, barred, and crisscrossed with wired glass—we were met by three familiar faces. I drew myself up and stiffened, but they held their hands high, palms out, in an apologetic gesture.

20

"Look, McGill…" began the skinny, balding Specialist. For the first time, I noticed his name was Turner. I hadn't bothered to read his name badge while he was assaulting me in my home.

"Look," he repeated, "I'm—we're all here to say we're sorry. For what that's worth. We don't know what went wrong at your place. But I think we can all agree that we've paid a price for it—whatever happened."

I stood stock-still, enjoying their discomfit for several seconds.

"I can accept your apology, Turner," I said finally. I turned to Natasha. "As to pressing charges, only Natasha here knows what really happened to her. She was assaulted as I understand it."

Natasha locked eyes with me for a second then turned to the three men in question. She drew in a breath and spoke. "I hope you gentlemen understand we're *all* legionnaires. We shouldn't let our petty rivalries pull us apart. We all serve the same world in the end."

"Yes, ma'am," said the fat guy eagerly. "We're really sorry for…for anything we did."

"You paid a horrid price," she said, looking at each of them with pity in her eyes. "You all died screaming. Turner, you even shit yourself at the end."

Turner's eyes narrowed making him look even less pleasant than usual. The other two fidgeted with their hats.

"Under the circumstances, I won't press charges," Natasha said finally.

They were all visibly relieved.

"Thank you, ma'am," fat boy said. "And for the record, I don't understand how this all could have gotten so out of—"

Natasha put up a hand, and they stopped talking instantly. "Try to control yourselves in the future," she advised, and we pressed past them.

I held my laughter until we reached her car. Natasha started up the car with a thrum and we glided through the city. My belly hurt I laughed so hard. I finally noticed she wasn't in as good of a mood as I was.

"Hey," I said, looking around. "Shouldn't we hit the auto-road? It's a faster way out of town."

"We aren't leaving town," she told me. "Official orders have come in—orders from Varus. You and I are to report to the local Chapter House."

"Great."

I tapped at my tapper, and my amusement died completely. Whoever had ordered my arrest had given up on having the local Hogs do it. They'd contacted my superiors this time. I was indeed ordered to report immediately to the Atlanta Chapter House.

For each of Earth's Legions, there were both Mustering Halls and Chapter Houses dirt-side. The rest of our organization existed up in space, usually in the form of a large ship that served to transport troops to their assigned worlds.

Mustering Halls were big buildings constructed in the largest cities, usually one Hall per Sector. They handled recruitment and operated as ready-stations for off-world missions. The major difference between a Mustering Hall and a Chapter House was in scale and scope. Chapter Houses were local sales outlets—a few veterans were posted there performing local recruitment for a single legion. The Mustering Halls were much bigger and were shared facilities used by all the legions.

I'd only been to the Atlanta Chapter House twice. Once was when I'd been thinking about joining up. The second time was to file my change of address info when I'd moved to Waycross. It was a dingy little place, and I wasn't looking forward to my third visit.

My legion's Chapter House wasn't much to look at. From the outside, it could have been a shoe store or one of those places that sells secondhand electronic goods from off-world. There was a row of similar Chapter Houses repping various legions. There were about fifteen in all that recruited locally and served the retired membership. Apparently a lot of my brothers and sisters came from the southern states, and this office functioned as a hub for them.

Natasha and I had suited up by the time we arrived. Smart clothing is great that way. You can dress in your car if you want to. All you have to do is wrap the cloth over yourself and wriggle a bit to let it worm its way around your butt and behind your back.

"What's our story?" Natasha asked me as she parked.

I eyed her worriedly. I felt confident I could bullshit my way past anything that was asked of us, but Natasha was a straight-shooter. She'd done all right against the Hogs as she didn't respect them, but with real Legion Varus people I knew it would be different for her. She liked telling the truth and doing as she was told when legit authority was involved. She'd helped me out back home and taken things way out on a limb. But I didn't trust her here. She'd crack under real pressure from one of our direct commanders.

"Uh...story?" I asked. "We've already got it down. Some goons came to the door, there was a struggle when they didn't identify themselves, and things went badly. Don't change even the slightest detail."

She looked worried, and she put a hand on the car door. The panel recognized her touch, flashed a colored light and the lock clicked open.

"Hey," I said, reaching over and giving her a kiss on the cheek. "Don't worry. We'll be fine."

"You murdered three men who someone sent to arrest you, James," she said with a tight look on her face.

"Yeah, well...they deserved it."

"I agree, but what if Graves is in that building? What if he's a little smarter than that Hog team? He'll *know* what happened. He knows us. He knows *you*."

"Graves won't give a shit if I got into it with a few Hogs."

Natasha sighed and rolled her eyes at me briefly. I got that sort of response often, especially from women.

She climbed out, adjusted her uniform so it fit properly, and straightened her spine. I did the same, placing my beret on my head and tilting it at an appropriate angle. The smart uniforms worked to transform themselves into a crisp arrangement by crawling over our bodies.

I led the way to the door, pushed it open, and stepped inside. At the front desk I got my first surprise. I recognized the man who sat there. He was a rat-faced guy with close-cropped hair that glistened with additives. His name was Winslade and he was Primus Turov's chief weasel.

Winslade had his feet on the desk. I looked at him, and he smiled back with sharp white teeth.

"Hey McGill," he said. "Nice of you to show up. You're wanted in back."

He directed me with a casual stabbing of his thumb over his shoulder.

"Adjunct Winslade?" I asked. "What's going on, sir?"

"You'll find out. There's only one closed door in the back. Go see who's waiting inside."

Winslade gave me a shitty grin. I passed him by, walking as coolly as possible. I wanted to maintain a solid front for Natasha's sake. She'd been rattled the minute we arrived in the parking lot, and there wasn't any point in giving her a weak vibe now.

As we passed his desk, Winslade's skinny arm shot out blocking Natasha's path. I felt like cracking him one, but I had to let it go.

"Not you, sweetie," he said. "You can wait out here and keep me company."

Walking to the door, I pushed it open and stepped inside. In the dim interior I met none other than Primus Galina Turov herself.

I should have expected this after seeing Adjunct Winslade out front, but somehow I hadn't figured it out. The Primus *never* came down to the sticks. She was a rare enough sight at the Mustering Hall up in Newark—but down here at the Chapter House? No way.

She took in my surprise with relish. I don't mean she was happy to see me, not by a long shot. Her joy was derived from my obvious dismay.

"Six months of leave and you've already forgotten how to salute?" Turov asked.

I jumped to attention and gave her a crisp salute. She didn't deserve it, but rules were rules.

Turov and I had never seen eye to eye. She was a small, shapely woman who was older than she looked and a whole lot

24

meaner. She'd been born a rule-stickler while I'd been born a rule-breaker. I figured we were destined never to get along.

She made a point of toying with her tablet before addressing me. I stood there, staring at the wall behind her head, waiting.

Finally, she set the tablet aside and leaned back in her chair.

"I suppose you're wondering why I've ordered you to come here. Correct?"

"No sir," I said.

A frown flickered over her features. She paused, but finally had to ask. "You *expected* to find me here?"

"No sir. I meant that I'm wondering who sent those three Hogs—excuse me, Hegemony officials—to my door this morning."

"Ah, that," she said, nodding. "I sent them."

For the first time since I'd entered the tiny, dim-lit office, I met her eyes directly. She'd gotten my full attention.

"Hegemony troops? On the eve of a critical vote concerning our independence? Can I ask *why*, sir?"

Turov smiled and steepled her fingers. Her nails were blood red, but cut short. "Because you are who you are, James. I was depending on that. Thank you for the assist. Now, if you would kindly get the hell out of my office and onto the lifter waiting at the Atlanta Spaceport, we can all move on with our lives."

I was confused. I'd expected a good reaming at the very least. But here she was, all smiles. Why had she bothered to come down here in the first place? Just to gloat about something? It seemed like she thought she'd won some kind of victory, but I was baffled as to what the prize was.

Then the implications of her new orders sank in.

"Sir?" I asked in confusion. "Did you say there's a lifter at the spaceport?"

"Yes. Get on it. Legion Varus is mustering out—immediately."

I hesitated. While I watched, she stood up and turned around. She removed a beret and jacket from the rack behind the desk. She put them on slowly, almost languidly.

As she turned away to gather her things, my eyes roved over her. I have to admit, although I was a young guy who usually didn't stare at women over thirty, I'd always kept Turov on my radar. She liked to wear her uniforms at the tightest, most form-fitting setting. Maybe even a notch tighter than that if the truth were to be told.

She turned back around and smiled. It was as if she'd put on a little show, and she'd known how it would affect me.

"Admiring my new patch I see?" she said. "Or maybe the suns caught your eye?"

My eyes flew wide. I'd been staring at her butt, naturally. Now that she mentioned it, however, she *did* have two gold suns on her collar and the wrong legion patch adhered to her shoulder.

Among the officer ranks, suns were the top insignia that could be achieved. Once you got to suns, it was just a matter of how many you had. I realized that Turov was no longer a Primus. She'd moved up two ranks, to the level of an Imperator. She could command her own legion now if she was assigned one. Or even multiple legions.

The promotion wasn't the biggest shocker for me, though. Her legion patch was what got me the most. Where the Wolfshead of Legion Varus should have been riding proudly on her shoulder there was now a blue-green globe.

I opened my mouth, but no sound came out for a second. When I managed to speak at last, I spoke rudely. "You bugged out? You joined Hegemony?"

"That's hardly an appropriate expression of congratulations," she snapped.

"Sorry sir."

"I've moved up in rank. There can only be one Tribune in Legion Varus, and that job is taken by Drusus. The council decided not to give me the legion, but rather to move me into Hegemony."

"I understand, sir," I said.

And I did understand. She'd been bucking for rank from the very first moment I'd met her, and now she'd finally gotten it. I'm a slow country boy sometimes, but today the light was going on inside my thick, dark skull.

I recalled all the times she and Winslade had made a huge production of filming the aftermath of battle. I'd also heard she wasn't above doctoring reports to make it seem as if every victory was due to her leadership. She wasn't the kind who liked to fight or even command in a battle—in fact I don't think I'd ever seen her fire a weapon or man a line in combat.

"Well, Specialist?" Turov asked, gesturing toward the door.

"One more question, sir?"

She nodded.

"I understand you got rank and I congratulate you, but what's happening to Varus? We're supposed to vote on our independence tonight, and—"

"About that," she said, walking to the door and opening it. "I know you're not the type to take good advice, but I'm going to give it to you anyway. Vote to disband Varus. Don't stand against what must be. Independent legions are a thing of the past. They're unwelcome anachronisms. Maybe you'll be allowed to keep your patches and unit names, but you'll soon be melded into Hegemony no matter how you vote today. I believe the plan is to assign each legion a number with the names becoming nicknames rather than official designations."

I was horrified. I had no interest in becoming a Hog from the 199th, or whatever they assigned us.

"I don't think that's such a good idea—" I began.

Sudden anger tightened her face. "McGill, you've had your warning, and you've had your explanations. Now, get the hell out."

She stood to one side, holding open the door. I saluted and marched past her into the hallway. She didn't bother to return the salute. Instead, she slammed the door so fast it almost hit me in the ass.

I walked down the passage trying to look on the bright side of things. At least Primus Turov—*Imperator* Turov, that is—was out of my hair. I should be celebrating. But somehow, things didn't feel quite right.

True to his word, Winslade was out in the lobby chatting up Natasha. She wore a polite but bored look on her face. Winslade didn't seem to have noticed. He was disappointed when I showed up.

"We've been ordered to muster out," I told Natasha. "Can you drive me to the spaceport?"

"Sure," she said, but she looked as confused as I'd been a few minutes earlier.

In the meantime, Winslade had stopped chattering and was now looking smug. He pulled a jacket out from behind his desk.

"Secret's out," he said. "I guess I can show you this."

There was a globe patch on his jacket shoulder.

"You too, huh?" I asked. I sneered. I couldn't help it. "True loyalty is a damned rare commodity, I guess."

Winslade's expression transformed in an instant. He hunched forward and showed me his teeth.

"You'll switch tonight if you're smart, McGill. Don't even participate in the vote. That's a ruse. The fix is in. If you vote the wrong way, you'll lose rank and be transferred to Hegemony in the end, anyway."

Natasha eyed him in concern. I sniffed.

"Thanks for the tip, Hog," I said, heading for the door.

"I'd kick your ass for that if you weren't mustering out," he called after me.

"Sure thing, sir."

-4-

Natasha followed me out to the parking lot, and we climbed into her car. She was freaked out, and frankly, so was I.

"What kind of crap have you gotten me into now, James?" she demanded.

"Don't worry, babe—" I began.

"*No!* Don't even go there. I don't want to hear any sweet-sounding talk about how everything's going to be fine. Turov—I always knew she was cast-iron bitch and that she hated you. But something serious is up, and I'm worried."

"Yeah," I said, making a forward spinning motion with one finger.

She caught the meaning of my gesture and started the car. We lifted up and glided out onto the road.

The conversation lagged as we both fell to brooding. I watched the streets whiz by out my passenger window. There were signs of Earth's newfound wealth everywhere. Atlanta's roads had all been dilapidated a year or two back. Now the weeds had been replaced with sapling trees, and the old crumbling asphalt had been paved over with puff-crete. I looked down, marveling at the alien building material. Puff-crete was colorful compared to plain concrete. The new road that slid under us was shot through with hints of pink and blue. Puff-crete was almost indestructible, and the stuff had been used all over the planet to give old roads one last, permanent pave-over. I knew the disintegrating roads of the past were hidden underneath that thin veneer. Here and there you could

29

see dark patches of old asphalt like rotten teeth glimpsed in the back of a mouth full of crowns.

"You think we have time to go back to your place and get your personals?" Natasha asked me.

I tapped at my arm. After a moment, I shook my head.

"No," I said. "Forget about my stuff—and yours. I'm checking the new deployment orders on my tapper right now. They've gone out to everyone. We're to leave Earth immediately by any means possible."

Realizing shore leave had come to an abrupt end, a flood of new thoughts occurred to me. I wasn't going to have time to say any goodbyes or even to lock up my place properly. I could only imagine what my parents were going through. I'd been killed on their property, and my body had been hauled away with the rest. I hoped my mom hadn't seen it—not even with a sheet pulled over my face. The sight would freak her out for life, I was sure of that.

I tapped a message to my folks letting them know I was fine, and that I'd been ordered to deploy. I grimaced when I sent that one. I'd said nothing about being killed, and that seemed like a pretty big omission even to me. My parents would figure I was in some kind of trouble and bullshitting about being deployed. The sad thing was they might be right.

We were going off-world. We were being mustered and deployed all at once, pronto. That wasn't the usual way these things happened. Normally, unless there was some kind of emergency, legionnaires were given a summons with a few weeks to comply. Once we made it to the Mustering Hall we were generally briefed, sometimes tested or trained, and only then sent into space. This time the process had been accelerated. I felt like we were moving much too fast.

Suddenly, Natasha pulled over. "You drive," she said. "I want to work my tapper."

I realized that fine brain of hers had been quietly churning. I switched places with her, and I was happy to be driving through downtown traffic. It gave me something to do besides think about Turov and her plans.

Natasha worked her tapper like a demon. Tech specialists were given better tapper units than the rest of us grunts—way better than civilians could buy. In addition to her tapper, she had various auxiliary devices in her kit to enhance her abilities. Fortunately, she'd brought them all in her car like a good legionnaire. Staying prepared was standard procedure for active duty personnel. We were supposed to carry around our basic kits. But in my case, as a weaponeer who specialized in big guns, I hadn't been allowed to take anything dirt-side other than my uniform.

She worked in relative silence. As an ex-hacker I knew she needed to focus if she was going to dig up anything that we didn't already know.

"The vote—I think this is all about the vote," she said a few minutes later.

"Yeah?" I asked. "Why would Turov care so much about the damned vote? She and that little ass-kisser Winslade spent the last hour telling me that it doesn't matter. We're all going to end up in Hegemony according to them, no matter what."

"Here's what I have from our official orders," Natasha said. Her voice had changed and become officious. She liked to line up her ducks before she knocked them down. "Tribune Drusus has ordered us all to muster out tonight and catch any transport we can to space. We'll gather aboard *Minotaur* tonight. Anyone who takes more than twenty-four hours to reach the ship will be left behind and disciplined."

We'd lost our old transport, *Corvus*, at Dust World. The legion had since arranged for a new ship named *Minotaur* to transport us. I hadn't gotten to see it yet, but it was rumored to be an improvement.

"Anyone who can't make it up in twenty-four is going to be flogged, eh?" I said. " Harsh. I know some guys are out climbing mountains and such-like."

Discipline generally didn't take the form of an actual flogging, but that technically *could* happen in the legions.

"I know," Natasha said. "We're going to leave some people behind, and they're on the forums screaming because they already know their screwed. But anyway, the interesting stuff on the boards and chat lines concerns tonight's vote. There's a new posting since your recommendation that they vote NO, and there are a ton of views on each side."

"A new posting? What's that about?"

Natasha tapped at it, and then hissed between her teeth. "I'm not going to show you this because you're driving—but there are pictures, James. Pictures attached to your name."

I huffed. "Pictures? What, did my latest gallery of selfies get out?"

"No. They're pictures of the men you killed."

That changed my grin into a frown. "Read the damned post."

"You sure?"

"Read it, girl."

She took in a breath and began reading. "'James McGill, Weapons Specialist, 3rd Unit. Three Hegemony MPs were dispatched to arrest Specialist McGill in the early morning hours today. He was found in a rundown shack in the countryside of Georgia District, North America Sector. Reportedly, he was met at the door armed with a large cutting instrument of some kind. Going berserk, McGill killed the three arresting officers but died in the process. The investigation is pending, and no reason was given for the arrest order. Drugs or other illicit behavior was hinted at by the officer who reported the incident.'"

As she read this aloud, I found myself hunkering over the steering wheel and gripping it more tightly with every word she spoke.

"That is one hundred percent horseshit," I told her. "Let me guess who released that message. Winslade, right?"

"Anon signature. But it does rank him as an Adjunct."

"Right, of course," I said. "I should have snapped his skinny arm when I had the chance—"

"James," Natasha said, putting a hand on me. "You need to calm down. I know how you feel, but this mess isn't the kind you can punch your way out of."

"Okay," I said. "Okay, right—but he's such a little rat-bastard."

"I know. Let's try to think. I'm piecing this together now. Turov got herself promoted—"

32

"Sure, by taking credit for negotiating Earth's new role in the Empire. She was there, but she was trying to stop us, not help!"

"I know, I know," Natasha said soothingly. "But now we need to figure out what she's going to do next. She got herself bumped up a rank and put into Hegemony. Now, she's trying to fold Legion Varus into Hegemony with her. Maybe that was her promise to the brass in turn for her new rank. Maybe she said she could use her influence to get us to join up willingly."

"I don't care why she's doing it. I want her to fail—now more than ever. Are there any polls on the vote?"

"Nothing official. But it's pretty obvious she didn't like your open statement to the Legion to vote no. She wouldn't be working so hard to discredit you if she thought the vote was going the right way."

It was dark when we reached the spaceport. I narrowed my eyes suspiciously as we pulled into the parking lot. Was this place even safe? I had to think like a conniving officer to anticipate what might be coming at me next.

We climbed out of the car, and Natasha swiped the "go home" command on her tapper. The car would carefully drive itself to her place hundreds of miles north. These days most cars could drive themselves on automatic, but riding that way made for slow, boring trips. I preferred to steer myself.

We walked toward the dark hulk of the waiting lifter which loomed nearly a mile ahead. I found myself looking around the spaceport as if I expected a gunman to show up and open fire on us. That's what it felt like—as if Earth wasn't neutral ground anymore. Even Atlanta felt like hostile territory. I told myself I was paranoid and tried to shake off the feeling.

A buzzing sound made me turn and look. There was a vehicle coming toward us from the entrance. It was moving fast—too fast.

I reached for my sidearm, but of course it wasn't there. Legionnaires didn't usually get to take their weaponry off-base. It was alien-made and too valuable. In most Districts, even a snap-rifle was illegal for citizens to own.

I gave Natasha a shove, spinning her around and out of the way. I stepped in the opposite direction. I figured that the driver of this small one-man machine might nail one of us, but there was no reason to let him run us both down at once.

"What—?" asked Natasha, who'd been tapping at her arm and not paying attention. Then she spotted the speeding vehicle and quickly stepped away in the direction I'd pushed her.

It was getting dark now, and the only thing I could tell about the driver was that he was short and reckless. He aimed his odd machine in my direction. He seemed to be slowing down, but not enough. At the last second he locked on his brakes and the vehicle went into a slide. He ended up lying it down and sliding past me as I danced to one side. Sparks came up from the fenders of the large single wheel that looped around the entire machine.

I reached out a long arm as he passed and gripped the visor of his helmet. It came off with a snap and his head jerked and flopped.

With the help of the nearby floodlights of the lifter I recognized the face. The strange vehicle came to a stop and when he climbed to his feet, I threw his helmet at him. He caught it, staggering and cursing.

"You about tore my head off!" Carlos complained. "You're an angry, violent man, McGill. The net doesn't lie about that!"

Carlos was a swarthy fellow built like a fireplug. He had thick limbs and a mess of dark curly hair. He was from Chicago and had plenty of attitude to prove it.

I wanted to shoot him right then, so it was probably a good thing I didn't have a weapon on me. I calmed myself with an effort of will and stepped closer to inspect his odd vehicle.

"What the hell is this thing, Ortiz?" I demanded. "And why were you trying to kill me with it?"

"It's a one-seat air-cycle," he said. "They're new, just out from Rigel. Fun to drive and humanoid-safe! Guaranteed!"

"Not moron-safe, unfortunately," said Natasha as she came close to glare at him.

Carlos looked from one of us to the other and threw up his hands. "What? Aren't you guys glad to see me? I got the mustering order while I was sitting on a beach in Florida. This is the closest District spaceport, so I came up as fast as I could. And baby, this thing goes *fast*."

"That's great," I said. "What are you going to do with it aboard a lifter? You can't just leave it out here on the ground. Not if you ever want to see it again."

Carlos grinned hugely. "That's where you're wrong. I *can* take it aboard the lifter."

He walked over and tapped at the controls. I could see there were colorful nodules displaying three-dimensional symbols rather than a screen. Lots of equipment that came from the Rigel area was built like that. We couldn't understand their natural language, but you could get used to their symbolic geometry-based sticks and buttons if you worked at it.

To our surprise, the cycle began to contract. It folded and twisted into itself. Like a deflating balloon, it kept shrinking. The single large tire that looped around the vehicle went limp and shriveled to nothing. The central motor became a bumpy cube of metal. The seat he'd been riding in folded away as if it had been so much paper.

Within a minute, the entire thing was down to shivering mass about the size of an orange crate. Carlos picked it up, tugged at the sides and they pulled up to form a carrying bag, complete with a shoulder strap. He heaved it onto his back and grinned at us.

"Pretty neat, huh?"

"Yes," I nodded, laughing. "That *is* pretty cool. Let's go up the ramp."

Together, we marched up into the gloomy interior of the lifter.

The lifter wasn't crowded. In fact, it was almost empty. That was strange all by itself. Burning fuel to boost less than a hundred passengers into orbit wasn't efficient, but the crew did it anyway without even announcing the lift-off was coming.

Only the warning tones and a few recorded messages warned us that heavy G-forces were imminent. Natasha, Carlos and I all strapped in, pulling down the safety bar over our heads and slapping the chest harness buckle into place.

"This is way too familiar," Carlos said.

When I didn't react right away, he had to emphasize his point. "You remember the first time, McGill? When we went up in one of these deathtraps and, in fact, died?"

35

"Yeah, I remember," I said. "Except I didn't die. Not that time."

"You expecting some kind of thank-you rubdown? 'Cause you're not getting it. Not this time. I repaid that debt."

"Shut up, Carlos," Natasha said.

He grumbled, but he did shut up—for a few minutes. Once we broke into orbit and the powerful weight of acceleration left our bodies, he perked up again.

"I got that message last night, big guy," he said. "A little love note just after midnight. The Primus must have been thrilled."

I looked at him. "What do you know about it? Why would she care so much?"

"Are you kidding me? She's Hegemony now. She figures Varus is just an embarrassment—a stepping stone from her past. She'd rather not have us do anything else dramatic now that she's out of our outfit. She has plans, baby. All the way to the top, and she doesn't care who she has to blow to get there."

Carlos had never been a tactful guy, but in this case, I figured he was dead-on target. "You think that's it? She's out of Varus, so if we screw up she'll get the blame?"

"Yeah, something like that. If we get sucked up into Hegemony, it's some other guy's fault if old McGill goes hillbilly on the Nairbs again."

I nodded slowly. "What do you know about this deployment?"

"Sudden and unwanted. I'd prefer to be back on Miami beach. This is total, sugar-spiked bullshit."

"Yes," Natasha exclaimed suddenly.

We glanced over at her. She was working her tapper as usual. She had a cable running from her arm into her pack which was sitting in the seat next to her strapped in like a toddler.

"What do you have?"

"I'm linking up!" she declared, eyes shining. "I can do it."

"Yeah, so?" Carlos asked.

"That means we can still vote," she said.

We looked at her for a second. Finally, I caught on. "You mean because we're up in space, our vote wouldn't count?"

"I say we do it right now," she said. "All three of us. If we don't, we could get disconnected again. I'm running on a thin tunneling-hack right now to get a stream off this ship and down to central."

"Could that be it?" I asked aloud. "Could she have called this emergency deployment just to scramble the vote? Once we're up here, we're out of range."

"Yeah, maybe," Carlos said doubtfully. "But that seems extreme."

I was tapping at my tapper. I fired off a message to every marine on the lifter. Carlos got it right away, and he read it aloud. "You've all been tricked. Vote now, vote fast, or you'll be silent hogs forever." Carlos looked at me. "Dude, you don't *know* that. You shouldn't spread rumors."

"It's already done," I said. "Are they voting, Natasha?"

She worked, tapping quietly with a fixed frown on her face. She nodded after a while. "About half of them have logged in to the voting page. I'm going to have to fight to keep this tunnel open until they finish. Don't bug me."

"Excuse me? Is there a stewardess on this flight?" Carlos asked no one loudly. "I need to move to another seat before McGill makes me dead again!"

I smiled at him. "Too late," I said. "Stop fooling around and vote to keep Varus independent."

"What if I vote for unity, for strength—to join the pride and glory that's known to us lowly rodents as Hegemony?"

I gave him an evil look. "If we lose, I'm going to ask that you and I serve together in a new unit under Winslade, damn you."

"Okay, okay."

37

-5-

When we reached *Minotaur* and docked, Natasha quickly repeated her hack. For a brief time, everyone aboard was able to navigate on their tappers to Earth and log into Central. I walked the promenades over the exercise deck spreading the word. It was time to vote—now or never.

I needn't have bothered because the news spread like wildfire. They didn't like the implications of the situation, and as far as I could tell there were a lot of angry votes shunting down the line to Earth. No one liked the idea that they'd been railroaded into not voting by being mustered off Earth on the eve of the vote.

"The loyalists are whipping the quitters five to one, I bet," Carlos said.

"I thought you were a quitter," I answered.

He looked at me in mock outrage. "That was just my charming sense of humor. I don't want to be a hog any more than you do."

I smiled at him, but inwardly I worried about what Turov had said. She'd indicated that it didn't really matter how we voted. It was only a method to identify dissenters. I hoped she'd been bluffing about that.

Outwardly, I clapped people on the shoulders and told them they were doing the right thing. I wondered about myself as I did so. Was I really into winning this vote? How much did it matter to me that we stayed independent? Sure, the dirt-side hogs were losers, but at least they didn't have to look forward to getting their guts chewed on by aliens once or twice a year.

"I hope you know what you're doing, James," Natasha said later, echoing my sentiments. She'd been eyeing me. I recognized the look. She knew me too well, and she knew when I was in over my head and bullshitting. This was definitely one of those times.

I took a moment to remind myself that Turov *deserved* to lose this vote even if it was only an embarrassment for her. She'd overstepped her authority, and right now she was coming off as petty despite her promotion. Defying her just for spite was a worthwhile cause in my mind.

"I joined this legion to see the stars," I told Natasha. "And I mean to keep doing just that. I don't want to be gelded and left in an office someplace."

She laughed. "Don't worry. I have a feeling no one in any office could put up with you for more than an hour."

I took her statement as a compliment, thanked her, and moved off to tour the ship. *Minotaur* really was an improvement over *Corvus*. Word was it had been shipped out from the Perseus spiral arm systems, from its old base about two hundred lightyears closer to the Core.

Whether this rumor was true or not, I liked the ship. It wasn't just a transport, it was a hulking warship. *Minotaur* had a broadside of guns, sixteen of them, strung down the starboard length of her thick, scarred hull. That meant this ship could fight if she had to. *Corvus* had been very lightly armed and built only to take a legion of humanoids to battle.

I managed to get to my bunk just before midnight. Over the last hour, every trooper I'd met had already voted. At the end they were telling me that they couldn't get through to Central anymore, and I assured them that that was normal—even though I had no idea why the connection had been broken.

Tired, I arrived at my quarters ready for bed. It had been a very long day. To my surprise, my roommate wasn't there. Instead, Centurion Graves stood in the middle of the room.

"Is there a problem, sir?" I asked, setting aside my bag.

Graves let his arm fall. He'd been watching his tapper. He stared at me coldly. "You tell me, Specialist."

"Sir?"

"You're late."

"Just got aboard, sir. Last shuttle up from—"

"Bullshit, McGill," he snapped.

I shut up. It had always been hard to bullshit Graves. I decided to quit while I was behind.

"I've been waiting here at the barracks for the last hour or two. Then I decided to hunt you down using your tapper to locate your position. Do you know what I found?"

"Uh...I was taking the grand tour, sir."

"Yes, you were. I've spoken to some of the people who were on your itinerary. Do you know what they said?"

I was standing at attention by now having come to realize this wasn't a social call. "I can guess, sir."

"They told me you've been out drumming up votes to keep Legion Varus independent. Is that right, Specialist?"

"In a manner of speaking, sir."

"Right... Do you know that the officers in the legion have all been specifically forbidden to sway the votes of troops in this matter?"

I glanced at him. "No sir. I wasn't aware of that."

"Well, it's true. That's why I'm here."

"Sir?"

"I want you to carry on, soldier."

"Oh. I see, sir. Will do."

Graves snorted. "As if you would listen to me if I told you to stop."

"The vote is pretty much over with anyway, sir," I said. "It's almost midnight, and they've cut our access to Central."

This seemed to amuse Graves. "No, Specialist. You're wrong about that. This is far from over. Now, if you'll please excuse me. I need to get out of your presence before the crazy rubs off on me."

He bid me goodnight and marched off down the passageway chuckling.

After my head landed on my bunk a few minutes later, I found it was hard to keep my eyes open. The vote was over, and I was pretty sure we'd won. If we hadn't won, I figured I could at least take comfort in the fact that I'd done my damnedest.

I wondered what Graves had been hinting about, but I hardly cared as long as we'd beaten Turov.

* * *

The next morning after breakfast we were summoned for a briefing. *Minotaur* was still in orbit, I was glad to see. I'd been worried they'd leave Earth during the night. I wanted the chance to tell my folks I was shipping out—once we were in a warp bubble there'd be no transmissions possible.

My unit stood at attention in a square inside our designated module. *Minotaur* was a big enough ship to allow each unit to have its own module. They were all linked together of course, stacked up like suitcases inside what had to be a single massive hold. But to us tiny humans, the modules were comfortable homes. There was an exercise chamber, sleeping quarters, and a mess dedicated to each. We were in the exercise chamber right now waiting for the mass briefing to begin.

Centurion Graves marched in from a side door at precisely 0700. Martial music began to play—I recognized it as the Hegemony anthem. A few troopers hissed, and their veterans silenced them.

A face flickered into being on the forward wall of the chamber. The image had to be thirty feet high. The face belonged to none other than Imperator Turov.

"Damn," Carlos said next to me. "That mole on her forehead must be a half-meter across."

"You should text her about it," I suggested.

Turov's face was tight and grim. She waited a moment then addressed the assembly. I knew she couldn't see us as she had to be looking into a camera pickup, but the effect of those gigantic eyes staring down on a man was chilling nonetheless.

"Fellow legionnaires," she began, her voice rolling out over us with the booming power of an amplifier. "As many of you

41

know, I've been transferred to Hegemony. I requested this opportunity to address my Varus cohort one final time."

Carlos nudged me, his eyes shining with excitement. "We've finally lost the old witch!"

I slapped him away and stared at Turov in concern. She had a reason for all this—of that I was certain.

"Your new mission begins today," the giant face told us. "You'll ship out within hours, and you won't be back for a year."

A general chorus of groans went up from the assembly.

"Because last night's vote was a failure," Turov went on, "Legion Varus will not be joining Hegemony. As a direct result, Central Command feels Legion Varus should be deployed immediately to Tau Ceti. There you'll serve as a color guard for the local aristocracy. The term of your contract will be, as I mentioned, one standard year."

She said these words with emphasis, and I figured she knew they would cause every soldier who heard them pain. We normally didn't deploy for more than six months at a time. A full year—that wasn't going to be easy. Worse, Tau Ceti was known as a dull world. They were a merchant's depot, a central clearing house for goods from twenty star systems. Most of the technology shipped to Earth these days filtered through Tau Ceti.

Although Earth legions often served there as bodyguards for rich merchant princes who wanted to show off to one another, service there wouldn't be anything to write home about. Effectively, Legion Varus was being put on ice.

"Legion Varus will be relieving Legion Germanica," she continued. "There will be a two week transferal period after which Germanica will be brought home aboard *Minotaur*."

"Marooned on Tau Ceti for a *year*?" Carlos complained.

I didn't glance at him. No one did. Carlos was always complaining about something—but this time I had to admit he had good reason.

"I wish you all well," Turov concluded with a smug smile, "and I regret that I'll be unable to accompany you on this mission. On a final note, I wanted to assure every trooper who privately texted me concerning certain irregularities in last night's voting process that the matter will be investigated. Thoroughly. The wheels of legion justice grind slowly, but in the end, no wrong will go unpunished."

Carlos slapped my belly. "She's talking about you, dummy."

I caught his hand and went for a finger-hold, but he managed to jerk it away before I could break something.

Veteran Harris turned his head, glaring. "You two knock it off. Is this junior high?"

"Sorry Vet," Carlos said. "McGill can't keep his hands to himself."

Shaking his head, Harris turned back around with a sigh. I was surprised he hadn't injured one or even both of us. Maybe he was too depressed to do so.

When Turov's giant face finally melted away, Graves made a speech about duty and honor, but I wasn't listening. The briefing broke up shortly thereafter.

All I could think of was the long, long year stretching out in front of me. We'd won the vote. Legion Varus was still independent. But it seemed like Turov had had the last laugh. She was sending us off to Tau Ceti for an entire year—a gulag assignment.

After the briefing, Harris was the first to "congratulate" me. He clapped a heavy hand on my back. His open palm landed so hard between my shoulder blades that the blow might easily have been mistaken for a slap.

"Well played, Specialist," he boomed in my ear. "Now I'll get to cool my heels twenty lights from home. I'll be wearing parade uniforms and accompanying drooling Tau while they go shopping in hostile townships. Lucky me. I'm so glad you kept us free and clear of the evils of Hegemony."

I looked at him in surprise. "I didn't realize you wanted to become a hog so badly, Veteran. Maybe you should appeal your case. They might let you off on a shuttle if you move fast. After all, we're still in orbit and—"

Veteran Harris' hand leapt from my shoulder as if I'd bitten it. He glowered and his eyes slid from side to side, glancing at the troops around us who were listening in.

43

"Shut up, McGill," he rumbled then quickly marched away toward the exit.

"Ha!" Carlos said, coming up to me and staring after Harris. "You smacked him harder than he smacked you. What do you think? Did Harris really vote to bug out and join Hegemony?"

I shook my head. "Hard to tell. If he wanted that, he could have bailed out after returning from any deployment over the years."

"Maybe it's a matter of pride," Carlos said. "He can't leave on his own because that would make him look like a coward to everyone in the legion. But if we *all* bailed out together, he could do it with dignity."

I looked at Carlos and nodded. "No one will ever accuse you of being insightful, but you might just have something there."

Carlos took my backhanded compliment well. He beamed and strutted. I guessed it was because, for him, praise was hard to come by.

6

The only person aboard *Minotaur* who didn't seem depressed was Natasha. She was excited to have the chance to visit Tau Ceti which she referred to by its nickname: Tech World.

"It's a techie dream," she told me. "They have stuff there you just can't get on Earth."

"Isn't it some sort of space station? A merchant clearinghouse in orbit?" I asked, making conversation.

"Yes, there is the orbital market. That's all most people know about the world. But there's much more to the system than that."

We were in line at the cafeteria, and I plucked an orange from a fake tree and rubbed it on my uniform. It was an old habit, one I continued to indulge even though I knew there wasn't a spec of dirt left on fruit aboard a legion ship.

"That's an example right there," she said, pointing to the tree I'd just relieved of its fruit. "These trees in the cafeterias are new tech marvels from Tau Ceti. Have you ever wondered how a spindly tree like that can grow fresh fruit every night?"

"This thing cost hard Galactic credits?" I asked, looking at the tree in surprise. "I figured the fruit was glued on there by the staff to make it more appealing. You're saying it actually *grows* like this?"

"Every night," Natasha said, plucking one of her own. "See the leaves? They're real. This tree can grow anything we want.

If we load it with a new DNA sequence it can grow new fruit *fast.*"

"Huh," I said. "The food has been better on this trip." I marveled briefly then carried my tray to a table and sat down. Natasha trailed behind and sat opposite me. She seemed to be almost in a trance as if her mind was working overtime.

"The possibilities..." she said. "There's so much tech out there, James. It's mind-boggling. We've lived on Earth all our lives while the vast galaxy has been just beyond our reach, wheeling around us, and creating new products we've never even heard of."

She proceeded to talk about tech miracles she'd heard whispers about but which she'd never yet seen. The gusher of money that had reached Earth had doubled the number of consumer and government products from alien systems, but rather than satisfying her, a glimpse of the true economy of the Galactics had served to inflame her desire for more.

I went to work on lunch, shoveling and chewing. For me, eating is a pretty serious business. She'd barely touched her meal by the time I'd reached the half-way mark on my plate, and I have to admit I was eyeing her portion and wondering if she was going to need help with it.

"Tau Ceti isn't like anywhere you've ever been," she went on. "It's more advanced than Earth in every way. The Tau have completely covered their planet with a single gigantic city. Even the oceans are crisscrossed with bridges and artificial islands. But that's only the half of it. Most of their world is hidden from the sky. It's an old world, and they never stopped increasing their population. They've been restricted from colonizing other systems like all frontier worlds, but they've become an impressive power anyway."

"You going to eat that orange?" I asked, unable to keep my true thoughts to myself any longer.

She tossed it to me and showed me a wry twist of her mouth.

"I have to admit, this is fresh-tasting," I said, peeling the fruit and popping pieces of the orange into my mouth in rapid succession.

By the time she was done talking about alien tech, I was leaning back and sighing. I'd eaten half her ration and all of mine. For me, that was the very definition of satisfaction. Eating with a girl often resulted in windfalls like that, one of the reasons I did it so often.

Natasha leaned forward and whispered to me. "You want to know what I'm going to do when we get to Gelt Station?" she asked.

I narrowed my eyes. "Something that you want to whisper about?"

She shrugged. "Nothing illegal—not exactly. I want to walk the markets and find something no one has ever seen on Earth. I'm going to buy it and take it home with me when our tour is done."

"Why?"

She made an exasperated sound. "To show it off, of course. I can tell already you're not going to be impressed."

"Depends on what it is," I said. "For instance, if you can score me a tree that pours out bourbon, or…I don't know."

"That's it? Your imagination ends with a daily booze producer?"

"Well, you'd have to admit that would be pretty cool in my little house."

"What else would you like to find?"

"Uh…" I looked at her and smiled in a predatory fashion. "How about a unique alien stimulation device? Something no one on Earth has experienced."

She looked at me in disgust and crossed her arms. "That's not what I meant, James."

"Training in five," I said, getting up.

All around us, soldiers were stirring and putting on their kits. Out in the passageway she turned to the left, and I had to go to the right. Techs and Weaponeers didn't often train together.

I reached out and caught her hand. She turned and kissed me. We traded smiles and parted company.

"Still nailing that one, huh?" Carlos asked, falling into step beside me. "Losing your touch, aren't you? I mean, shouldn't you be chasing some fresh tail by now?"

"She's a good friend."

Carlos walked backwards for a half-dozen steps, making guttural sounds. "Yeah, I can understand the attraction better as she walks away. Tasty."

I tripped him without even breaking my stride. It wasn't hard since he was walking backward. He sprawled, then bounced back up.

"Asshole," he muttered.

"Have you heard anything about our unit's assignment?"

"Not really. We're all breaking up, I know that much. We're spreading all over Gelt Station playing soldier for any tax-cheat, payroll courier, or merchant princess who wants a color guard."

"I have to admit it does sound a little dull. But I'm looking forward to a vacation from serious combat missions. Isn't it about time we got a cush assignment?"

"Yeah, maybe," Carlos admitted. "We can't always play hero on some primitive dirtball of a planet, I guess. It just seems wrong for Legion Varus, you know what I mean?"

Looking down at him, I frowned and nodded. "You've got a point there. As I see it, there are two possible reasons for this assignment. Either Turov just wants to put us on ice out here so we can't embarrass her further, or…"

"Or what?"

"Or there's more going on out there than we've been told about. Maybe there's a reason why they're retiring Germanica from this world and putting in the goon squad instead."

"Ha! The goon squad. Yeah, that's about what we are, isn't it?"

We reached the exercise room, took up live weapons and slouched against the wall. Above and ahead, we could see space. It was vivid but fake. I knew there was only a titanium wall there, no stars, no swirling planets or nebulae.

When a warp ship was inside its bubble, sliding between the stars at amazing speeds, it was impossible to see light in a normal way. An actual window to the bubble field outside would only show a glowing white haze. But as it comforted the occupants, human ships tended to display portals and even large panoramic views of what the passing universe *should* look like—if it were physically possible to see it.

"What's on the menu today?" Carlos asked me.

"Another squad of recruits," I said, shouldering my belcher, a heavy plasma cannon.

"You don't sound happy about it? You scared?"

I glanced at him and gave him a disgusted look. This kind of training had always delighted Carlos and disturbed me.

"My only fear is that you'll shoot me in the ass somehow," I said.

Carlos belly-laughed. "That's more likely than getting hit by the noobs!"

The exercise room began to warp and dim. I knew that was our cue. Carlos and I jogged forward and selected a position behind a rock that had grown up out of the floor over the last thirty seconds. It was solid enough even though it was just a pack of smart metal with a pixelated texture projected over it.

Veteran Harris' voice crackled into my ear as I adjusted my helmet and the built-in headset.

"All right, ambushers. The recruits are entering the passage to the west in one minute. No one is to fire until they are all in the room, armed, and on alert. Is that clear? No pasting them early this time."

I heaved a sigh. The exercise room was about two hundred meters square, but it seemed bigger because of all the illusory scenery on the walls. Trees, rocks, even tall grasses that rippled in a non-existent wind now surrounded the fire team I was hiding with. Including Veteran Harris himself there were only six of us against thirty recruits, but this wasn't going to be a fair fight.

The noobs came in, armed themselves with snap-rifles from a rack, and were told to patrol to the far side of the exercise area. The Adjunct leading the group was a thin female with big eyes and a small, mean mouth. She ordered them forward but didn't step into the room herself.

As an experienced soldier in Legion Varus, I could have told these poor bastards to keep their eyes on their own officer for clues. Whatever she did—or didn't do—could be critical to their odds of survival.

"Hold your fire, troops," Harris said in my earpiece. "Let the babies march in close. We want to scare them good."

Scare them? That was a laugh. We were going to tear them apart. For the first time, my mood shifted. I watched as the confused recruits walked forward. They looked around warily but without proper appreciation for the danger they were in. It didn't seem right that they should be blasted without warning.

I reached up and cranked the aperture on my weapon down to a tight beam. An instant later, Carlos slapped a gauntlet on my shoulder.

"Are you going to screw me?" he asked quietly, his helmet uncomfortably close to mine.

"Take your position, trooper," I said. "This is gonna be a real fight."

"Shit McGill—shit!" Carlos broke off and belly-crawled away from my position.

I almost chuckled. There was one man who knew me well.

Sighting carefully with my cannon balanced on the back of a fake rock, I targeted the approaching platoon. I was supposed to start this with a wide-angle blast that would engulf the front troops in a cone of hot plasma. Ambushing them and taking out half their number in the opening volley was part of the procedure.

Instead, I aimed through them to the very back rank. There, slinking along with her pistol drawn and looking very tense, was the thin Adjunct.

She knew the score, of course. She was leading her platoon into an ambush to teach them a "lesson".

"McGill leads," Harris said. "Fire when ready, weaponeer."

I couldn't get a clear shot. The hapless recruits were all over, bunching up, not even keeping their distance from one another. I watched as they jostled one another, laughing. I had to admit these pups needed a little training. I felt sure they were going to get it before this was over.

"McGill?" Harris said a second later. "Fire, man!"

It was like threading a needle with a fire hose. I nudged my weapon right, then left. Damn, that Adjunct was a skinny little thing. It was almost as if she knew what was coming.

Finally, I got my clear shot, and I took it instantly. A gush of brilliant energy leapt across the short distance between our converging lines. It lanced between several startled recruits and caught the Adjunct full in the upper body. Her head was completely gone, and most of her narrow shoulders were burned away with it.

My dad used to talk about how chickens ran around the yard after you cut their heads off. That didn't happen in this case. The Adjunct flopped down stone dead. But the rest of her platoon certainly did remind me of frightened fowl as they scrambled for cover screaming and shouting to one another.

All around me, my dastardly comrades sighted, but held their fire, waiting for the order. We had heavy armor, experience, and surprise on our side. But there were only six of us against thirty.

"What kind of a chicken-shit shot was that?" Harris demanded. "Take out that front line before they disperse!"

I set my plasma cannon aside and released the heating coil, letting it drop out onto the camouflaged deck, steaming. It sizzled there and sent up a tendril of gray smoke.

"Weaponeer reporting weapon failure," I said calmly. "Repeat, weaponeer McGill reporting—"

"Damn you, McGill!" Harris roared. "You think you're funny? The rest of you fire at will! Tear them up!"

A hail of fire erupted from both sides almost simultaneously. The recruits had gotten over their stunned status and were back in the fight. Their commander was down, but they were past their initial shock and they responded by getting low and crawling toward us.

The metallic trees around us were splattered with countless rounds. I returned fire with my secondary weapon taking out two before I was hit multiple times and forced to retreat. I don't like to die any more than the next guy. Really, I don't.

My heavily armored team was pushed back. We couldn't be taken out with a single snap-rifle pellet but there were thousands rattling against the skin of our suits now. If they hammered one spot several times in a row, they could penetrate and kill even a heavy.

We retreated until our backs were against the far wall. Three heavies were down by that time including Carlos. I was breathing hard.

This wasn't looking good. We'd taken down at least half the recruits, but the rest had blood in their eyes. They were angry, semi-organized, and pushing hard.

A massive clang sounded and I thought I'd bought the farm. But it was only Harris smashing his gauntlet onto the top of my helmet.

"I should shoot you myself!" he roared.

"We have to pull out to the north wall, Vet!" I said. "There's a pile of rocks to hide in over there."

Harris had a crazy look in his eye. "I'm going to do it," he said, putting his gun to my head. "I'm going to finish you off."

"Your odds of survival will be much better if we cover each other's retreat to those rocks, Veteran."

Harris roared in frustration, and he ran for the rocks. I covered his retreat by lancing a recruit who'd crawled too close with a hot poke from my suit blades. Then I fell back while Harris's gun beamed down my pursuers.

In the end, we reached the rockpile, holed-up, and let the enemy patrol pass to victory.

For the first time in Legion Varus history, the recruits had won the ambush scenario.

7

It wasn't my first dressing down, and I knew it probably wouldn't be my last.

I'd been summoned to Centurion Graves office about an hour after the vicious firefight in the exercise room had ended in a loss for my team. I wasn't under any illusions about what was in store for me when I reported to my commander.

Normally Harris would have given me a nasty grin when he saw me show up on a day like this, but he was too pissed-off to enjoy the situation. He glared at me, and I knew he'd as soon put a round between my eyes as spit on me.

Graves saluted us as we stepped into his office, but he didn't tell us to stand at ease. We remained rigid and staring while he eyed us both. Finally, he heaved a sigh.

"McGill," he said, "I'm sorry to say that Veteran Harris has requested a formal reprimand for your conduct earlier today. I've already heard his side of the story. Please relate yours as concisely as possible."

"Sir," I began, "at 0800 hours today I joined Harris' team of heavies in the exercise room. We planned to stage a mock ambush on an unsuspecting platoon of lightly armed recruits. Unfortunately, my weapon didn't operate as I'd—"

"Bullshit, McGill!" Harris interrupted with sudden vehemence. "Don't you even *dare* go there. We're not a pair of desk-flying noobs, you know. We've seen your act plenty of times before, and—"

"Harris, please," Graves interrupted.

"Okay," Harris said. "Okay. I only wanted to point out the obvious—that McGill is full of Grade-A shit, sir." After that, Harris clamped his mouth shut. I could tell it wasn't an easy thing for him to do.

"McGill," Graves said, "I have to agree with Harris' assessment in this instance. I'm not buying any nonsense about the status of your weapon. It operated perfectly before and after the exercise—just not while it was in your hands."

"Well sir, in that case I'd like point out the general rule followed by heavy weaponeers in combat. The commanders give the orders, but we're in charge of executing the technical details to the best of our ability and at our discretion. My actions were due to a personal judgment call. While I can understand how someone could see my decisions as…flawed, I believe the end results were positive."

"You didn't follow orders!" Harris exploded. "You know damn well—"

Graves waved him to silence again. "McGill, half the heavy troopers lying in ambush were killed by the enemy patrol during the exercise. More importantly, the recruits made it to the far wall achieving their goal and a clear victory in the game. How can these results be looked upon as 'positive?'"

"It's true, sir, that my side failed to stop the enemy in the exercise. But that's only one way of looking at it. The real purpose of the mission was to train troops, and to shape them into battle-hardened fighters before their first real battle. I believe my approach managed to do just that."

Graves frowned slightly. "Could you elaborate?"

"The enemy light troop officer in this mock firefight played her role poorly. She knew what was going to happen. She didn't spread out her men or give them any orders that would improve their odds. Instead, she hung back and offered them no guidance. If she'd led her team to the best of her ability, we might have lost the exercise fair and square."

Harris lost his cool once again. "That's the whole damned point! The recruits are *supposed* to lose. They're supposed to be *slaughtered*. It's a good hard lesson for them and puts the fear of live rounds into them before they wander out onto an alien battlefield. Are you trying to outthink Legion Varus'

54

training techniques? Is that it? Do you know better than your officers? I—"

"Hold on, Harris," Graves said. "McGill, explain yourself."

"I don't think the exercise is well-designed. If the purpose is to train both sides, then my alteration of the script achieved that goal. In fact, I think both sides gained from the action today. The surviving recruits got a morale boost out of it. I even provided their commanding officer with a little education. Next time she might take the exercise seriously rather than hanging back and letting her troops march into a slaughter. Maybe she'll try to win and stay alive in the process."

Harris sputtered and scoffed, but no intelligible words came out of him. Graves looked at me, frowning and thinking hard. Finally, he spoke again. "McGill, Veteran Harris was your commander in this exercise. You owed it to him to follow his orders. Regardless of your complaints about the opposing officer, Veteran Harris had the superior strategy. You ignored his orders and your side did poorly as a result. Since this combat wasn't with an actual enemy, your mistake doesn't warrant a demotion or other punishment. I'll keep it out of your permanent record, but it will cost you big-time all the same."

"Yes sir," I said. "Uh, cost me what?"

"McGill, I regret to inform you that I'm removing you from the promotion roster. Up until today, you were on my short-list for the rank of veteran."

"Say *what*?" demanded Harris, flabbergasted.

Graves stared at him coldly until he quieted.

"That's right," Graves continued, "I'm going to have to rescind my recommendation. This prank has cost you rank—do you understand me, Specialist?"

I felt a wave of shock. *Veteran? Me?* Such rapid advancement was highly unusual. In most cases, even a stellar trooper had to work his way through his first enlistment and be accepted for his second active duty stint before he had a chance of achieving advanced rank. Learning that I'd been considered for rank and lost my chance came as a stunner to me.

Graves was still eyeing me, and I realized he expected a response.

"Yes sir," I said. "Right. I understand, sir."

"Good."

My face was a flat mask. Internally, I didn't know what to think. Should I argue? Had I been a fool to go off-script in the first place? Did I even *want* to be a veteran? I wasn't sure how to answer any of these questions which were popping off in my head.

"Centurion?" Veteran Harris said, leaning forward, "I'd like to request a private word with you after this. Would that be possible?"

"Request denied," Graves responded immediately. "I already know what you're going to say, Harris."

"Sir, I just can't understand how you could—"

"Veteran," Graves said, cutting him off, "you've made your point. Your report has been taken into account and considered carefully. Specialist McGill has been reprimanded and materially punished. I think you should take that at face value and leave it alone."

"Yes, sir."

"You're both dismissed."

Harris and I walked out of the Centurion's officer together. I was in a daze, and I think Harris was, too.

Harris turned to me with a savage look on his face.

"I want you to understand something, McGill," he said. "I don't care what happens. I don't care what dumbass idea the brass comes up with in the way of promotions. I'm *never* going to salute you."

I wasn't sure how to take this, but I was beginning to get a little angry with him myself. It's hard to stay cool with someone who's raging at you all the time.

"Veteran Harris," I said. "Do you remember the day we met? I came to the Mustering Hall and you personally talked me into signing with Legion Varus."

"How could I forget? An hour never passes where I don't regret that day."

"Well, do you recall telling me that I wasn't fit for the other legions because I was a misfit? A square peg that didn't fit into their little round holes? You told me Legion Varus values troops that think for themselves. You said this outfit seeks misfits and upstarts, and that my kind is welcome here."

"That was a sales pitch," Harris snapped.

"Well, I think there was a grain of truth in your pitch because that's what I am. It's in my nature to think outside the box and to cause trouble for those who don't. Maybe that's why I've moved up in rank quickly, and why I may well continue to do so."

Harris grunted unhappily. "God help us all."

We went our separate ways at the next intersection, and I found my way back to my quarters. Carlos was there to greet me—lucky me.

"Here he is!" he shouted, throwing his arms wide. "My favorite backstabbing traitor! What was it this time, McGill? Did you spot a piece of rookie ass you couldn't bear to gun down? Or were you dying to hear the centurion's big-dog bark again? I know it's been a month or more since you've been reprimanded. Things must have been getting dull in that swamp-shack of yours down in Georgia."

"Not really," I said, grinning. "I killed three men in that shack the day I left Earth."

"I heard about that. Same old crazy. I hope you save a little of that for the shop-lifters on Tech World."

"Is that all there is going on down there?" I asked him seriously. "Shoplifting, smuggling, maybe a little tax-evasion? Is that what they want us to guard against?"

Carlos shook his head. "Really, it's worse than that. From what I can tell reading a few old online tour summaries from Germanica commanders, almost nothing ever happens on Tau Ceti. We're for show, and that's why those Germanica pukes have always loved the assignment."

"I'm pretty stunned to hear you read up on our mission world."

He shrugged. "Reports of my retardation have always been exaggerated—unlike those with your name on the top."

It was classic Carlos, but somehow I didn't feel like punching him this time. I was too distracted by the results of my meeting with Graves.

"You want to hear a shocker?" I asked him.

"You know I do. You're gay, right? I always suspected it. I'm going to win the Unit pool this time."

57

I couldn't really see Carlos. I certainly wasn't listening to him. I walked to the far wall of our small quarters and tapped on it. Obediently, the wall displayed Tech World. Our destination was a blue-gray planet that sparkled like a Christmas tree on the night side. An endless city they said, with a native population that was pushing a trillion humanoids. From space it looked interesting, but I could already taste the canned air.

"You know that picture's fake, right?" Carlos asked.

I didn't say anything, and he stared alongside me at our destination.

"Graves said I was on his short list for promotion to veteran," I told him. "But he canceled that because of the exercise."

"Ouch," Carlos said. "That sucks for you. But you know, now that I think about it, I'm not the least bit sorry for you. In fact, the idea he'd been about to promote you again before he gave me a Specialist rank—man, that's bullshit. You piss off half the legion every day, and I'm on his permanent shit-list. What I'd ever do?"

I glanced at him. "For one thing, you never shut up."

"Well, yeah. But that's not as bad as disobeying orders all the time."

"I don't disobey orders—not often, anyway. I just tend to interpret them in my own special way."

Carlos rewarded me with a dirty chuckle. "Officers love that." After a second, he frowned. "Do you really think my mouth is holding me back?"

I nodded. "I'm sure of it. Free-thinking actions annoy them, but they partly admire initiative. What they really hate is a loud smart-ass."

Carlos grunted. "I've got to work on that."

Turning my attention from the glimmering projection of the world we were heading toward, I eyed him in surprise. I couldn't recall Carlos ever accepting criticism much less suggesting he needed to mend his ways.

I guess there's hope for everyone.

-8-

A month passed before the big day came. *Minotaur* came out of warp, paused for a moment to get her bearings, and then glided like a stalking predator toward Tech World. Crawling across the star system in normal space, it took a full day to get from the designated warp-in point to the target planet.

During the final hour of the approach, every trooper was on deck and wearing their full kit. A massive power pack humped my back like a bloated camel. On my shoulder rode my belcher, a venerable piece of legion armament. It was a powerful infantry weapon and the heaviest a single earthman could carry. But I had to wonder if a better heavy gun could be found somewhere else in the Empire.

Maybe, just maybe, we could find one and order it on a place like Tech World. If we could find a better weapon, shouldn't we buy it and use it instead of these older weapons systems? We had the credits, I was sure of that. The belchers were reliable most of the time, but they had notorious problems with heat. They also took powerful hands and arms to operate which was why I suspected they were originally designed for much larger beings. Maybe my belcher was nothing more than a hunting rifle on its distant world of origin.

Schemes to gain better weaponry wormed in my head as I stood at the far left end of my unit's third rank. Together, we formed ten ranks of ten troops each. A perfect square on parade.

My unit's square was one of nearly a hundred such formations. There was only one chamber big enough to contain so many of us at once, and it wasn't a spot I liked much. We were in the open hold standing on top of our unit modules. There were gaps between these modules—alarming crevasses five meters wide. Above us was the "roof" of the ship, the top of the main hold. Dull and crenulated with equipment, the roof was really the inside of the primary hull. Beyond that was open space. Assembling our entire legion on top of these modules seemed dangerous to me. If there was a hull breach, we'd be hurled out into the void like so many motes of dust.

But no one had asked me about the pageantry of legion rotation. It was a tradition for the arriving legion and the legion being relieved to stand in full dress in a single area if at all possible. I knew our Tribune Drusus wasn't about to let Germanica look more formal than we did.

There wasn't any artificial gravity in the hold, so we had to use our magnetics to hold us down. We braced ourselves against the jolts of deceleration and course adjustments as we eased our way closer to the gigantic space station outside.

Throughout the lengthy docking process, the brass wanted us all on parade. There were camera drones buzzing everywhere. I had to smile at that. Drusus had even told us to hold up our unit flags. The rumpled banners displayed our Wolfshead emblem and our unit numbers, but the flags themselves hung oddly in null-G, looking as if it was the most shockingly windless day in history.

All this sounded more exciting than it was. In practice, it meant standing around at attention on the flat roof of a module for an hour or two waiting for something, *anything*, to happen. I was left with plenty of time to think. I was excited to be arriving at Tech World. This would be my third visit to a new planet.

There was so little we knew about the Galactic Empire as a whole. I'd been impressed by the influx of funds, but so far I hadn't heard much in the way of new information from the Empire beyond Frontier 921. Natasha was excited by the new gadgets we'd gained access to, but I wanted something bigger. I wanted *information*—preferably in its rawest form.

60

I was jolted out of my reverie. Without warning, a tremendous clang rang out sweeping the hold. It was a sonic blast of such power it might have deafened the exposed troops if we hadn't been sheltering inside helmets and suits. Even so, I saw men put their gauntlets up to the sides of their heads futilely trying to protect their ears.

Somehow, I knew what might happen next. I bent my knees and spread my feet a half-step wider. Even so, I was almost thrown flat by the rippling wave of vibration that swept through the ship. My feet felt like they were buzzing, and my head hurt.

"We've hit something!" Carlos shouted. I walked over to him, threw a hand out, and hauled him back to his feet.

Harris was marching the line, kicking and shoving troops back into line.

"Up, up!" he shouted. "It's nothing—we've arrived, that's all. Get up off your cans! You look like a bunch of recruits crying for mama!"

Within seconds, we were back in formation, but we were wary now. Every helmet rotated to watch for cracks in the hull overhead.

My audio crackled, and Graves' voice came into my helmet. "That was a dirty trick," he said. "Germanica is operating that boom. I can almost hear their people laughing."

I frowned. Could he be right? Legion rivalry had always been strong, and there was no legion more reviled than Varus. Germanica troops, on the other hand, had a pretty huge opinion of themselves. If they'd played a dangerous trick to knock us all on our butts while the cameras were running—well, that didn't bode well for a smooth transition between the legions.

What felt like five minutes later, the ceiling lit up. We all gawked and stared. There they were, projected on the ceiling like a mirror in the sky, ten thousand strong. Legion Germanica in all its glory was displayed directly above us. I didn't know where they'd managed to assemble, but they looked good.

Reluctantly, I had to admit they were sharp troops. Their blue-white flags fluttered majestically whereas our red and gold equivalents hung like limp towels. Every suit of armor shined like it'd been polished and dipped in chrome. Not a

61

trooper was out of place. Not a hand or a helmet was out of alignment with the next man in line. In comparison, we were a ragged band of tarnished yokels.

"They must have fans or something to keep their banners up like that," Carlos marveled. "Conceited bastards."

"They're pretty, aren't they?" asked Veteran Harris loudly. He held the staff of our banner. As the senior non-com in the unit, the honor had fallen to him. "Their armor is unscratched because they never fight! They'd run like beetles if faced with a real battle."

A roar of approval went up from our unit members, and I joined them. But I knew better. Germanica wasn't as hard-scrabble as we were, and I'd bet our troops had twice the combat experience as their troops on average—but they were still the real deal. They were disciplined, organized, and deadly when a fight really came down.

All across the hold, Varus troops were waving fists and lofting weapons over their heads. Germanica troops stood in perfect ranks, motionless. They didn't respond to our taunts which they were surely able to see. They stayed at attention and ignored us, and I came to understand we looked like so many apes making an embarrassing spectacle of ourselves.

The hullabaloo went on for a full minute before our officers roared for quiet. They got their wish, and we tightened up standing in silent neat rows again.

Above us, the projected image of shining ranks of ant-like troops was overlaid with another image. A huge, leering face appeared.

The face belonged to Germanica's tribune, Maurice Armel. The first thing I noticed about him was that he was he looked like he smelled something bad. Real bad. His aristocratic nose was pinched up over pursed lips. His whisper of a mustache lay over his lip like a humped caterpillar, and his eyes were narrowed in disgust.

Carlos whistled. "That's Armel all right," he said. "I've read about him on the net. He thinks he's pretty hot stuff."

"That just means he's soft," I said without conviction.

Despite my words, those eyes didn't look soft. They looked as hard as a man's eyes could look. And considering that his face loomed directly above us like the very face of God himself, it was hard not to feel overawed by him.

"Legion Varus," Tribune Armel began solemnly. "Legion Germanica welcomes you to our long-term station. May you perform your mission here as flawlessly as we have."

Inside my helmet, my lips twisted themselves up like a pretzel. This guy sure did think a lot of himself. Standing watch at a quiet post didn't indicate heroism—not in my book, anyway.

"Let's play a game," Carlos said. "Let's count how many times Armel gives himself a compliment."

I smiled despite myself. "I'd rather count how many times he slyly insults our legion."

"Would you two shut up?" Harris demanded suddenly. "If I wasn't standing in perfect ranks right now, I'd come down there and kick your butts off this module. Do you want to play that game?"

"No, Vet," we muttered together. Others in the ranks chuckled at our expense.

The speech did go on for what I counted as twelve full minutes. Later, Carlos claimed it was fifteen. Whatever the case, he managed to pat himself and his legion on the back multiple times—while subtly suggesting we were substandard cretins barely capable of standing on two legs.

Finally, it was Tribune Drusus' turn. His own face was alarmingly youthful and unimpressive in comparison to Armel's, but I knew that wasn't an accurate reflection of his capacities. He'd died a number of times in service to Legion Varus, and he wore his apparent youth like a badge.

His speech was blissfully brief and to the point. He accepted the mission from Germanica and formally requested permission to disembark. Armel gave it, and that was that.

The big screen overhead faded with the final images showing Germanica troops cheering and congratulating one another.

We were allowed to break ranks as well, and Natasha found her way to my side.

"They look pretty happy to be going home," I remarked.

"They aren't out of here yet," Natasha said.

The ranks had broken as the cameras buzzed away, and we were left to file to the roof exits. I fell into step alongside her. I felt like an armored oaf clanking along beside the relatively tiny tech specialist.

"How long will the switchover take?" I asked her.

She shrugged. "A few weeks. Legion Germanica has to be satisfied that we're capable of performing the mission then they'll officially pass the duty to us."

I snorted. "Compared to hot-dropping on a hostile world, this is a joke."

"They don't see it that way."

Nearly ten long hours later, I was finally allowed off-ship and onto the massive space station named *Gelt*. There were several of these stations hanging in space over Tau Ceti. They were unbelievably huge and tethered permanently to the planet with an umbilical. The stations were called 'megahabs,' as they were capable of housing millions of humanoids each.

Transferring to Gelt Station was a daunting experience. The structure was an amazing sight. Built like a spinning top, it had artificial gravity due to centrifugal force. The lower portion that hung down near the atmosphere contained all the machinery to keep the internals working. Power, water, atmosphere—it all came from the conical section at the bottom.

The planet had three small moons, the configuration of which allowed for La Grange points close to the planet. These were points where relatively stable orbits could be found for objects like this massive station.

The planet itself was almost as impressive as Gelt Station. Stretching out in an impossibly broad arc, the world was bigger than Earth, but due to a different composition, the gravity was reasonable. I wondered if I would ever get the opportunity to set foot on that gray-green, cloud-shrouded world.

Gliding aboard our lifter into a massive landing bay, we soon disembarked. Every head was craning and every mouth was gawking. The interior of the station was amazing. There were colored lights and holograms everywhere. The interior space was so vast it was as if we'd entered a new world. In a way, we had. The sheer number of galleries, holds, workshops, and massive cylindrical passageways we marched by kept everyone in awe.

The interior of Gelt Station was a single massive city. It was probably the largest city I'd ever visited in my life. There were countless marvels to see. The transportation system by itself made me feel like a primitive.

By setting foot on a broad flying disk, I was able to state my destination to the pilot, apply my tapper to a credit voucher to the console, and be whisked away to anywhere I cared to go.

The pilot was a fast-talking guy who looked like a blue turtle. He gestured and chattered until I stumped up to try one of the disks. We'd been ordered to find our own way to our new quarters which were currently located on the sun-side of the station. Due to Gelt Station's stable orbit, part of the megahab faced the planet while the other half faced the local star, but as the station rotated, everyone had a day-night cycle. As a species that preferred warmth, we'd been given living space on the upper rim, a region of the massive structure that tended to stay warmer.

Natasha caught me before I touched my credit voucher to the console.

"Just a minute," she said. "How much is this little ride going to cost?"

The turtle-guy threw up two stump arms—or were they legs? "A pittance, citizen. A pittance. The exact amount is impossible to calculate until you've arrived. Traffic conditions may lengthen the journey, you see."

I frowned. "You mean I'm paying for time spent in transit?"

"Of course, sir! Naturally! Would you deny my children their feed?"

People on Tech World often talked like this according to the briefing. Anything you suggested that might lower a price was considered offensive and downright miserly. All the same, haggling was expected.

"Maybe you could share the fare," I suggested to Natasha.

She shook her head. "How much per minute?" she asked.

"Always the questions! Always they doubt me, they suspect me. Already I've lost a full credit's worth of time talking to you two. Would you deny me my next meal just to stand here and chit-chat?"

"That's what I thought," she said. "Come on, James."

"Wait! A credit, a single credit piece per minute! You'll not find anything cheaper."

"A full credit per minute?" I demanded incredulously. "You *are* a cheat."

We turned to go. A credit on Earth—a Galactic credit—was easily a full hour's wage for a skilled human worker. You could rent an apartment for a ten credits a week—a good one.

"Wait!" cried the turtle again. "I give you bargain. Five credits, whole trip. You can't walk. It's thirty kilometers at least."

"All right," Natasha said. "But we're sharing the fare."

The turtle grumbled, but at last we climbed aboard his disk and shot off, beginning the wildest ride I've ever been on. I can't tell you what it was like because there aren't any earthly equivalents. Imagine, if you will, a rollercoaster car without tracks that's let loose in a modern major city—but this rollercoaster flies and is piloted by an insane blue turtle that moves like a mongoose.

We were almost sick by the time we arrived at our quarters ten long minutes later. The turtle threw us out then shook a stumpy appendage at me.

"What?" I asked.

"A gratuity is customary in your culture," he explained.

I scoffed. "You just got a day's wages off me for a ten minute flight. Here's your tip: don't gouge people."

The turtle flew off in a huff, and we were blasted by a wash of ozone-tasting exhaust.

-9-

The majority of Tau Ceti's population wasn't made up of turtles, blue or otherwise. Most citizens were a humanoid race known as the Tau. They roughly matched the size and dimensions of an Asian person from Earth. That's where the similarities stopped, however. Up close, they were pretty alien-looking. They had reddish-pink skin, black bug-eyes, and fringes of squirmy eating-tentacles that surrounded their mouths like a fleshy beard. Frankly, to me the tentacles were disgusting.

If you didn't look at their faces they looked human enough. But as I understood it, if you eyed them closely (something I'd never done) the differences became glaringly obvious. For one thing, they had a lot more visible ropy veins than we do. The bio people said that was because Tau stored their body fat internally rather than as an outer coating under the skin. When their muscles moved or their organs churned, you could watch the action right through their thin hides.

It was the Tau who had built this amazing space station. A megahab floating in orbit over the sole habitable planet in the Tau Ceti system, Gelt Station was an amazing achievement by itself. The Tau had also developed the amazing level of commerce that trafficked here. As far as I could tell, every alien product that Earth purchased each year, plus our banking connection to the Core Systems, funneled through this single structure. As a result, the Gelt space station was the mercantile capital of Frontier 921 serving our local network of a few dozen inhabited star systems. For that achievement alone, I found the Tau to be an impressive species.

Unfortunately, their individual personalities were lacking. They were a universally self-serving and suspicious people. They fawned over anyone who had money and reviled those who didn't. In their society, everything had a price with wealth being the sole indicator of social status.

The neighborhood surrounding our barracks was a case in point. There were countless salesmen manning booths as well as fully automated kiosks all of which relentlessly hawked all sorts of garbage to relieve the troops of any credits they may have brought with them. The products sold looked to be high quality at first glance, but a cursory inspection of "genuine saurian leather boots" turned up a cheap synthetic with bad stitching. Sexual aids shoved into boxes with human anatomical imagery on the label contained devices obviously incompatible with our physiology. The list went on.

Worse, the selling-machines were noisy. There seemed to be no limit to how gaudy, irritating and loud you could make an advertisement on Tech World. I had to push my way past a grasping mechanical hand that played loud discordant noises, which apparently passed for music somewhere in the universe, just to get into the lobby.

Inside the barracks, relative quiet reigned. I heaved a sigh and turned to Natasha.

"It's hell out there," I said. "I'm disappointed."

"Why?"

"Because we're stuck here in this loony bin for a whole year, that's why."

She seemed incredulous. "To me this place is *fantastic*," she said with feeling. "I'm looking forward to searching every inch of Gelt Station for good products to take home. Don't worry about those vendors at the door they'll be gone in a few hours. Whoever owns them probably bought a short-term permit to catch newcomers. Every major Earth city has stuff like that to watch out for. You just have to keep your hand on your wallet—and don't get too drunk."

I shook my head, annoyed. I hated cities in general, and this one was worse than any I'd ever seen. Alien-filled, noisy, overrun with traffic and confusion—and I was stuck here for an entire year. I was already missing home.

"Don't tell me you'd rather be squatting in your shed drinking beer," Natasha said.

With a shrug, I turned toward the looming interior of the barracks. I frowned, then stared, then finally cocked my head.

"Is this a joke?" I asked. "Don't you think these modules are familiar-looking?"

They were, in fact, the same modular living quarters we'd left behind on *Minotaur*.

"Of course they are," Natasha said. "That's why we were shipped out here in these things. They unload the living modules here at headquarters and plug the habitats right in. It's an instant home for our species. They're preset for a comfortable temperature, air pressure—the works. Don't tell me you were hoping to live like a native out on the streets."

I turned to her in amazement. "But...why didn't they just drop the modules off here with us in them?" I demanded. "That would have been so much easier. All these troops crossing Gelt Station on their own dime, getting lost, wasting time..."

Natasha laughed and shook her head. "I can see you have a lot to learn about this place. The Tau would never permit ten thousand suckers to slip by them like that. I'm sure they denied *Minotaur* landing permission for cargo and passengers at the same location. They probably directed them to let us off at customs then sent the ship around to unload our modules here—on the opposite end of the station."

"Customs?" I asked. "I don't remember much in the way of searching and document-checking.

"There's none of that here. If you have enough money to get to the station, you belong here. That's the Tau rule. They have a few automated weapons detectors and the like at the entrance, I'm sure, but that's about it."

I nodded slowly as we climbed a long flight of steps up to our unit module. "I'm beginning to get it. If they delivered us here efficiently, they'd have missed out on fleecing noobs at the door. This way, who knows how many turtles made a profit on pointless transportation alone. What a waste."

"One creature's waste is the next creature's profit," she said.

I frowned at her.

"It's a local proverb," she explained. "I've been reading up on these people since Turov announced our mission objective."

"I can tell."

When we found our way up to the unit module, I was recognized by the entry system and ordered by my tapper to head to a briefing in the wardroom. Natasha received the same orders, but Carlos and Kivi didn't. We met up with them in the hallway and Carlos complained that someone should have warned him that his newly purchased "real life human sex partner" would be a balloon with feathers glued to it.

We headed to the meeting, and I realized by the nature of the crowd accompanying us that only the officers and noncoms had been summoned. Grunts hadn't been invited. Lucky them.

When we'd all assembled, I half expected Turov to project herself on the wall again. But instead, Centurion Graves arrived last with someone I didn't know in tow behind him.

The guest was an officer, and he was an old guy. Shockingly old. White hair frosted his naturally wrinkled skin and even his neatly trimmed fringe of a beard was a salt and pepper mix like my own granddad wore. I was fairly certain no one in Legion Varus was that old—at least not outwardly. His body was probably fifty-plus and we found it shocking to see someone that old in uniform. I saw the bullshead emblem of Taurus on his shoulder and realized he was a member of Legion Germanica.

We came to attention and saluted. Centurion Graves ordered us to stand at ease and introduced his guest.

"This is Adjunct Claver," Graves said. "He's been assigned to our unit during the handover of the mission from Legion Germanica to Legion Varus. Adjunct, if you please."

Claver took a step forward and gazed at us with ice-blue eyes. His silver hair was cropped down to a square shape on his skull, and his heavy lips were drawn into a tight grin.

"Welcome to Tech World, troops," he said in an alarming baritone with a mild Texan accent. His voice was one of those that naturally carried overriding all other speech in the room.

"Most of my friends call me Old Silver—but you aren't my friends so don't bother. I'm here to explain your duties and help make this transition as easy as possible for all parties concerned. I've spent no less than nine tours here on Tau Ceti over the years, and I know how this place operates. Consider me to be your local guide."

Claver made a little speech about avoiding certain regions of the station when alone and off-duty. The most prominent of these was a region known as "The Vents" which was apparently a low-oxygen region far down in the bowels of the station. He also told us that any bargain that seemed too good to be true definitely *was* on this planet.

When he finally got around to explaining our specific assignment, I was happily surprised.

"Light units are being assigned to police duties," he said. "But the heavy troops are going to be hired out on an individual basis as bodyguards and for other special duties. The inhabitants of Gelt Station are an odd group. They'll pinch a penny until it bleeds one minute, then blow a thousand credits on some extravagant display of wealth to impress their peers the next. Heavy troopers are our real cash cows in this system. With all that armor and weaponry, you don't really fit in standing on street corners. But you *look* scary, and that's worth credit!"

Claver laughed loudly and didn't seem to notice or care that none of the rest of us were joining in.

"Honestly," he continued, "for a heavy unit like this one, I'd recommend you invest in polish. Buff out every battle scar on your armor, and consider having it dipped in chrome. Down on violet deck they have some excellent metal smiths. They can do damn well anything."

For the first time, I began to frown. This wasn't what I'd been expecting. I'd been waiting for a list of active threats—for a battle plan, maybe. But it was sinking in that we weren't here to fight anyone. We were here to babysit merchant princes and polish our armor. It was quite a letdown.

At last the question and answer session began. I immediately raised my armored hand high.

A long arm reached up behind me and gripped my shoulder, attempting to force my hand down. I resisted automatically, and due to my superior height and the whining power-assist motors in my suit, my assailant was unable to force me to comply with his wishes.

"Dammit McGill, put your friggin' hand down!" Harris hissed in my ear.

"Oh, sorry Veteran," I said, turning him a pleasant look of surprise. "I didn't notice you there."

Harris glowered at me, and I finally lowered my arm—but it was too late.

"Yes?" Claver asked loudly. "You there, that telephone pole of a man. Speak up."

I turned back to the adjunct and I could feel Harris' breath on the back of my head.

"Sir, could you do a rundown on local threats?"

"Local threats?"

"Yes sir. I understand we're to bodyguard a local merchant princess. But who are we to protect her from?"

Claver chuckled. "A groper on the subway, maybe," he said. "Or a bad piece of fruit she might purchase. Really, there aren't any significant threats on this station. The Tau allowed to work and live here are the best of their species. There are no youths, no children. Only successful adults from below can reach this station if they meet the stringent qualifications. Even then, there are a few thieves and robbers around—nothing organized, however."

I frowned, nodding. Claver turned to Centurion Graves, and I sensed they were about to wrap things up.

My hand rose again. I heard Harris make a choking sound behind me.

"Sir?" I asked. "What about down on the planet surface? Is there any trouble down there?"

"Ha!" Claver said. "Yes, loads of it. Rival gangs burn entire districts sometimes. Rebels hold chunks of land and even some of the underwater stations. Don't know why they don't just flush them all out into the ocean."

I frowned. That didn't sound like a trouble-free environment to me. But I guessed that if we'd been hired to guard people on this station only, we didn't have much to worry about.

At least, that's how things had worked out for Germanica whenever they'd been assigned out here for a long, dull year.

-10-

On our way to our new duty station that afternoon, Carlos fell into step beside me. We were marching down a very long, gently curving street. Only losers walked on Tech World, and we were right in the middle of them.

Aliens who resembled animals, insects, and just plain freaks hobbled by. All of them looked destitute and sour. They scuttled out of our way like cockroaches when we came near them in clanking armor.

As per Centurion Graves' orders, 3rd Unit had split up into platoons. As I was part of Adjunct Leeson's platoon, I followed him and Claver into the city.

"Can you believe this joker named Claver?" Carlos demanded, gesturing to the front of the column where the officers were walking. "Old Silver is a good nickname. He must be ninety-nine years old!"

"I bet you're close to right," I said, "at the very least, he must not have died for thirty years or so in order to look that old. No one in Varus has silver hair."

"Might be kind of cool to get old," said Carlos in an uncharacteristically thoughtful tone of voice. "I'd be willing to try it just once. Then I'd get myself killed at around forty to start over fresh."

"I have to admit that sounds like more fun than dying all the time."

"Platoon halt!" came the order from up ahead.

We all stopped marching and shuffled ourselves back into an organized column, two abreast. I was at the midpoint of the column, and I felt secure enough to do a little sightseeing.

Unfortunately, the best vistas were above us. On the street-level, I felt as if we were walking in the gutter. There was trash everywhere, and aliens slept in makeshift shelters against the foot of every towering building.

Tilting my head upward, things looked better. A false sky hung about two kilometers above our heads. Soaring structures loomed all around us reaching for that synthetic heavenly blue.

The buildings we passed were like buildings on Earth. They were more open than structures on my homeworld as they didn't need to be completely sealed the way a building had to be when it was on a planetary surface.

The towering structures resembled networks of girders built with puff-crete and metal struts. There were gaps in the walls—big ones. Rather than going to the trouble of building a true window or door, the natives often just left a large square missing. These gaps were up to several meters wide and served the purpose of allowing entry, exit, and ventilation. There were a lot of balconies too, as there were great views to be had everywhere on the station.

In between these towering mountains of metal and puff-crete, vehicles buzzed. Walking on the street, we were a good fifty meters below the lowest echelon of air traffic. There was occasional ground traffic as well, mostly made up of cleaning machines and rickshaw-like carts pulled by the poorest of folks.

The column was called upon to halt, and we were left standing in line. Up ahead, Claver and Leeson were talking. As grunts, it was our job to stand around and wait for orders.

"Do you think it ever rains in here?" Carlos asked me.

I shrugged. "How the hell should I know? It's plenty big enough to have water condense up high, I guess. But they might employ enough reprocessing systems to stop it."

Carlos pointed to the structure we had halted at the foot of, and I saw what he was talking about. There was a large thick pipe that ran down from a kilometer or more above us. The pipe opened with a flared tip at the bottom. I could see liquid dribbling from it in a trail to the gutters and drains that lined the street.

"That pipe could be for rain," I admitted. "Or, it could be a cheap, alien-waste removal system. We seem to be in the low-rent district."

Carlos made a sound of disgust as he stepped gingerly out of the pools of unknown liquid his boots were soaking in.

"Back in line, Ortiz!" shouted Harris.

Grumbling, Carlos stood in the puddle again. "What the hell are they doing up at the front of the column?" he demanded.

Being a head taller than anyone else between ourselves and the officers, I was able to give him a report on the situation. "Looks like they're arguing about something."

"That's great. I'm standing here in alien piss and Adjunct Leeson is bitching out Old Silver."

"Shut up in the ranks!" shouted Harris.

Carlos and I both knew that the next step would involve Harris breaking ranks to come close and chew on us, so we fell silent. Staying quiet had always been hard on Carlos in particular, but fortunately, the line began moving again soon.

The column took a right-angle turn into the structure that loomed overhead. Old Silver seemed to have gotten his way as he was leading the platoon inside through a wide opening between two massive metal struts. The struts were rusty and thick liquids trickled down both of them onto the sidewalk from God knew where above.

"What is this place?" demanded Carlos. "An alien poorhouse?"

"Beats me," I told him. "I thought we were supposed to be guarding a fancy-pants merchant prince."

Things went from bad to worse once we were inside the building. It looked like an abandoned skyscraper, and we were on the ground floor. Things that must have passed for rodents hopped and scurried around us—but they weren't mammals. They were more like beetles or cockroaches the size of rats. They had horns, too—honest to God *horns* on their heads—right between their feelers.

76

"Ugh," Kivi said, pointing her weapon at one that reared up and gazed at us in silent, frank appraisal.

"You think you can take him, Kivi?" I asked. "I hear that's a new kind of citizen down here."

"You're kidding me."

"Yeah, I am."

"Bastard."

She moved off, and I shrugged my armored shoulders. I followed her with Carlos right behind me. Kivi and I had an on-again off-again thing that had been going on for years now. I knew I wasn't the only man in that category, either. The nature of our interactions all depended on how annoyed she was with me on any given month or day. Taking her measure, I judged I was out of favor with her on this mission—but you couldn't blame a guy for trying.

Water—or something worse—dribbled from the ceiling onto our heads. People cursed and flapped their gauntlets all up and down the line.

An order soon came down the column from the front: "Helmets on, visors open!"

Everyone complied quickly enough, but I adlibbed and slammed my visor down too. My suit air conditioners kicked in on automatic, and I felt better immediately. Being inside my suit was almost like driving a small car through the nasty building. It gave me a feeling of comfortable distance from the exterior world.

It got darker, and danker, and then we finally reached a downward slanting ramp.

"Oh, *hell* no!" Carlos exclaimed, echoing my own opinions. For once, Harris didn't tell him to shut up.

Suit lights snapped on. My twin beams bracketed my helmet and shone brilliant light wherever I turned my head. Like most of the troops, I sent my lights stabbing down toward the bottom of that ramp.

We all stared down into what could only be described as a brownish-green river of slow-moving sludge.

Leeson must have sense our mood, so he clicked onto the general tactical channel and started talking. He spoke calmly and matter-of-factly sounding to me like an airline pilot discussing a passing cloud.

"What we have here is a mission-barrier," he said. "Adjunct Claver has informed me we need to cross this barrier in order to reach our objective."

"Uh, sir?" came a voice. I recognized it as Veteran Harris. "Just what objective can be found on the other side of this shit-river, if you don't mind my asking? Some of the boys were wondering."

"Our clients are waiting on the far side," Leeson said flatly.

We all looked at one another in surprise and confusion.

"Good thing I spent an hour polishing my armor," Kivi said bitterly.

"Now *this* is Legion Varus' luck in action, people," Carlos said. "We got ourselves hired by some kind of sewer monster. I bet it wants us to lather up in this river of filth then it'll ask us to escort its slimy butt to the fanciest hotel in town."

"Shut up, Ortiz," Harris ordered without conviction. We all knew Carlos could be right, and Legion Varus' misfortunes *were* legendary.

How can I describe the next step of our mission? Crossing the shit-river was grotesque and humiliating. We held our weapons over our heads and waded in. Fortunately, the current was slow and no one got sucked under. They even ordered the troops to clamp their visors down tightly—mighty nice of them to think of that.

When we reached the far side there was a ramp going up and lights ahead too. We struggled out of the muck onto the ramp, cursing and slipping.

A gush of mist sprayed down onto us without warning. I wasn't the only one who had his weapon out, aiming this way and that—but there were no enemies in sight. The spraying system seemed to be automated, and I had to admit it was cleaning off my armor.

"Keep moving! Up and off this ramp, people!" shouted a now-familiar voice. It was Old Silver himself.

We marched upward, and it was like walking through a carwash. At the top, we gathered and stood more or less in a square. Everyone had their weapons out and cradled. We weren't aiming at every shadow, but we were alert. This wasn't our first mission after all.

A hissing release of gas sounded, and a whirring sound followed. A large portion of the ceiling lowered itself slowly into our midst. We backed up, forming a circle around it. We watched these developing events with unblinking eyes.

Creatures stood on the platform as it came down. There were six of them, and they were all Tau. Bug-eyed, they were well-dressed in shimmering riots of color. Tau didn't wear clothes—at least, the rich ones didn't. They wore projected articles of clothing in various colors. An illusory mass of moving shapes and designs. I could tell from what little I knew of Tau society that these guys were rich. They had a color shield that was very thin—but completely opaque. Illusionary suits that were both thin and opaque cost the most.

The details of the suits each cost extra as well. If you wanted shoes of a certain style and form, you could have them. But it would cost you. It was all artificial, of course, and sometimes Tau hacked their suits and displayed wealth they didn't have. To be caught doing so was a humiliation, however.

The six aliens eyed us critically.

"Weapons aimed down with safeties on, fools," Harris said to the troopers as he strode along the front of the line.

Soldiers reluctantly aimed their weapons away from our benefactors.

Old Silver himself stepped up to greet the six aliens. He buzzed and clicked, and after a second I realized he must have a personal translation device on his suit. That was unusual and expensive.

My next thought was to wonder what exactly these characters did to amass wealth and why the heck they had to have us march through a sewer to meet them.

"This stinks worse than the shit-river," Carlos said to me.

"My thoughts exactly."

Old Silver turned around and smiled at all of us. In his hand was something—could that be a credit stick? It vanished before I could identify it with certainty.

"Platoon," he said, "you're the luckiest men on this station. These clients understand the rarest of customs here on Tech World: *tipping*."

We looked at one another in bewilderment. Were we soldiers or waiters?

"All we have to do to conclude this contract is escort these gentlemen—or ladies as the case may be, I'm not always sure with these guys—to The Vents then back up to the financial district. That's it. We'll be done in few hours. After that, you can all spend your share of the credit anyway you wish."

"How big of a tip are we talking about?" Carlos asked.

Harris didn't shout at him, which surprised me. I guess he wanted to know, too.

"Uh..." Old Silver said, looking around at the assembled troops. "I've got enough to distribute two thousand to each of you. Double that for your commander."

The reaction the sum generated was immediate and gratifying to Claver. The assembled troops whooped and shook their gauntlets over their heads in approval. Two thousand Galactic credits was a lot of money to us. Translated into local cash on Earth it would be worth millions.

Only I and a few others reacted with comparative reserve. I looked at Leeson. He was quietly frowning at the aliens. Harris looked absolutely paranoid, and he wasn't even looking at the Tau. He was staring around us into the surrounding subterranean darkness.

I considered the offer. It sounded like easy money for a tour of the sewers, the banks, and the bad side of town. A nice Sunday stroll in combat armor.

All you have to do is look the other way and take your bribe, trooper. Nothing funny going on here!

I didn't like it—and I finally said so when Old Silver came close to transfer my share of the credits from his tapper to mine.

"Sorry sir," I said. "I'm going to pass."

Claver eyed me with a mix of surprise and disdain. "What do we have here? A boy scout who thinks he's better than the rest of us?"

80

Carlos leaned forward extending his tapper suggestively. "He's no scout—but he does think his crap is odorless. Can I have his share, sir? I'll watch over him and make sure he doesn't get into any trouble."

Claver ignored Carlos entirely. His steely eyes were locked with mine.

"Two *thousand* credits," he said, giving a whistle. "You can afford to pass that up? Maybe you're one of those rich legionnaires I'm always hearing about. One that just joined up with Varus, the worst of the shit-outfits, to see the stars in style. Is that it, boy? Are you rich?"

"No sir," I said. "I just don't like taking money from people when I don't know where it came from."

He nodded slowly. "A rules-lawyer, eh? A stickler?"

Carlos laughed until he coughed.

"No sir," I said to the Adjunct. "I'm going along, but I'm skipping my 'tip'."

Claver hesitated. The rest of them watched with interest. I'd half-expected Leeson or Harris to jump into the conversation, but they didn't. They'd taken the money quietly, but maybe they were curious how a contest between me and Old Silver would go.

"All right," he said at last. "But don't come crawling back to me later for your share. And don't think this will give you some kind of a lever over me. Hell, boy, we're mercenary troops. That means we fight for pay. What difference does it make if your Tribune arranges a contract for your benefit, or I do?"

"Point taken, Adjunct," I said.

Claver sighed and walked down the rest of the line, distributing funds. Natasha was the very last one in the group. She glanced at me then looked down as she extended her tapper. Claver touched his arm to hers, and the hot-link was formed. The funds were transferred instantly.

I knew that Natasha had money troubles back home. Her parents always needed cash for medicines and the like. She also had big ideas concerning what she might find here on Tech World to take home as a souvenir.

81

Deciding I wouldn't hold anything against them, I put a smile on my face. But it didn't come naturally to me. I didn't like Claver, and I didn't like anything about this little side job he had gotten us involved with.

-11-

Half an hour later we were back up on the streets marching in a square. In the midst of our formation were the Tau, protected by our armored shells.

Our employers had toned down their plumage. Their fancy illusionary garments had turned to muted colors—why, I wasn't certain. Their projected outfits were supposed to depict their mood and demeanor. Right now, they were all grays, blacks and shiny copper. I wasn't sure what that was supposed to mean, but they looked as if they didn't want to be noticed. Maybe that was how one dressed when one was nervous on Tech World.

"That old buzzard is holding out on us," Carlos complained.

"How much do you think Silver kept for himself?" I asked Carlos seriously.

"How should I know?"

"When it comes down to lies and bribery, you're the closest thing the unit has to an expert."

Carlos made a face, but he lowered his voice and whispered his answer. "Half," he said. "That would make it easy to do the math. I bet he paid out around fifty thousand and pocketed the rest."

I whistled, impressed in spite of myself. No wonder Germanica had always come home to Earth in finery with the best barely used equipment stowed aboard their ship. They'd found ways to supplement their budget that I'd never realized were possible until today.

We came to another ramp, but this time it didn't lead us down into the sewers. Instead, it rose up and up at a steep, forty-five degree angle. As we came out onto a higher level street, I could tell right off we were in a nicer part of town. The streets weren't dirty, they were shiny. There were a lot more garish lights flashing ads, and the buzzing air traffic was just over our heads instead of a kilometer above us.

We entered what looked to be a merchant warehouse. There were massive crates everywhere, reminding me of containers for mass-shipping back home. They stacked perfectly and even gripped one another when they came close with automated magnetic clamps. What surprised me, however, was that the crates didn't appear to be made of metal. They were some kind of strong, lightweight polymer. Like puff-crete, but thinner and more uniform.

"What are these things?" I asked aloud.

Old Silver must have overhead me. He was walking down the line, instructing troopers to stand at each corner of a given crate and pick it up. Four men were enough to carry one, but they would have to shoulder their weapons while the rest stood guard.

"They use gravity adhesives," he explained. "I don't think we have that kind of technology back home. Think of a magnet that works on anything—like gravity. If you have two of them, they attract or repel each other depending on relative polarity. These crates are sealed closed by terrific gravitational force, and you have to be careful when you move them close to one another—they can crush you like bug."

"I'll keep that in mind, sir. What's in these things?"

Old Silver's smile faded instantly, turning into a frown. "That's not for any of us to ask, son. The Tau have paid the freight. We're going to move their shipment down to the Vents then escort them back to civilization. What they're trading is their business. Understand?"

"Yes sir," I said without conviction.

The adjunct moved away, exhorting more effort out of the next squad of troops. Several troops were assigned to each crate, and there were six of them in all. As a weaponeer, I was given the assignment of walking nearby and cradling my plasma tube.

Carlos wasn't so lucky. He and Kivi were both tasked with carrying a corner of a crate. They staggered under the weight even with powered armor and gravity-assisted technology.

"This is bullshit," Carlos complained. "Why do you get to parade around while we grunt and struggle, McGill?"

I shrugged. "I guess the officers can recognize a winner when they see one."

We began a less comfortable part of the journey, escorting our cargo to a waiting skimmer. The skimmer was one of the open-air types, essentially a flying barge. The back was open and bigger than a freight car on an old railway. We loaded up the boxes and stood around them bracing our feet and looking worriedly at the railing. It was only about a half-meter high, not enough to keep a man safely on the back of this thing if it took a hard turn.

There wasn't even a warning siren from the pilot when we took off. Worse, the initial launch was anything but smooth. We powered up into the air, swirled around, slewing and heaving, then leveled off and flew at great speed into the hurtling air traffic.

"What the hell is with this pilot?" Kivi shouted, coming to stand near me. She put a hand on my shoulder to steady herself. My heavier weaponeer's suit was equipped with auto-levelers, and could serve a regular trooper as an anchor in a pinch.

"I don't want to let my feet move," I said. "You take a look...is he by any chance a bluish turtle-looking guy?"

Kivi stretched and leaned out to get a look at the creature at the helm up front. She nodded.

"Yeah," she said. "Bluish, and that's definitely a shell."

"Crap. These guys are crazy drivers. Hang on everybody!"

I eyed our guests. It was better than looking down at the heaving streets a kilometer below. They seemed to be in a better mood now. The somber colors were gone. Their suits ran with rippling pinks and blues over their bodies, and their shoes were a distinctive shade of gold. I had no idea what any of that

85

meant, but I surmised they were happier than they'd been when they were marching through the streets.

About then, everyone yelled in alarm in my headphones. A sickening feeling of falling had freaked out all of us. We plunged down, like a leaf dropped from a tree, directly toward the ground. We didn't tip over or nose downward—it was more like we'd lost power.

"Platoon, brace yourselves!" Leeson ordered.

He needn't have bothered. Both Kivi and Carlos had decided to hang onto me. Others had found cables, protruding equipment—anything. I didn't think it was going to matter if we hit at this velocity.

Leeson came on platoon chat, and he sounded worried. "Can anyone raise Claver? I'm not sure if we're out of control or what."

We tried, but no one could connect with the Germanica Adjunct.

"Should we try to take over the helm, sir?" I asked on platoon chat.

"Can you fly this thing, McGill?" answered Adjunct Leeson.

"Probably better than that crazy turtle."

"All right, if you can move without falling overboard, recon and take appropriate action. I'm down to crawling myself."

Most of the troops were crawling. I commanded my feet to move and they did, dragging Carlos and Kivi with me.

"Let go, that's an order," I told them, and they reluctantly grabbed for less stable handholds. Strangely, the crates seemed glued into place as did the Tau. Kivi and Carlos along with most of the others had figured this out and began clinging to the crates.

I marched carefully in an effort to keep my magnetized feet close to the deck of the skimmer so they could clamp on with every step. Fortunately, it was made of metal unlike the crates. To speed things up, I grabbed the nearest crate and hand-over-handed my way toward the front of the vessel. As I came up to the last crate, I was surprised to see Old Silver standing there among the Tau. He seemed to be chatting unconcernedly with our employers.

"Sir?" I asked him. "Why are we falling like a stone?"

He craned his neck around and looked at me. His hair shone like liquid mercury in the artificial sunlight.

"What are you doing up here? Get back to your post, Specialist."

I was confused, but I could see the blue turtle was still at the helm flying with vigor.

"The platoon commander sent me up here," I said. "He thought something might be wrong with the helm controls."

"Good lord, what a bunch of old women!" Claver said.

I blinked at him and frowned. "If you don't need assistance, I'll get back to the crates."

"You do that—and tell Leeson I've got a spare set of balls he can use until he locates his own."

"You can tell him that yourself, sir," I suggested. "I'll open a channel for you."

He made a dismissive gesture, waving me off, then turned back to his alien buddies. I made a gesture of my own behind his back. Every time I interacted with this guy, I found I liked him less than before.

I'd no sooner turned around and taken my first step back toward the crates when the world was plunged into blackness.

My first thought was that we'd hit bottom but there was no impact, no screams—well, maybe there were a few of those from our less brave members, but we were definitely still flying.

I looked upward as my eyes were drawn by the only source of bright light. Above was a shrinking square of brilliance. We'd dropped into some kind of a shaft.

There was no sensation of slowing down. If anything, we were going down faster than before. It occurred to me then that after we were to pick up our cargo we were to transport it to the Vents. By all accounts, they were at the very bottom of the station. Suddenly, everything made sense—at least, it did if you were an insane turtle.

"Sir?" I said, linking with Leeson privately. "I think we're okay. The pilot is taking us down a shaft to the bottom of the station."

"Is that what Claver told you? He's still ignoring my com requests."

"Uh, more or less," I answered. "He put it more colorfully, sir."

"What does that mean?"

"He mentioned your genitalia—making an unfavorable comparison with his."

Leeson didn't often show emotion of any kind, but I began sensing a current of anger.

"I see," he said. "We took the money he arranged so now we're his whipping boys. He's having a laugh and taking us on a joyride. Fine."

He gave a general order to seal our suits. Helmets were to stay on and visors were to stay shut. I recalled from the briefing that the air was bad down below the station's street level, and I thought it was a sensible precaution.

We halted soon after that creating a mixture of relief and pain for everyone aboard. Relief because we were no longer rocketing down into darkness, and pain because the stop was so bone-shuddering hard that our legs barely supported our bodies when we hit bottom.

"Come on, come on!" shouted Claver, slamming his hands together and walking the length of the skimmer. "Get your crates off the skimmer, you lazy sons-of-bitches. We've got a schedule to keep!"

This was the first I'd heard of a schedule, but it made a kind of sense. We certainly seemed to be in a hurry.

"Are we late to meet the freighter, sir?" I asked.

Claver peered at me. "You again," he said. "You ask too many questions, you know that? You'd never make rank in my outfit."

It took a few minutes, but we managed to get the cargo off the skimmer. The aliens strolled down the ramp after their crates. They no longer seemed nervous. They were pleased with themselves instead. Most of them were wearing a shimmering green now—a favorite shade among their species.

88

I looked around, and the sights were indeed impressive. Massive machinery rotated and spun around us. Devices as huge as they were mysterious clanked and made pounding sounds. As far as my eyes could see, the equipment stood in ranks and rows. Between the machines were crisscrossing lines of metal as if terrifically huge grates covered the landscape.

"This is the Vents," Claver said. "If you look closely down at the Vents themselves, you'll find the most wretched members of society in the star system. Those are what we call *breathers*."

We looked, and indeed I did see individuals here and there. There were all sorts of creatures down here. The variety alone was impressive. Most were sitting along the metal walkways that I now realized made up the Vents themselves. Misty gasses gusted up now and then from the depths below them obscuring the unfortunates.

"You see, oxygen costs money," Claver said. "Nothing is free on Tech World. If you hit rock-bottom, they let you come down here to breathe for free—but you won't last too long."

"What do they eat?" Carlos asked, fascinated by the pathetic breathers.

"Each other, mostly," Claver said. Then he cackled. I wasn't sure if he was joking or not, but he clearly thought his answer was hilarious.

Another skimmer arrived about two minutes later. It didn't come right out and land next to us, however. Instead, it hovered a distance away over the Vents. I caught a flashing of lights between the aliens and the second skimmer.

Finally, cautiously, the second skimmer approached ours. It set down nearby—and crushed a breather callously.

"Did that pilot just kill a guy?" I asked Carlos.

"Yeah, I think so."

Frowning, I watched as a second delegation of the Tau approached. They carried a single crate that was smaller than ours.

"I feel like I'm watching a ransom being paid," I said.

"Maybe you are," Carlos agreed.

The two groups of aliens met, and their clothing changed from one color to another in rapid succession. I knew they used these colors to communicate moods in subtle ways. It was almost subconscious behavior for them. For them, it was similar to our body language.

Finally, a signal was given. The bargain—whatever it was—had been approved. A group of figures carried the smaller crate closer at the same time we carried our larger boxes to them.

I got the surprise of my life when I recognized the people carrying the smaller crate. They were legionnaires—Germanica legionnaires.

-12-

The Germanica troops eyed us, and we returned their gaze levelly. There was only a single squad on their side whereas we had a full platoon. We stared at one another uncomfortably across big gaps between the crisscrossing steel roadways that made up the grate we were walking on. Thick vapors drifted around us before being sucked into the giant squares of the grate and down into a hot abyss below.

I could only imagine what it would be like to step off the side and fall into the oxygen reprocessing systems. I heard gears and grinding sounds down there on top of the bubbling of unknown liquids. Falling could only result in an unpleasant death.

The two groups of Tau were still talking, and their suits flashed displaying their excited moods. I hoped the negotiations were going well. I wasn't about to shoot a Germanica trooper just because some alien had paid my team a few extra credits.

Fortunately, the deal went smoothly. Both sides parted, and we were left with the small crate. The other troops loaded our larger, heavier crates one at a time onto their skimmer.

"What the hell do you think is in these things, Carlos?" I asked.

He appeared thoughtful. "There are only a limited number of possibilities. It must be something valuable enough to be worth all this security and sneaking around. Probably something illegal—otherwise why are we doing the deal on the Vents?"

"Why indeed?" asked Adjunct Claver. He'd come up to us while we stood and talked. "I hope you two gentlemen are comfortable and well-rested."

"As a matter of fact, I'm feeling a little sleepy, sir," Carlos said. "Maybe we should all take five on this lovely—"

"Shut up and get up that ramp! You two are an embarrassment. Look at my troops over there! One single squad of my men from Germanica is shouldering that load without a complaint in the bunch. Now, *those* are what I call soldiers!"

"Sir?" I asked. "Did you say those men are under your command?"

He looked at me sharply. "Not right now. You rookies are my babysitting mission for the day. Get moving."

The Tau rushed forward when the Germanica people retreated and were soon grunting and heaving with effort as they lifted the single, small crate. They didn't let us help them. They loaded the small box by themselves.

The minute we were all back aboard the skimmer it took off with a sickening lurch. We didn't even have the larger grav-locked crates to hold onto this time, but at least we knew we weren't going to die—not unless the turtle screwed up.

We zoomed up the shaft until we popped out into the open again blinking in the artificial sunlight. I opened my visor and sucked in the relatively fresh air. We flew with relative grace toward the financial district. There, massive structures like pyramids stood in rows. I recognized them from Natasha's discussion of landmarks. The buildings were the Imperial banking outlets.

Financial institutions were technically independent within the Empire, but the Galactics kept a pretty tight leash on them. All large credit transactions were recorded and reported back to the Core Systems. Or at least, that's how it was supposed to work.

We landed at the foot of the largest pyramid. For the first time, I saw Old Silver was alert and even concerned. "Okay, look alive, troops. Circle up, guns pointed away from the cargo."

"Are there any dangers we should be made aware of, Adjunct?" Leeson asked.

"No, nothing in particular, but this is the moment of truth. We're earning our pay right here, right now."

The aliens swarmed around the small crate on the skimmer and spread their hands out, urging us back with clicks and translated statements of "no". They didn't want any more help from us.

We let them circle around the small crate and watched them lift it with difficulty. I unlimbered my heavy cannon and put it on my shoulder. I wasn't too worried as I watched the surrounding crowd. Some looked like your typical pack freaks that wandered the station's streets, but most were Tau and there were plenty of them. In fact, most of the passersby wore rich shimmering clothing that dazzled the eye.

Natasha had spent most of the day with the auxiliary personnel. Techs and Bio Specialists usually didn't carry crates and threaten people with guns. She had been apart from me, but now she came to my position and pointed into the crowds.

I followed her gesture, but didn't see anything unusual. It was just a knot of Tau on a walk. Sure, the group she pointed to were moving in a pack of perhaps twenty individuals, but there was nothing unusual about that.

"Hi Tasha," I said. "What's wrong?"

She frowned at the group. "Their colors, that's what's wrong."

I looked again and saw maroon bodies with silver shoes. I shrugged. "So they like purple. So what?"

"That's not right for going to the bank. That's a color worn at solemn events like funerals or weddings. And I don't understand the silver shoes. That's not even on the list."

I laughed. "I can think of plenty of reasons to be depressed in front of a bank," I said. "Maybe their apartments were foreclosed on."

"I'm reporting it to Leeson anyway," she said, activating her com link.

Just to be sure, I swung my weapon to cover the knot of Tau in question. They were approaching, walking down the street toward the same cavernous bank entrance that our charges were now heading toward.

"All right," Veteran Harris shouted. "Our orders are to hold our ground. The Tau are going to carry their package into the bank. Once it's there, we've completed our mission. Stand by."

I clanked to the edge of the skimmer stepped over the low rail and hopped down onto the street. A few other troopers positioned themselves on the ground after I did. No one really wanted to be close to where they were just coming down the ramp. Our clients were straining, heaving—I wasn't sure why they didn't let us help them with their load. With exoskeletal strength and auto-assist servos in our arms, I was sure we could lift that box like it was nothing.

Perhaps it was chance, or maybe some part of me had done it on purpose, but I found myself positioned directly between the approaching group of locals and the struggling group carrying the crate.

Then I heard a cracking sound. I turned around, realizing it had come from the crate. The Tau had dropped it, and it was flat on the ground. One of them was screeching, and I saw his foot was pinned underneath. Syrupy black blood flowed.

"Help them out—McGill, lend a hand!" Adjunct Leeson called to me.

I was close, so I clanked over to them. I tossed a glance over my shoulder, and noticed the mob with the odd colors showing had halted. They'd stopped walking closer and were just standing there watching the spectacle.

The Tau struggling with their box hissed at me but then waved me forward when I pantomimed lifting their box. I could tell they weren't able to move it any further by themselves.

Heaving on the crate, I was shocked at how heavy it was. I grunted and strained, managing to get a corner up. The Tau who's foot had been trapped managed to pull it out, but then I lost my grip and the crate slammed right down again. I braced myself and tried shoving it. I thought maybe it might be stuck on something. If I could slide the box to one side, it might

94

come free. My suit registered three tons of lateral force, and I smelled a hot odor—then, finally, it shifted.

Like an object breaking free from a frictional hold, it slid about a meter forward. The Tau chattered with enthusiasm. One of them spoke to me.

"Big man, push more!"

I activated my headset. "I need a little help, Adjunct. This thing is stuck on something."

"Right. Carlos, Kivi—get up there and push."

"Sir!" I heard Sargon shout. "Request permission to man-handle that box. McGill is a known weakling."

Sargon was the other weaponeer assigned to my platoon. He was large, strong and a terrible braggart.

"Denied. Stay here with me on the skimmer, Specialist. I don't want both my weaponeers farting around with a box instead of manning their weapons."

Kivi and Carlos arrived. Carlos kicked me in the ass as he stepped close, but I could hardly feel it through my armor.

"You're like a mule put out to stud, McGill—useless," he said.

I would have liked to kick him back, but there was a crowd forming now and I didn't like it. Kivi and Carlos threw their shoulders into the effort, but the crate did little more than rock from side to side.

"Damn! What's in this thing?" Carlos asked.

"It must be stuck on something," Kivi said, getting down on her knees to look under it.

"That's not it," I said. "Seems like it's gotten heavier, somehow…"

Using a private channel, I contacted Natasha. "Hey, could you see if there's something wrong with these grav-clamps?" I asked her. "I think that's what's going on. They've malfunctioned and they're trying to clamp the box down to the street."

"Ah," she said. "That would explain a lot."

She asked permission to move forward to my position out in the open, and Leeson reluctantly gave it. After a second, she was running instruments over the box.

95

In the meantime, the Tau were losing patience. They were so close to their goal, and yet unable to reach it. I could tell they were debating among themselves and becoming increasingly nervous.

Claver, growling in frustration, marched down the ramp toward us.

"Great," Carlos said, "look who's coming. Maybe he'll add a few ounces of lift and fix everything."

Natasha looked up at me in bewilderment after she'd finished her examination. "You're right," she said. "The grav-clamps are active. This crate has been glued to the ground with about five thousand kilos of excess force."

"Well, turn it off!" roared Old Silver. He now stood among us with his leathery hands on his hips. He was the only man not wearing armor in the unit. I wondered how he'd survived so very long with the kind of attitude he'd displayed thus far.

Carlos was ahead of me for once in his life. "We've got a local with a weapon, sirs!" he shouted. He lifted his rifle and directed it toward the group of Tau who were watching us intently.

"Sling guns!" shouted Claver. "No firing here, too many civvies!"

Reluctantly, we all slung our guns.

That was the moment they'd been waiting for, I think. Looking back, I figure they'd been worried about our presence and had been hoping we'd pull out and leave our clients struggling with their impossible burden on the steps of the bank.

The strangely colored Tau moved with sudden decision. They pulled out short-barreled stubby weapons and spread out, filtering into the crowd.

To my credit it wasn't me who reacted first. Carlos had always been the jumpy sort. He unslung his weapon and aimed it in their direction. He didn't fire—but he was clearly threatening them.

"Don't shoot!" roared Claver. "I can talk to them! Leeson, control your men! We can't afford to have an incident right here in the middle of—"

A shot rang out from the crowd, sparking and burning a scorch mark on Carlos' armor. That was all it took to put everything into motion.

We were Legion Varus troops. That's all I can say. We're not like other legionnaires—I'd be the first to admit it. But I don't blame our heritage or our training. We were so accustomed to deadly danger, so familiar with death, that in the thick of combat we obeyed animal instincts more than we did the orders of an officer. Especially orders from someone like Old Silver.

We unslung our weapons as a group and aimed them at the Tau that were moving to surround us. The crowds were surging away and trying to melt into side streets, but the bandits who'd pulled out their sub-machinegun-like weapons grabbed individuals to use as shields.

I can say with near certainty that it was their side that opened fire. A strange sound ripped the air. It wasn't like a gun, not exactly. It was more like a rapid series of gas releases. A loud series of chuffing sounds that were quickly joined by many others.

Explosive pellets rained on my squad mates. Kivi spun around and fell, but got back up again. Her armor had taken the brunt of it, but she seemed to be moving slowly. Carlos took shelter behind the crate, laying his rifle over the top of it. Natasha was crawling on the ground.

I brought around my plasma weapon, but I didn't fire. Claver was right on one count—the area was full of innocent bystanders. If I released a charge into the crowd, I'd splatter a dozen unfortunates.

On impulse, I aimed my belcher at the ground and discharged it. A blaze of light gleamed, and the puff-crete melted away. A smoking hole revealed the level below the street we stood on.

I'd been hoping that my display of firepower would cause our assailants to retreat, but it had the opposite effect. They seemed to believe the fight had turned into all-out war, and they all blazed away spamming us with pellets that popped and flared against my armor. Our Tau clients weren't armored, and things went badly for them. A glance told me they were all

97

down. Their shimmering, nonexistent clothing wavered and blurred over their bodies which lay all around their precious crate in various states of death.

"Return fire!" Leeson shouted. "Single-shots only, mark your target!"

"NO dammit!" shouted Claver.

I'd figured he was probably dead by now, but even without armor he'd scuttled like a rat and was lying at the bottom of the steps, sheltering between two dead Tau.

Once we were away from Earth, Legion Varus troops were only obligated to follow the orders of Galactics and our own officers. That's what independence was all about, and we'd voted to keep it just a few weeks ago. Ignoring Claver, our troops shouldered their weapons and sighted carefully. They popped shots steadily into the enemy, who seemed like untrained amateur thugs to me. Six or seven of them went down, but there were plenty more, and they didn't look like they were running away.

For me, the fight was frustrating. My big gun was anything but precise. All I could do was absorb fire. I decided to change tactics.

Slinging my cannon, I spread my arms wide and extended two force-blades, one from each wrist. Then, I charged the crowd.

This development startled everyone. I found I'd even surprised myself when I reached the lines of screaming civvies and thugs. I'm sure the innocents figured death itself was charging them in a metal cocoon with swords of fire in either hand.

I caught half a dozen pellets before I reached them, but I was still on my feet. As a weaponeer I'd been issued heavier armor than the rest of the unit, and I was relying on that extra layer of metal now.

Once into range, I cut and thrust. A force-blade is far from a precision instrument, but it's a lot cleaner than a plasma cannon. I jabbed into soft unarmored flesh, opening up chests and lopping off heads. Between my efforts and the careful marksmanship of my fellow squaddies, the enemy lost half their number and most of their nerve.

In a last act of defiance, one of them lobbed a brightly glowing, blue-white object toward the group huddling around the crate.

"Grenade!" I shouted.

Troops scrambled, crawling and dragging themselves away. The crate was left smoking and black.

Our assailants ran every which-way. I felt like chasing them down, but was ordered back to the skimmer. I rejoined Leeson there as he walked down the ramp to the broken crate.

"Let's see what the hell we've been fighting over," Leeson said, peering through the hole in the roof of the crate. "Holy crap..." he whispered.

I shouldered close to him and peered inside. "Disks of metal?" I asked. "What are those—wait a minute."

It took me a second before I recalled a museum trip from long ago. "Those are Imperial coins. Galactic credit pieces."

On Earth we still used cash in some cases for local commerce. But Galactic cash had been outlawed nearly a century back. All Imperial currency was accounted for in electronic form. Originally this had been sold to us as an economic and environmental boon. Over time, however, many had come to suspect that if all money was a figment inside a remote computer, it was all really under the control of Hegemony—and beyond them, the Galactics.

"That's money—*real* money," I said.

"That's right, son," Claver said, walking up to the crate and staring inside it with the rest of us. "Untraceable Imperial cash. Each of those coins is worth more than your annual pay, and they're not ours. Keep your hands off."

Leeson frowned at him. "You're right of course, Claver. We're not thieves."

Claver gave a nasty laugh.

Leeson's frown deepened. "Our clients are dead and we're stuck out here in the street with this shattered box," he snapped. "Do you want us to walk away?"

"No. My clients are plenty rich enough to afford a second life. When the clean-up crew shows, they'll scan them and order revivals immediately. They'll be billed and released. I'd be surprised if they don't show up again within two hours."

"Isn't there going to be a bit of tough explaining to do when the local police arrive?" I asked.

Claver gave me another of his unpleasant laughs. This time, it was louder and more insulting.

"What are you? Some kind of dumb cracker? We *are* the police, boy. At the very least, we outrank any local badge they'll bother to send out here. Why do you think these people wanted to hire us in the first place?"

Looking around and examining the bodies, I lost count at around seventy. There were only a few legionnaires among the dead.

I reflected that when I'd helped arrange for Earth to become the local Enforcers in the Galactic Empire, this wasn't exactly what I'd had in mind.

-13-

Once the violence had ended and we'd established a perimeter, officials began to arrive. The first responders were Tau in the medical personnel colors of blue with yellow lateral stripes. They ignored us and moved to inspect their dead fellows. Checking each citizen's DNA with instruments, they began to chatter excitedly amongst themselves.

Old Silver watched with interest. "They're pretty happy. This bunch of stiffs must be worth thousands to them."

"I bet. After all, they dumped about a million Galactic credits out of that box."

"Yeah, but that doesn't mean that they own the cash. They could be couriers just as we are—but I would bet they aren't. Couriers wouldn't rate a revive. They seem to be actual traders. They'll have the coin to buy their lives back, and it won't come cheap. They base the price on a percentage of net worth, you know."

I frowned thoughtfully, and dared a question. "May I ask, sir, what were we transporting for them?"

"Are you stupid, son?" he demanded. "Guns, of course. They're gun-runners. What else would be in crates of that size that would be worth hauling down to the planet surface?"

Stunned, my eyes widened. "Guns? So this is an illegal operation, and we're aiding some kind of rebel force on the planet below?"

Claver shook his head. "You make it sound dirty. What do we care? Maybe the guys downstairs are freedom-fighters.

Maybe these fat cats up here on Gelt Station are lording it over them, hoarding all the trade-money. I don't know which side is heroic—I don't even care. I'm here to collect some pay and get out. I suggest you do the same."

"But isn't this against the law, sir?"

"Law? The only laws that matter out here are those imposed by the Galactics. And you know as well as I do they don't give a rat's ass about the internal politics of any star system. As long as these Tech Worlders don't go off and attack another system, the Galactics don't care. And we shouldn't either. Other than us, there are only a handful of humans within lightyears. Grow up, McGill."

"But sir, these are Imperial credit coins. Trading with them is illegal."

I could tell he was getting angry, but he answered me anyway. "We didn't do that. They did. We were just the bodyguards. We were paid with legitimate, digital credit. Don't you forget that."

I wasn't sure that the Nairbs would see it that way, but Claver had actually presented compelling points. I knew that the Galactics couldn't care less what happened here in the Tau Ceti system. Star Systems were free to have all the civil wars, rebellions and even vigorous genocides on their own turf they felt like. The Empire was too huge and spread out for any central governing body to get into fussing with local politics. As long as the Tau kept their trade goods flowing and didn't build starships to bother other members of the Empire, no one would do anything about their behavior.

Still, I felt as a part of the local enforcement branch of the Empire we owed it to our neighbors to do better than taking bribes and participate in gun-running. Hadn't we moved on past taking any job we had to just to survive? What was the point of being official representatives of the Empire if we didn't improve the lot of other species when we came into contact with them?

"I believe reputation matters in the long run," I told Adjunct Claver. "These Tau are weasels, I'll give you that, but I have hopes they might come to trust and rely on us in time. Maybe I'm being naïve, but that's the way I feel about it."

Claver rewarded me with a long, hard laugh.

"You've gotta be kidding me!" he said. "Listen son, the bigger the city, the worse the people behave. This whole planet is nothing but one endless city! Any local will cut your throat just for the privilege of selling their own mama—and they'll take a bent credit-piece for her, too. The ones that live downstairs on the planet's surface are even worse."

What he did next surprised me. It wasn't the act itself, but the brazen quality of it. He walked over to the cracked open crate, reached in a hand and scooped out a jingling handful of coins. His hand dipped in again—but by that time, I had my gauntlet clamped over his wrist.

"What are you doing, Specialist?" he demanded in a growling tone.

"I'm stopping a blatant attempt at theft, sir."

He looked at me in disbelief. "What, are you stupid? We can't leave these coins sitting here in the street. I'm going to fill a sack, and I suggest you do the same. Together, we'll get this cash to safety."

The adjunct was getting under my skin. I felt I had to say something that would worry him. "I think I should inform you, Adjunct Claver, that I'll be reporting this incident to Centurion Graves."

He snorted. "Let me give you a piece of advice, kid. Your outfit is going to be left here on your own in another week. I didn't get silver hair by making mistakes. You should learn all you can from an old hand rather than trying to screw with me."

I made a sweeping gesture. "We've lost several men. We've been taking bribes and aiding gunrunners. You don't think that's worth reporting?"

He struggled with me, but I shook his arm until the coins dropped back into the crate. He growled in frustration.

"You're the one that wouldn't take the tip, aren't you?" he asked me. "You don't want your cut? Fine. You run off and tattle. In fact, I don't care if you tell your prissy tribune as well. Germanica will be gone soon enough."

When I was sure he didn't have any coins in his pockets, I let him go. He stalked away, got into the skimmer, and said something to the blue turtle. To my surprise, they lifted off and flew away. I watched him leave with my mouth hanging open.

Adjunct Leeson left his position on the steps of the bank and rushed over to me.

"What did you do?" he demanded.

"Uh…I guess we didn't see eye-to-eye, sir."

"No shit," he said. "He just took off? What the hell are we supposed to do with these 'clients' and their money?"

"About the money," I said, "he tried to take that with him."

Leeson glowered at me. "You pissed him off, didn't you? Did it occur to you that he's our guide on this planet? That neither you nor I have a clue how this society operates while he's been here for several tours over decades?"

"He did say something to that effect," I admitted.

Once Claver was gone, the attitude of the Tau officials around us changed. The officials who'd been inspecting our dead clients stepped up and said something in their clacking language. Claver had taken the translator with him, but we got the gist of it when he put out a hand, palm up, and made a grabbing motion with it.

"I think he wants to be paid, sir," I said to Leeson.

Leeson threw his arms wide. "This is a frigging mess. How can we pay him? How do we know how much we owe?"

The official pointed toward the cracked crate of cash on the bank steps.

"No! No way," Leeson said. "That's our clients' money."

Irritably, the Tau medical people left us there. They took the bodies with them and I watched closely to make sure they left the cash in place. Other officials had removed the bodies of the thugs and civilians. In each case, they tested them to see if they were worth reviving. A few were and were carefully loaded aboard flying machines. The rest were piled onto a single cart and dragged away. I had the feeling they would end up in that river of sludge that flowed everywhere beneath the streets. The Tau weren't much for respecting their dead— unless the dead were rich.

"What about Claver?" I asked Leeson.

Harris answered my question. "He's forwarded his data-link to some bullshit box that's full of messages. How's that for a hint, McGill? He's too pissed off with you to help out!"

"What about headquarters? When can we expect relief?"

Adjunct Leeson sighed and came close. He put an arm around my shoulders—but it wasn't a friendly gesture. He spoke directly into my ear.

"Did you see me take a bribe, soldier?" he asked me.

"I'm not sure, sir," I said. "Some people might see it that way."

"Do you think that I want to explain all this to Graves—or anyone else?"

"Uh...no, probably not."

"That's right. We're not calling headquarters. We're handling this by ourselves. You're a big boy. You shouldn't be worried about a little bank-robbery attempt."

Adjunct Leeson gathered up the group, patched up the wounded, and talked over his options with Veteran Harris in a low voice.

The sky darkened as we stood around over the next half-hour. I got the feeling Veteran Harris and Leeson weren't sure what to do. Maybe they were waiting around to see if our clients did return to claim their cash. After all, Claver had said they would.

As night fell, businesses closed and the streets emptied. Then a new delegation appeared. This time they stood at the top of the steps of the bank. A group of lightly armed bank guards from the pyramid-like building we were squatting in front of came down toward us.

We eyed them warily, kept our fingers on our triggers, but we kept the muzzles of our weapons aimed downward.

It was about this time that I realized Claver had screwed us by dumping us here. He'd guided us across the city, a place he knew well while we were completely out of our element! We'd been left with the credits we'd been guarding, but we had no idea what to do with them. Should we take them back to base? Not easily done, even if the crate hadn't been damaged. We couldn't just leave the money out here. What client for any future subcontract would trust us after news of that got out?

We were armed guards, our clients were dead, and the crazy officer who'd made the deal had bugged out. We were well-armed but clueless. It was an uncomfortable situation.

The bank guards came closer one step at a time. They looked at us as if we were feral zoo animals somebody had let out of a cage.

Leeson stepped forward to greet them, reaching toward them as if to shake hands.

At first, they drew back. They chattered amongst themselves for a second then one of them produced a local, Tau System ten-credit piece and slapped it into Leeson's hand. Leeson looked at it in confusion.

The guards moved forward with more confidence after that. They approached the broken crate and peered inside. Immediately, they became excited and spoke rapidly amongst themselves.

"Sir?" I said to Leeson, who had been watching the guards without comprehension. "I think they're trying to take the money."

"Good," he said. "That's what we're supposed to do, isn't it? Deliver the funds to the bank. If the guards take it up those steps, it's their problem. Then we can focus on the walk home."

"I don't know if that's a good idea, sir," I said.

"Uh," said Harris, stepping into the conversation. "I have to go with McGill on this one, sir. The yellow light of greed is shining in the eyes of those guards. They'll steal it all the second we turn our backs."

"If you can't trust a bank, who can you trust on Tau Ceti?" Leeson demanded.

"This money isn't in the bank's hands, and it's cash," Harris said in a low voice. "Untraceable old-fashioned *Imperial* coins. There aren't too many guys back home I'd trust, either."

Leeson made a sound of disgust. I could tell he'd been hoping to unload this problem onto someone else. At least he hadn't spent all his time trying to figure out how to steal it. I had to give him high marks for that. All of us knew we'd never get these coins home to Earth much less get away with spending them on anything.

Leeson approached the bank guards making shooing motions. "Back!" he shouted. "Back into your bank you thieving rentals! That's not your money."

The guards chattered at him in irritation and didn't move. I stepped back a pace and looked around the street. It was surprisingly quiet. During business hours, there had never been less than a thousand people in sight. Now, there were only a dozen or so.

"Here," said Leeson irritably, producing the ten-credit coin and handing it back to the bank guards.

Reluctantly, they took it and retreated when Harris prodded a few of them with his gun. As the last man walked by, I reached out and clamped onto his wrist with my gauntlet.

"Just can't let a fight go by, can you McGill?" Harris demanded.

"Check his pocket."

Harris did, while the man hissed and sputtered. Three of the thousand-credit coins jingled into his hand. Harris tossed them back into the crate and I let the guard go.

Rubbing his hand and flaring his mouth tentacles at me, the guard walked back up the steps and into the bank. I was pretty sure he wasn't blowing me kisses.

"All right, McGill," Leeson said. "I've requested a private skimmer. It'll be expensive, but I'll pay for it. Unfortunately, I've just gotten the word it won't get here until morning. Apparently, flying vehicles are shot down automatically by these banking structures after business hours—too many robbery attempts. Lucky us, we get to spend the night out here."

"Hmm," I said thoughtfully. "Where are the local cops, sir?"

"We don't get support from their kind. First off, you have to *pay* cops on Tech World to help you out. They charge by the minute. Secondly, they avoid us like the plague. We're now officials of the Empire. We're like royalty, but royalty despised and feared by everyone. They don't want to mess with us, so they're staying away. We're on our own for good or bad."

"Only one choice then," I said. "We've got to get these coins off the street and back to headquarters."

"This part of the city shuts down after business hours, Specialist. Headquarters is at least a ten-kilometer walk. We'll wait for the skimmer."

"Let's carry the coins toward the foreign quarter," I suggested, not liking the idea of spending hours out here in the dark. "Rentable transportation is available non-stop in that district. We'll find a local skimmer with one of those crazy turtles driving and make their day."

There were a number of complaints, but the idea was finally accepted by everyone. We reached into our armor and pulled out our own shirts tying off the sleeves to make sacks. Each man filled a sack half full, and the coins were jingling over our shoulders as we set off.

Kivi marched at my side. "This has got to be new ground on your list of crazy ideas, James," she said.

"Would you prefer to stand guard next to that broken crate all night?"

"No," she admitted. "We do have to keep moving. You understand that Claver will be coming back for these coins, don't you?"

I glanced at her, startled. "He can't get past us."

"Of course not, but a full Unit of Germanica troops could. Or even a thousand more locals."

I frowned, alarmed by her ideas. "You really think this place is so lawless? That our legions are that corrupt?"

"Think it over," she said. "Why would Claver come to us and gather us together to do this job? Why not use Germanica troops? I don't know the average size of a crooked deal on this planet, but this has to be a big one. Claver sought us out and tricked us into escorting money blindly. Now, he's disappeared. I think he *likes* money. What do you think?"

Turning that one over in my mind, I had to admit Kivi had a good point. She'd been thinking it through, as I should have. I'd been so concerned with the situation at hand I hadn't been worrying about the bigger picture.

"Maybe…" I said, "he was the one who'd orchestrated this disaster from the start. How did those grav-clamps malfunction? Germanica troops had the crate before we did.

And, as I seem to remember, he knew those legion troops by sight when we met them."

Kivi nodded. "Now your brain is working again. We're in the middle of something big—and we aren't in control of the situation."

I relayed Kivi's fears to Leeson, but he didn't seem very receptive. Sometimes, an officer doesn't want bad news so much they'll ignore it completely. Leeson was in that mode now.

"Just keep marching!" he shouted at me. "Stop making things complicated. This was your damned plan, McGill, so live with it. If someone shoots at us, we shoot back. If they kill us all, then we'll get a revive and I'll kick your ass afterward."

If you've ever wandered a strange alien city at night, you know how unfriendly such places can be. There were drifting masses of people most of whom avoided us. When we posed questions to passersby, a few had the guts to offer us random goods for sale but most scampered away as if we were a gang of potentially violent lepers.

Once we'd left the financial district behind, I'd half-expected a rescue vehicle from headquarters to locate us—but it didn't.

I was worried as I trudged near the end of the line watching for trouble. My suit was at half-power already, and I didn't like the idea of running out of juice out here.

Veteran Harris drifted back to me, and I winced at his approach. He hadn't been too sweet on me since the training incident aboard *Minotaur*. Come to think of it, he'd never been too happy with anything I'd ever done in service to the legion.

"McGill?" he asked. "You asleep in that suit of yours?"

"No Vet. Right as rain."

"Ha! You're as crooked as that nut Claver if you ask me."

I eyed him wondering why he'd come back to talk to me. As he wasn't making it obvious, I figured I'd prod him a little.

"Hey Vet, why haven't we met up with any of the other units out here?"

Harris snorted. "You should be able to figure that one out by yourself," he said in a lowered voice. "And if you do, keep quiet."

I thought about that for about thirty seconds. As I pondered, it began to rain. *Real* frigging rain drops! I couldn't believe it. Carlos had been right. If the Tau had set up dehumidifying fields on the distant roof, they were failing utterly.

Suddenly, I looked to the front of the platoon. There was Adjunct Leeson marching alone. At last, I figured it out.

"They're in cahoots," I said.

"Ca-what?"

"I mean Leeson and Old Silver. They're in this together and now—we all are. Locked in tight. He doesn't want anyone coming to rescue us. He—did he even call in and report what happened, Vet?"

Harris looked upset. "Just keep quiet about that," he muttered. "Leeson did what he had to. He's a good man—if a little slow to see a trap when it's laid at his feet."

Nodding to myself, I figured Harris was right. We'd taken bribes, lost men, and we were marching around with high-value credit pieces slung over our back in wet sacks. For all I knew, the coins were as illegal here as they were back on Earth. There had to be a serious reprimand in Leeson's future if anyone higher ranked figured out all these details. The first thing they'd want to know was what idiot was in command of this fiasco.

"Leeson's scared," I said.

"Shhh! Shut the hell up! You can't say that about your officer—especially if it's true. Why do I even talk to you, anyway?"

"Because deep down you have feelings for me, Vet. No, no—you don't have to say a thing, 'cause I know it's true."

That was the sort of thing Carlos would have said, but I didn't care. It had the effect I was hoping for. Harris flipped me off and moved back up the line, slapping at troops who were about to let their bags rip. He demanded that each of them keep their heads, weapons and peckers upright.

It was about midnight when we finally reached a more civilized region of the city. Here, we found buzzing skimmers for rent. I longed to climb into one of those flittering taxis. I didn't even care if the pilot was a mad alien who made me puke. I just wanted to get back to my bunk and crash.

110

Adjunct Leeson trotted forward flagging down the first transport he saw. He waved and the craft drifted closer. Suddenly, just as the skids touched down in the stained street, it reversed itself and lifted off again.

I could hear Leeson's curses even without squad chat turned on.

"Did you see that?" he demanded. "What the hell kind of a civilization are these aliens running here? They must know we have money. We can pay, but they don't want to pick us up."

"Maybe they know trouble when they see it, sir," I suggested.

Leeson marched back along the line toward me. I guessed right then that everyone who'd ever told me I had a big mouth had had a good point.

Leeson's eyes were more than a little tired and crazy when he got to me. "What do you suggest, McGill?" he asked dangerously.

I unlimbered my sack of coins, reached inside and pulled one out. It gleamed and flashed in the rain, reflecting the city lights.

"I'll go up to the taxi station at the end of the block. I'll wave this around until one of these greedy bastards takes the bait. He'll have to take the rest of us to get it, but by that time, I'll be aboard his skimmer."

Leeson's face changed. His rage subsided, and he nodded. He reached out and snatched the coin from me.

"Good plan," he said. "But I'll do it. You look like some kind of armored ape and I don't want to spook them."

We huddled up while we watched Leeson march to the taxi station. He mounted the steps, which clanged as if they were made of black iron. He reached the top, which was unmanned, and lifted his coin into the air.

The effect was immediate—but unexpected. Someone did notice but not the *right* someone.

An air car packed with a half-dozen Tau swooped and a nose-mounted beamer flashed blue-white.

Leeson didn't even know what hit him. He was burned down to his boots. The golden thousand-credit coin rolled back down those black metal steps, clinking and clattering.

-14-

"Ambush!" roared Harris. "Take cover!"

Troops separated and crouched behind anything they could find. I straightened my back and unlimbered my weapon.

The air car did a loop and came cruising back toward us picking up speed.

What can I say? It was luck, really. I fired first because I had to. The lucky part was that I had my beam cranked down into a narrow field, and I managed to hit them with my first shot.

The air car lost its stabilizers on the left side and it was thrown into a spin. I found myself sprinting and diving for cover.

It splashed down with a cascading sheet of white fire onto the street. We lost a man there, and I felt bad about that, but the rest of the platoon clapped me on the back and even Sargon came to me shaking his head.

"That was class-A shooting, kid," he said.

"You should try dying more often," I told him. "I find it sharpens my reflexes."

Sargon laughed and moved off. Generally, in small unit actions it was standard procedure to separate specialists so they didn't all get wiped out at once. Natasha broke that rule by hurrying over to me.

"Are you okay, James?"

"I'm feeling better than those guys," I said, gesturing to the burnt Tau corpses lying in the wreckage of the air car.

Harris called us together and ordered us to retreat from the open street. We moved into a long, low structure that appeared to be abandoned—or maybe it was just under construction. It was hard to tell the difference on Tech World.

Natasha followed along talking fast. "I was worried about that possibility."

"What possibility?"

"They were waiting for us," she said. "Didn't you see that? They knew we had to come this way, and they knew the financial district was a no-fly zone. So, they waited here in the tourist section until we showed up. I bet every skimmer driver on the street has been paid to tip off whoever is hunting for us."

"Who are 'they,' exactly?"

She looked at me as if I was being dense. I get that often, but I think it's because if I don't get something I confess ignorance right up front. A lot of people prefer to pretend they know what's going on even when they don't. As a general rule, I only fake competence when I'm flirting with women.

"I'm talking about those gangsters—whoever they were— the people who tried to hijack this cash at the bank."

"Hmm, maybe," I said.

"Who else would have been ready to swoop down on us that way?"

"Just about any thief on the station. If you haven't noticed, they're a little obsessed with shiny coins."

"We should just dump this cash," she said with sudden feeling.

"Why?"

"Why get ourselves killed? We did our job. We aren't getting paid anything extra for dying over some crook's treasure."

"You have a point there, but the platoon took payment. We've got a rep to establish on this world. If these people think they can chase us off over this—how do you think the rest of our year-long tour is going to go?"

Natasha chewed over that thought. "You're saying we have to show how tough we are and return the coins to their owners even if they're crooks themselves?"

"At the very least we should return to headquarters and show we weren't beaten."

"About that, why haven't we been picked up? Someone must have been dispatched by now."

"Haven't heard about that yet, huh?" I asked then filled her in concerning Harris' hints.

"You mean Leeson never called us in? That's unbelievable. I'm patching into command right now."

Natasha was our platoon tech, and I knew she could do it. I put a gauntlet on her arm.

"Let's talk to the commander first," I said.

"Leeson's dead."

I gestured with my chin toward Harris. He was trotting along the line looking over his shoulder at the sky every few seconds.

"Vet?" I called. "You got a second?"

Harris turned to shout back something rude, but then he saw the two of us together. He frowned and trotted to our location.

"This better be short and good. We're in a combat situation, and God knows who else is looking for us."

"Vet," I said, "Natasha is patching into command. She's going to call for support."

Harris hesitated. His eyes widened, and he opened his mouth uncertainly. Finally, he nodded.

"Fine. Leeson's paste anyway. It's his own damn fault if they bust him on this deal. Call in the cavalry, Specialist."

Natasha worked her magic. She was on the line with Graves in ten seconds flat—and he was pissed.

"I've been waiting for this contact for hours," he said into every headset in the platoon. Put Leeson on the line, Tech."

"Sorry sir, he's gone."

Graves was silent for a second. I saw Natasha dialing down the number of people in the channel. It went from everyone to just the noncoms and officers—only, we didn't have any officers left.

"He's gone? Oh yes, I see that now on the system—he's queued up for a revive. I think I'll postpone that until morning. He can sit in limbo for the time being."

A chill ran through me. Could he really do that? Just leave a man dead overnight because he felt like it? That seemed like an odd, godlike power to me, but then, the process of reviving the dead into new bodies was freaky under the best of circumstances.

"So," Graves said. "I show Claver as in command. Why isn't he on this channel?"

"Uh," Natasha said. "He's not available, either."

"Who is in charge of the platoon?"

"Veteran Harris, sir."

Graves sighed. "Harris, stop hiding. Talk to me. What the hell happened to your officers?"

With a look of obvious pain on his face, Harris began his report. "Claver took off on us, sir. He took the skimmer we left headquarters with and bugged out when things went wrong at the bank."

"The bank? What bank?"

"Uh, are you aware of the mission parameters we've been working under, sir?" Harris asked.

"Apparently, I'm aware of frigging nothing. It's midnight, and you guys are out there cluster-humping in the streets. That's what I know."

Harris showed his teeth and squinted his eyes in anguish. I knew there was nothing he hated more than being left holding someone else's shit-bag of mistakes. Nothing, that is, except for dying.

Natasha tapped on my shoulder and I turned away from the drama as Harris tried to explain how our day had gone thus far. Graves peppered the report with curses and threats.

"What's up?" I asked Natasha.

She pointed, and I followed her finger.

I saw a mass of people. They were Tau, what looked like an army of them.

"Behind us, too," Natasha said, pointing the other way.

I looked, and she was right. They were gathering on the streets in every direction. They all wore the same maroon-colored holographic suits. These weren't expensive projectors, however. The illusory suits flickered with dark, deep vibrancy.

The effect was a ghostly one. It appeared as if they wore shimmering wraps that were the color of dusk.

They shuffled forward, readying weapons. They were closing in.

Shouldering my belcher, I slammed my gauntlet on top of Harris' helmet. I knew he liked that.

"What the frig, McGill...?"

Then his eyes crawled over the scene, and all around us troopers hunkered down and unlimbered their weapons.

"Ah, dammit," Harris said. "Tell me those are civvies, someone?"

"I think they are, Vet," I said. "But they're armed and well-paid if I had to guess. Or maybe they're driven by greed."

This time, we opened up first. As soon as we saw them expose the short-barreled automatic weapons they had under their shimmering non-clothing, we didn't wait any longer.

Someone must have told these fellows we were packing a fortune—which was true. Probably they'd been told we were leaderless and lost—which was partly true.

But the one thing we weren't was weak. We had firepower and training this mob of thugs could only dream of. We slathered them with beams and bullets until the front line fell, shattered.

I have to admit, I fully expected them to turn tail and run screaming at that point. I even let my weapon dip—but when the smoke cleared, there were even more of them than before. Any mob on Earth would have broken. But these people weren't human.

I could only surmise that greed was such a powerful motivator among the Tau that they could be driven to reckless behavior by it. Apparently the emotion was akin to hate, or even love, for these beings.

Instead of fleeing, they charged in a convulsive mass. The front line showered us with explosive pellets. A few on my team had been surprised enough to forget to slam down their visors. Pellets popped into two troopers' faces and provided them with an instant, gory death.

Cranking my weapon aperture as widely as it would go, I set it for a broad cone dispersion pattern. My next blast hosed down a hundred of them, giving their unshielded skin about a thousand degrees C of energy. I didn't feel good about doing it, but I hadn't started this fight.

After that, they rushed in too close. I couldn't get off another effective blast. I had to drop my cannon, set my legs, and extend my force-blades. All around me, troops were doing the same.

We fought in close-quarters. It was a vicious struggle with ghostly people that quivered and wore colored lights for clothing. They flickered as we fought them. Only when they died and the power to their illusionary circuits was cut could we see the reality of their bodies underneath. Pink, covered in ropy veins, they shivered and died at our feet.

They formed a howling wall around us for maybe two minutes. That was all it took. After that, sanity returned. The fight was over, and about half of us were still standing—I guess that meant we'd won.

Sargon had gone down. Natasha was hurt but able to stand while hobbling on one stiff leg. Veteran Harris was on his back but still breathing. Carlos had made it too, and for once, he didn't have anything funny to say.

"That was unbelievable," he said, staring at the bodies. "Can they really want Galactic credits that badly? So weird."

"I don't know," I said. "Maybe something else was driving them. The bank guards weren't this crazy. Why these folk? Why now?"

Carlos shook his head and went to help the survivors get on their feet and gather up the fallen equipment and coins.

"Can you get up, Vet?" I asked Harris, moving to where he lay on his back like a beached turtle.

His face was sweating and his visor was open. His breath came out in puffs.

"Does it look like I'm getting up?" he demanded in a wheezing voice.

I peered into his face and checked his vitals. As far as I could tell, his spinal cord had been severed somewhere down the line. The back plate of his armor had taken a lot of rounds, and it looked like someone had beaten on it with a jackhammer.

117

Harris looked at me and laughed suddenly. He sounded half-mad. His tongue showed pink and his teeth were outlined in red.

When he was done laughing, he didn't close his mouth again. His eyes just stared at me, and his lips froze wide, still in the midst of a belly laugh.

He was as dead as a dead man could be.

Natasha put a hand on my shoulder. Her face was dirty, and she looked bloody and stressed.

"You're in command now, McGill. You're the senior noncom."

"Crap," I muttered.

-15-

I've fought and died on several planets in my lifetime, but Tech World had to be the strangest. About ten minutes after the battle was over, the death-officials arrived. As before, they didn't ask questions or fill out reports. They made no effort to figure out what had happened or who was at fault. All they wanted to know was who had died and whether or not they could make a buck off of the corpse.

Apparently, the reaper had brought in a pretty poor crop this time. Unlike the relative excitement these ghouls had exhibited when our original clients had died on the steps to the bank, this time they were disgusted. They kicked at the bodies and shoveled them wholesale onto a skimmer. There would be no expensive revival processes tonight.

I approached the nearest of them, and he watched me warily.

"Speak English?" I demanded.

"Little bit," he said. "No deals."

Snorting, I reached out and showed him what I had in my hand. It was a golden coin. An Imperial coin that apparently everyone on Gelt Station knew was priceless.

He snatched for it, but I was quicker. I closed my gauntlet over the coin and pointed to the skimmer they were loading with bodies.

"Give us a ride on that thing. You get this coin now and one more when we get home."

"Two?" he asked, as if he couldn't believe his ears.

"Two," I said firmly. "Deal?"

His eyes darted over to the corpses. I knew he was calculating the profit he could make here, weighing it against what I was offering. I had to wonder what value a pile of still-warm corpses would bring on this station and to what purpose they might be applied. When credit-values were compared, however, there wasn't any contest.

"Move, quickly," he said, pointing to his skimmer and chattering into a communications device. Immediately, the ghouls reversed their work. They shoved bodies off the skimmer even faster than they'd loaded them a moment earlier.

I waved to my men. Each of us dragged one of our fallen troops letting weapons dangle from straps. We valued the dead even more than the ghouls did—we needed to recycle their equipment.

"Don't leave a single bag of coins behind for these monsters," I ordered.

No one argued. They followed me as quickly as they could. We slipped and staggered as we waded through bodies. When we were aboard the skimmer, I gave a coin to the guy who I'd cut the deal with.

"No funny business," I said. "Or we kill you all."

He sneered at me, spreading his mouth tentacles wide. "Nothing is funny here on Tech World, big man."

We lifted off then, and I found Natasha tapping at me again.

"It's Graves," she said. "He wants another report."

"Tell him we're fine," I said. "We'll be home for breakfast."

Air travel always seems like a miracle after a man has been slogging on foot. The skies were a different place, another world. We flashed at the usual madcap pace toward our destination. I now suspected that people on this planet piloted their vehicles like madmen for a good reason: they didn't trust passersby not to attack them. It was difficult to accost a vehicle that zoomed by in the blink of an eye.

We landed on the roof of the square block of puff-crete that was our headquarters. Legionnaires were up there. Some were on guard duty while others were just taking a break. They eyed us in surprise and curiosity, but when they saw half of us were limp in our armor they rushed to help.

Our bio specialists are a unique breed of soldier. Part corpsman and part mortician, they patched the injured among us and stripped the dead. I eyed the corpses as they were hauled away below, especially Harris. It still felt odd to know he'd be yelling at me about something in the morning despite the fact he was flopping dead meat right now.

How different were we, I asked myself, from the death-merchants that swarmed any scene of violence on Tech World? They were seeking profit while we sought raw materials to rebuild a new version of every fallen man.

I knew more than most troops about the process. The bio people liked fresh bodies. They fed them into the maw of their machines like fresh wood cast upon a fire. They called it "recycling", and thinking about the process could still make me shudder if I pondered it too long.

Finding my bunk at last after a few bites to eat, I patched up a few minor injuries and took a long draught on a warm beer. Then I crashed and fell asleep instantly.

A kick in the side awakened me in what felt like seconds later. I looked up fully expecting my tormentor to be Harris, but it wasn't. It was Centurion Graves.

I probably would have told anyone else to screw off at that moment, but you just didn't talk to Graves that way—not when his eyes were dark and his lips were drawn into a single tight line.

"Sir?" I asked, heaving myself awake.

"What happened out there, Specialist?"

I looked around the room blearily. It was empty. Several of my fellow troops had died during the long night, of course, but not all of them had. Graves must have chased them out before he prodded me with the loving tip of his boot.

"Lots of stuff, sir. Claver led us into a series of unfortunate encounters."

Graves produced a gleaming golden disk. He tossed it to me, and I caught it. Curvy Galactic number symbols were engraved on both sides.

"Two to the tenth power worth of credits," Graves said. "One thousand twenty-four, in our number system. Why are there twenty sacks of these in my office?"

"Only twenty?" I asked in alarm. "Every man had one...I hope none have found their way to another location."

Graves waved his hand in my face as if to erase my words from the air. "I didn't count them all. Tell me what the hell they're doing in our possession."

I gave him a full accounting at that point. I didn't bother to add my assessment of Claver's part which seemed obvious. Finishing up, I asked him if Claver had returned to headquarters.

"No," he said in a venomous voice. "He's rejoined Germanica. Oddly enough, he seems to be among the few Germanica legionnaires who are already aboard *Minotaur*. That's where you come in, Specialist."

"How's that, sir?"

"In the morning, you and I are going to pay him a visit aboard ship."

Grunting unhappily, I rubbed my eyes. "How long until morning, sir?"

"About two hours. Get some sleep."

I flopped back onto my bunk and sighed until my lungs were empty. Sometimes I wondered if I even wanted to be revived the next time I was killed.

* * *

The next day dragged until we reached *Minotaur*. Watching Graves, I had to admit being an officer had privileges that often surprised me. Rather than taking public transport at his own expense, a pinnace was dispatched to pick up Graves and me.

We boarded the small ship just before noon and were whisked away toward the dark hulking shape that was *Minotaur*. From the outside, the warship was more imposing than I'd realized. She was fully armed with a broadside of heavy guns. I didn't understand her armament, but I'd heard it was made up of accelerated particle cannons.

122

Earth had never had control of a real warship before, but now they were becoming increasingly common. *Minotaur* wasn't just a transport, she was capable of battle in her own right. She was a capital ship, an engine of destruction.

Graves sat in a gloomy silence aboard the pinnace as it shuddered and lurched attempting to dock.

"Sir?" I asked. "Why are all *Minotaur's* weapons on one side of the ship?"

He glanced at me as if remembering he'd brought me along. I could tell he was thinking hard about something. He'd been poking at his tapper and staring out the windows of the pinnace the entire time.

"That's pretty standard design," he said. "If they're bombarding a world, the world is only on one side of the ship. If they meet enemy vessels in combat, a big ship generally places all of its heavy hull plating and weaponry on one side. The distances are so great it's unlikely a ship will be surrounded by enemies and fired upon from more than one direction at the same time."

"But what if that situation were to occur?"

"Then the ship is probably doomed, anyway."

I nodded as I thought about it. Combat in normal space—the only place that combat could occur as far as I knew—usually played out at a range of one hundred thousand to one million kilometers. At that distance, only one flank of each ship mattered.

As a result of her design, *Minotaur* was a lopsided vessel. It looked as if it had a huge hump on its back. We sailed around and underneath it into a bay located on the side opposite the weapon mounts.

Disembarking, Centurion Graves went first. He'd brought me along in full combat armor which even I knew wasn't the norm when making a friendly visit to another legion's territory. I hadn't argued the point as I always felt more comfortable among unfriendly faces when I was packing firepower.

Minotaur felt deserted as I walked through the ship's gigantic hold. Our boots echoed and rang from walls a kilometer or more away. There was no one here to greet us, but that didn't deter Graves. He marched resolutely toward the crew quarters as if he owned the place.

Five decks aft and two above the floor of the hold, we found three units from Germanica holed up. They were busy planning and arranging equipment. A centurion named Dubois met us in the wardroom. He had a slight French accent and his demeanor was anything but friendly.

"Centurion Graves," he said. "I understand that you have some kind of problem with your new contract. This is unexpected."

"I was under the impression that Germanica was to help us during the transitional period. Am I mistaken?"

Dubois shrugged. "We didn't expect an experienced legion to make serious mistakes at such an easy post."

Graves' eyes narrowed. I could tell he was pissed, but it took experience to recognize the signs. He wasn't an overly expressive man.

"Our trouble isn't with the post," Graves said. "It's with our liaison. Claver has gone off the rails and as I understand it he's hiding here on *Minotaur*."

Dubois laughed. "Hiding? Hardly. He's busy performing last-minute critical adjustments to the biosphere. I'm afraid I can't spare him."

Graves took out a handful of coins and let them fall on the deck-plating. They rang and flashed with golden beauty. I'd never seen coins outside of a museum back on Earth and hadn't understood their luster and mesmerizing effect.

Dubois wasn't immune. He watched them until they stopped rattling and spinning.

"Is this some kind of bribe?" he demanded.

"This is what was in the last crate your man Claver had us transporting. The first crates contained weapons—weapons of unknown origin. They were transferred to a group guarded by Germanic troops down at the Vents. The gunrunners gave my platoon a great deal of illegal funds which my men neither understood nor approved of. My troops were later attacked repeatedly by thugs from every part of the city."

"Nothing surprising about that," Dubois huffed. "Every fool knows you can't walk around with that kind of money in any city, on any planet. You could hardly pick a worse place than Tau to pull such a stunt."

Graves and I exchanged glances. "I don't think you're quite getting what I'm saying, centurion," Graves said. "Your man Claver—"

"—is otherwise engaged," Dubois interrupted, sighing. "Now, I must thank you for your visit, which is at an end. I'll thank you again when you're back on that pinnace and flying out of here."

Graves shook his head slowly. "That's not going to happen. If you aren't going to take disciplinary action, then I'm going to have to take matters into my own hands."

"And what does that mean?"

"I want Claver. He was attached to my unit, and he was under my orders. As far as I'm concerned, he's one of my legionnaires and he's AWOL."

Dubois laughed again, grinning. "I'm sorry, but I have to deny your request. His assignment with your unit has been terminated. Now, if you'll excuse me, we've got a journey—"

"Not so fast. I've contacted Hegemony using an expensive FTL link system the Tau rent out for emergencies. They're sending brass out to investigate the situation."

For the first time, both Dubois and I were surprised.

"And why would Hegemony care about this situation?" Dubois snapped.

"Because I reported a Galactic violation to them, and they had no choice other than to respond."

Dubois' face changed. His jaw sagged. "You did *what*? Don't be absurd. This is Tech World, man. I can't believe you're going ballistic over a bit of gunrunning. There are bribes and illegal activities going on every day on this planet. Didn't someone brief you?"

Graves nodded. "I was briefed. Apparently, it's your legion that didn't get the memo. Centurion, this isn't about the gunrunning—although it is the height of insanity for a peace-keeping force to get involved in something like that. The problem is that Earth is now the Enforcement arm of the Galactics in this part of the galaxy. In case you haven't heard, ownership and trading with Galactic credit coins is illegal in

125

Frontier 921. It's not just illegal on Earth. The coins have been outlawed by the Core Systems and mere possession constitutes a Galactic-level offense. An Imperial crime has thus been committed by the Tau and Imperial enforcement personnel— we're now representatives of the Empire, remember? Your man Claver facilitated this operation. Are you listening, sir?"

By this time, Centurion Dubois finally *was* listening. He lifted a hand and snapped his fingers. An adjunct appeared next to him. "Get Claver's ass out here."

The adjunct disappeared. We didn't have long to wait. Claver soon came out of a nearby passageway, sauntering as if he didn't have a care in the world.

"Ah, there you are, Graves," Claver said. "Kind of odd to see you here aboard a Germanica ship."

Graves ignored him as he turned to centurion Dubois. "Do I have your permission to assert command over this officer?" he asked Dubois formally.

Dubois nodded.

Graves turned to me. "McGill, arrest this man. We're taking him back to his post."

I smiled and came clanking forward. I suddenly understood why he'd brought me along. I was the muscle—and I was well-motivated.

Claver's upper lip curled as I raised a powered gauntlet toward him.

"Unnecessary," he said. "This is all a misunderstanding."

"We'll talk everything out on the way back to the station," Graves assured him.

I removed Claver's sidearm, and he did nothing to resist. Graves led the way back toward the pinnace with Claver grumbling along after him, and I brought up the rear.

My grin stayed in place as we returned to the pinnace. I don't think I've ever enjoyed arresting someone so thoroughly.

-16-

Once we boarded the pinnace, Graves' promise to talk things out with Claver evaporated. Taking my cue from him, I stoically ignored the mixture of scoffing, insults and veiled threats the Germanica Adjunct dished out.

"There's never been any love lost between our two organizations, Graves," Claver said, throwing out his latest barb. "But I don't see any reason to take things to this extreme. Your men made it back to base without anyone getting permed. The mission was completed—despite poor management on the part of your man. What was his name? Adjunct Leeson, that's it. He resisted every step of the way, but I managed to hold it together until we reached the foot of the bank steps."

Graves was as silent as space. I didn't even look at Claver. I tried to do the same, but I did grin just a little. I couldn't help it.

"Look," said Claver, edging closer to the Centurion's chair. "I imagine I know what the real problem is. You don't know how to handle those credit pieces. I can help you there. Sure, I know you can't just take them home to Earth and spend them at the corner store. But you can get good value out of them. Ten percent maybe, if you go through me."

Graves finally glanced at Claver flatly. The Adjunct lit up, misinterpreting the look. I could have told him he was on the wrong track, but I was having too much fun enjoying the show.

"Yeah, that's right," Claver said quickly. "Ten percent of face value. How? First, we'll contact the dead clients. They'll all have been revived by now and anxious to reclaim their goods. A finder's fee under extenuating circumstances like these will be expected. They'll pay in clean credits, dumped right into your tapper. We're talking about a lifetime of credit, Graves."

"McGill," Graves said, staring at Claver like he smelled filth.

"Sir?"

"Did you overhear Claver's remarks?"

"Yes sir!"

"How would you characterize them?"

"I heard a confession, sir. Bribery, extortion, fencing illegal goods—a laundry list of crimes, Centurion."

Claver laughed nervously. "You guys have to be—"

"I recommend you shut up, Adjunct," Graves interrupted. "For your own good—although I doubt anything you do will matter at this point."

Claver frowned. "What are you talking about?"

"I said that I contacted Hegemony. They've dispatched a flag officer. Have you heard of Imperator Turov?"

Claver squinted. "Oh, yeah. Is that the one that used to be your Primus? Tribune Armel called her a real bitch."

"A poor choice of words," Graves said smoothly, although I didn't believe his heart was in it. "She's coming out on one of the new corvettes. She'll be here within hours."

I was as surprised as Claver by this statement.

"Hours?" Claver asked.

"Hegemony has been busy purchasing new hardware," Graves explained, "and the corvettes are their latest naval toys. Flag officers can travel first class now if they need to."

Claver nodded slowly. "Good thinking," he said. "She'll know how to sweep this business under the rug. Nothing like an Imperator for that."

Graves turned to me. "Specialist, tell the Adjunct how Turov handled the last Imperial crime she discovered."

"Uh...sure. She had me executed. I caught a quiet revive afterward because it was all a misunderstanding—but then she went for me again anyway. Court martial, the whole deal. She almost got her way and had me burned all over again. Fortunately, Tribune Drusus managed to stop her."

"That's how I recall the sequence of events," Graves said. He gave Claver a nod and a grim smile. "The only difference is that this time she outranks Tribune Drusus *and* Tribune Armel. On top of that, I doubt either of them would lift a finger to save your hide, Claver."

Graves turned away again as if satisfied. Claver was quiet for a moment, but he sighed heavily after a few minutes.

"So you're going for broke on this? Bringing in Turov to screw me permanently? That's unfortunate—for everyone."

Graves ignored him and the rest of the flight went quietly. I took the opportunity to eye Claver in concern. He fingered his tapper now and then, but said nothing. He was no longer smiling and cajoling anyone—but he didn't seem defeated, either.

It occurred to me that a man like him didn't get a full head of silver hair without being resourceful. I watched the instruments and kept checking on the crew, but nothing seemed amiss.

We reached our destination a few minutes later and landed on the flat roof of legion headquarters. All this time, Claver hadn't tried to escape or do anything else unexpected. When we disembarked, he marched along in front of me without missing a step.

Just as we reached the elevators an emergency message came in over Graves' tapper. The centurion halted and lifted his arm, frowning.

"Something on command chat..." he said. After a few moments, he looked up at me. I saw a hint of alarm on his normally stoic features. "Specialist McGill, what kind of weapons did you deliver to the gun-runners down at the Vents? I thought they fired explosive pellets."

"I can't say the guns in the box were the same type, sir. We never saw them. I only have Claver's word that they were guns at all. Whatever was in those containers, the items would have to be unusual and valuable to warrant all that credit."

"Indeed. I've just received a priority message from Drusus. There's an attack underway at the umbilical transport hub and the weaponry involved is quite unusual. In fact, no one who's seen it can identify the technology."

Both of us looked at Old Silver. He smiled back faintly and shrugged. "Can I help you gentlemen?"

"You better not be behind this, Claver," Graves said.

Claver laughed coldly. "What are you going to do? Hold me in contempt in some Galactic court run by Nairbs? Or maybe you'll perm me on the spot? What's the difference to me at this point? You've played your last card, Centurion."

Graves turned away from him and back to me. "The Tribune has heard about your jog across the city, the gunrunning—everything. He's not happy and he's already done the math. He's blaming our new Primus, who in turn is blaming us. Our unit is to deploy in a police action to stop the riot at the umbilical transport hub."

Claver chuckled. "A riot, huh? Is that what it is?"

"We're bringing this man to the line with us. I don't trust anyone to watch over him—not even you, McGill."

"Don't worry, sir," I said. "You can give me his leash. I hate him more than I love money."

The corners of Graves' mouth twitched upward. "Good to hear. I've arranged air transport. Three units are deploying at once."

"Air transport?" I asked. "The pilots wouldn't be hired locals—guys who look like turtles?"

"What the hell difference does that make?"

I sighed. "None at all, sir."

* * *

We arrived less than an hour later at the umbilical transport hub. The place was eerily quiet. It wasn't empty, however. There were corpses everywhere.

Most noticeable to me were the corpses of the ghoulish revival squads. They had attempted to search among the dead for good clients and quickly paid the ultimate price.

130

Hanging back now along a perimeter a block from the cavern-like entrance to station, the surviving revival squads complained and stayed behind hastily erected barriers.

I followed Graves who met up with Adjunct Leeson. I rejoined 3rd Unit, with Old Silver at my side. He was in a fine mood for a man condemned. I couldn't explain his attitude, but I knew I didn't like it.

Leeson didn't hesitate to put his face into Claver's face. It was an odd spectacle, one man screaming and red-faced, the other smiling and unconcerned.

"I know how you feel, kid," Claver told Leeson. "I've been there, believe me. Really sucks to be in the dark when the shit starts to fly. If you live through this one, take notes and learn for next time."

Leeson finally stalked off, and I relaxed a little. I'd been charged with watching over Claver. He was unarmed, unarmored and under arrest. Officially, he was an officer who had yet to face trial. Unfortunately, that meant I was in the odd position of protecting him.

I followed Claver to the front lines. Harris was there, and he gave Claver a deadly stare. For the second time within a minute, I knew my prisoner's life was in jeopardy.

Harris was good, I have to admit that. He knew the score. He knew I was Claver's jailor and bodyguard at the same time. What I should have seen coming was an underhanded move. Harris was a master at putting the hurt on a man when he least expected it. I should have, in retrospect, figured out what was going to happen. I'd been the Veteran's victim often enough myself.

Harris turned to me, ignoring Claver. "Nice of you to join us, McGill," he said. "You know what we get to do now? We're going into that bat-cave over there and down to the bottom of the station. The only thing lower than the Vents on this megahab is the umbilical transport hub, and we're going to visit it personally."

"It's been on my list of tourist destinations since we got here, Vet."

Harris shook his head, stood up, and turned toward the cavernous entrance to the transport hub. Naturally enough, I moved to stand next to him, and Claver came up behind the two of us.

That was all the proximity that Harris needed. He took a step backward and stomped his boot down onto Claver's right foot with grinding force.

Now, stomping on another guy's foot is all fun and games back on Earth. But when you're wearing heavy armor weighing in at a ton or more, and you engage the power-assist mode when you stomp—bones break.

Claver went down, hissing and screeching.

Harris whirled, almost catching him before he hit the ground.

"Oh, *damn*," he said, "did I do that, Adjunct? I'm sorry, man. I backed up right onto your foot. I'm so *sorry*, sir. Please accept my heartfelt apologies."

I put a gauntlet on Harris' forearm. Harris already had a short, white-hot length of force-blade sticking out of it. He looked at me, and I shook my head.

"Can't let you do it, Vet. Much as I'd like to."

The force-blade vanished. Harris' face shifted to one of innocence. "McGill," he said, "you're a guardian angel. Did anyone ever tell you that?"

"No Vet, I don't believe they ever have."

"Well, it's true. And do you know when people see angels? Old people like you see them all the time, Adjunct Claver. Right before they die. Did you know that, Adjunct Claver, sir?"

"Come on, Vet," I said, and I finally got him to retreat.

I noticed Claver was tapping on his forearm again. His expression was grim but that might have been the pain.

"If you pricks are done laughing," he growled, "help me up and get a bio over here."

I signaled the bio people, one of whom had seen the fall and was already on her way. I tapped a short text to Natasha as well. She arrived and they worked on Claver together.

The Adjunct was on his feet again shortly, but limping. The bones wouldn't knit up for hours, but his boot had been turned into a cast, holding his foot so tightly he was able to walk on it.

Out the corner of my eye, I saw Claver working on his tapper again. He paused, cursed, then repeated a series of gestures. Finally, he looked around after Natasha, then at me.

"Did that bitch disconnect my tapper?" he demanded.

"It's for the best, sir," I said.

"You don't have the authority to do that!"

"Should I contact Centurion Graves? I'm sure he'll be glad to have our techs look over all your recent activity. If there's nothing unusual recorded, I bet he'll turn it back on."

Claver bared his teeth at me then nodded after a few seconds thought.

"All right," he said. "Why not? We'll ride this out blindfolded and see how it ends."

I cocked my head, unsure of what he was talking about. Before I could ask anything else, an explosion rolled up against my back. My faceplate was open, but my armor took most of the heat and pressure. I turned, flipping down my visor, and unlimbered my belcher. My ears stopped singing and started working again a second later.

A horde of Tau were boiling up out of the transport hub entrance. They were wearing a shifting maroon light for clothing and nonexistent silver shoes. Many of them had slim metal rods in their hands with knobs at the end. From these they released bolts of energy that looked to me like…lightning?

Whoever these people were, they were pissed. They fired their strange weapons toward us, and each strike landed like a mortar. I think the only reason they didn't clear our line right off was because they barely knew how to aim their lightning rods.

A bolt struck a puff-crete barrier right in front of me. It jumped as if kicked and was left smoking. I was knocked flat from the jolt, falling onto my face.

Hunkering down there at my side was none other than Adjunct Claver. He didn't talk to me or even look at me. Instead, he crawled on his belly away from the action. I couldn't really blame him for that. He was as good as naked and didn't even have a sidearm.

133

All around me troops opened up in a blaze of fire. The front rank of rebels, terrorists—whatever they were—went down in a heap. More came up behind them, raving. They snatched up fallen lightning rods and spread out taking cover on both sides of the street. Bolts flew overhead sizzling in the air.

As a weaponeer, I was torn. Should I fire on this charging enemy or go after Claver? I'd been put in charge of him, but as far as I could see all he wanted was to keep breathing.

I made a decision, and later I came to regret it. But there it was. I got to my knees, leveled my heavy weapon and beamed the crowd.

My weapon was set for a mid-range cone and it caught the front rank squarely. At least eight of them smoked and fell. Their eyes boiled in their sockets like eggs. A few more bolts flew from this group, then they were nothing but dead ash on the street.

It was a good shot, but it wasn't enough. We were being overrun. Looking around, I saw that at least half our heavy troopers were down and not moving.

"Fall back!" roared Leeson, standing over me suddenly. "3rd Unit, fall back!"

Clanking along in a half-crouch, I did the best I could do in heavy armor to follow his orders. But then, a moment later, something came up and kicked me in the ass. I'd been struck by artificial lightning. Falling again, I found I couldn't get back up.

Systems failure—not in my body but mechanical. My suit had shorted out, and I realized an instant later that this is what had happened to many of my fallen comrades. The lightning strikes not only blew things up, they operated as EMP blasts to fry our equipment. Overloaded couplings smoked all around me inside my suit, and the stink of burning insulation rolled into my nostrils.

A face loomed in front of me then. It was none other than Old Silver.

"You like it in there, punk?" he asked.

I felt a jostling as he worked my sidearm out of its holster.

This pissed me off. I'm a large, strong man and I'd worked out like a man possessed to become a proper weaponeer. All that training had made me twice as strong as the day I'd joined Legion Varus. Despite the fact my power-assist was dead, I snaked out my arm and clamped onto Claver's hand with my dead gauntlet. It felt strange, as if I was grabbing someone with two shovels, but I managed it.

Claver cursed me desperately and tried to aim my own gun into my face. At this range, it would go right through my visor.

My next action came without thinking. It was self-defense, pure and simple. I fired the explosive bolts on my suit.

As far as I knew no one had ever done that in combat, but I was trapped in a dead suit. I didn't feel like waiting around for Claver or one of these crazed rebels to finish me off.

Not every suit has explosive bolts. Only weaponeers were so-equipped. Because our kit was so heavy, they'd been installed in case of a power failure like the one I was experiencing.

The two halves of my suit popped apart, and I was freed. I did a push-up, and the back half of the suit fell away.

Claver looked startled, and I managed to slap away the pistol before he could pull the trigger. I grabbed him by the shirt and dragged him after me as I ran from the front lines.

The battle was clearly over, and Legion Varus had lost. Chattering excitedly, the Tau killed everyone they caught. I ran with Claver stumbling and hobbling on his bad foot right behind me.

"You don't die easy, do you son?" he asked when we found a spot to hide and gasp for breath.

I looked at him. "I'll probably never have your silver hair, sir, but I don't like to die any more than the next man."

"Then you should take my advice, kid," he said. "Get off this station."

I frowned at him but didn't get a chance to reply. Something dashed against my skull. I spun around and slumped onto my back, staring up at the artificial sky. Claver fled.

Stunned, trying to get up, I saw the rebel Tau were overrunning my position. Several of them ran past me ignoring the unarmored human who couldn't even stand.

But one man noticed me. He paused, aiming his lightning rod at me. He turned to chatter something to his fellows—perhaps it was a joke, or maybe he was bragging.

While his attention was diverted, I kicked his feet out from under him. Tau are skinny fellows, and he went down with a surprised squawk. On my knees and elbows, I made it to the lightning rod before he did. I shoved the butt end of the weapon into his mouth tentacles and dark blood fountained.

Heaving myself to my knees, I took a look around. There had to be seven of them nearby and another seventy within earshot. Already they were pointing and converging.

I lifted the unfamiliar weapon, aimed at the biggest knot of rebels in sight, and depressed a firing stud. Nothing happened.

One of them returned the favor and a bolt exploded an air car nearby. They were shooting at me. I didn't have much time to figure out an unfamiliar weapon.

The controls weren't anything special to look at. There was a knob on top, but no sights, no readouts. There were only two studs that I could find—one at the end and one at the front. I'd pushed on the front one and it hadn't worked.

I moved my hand to the rear one, but hesitated. A detachable-looking apparatus sat there like a battery-pack at the rear end of a flashlight. Might that not be a release for the power-source? These things had to use a fantastic amount of power very quickly.

I tried pressing the forward stud again. This time I held it down—and that did the trick. Apparently you had to hold it depressed for a full second. Or maybe, when it was low on its charge, it took that long to cycle up and fire. I really didn't know.

The bolt connected me to a group of three victims briefly. My newfound weapon, their bodies, and the street formed a closed circuit. They died in an instant, and I had time to grin with blood in my mouth.

The moment passed, and the rest of them fried me down to ash.

-17-

Awakening after a bad death is something I'll never get used to. But I didn't think of this one as a *really* bad death. After all, I'd taken more than my weight in enemies down with me, and I doubted any of them were going to get a revive of any kind.

I woke up gasping, and even after I got that under control I had trouble breathing. There's always liquid in your lungs when you're reborn, thick stuff like snot—but this was worse than usual. I lay there hitching and trying to suck in air like a dying fish. I didn't open my eyes. New eyes were always painfully dazzled by the bright lights of the revival room.

"He's a good grow, but there's an obstruction," said a male voice. It was probably one of the orderlies.

"Where?" a woman asked. I found her voice vaguely familiar to my fuzzy mind.

"Right lung. Might be a clot."

"Let him sit up. Let him cough it out. Sit up, McGill."

I squirmed but couldn't sit up on my own. My rubbery muscles wouldn't obey me. I rolled off the platter-thing they'd used to pull me out of the machine, and I went down on my hands and knees. I coughed and spat until I vomited—but nothing came out of my stomach or my lungs. Absolutely nothing. Not even a trickle of bile. My guts were brand new and completely empty.

"Cough, don't puke," said the woman. "Cough, damn you."

I recognized the voice then. She was Anne—Anne Grant. A senior bio specialist who'd fought two campaigns with me. We'd both gotten each other killed and rescued on multiple occasions.

"Anne?" I sputtered.

Before she could reply I began the coughing fit she'd been hoping for. Talking had triggered it. Blood and slime splattered the floor.

"You good to go?" she asked when I was finished. Her voice was softer than before, and I felt her light touch on my hair.

I forced my eyes open at last and squinted up at her. The operating room lights were like twin suns behind her head.

"Never better," I rasped.

She laughed and put her hand on the back of my neck. "Good. We need you back in the streets."

I sat up and dragged in ragged breaths. My lungs were clearing, but they burned inside. "What's happening outside?"

"Lots of people are dying, that's what," she said with a trace of bitterness. "This entire orbiting city has gone mad."

I looked at her, frowning. "Because of the transport hub attack?"

She shook her head. "That's old news. The unrest has spread."

"But…how long has it been?" I asked in confusion. To my mind, the attack was moments ago. "How long was I out of the picture?"

Anne looked regretful. "We couldn't revive you right away. Turov placed a limit on troop revivals. She's using legion equipment to revive Tau civvies. Only the important ones, of course. By important, I mean rich ones who are paying for the service. Can you believe that? She's spouting some crap about diplomatic relations."

I shook my head, confused. "Imperator Turov? She can't have come out here so fast. Wait—how long was I dead? You didn't say."

"Three days," Anne said with a hint of an apology in her voice. "You were gone for three days, James."

I put my face in my hands. I didn't feel well all of a sudden.

Anne watched me and sighed. "Don't tell me you're going to freak out. You're fine. You're *back*. Don't think about the rest of it."

I knew her advice was sound, but I couldn't help myself. I'd been dead and gone for three whole days. My old body had probably been mulched by this time—maybe burnt or eaten or sold for fuel—who knew with these people.

What had happened to my existence during those long days? Could I really be the same man if I'd been dead for that long?

Anne knelt beside me checking my eyes and shouting orders now and then over her shoulder to her helpers. They were reloading the machine and filling tanks with protoplasm for flesh and calcium to grow fresh bones.

Three days. I'd been in limbo for longer than I'd ever been before. I couldn't get over it.

Anne came close and stopped talking. I could feel her concern. She was one of those medical people who could compartmentalize her empathy and emotions but who could still feel them.

I gave into a sudden impulse. I leaned awkwardly forward and kissed Anne. She blinked at me in surprise then she gave a little laugh.

"That was inappropriate," she said.

"No, it wasn't. I wanted to do it—I've been wanting to for several existences. I thought I should give this version of myself a shot since I don't even know how long he has to breathe. In fact…you know what? I think the last version of me died a virgin. Isn't that sad?"

Anne looked troubled. She ran her hand over mine and then gave me a light slap on the cheek.

"You're good to go, Specialist. On your feet!"

I stood up and pressed my body into clean clothing. My fingers were rubbery, and it took me a full minute to get dressed. I think I would have failed entirely if the clothes hadn't been smart enough to help wrap them over my skin.

"I'm sorry about that," I said as I stepped toward the door. "I mean the kiss."

Anne turned away from her devilish machine and walked up to me. She gave me an odd look. Her expression was thoughtful—but I believed I knew what it meant.

"You want a date tonight?" she asked.

I pointed toward the machine. "With you or with that thing?"

She laughed tiredly. "You know what I mean."

"Okay then... When do you get off?"

"When the shift ends or when this thing stops giving birth. I'll text you."

I gave her an awkward, slimy hug and left the chamber. When I reached my bunk, all I wanted to do was crash into it. But that wasn't meant to be.

"There you are, McGill," Leeson said as he followed me to my bunk. "Had a nice rest?"

"About three days' worth of nonexistence, sir. I recommend it highly if you're feeling low."

Leeson's lips twisted into a grimace. "Never mind about that. This platoon has been short both of our weaponeers for a long time, and we haven't been deployed. Sargon still hasn't been farted out of that machine yet. Turov is driving every commander in the legion nuts with the slow-downs."

"She excels at that, sir. Do you want me to pass your opinion on to the Imperator next time I meet her?"

Leeson's eyes widened. "Hell no! Has she contacted you?"

"Not since the legion left Earth. But she had a private meeting with me the morning before we lifted off."

"About what?"

"She wanted me to throw the vote concerning our legion's independence. She asked me to come out online as a supporter and reverse myself."

"Ah, I remember your original post. Pretty funny. You were drunk when you wrote that, weren't you?"

"Maybe a little."

Leeson nodded and crossed his arms. "A man's true feelings come out of a bottle, sometimes. Anyway, I'm glad you posted your little rant, and that you didn't back down. Most of all, I'm glad the troops voted with you."

I sat up. "That's just it, sir. I don't think they really did—I mean, I probably had some effect, but I don't think they were going to vote to join Hegemony anyway."

Leeson narrowed his eyes at me and grinned. "Yeah, maybe not. But then you sealed it when you connected the enlisted people up to file their votes with Central before we left orbit. Just before the deadline there was a flood of votes, you know. That took crazy balls. I'm glad it was you. I'd have been stripped of my rank by now."

I didn't mention to him that I'd suffered plenty of abuse from Turov already over the vote. I'd even been murdered in my own house. A nice calm demotion would've been preferable.

"Is there a special reason you're paying me a visit right now, sir?" I asked.

"Yeah, we're moving out. I've been waiting for a weaponeer before deploying. Now that you're back, we're heading back into the streets at dawn."

"Dawn," I said, checking my tapper. I had six hours to rest. My eyes closed and I saw strange images. I was so tired that my brain was playing dreams on the inside of my eyelids despite the fact Leeson was still talking to me. Dreaming or not, I was awake enough to respond to Leeson.

"Don't you want to know where we're headed?" he asked.

"Not really, sir."

"Damn, you're one cool customer, McGill. I didn't think you'd turn out this way when you first mustered in. To me, you looked like a giant screw-up. Oh, and thanks for covering for me with Graves about that debacle at the bank. I was worried that when I caught my revival I'd be put right back down again."

I opened one eye and looked at him blearily. I realized that was why he'd really come in here to talk to me the minute I'd come back from the revival machine. He wanted to thank me—and maybe to make sure I wasn't going to screw him at this late date by talking about Old Silver and his bribes.

The odd thing was I hadn't tried to protect Leeson when I'd made my report. I guess I could have told Graves what I thought of Leeson's decision to go along with Claver. But I was so pissed at Germanica's silver-haired devil that I hadn't even considered my immediate commander's lack of good judgment. Funny how things worked out sometimes.

I forced an upward twitch of my lips and closed both eyes again. "No big deal, sir. Could have happened to anyone."

"See you at dawn then," Leeson said, and left.

Lying on my bunk I thought about what had happened out there with Claver and the rest of my platoon. Was Claver involved with all this violence spreading across the city? I didn't see how he could be at the bottom of it, but then, he was a wily old bastard.

As I passed from wakefulness into a deep soulful sleep, I wondered if Claver was still alive out there somewhere. The odds were against it with enemy rebels killing every legionnaire they caught in the streets.

Claver's silver hair represented an amazing accomplishment in survival, but I'd realized by now it wasn't a heroic achievement. It had been done through trickery and deceit.

Yeah...he could be alive. The more I thought about it, the more I thought it was likely.

Old Silver was as impossible to kill as a slippery river-rat. I felt sure he'd survived out there somewhere, somehow.

* * *

I woke up late with about twenty-five minutes to shower, dress, and shove food into my mouth. I was still chewing when I rammed my helmet down over my head and jogged down to the rally point.

"All right, line up!" Harris roared, marching along the line like we were a bunch of day-old recruits.

I resented his attitude—nothing new for me—but I lined up with the rest of them. Harris paused in front of me and narrowed his eyes. "Glad to see you felt like joining us today, McGill."

"Wouldn't miss this for the world, Vet."

Carlos was there—as were Kivi and even Natasha. It was old home week and as always I felt strange looking at faces I'd seen dead in the mud what seemed like only a few hours ago. That is not to mention the disconnected feeling that came along with knowing my own eyes had been as dead as rubber just last night.

I did my best to shake it off and get into the mission. Whining about a death was amateur-hour in Legion Varus.

When we'd all gathered, Centurion Graves appeared and stepped calmly forward to address the unit.

"People, I'm not going to lie to you. Just about everyone here has died at least once over the last seventy-two hours. I'm here to thank you for your commitment to the cause and to inform you—regretfully—that your sacrifice is not yet done."

We tried to stay cool, but this wasn't Graves' usual sort of opener. I sensed more than saw people fidgeting and exchanging glances all along the ranks. Graves wasn't sounding as overconfident as he often was—he was downright apologetic. I couldn't recall a similar briefing.

The screen behind him lit up from the floor to the ceiling. I was glad not to see Turov's leering face up there. Instead, a diagram of the city appeared with varied colors for levels of conflict and numbers indicating districts. Our position was in the middle of district-14, a relatively calm region of the city that glowed a cool green. I was surprised by how many areas were yellow, orange, red—even purple, a color that indicated we'd lost the zone and given up on it.

"As you can see here," said Graves, gesturing with his hands as if he were grabbing leaves and plucking them from an invisible tree. "The lower decks around the Vents and the umbilical region have been lost to the enemy and are now shown in violet. The red zone contains enemy troops, but fighting still goes on there between government forces, legion troops and the rebels."

By my estimate, I'd say a third of the city was violet or red. I immediately suspected that the enemy controlled all of that, and that we were making incursions and patrols now and then to look like we cared.

His hands shifted, spreading his fingers, and the view zoomed sickeningly. The see-through outline of Gelt Station itself whirled around like a top, and we came in from a different angle focusing on the orange zones.

"The mid-decks are residential," he said without any inflection. "We're fighting in the streets there, block-by-block. The fighting is heavy at times, but quiet right now. Tonight's mission involves residential-6, an affluent neighborhood directly below the financial district. Intel estimates this region is a key target for the enemy."

I had to suppress a snort of disbelief. I wondered what kind of genius adjunct had figured that one out. These Tau thought of nothing but money most of the time. I wasn't at all surprised they were trying to take over the banks. Hell, that might be the whole point of the uprising in the first place.

Graves made an erasing gesture, and the three dimensional image of the station vanished. He brought up camera feeds from the streets.

My interest immediately rose. Here were the faces of the enemy. I could see them, and they looked grimly determined.

There were more of them in the streets now. Throngs. They were suited up in dull maroon and shimmering silver. I again wondered at the significance of those colors.

I figured they must be the working class proles from the planet's surface. Only one in ten of them were armed with anything other than a makeshift weapon. Of those officially armed, a few carried lightning-rod devices. Others carried—my eyes widened in shock.

"Excuse me? Sir?" I called.

Graves looked at me for a moment before waving for me to speak.

"Sir, are they carrying legion regulation weapons?"

"Yes, yes, very observant," Graves said. I couldn't tell if he was being sarcastic or not. "They have snap-rifles for the most part. They took down two full cohorts of our light troops last night and distributed the weapons. Notice also that most of them are unarmed. Entire squads follow one leader with a real weapon. When he goes down, they pick it up and keep fighting."

I shook my head in disbelief. Snap-rifles weren't much—but they were better than regular gunpowder-based ballistic weaponry. They accelerated tiny needles of mass to great speeds and operated with a high rate of fire. I didn't want to have to face a mob armed with the same weapons we had. To be shot to death by our own weapons—that would be a tough way to go down.

What was surprising was that they'd managed to get so many weapons from our troops. They must have killed the light troops pretty fast to keep their grip on them. Our legion recovery teams put a priority on weapons retrieval. They were much more important than bodies or uniforms.

"Perhaps I should recap what we've learned of this conflict for those of you who've been out of the picture for a while," Graves said, pointedly looking at me. "The unrest on the surface has been growing for years. Tau is a world of contrasts. A few have great wealth, but due to their unrestricted population growth, most are poor. Only the wealthy few make it up here into space to seek their fortunes. All of that background information was available on the legion website, and you should have read it on the flight out here.

"What's different today," he continued, "comes down to two key elements. One, they managed to get a large shipment of powerful alien weapons. Two, the population of this world has learned of Imperial weakness. It was bound to get out, and the first world to hear about it was this one, a merchant hub of local trade. They know that the local Battle Fleet has been called to the Core Systems. We've been left in charge. How does that look to them? Well, they've seen a scrim of fancy troops courtesy of Germanica for years. The rebels on the planet surface weren't impressed. They decided to make their move before the Empire ships come back."

Carlos, of all people, raised his hand. Graves ignored him and pointed to Natasha.

"Sir," she asked, "why were they holding back? I mean, the Empire doesn't care about the purely internal affairs of any system. They could have a civil war and a blood bath without a threat from the Imperial Fleets."

"That's not true in this case," Graves said. "Remember that Gelt Station is the hub of interstellar commerce. Aliens are here on legitimate Imperial business. If they destroy an alien trade ship without good cause, they risk sanction by the fleets if they come back. The *ultimate* sanction."

Natasha frowned. "Did you say 'if' the Imperial fleets come back?"

"I should have said 'when.' In any case, their return might take a long time."

The entire subject of warfare among the Core Systems was the topic of countless whispered conversations among the troops, but our officers rarely brought it up. I was alarmed at the idea that Imperial ships might never return. How could the Empire hold together in its current form if they didn't? At some point, an alien civilization would grow bold and attack another. At that moment, the galaxy would change forever. I hoped someone back on Earth was thinking about these things and working up some kind of plan to deal with the situation.

"A long time, sir?" Carlos blurted out of turn. "The fleet might not return for...what? Are we talking years, here...or centuries?"

"A trip to the Core Systems takes over a year each way," Graves said. "Beyond that, we have no way of judging the situation. If anything, the Galactic Net is more closely policed than it was before. We're not getting any formal news from the Nairbs or anyone else."

I found it remarkable that Graves was freely passing on this information. I wasn't sure why he was doing it. Maybe it was part of the same disease that had infected the local Tau. They'd figured the cat was gone and may be dead, and they were partying harder every day, celebrating the absence.

How long would it be, I asked myself again, before more worlds went wild?

-18-

Graves slammed his hands together, ending the briefing and dismissing us with one gesture. We hustled for the armory and loaded up. I decided to go with a heavy kit today. I was done fooling around. I asked the quartermaster for a light artillery emplacement, a floater cart to carry it, plus another cart for ammo.

"You know this 88 has a kick?" the quartermaster asked, as if I was some kind of rookie. "You can't just put it up to your shoulder."

"Yeah?" I responded. "Do you think that's why it has a tripod base?"

He looked at me with twisted-up lips for a few seconds, then sighed and contacted Leeson for approval.

Adjunct Leeson backed me up without a moment's hesitation. I was gratified that I had a favor to pull in from him, and I hoped that state of affairs would continue. To my mind, it was best to immediately turn gratitude from a superior officer into something tangible. They tended to forget who they owed very quickly.

I had Carlos assigned to drag my ammo cart around for me. You would have thought I'd put a dog collar on him and sent him into the snow under a heavy lash.

"This isn't cool," he said, dragging the tether line.

The floating cart barely weighed anything from the point of view of the soldier guiding it. The cart even had enough automated brains to follow a man on its own if you let it. But none of that stopped Carlos from complaining.

"I've got a cart of my own," I told him, tugging on my tether. My burden was, if anything, bigger and more unwieldy than his was. The entire gun emplacement rode on it. It looked squatty and had a bulbous nose on the front projector. The tripod of legs had a distinctly insectile appearance. Alien 88s always reminded me of beetles with nozzles, but they were deadly at mid-range against large formations.

"I'm supposed to be your friend, not your slave," Carlos continued. "I don't get this at all. Do you hate me, McGill?"

"I just wanted to team up with someone I could talk to," I said. "I guess I was wrong. I'll contact Adjunct Leeson and get you reassigned on point with Kivi."

"Fine, fine, I'll pull your damned cart. No need to get pissy about it."

Carlos was an acquired taste. For some reason I liked the man. We were still friends despite all the trouble between us. I think it was the fact we'd faced death together so many times. Serious combat welds men together. In our case, it gave us the fortitude to overlook one another's faults.

"We pulled the lucky card on this deployment," Adjunct Leeson's voice crackled in my headset. "We've been assigned the high ground. The best part is we're not going anywhere near the financial district."

This was news to me and Carlos. We exchanged glances and continued to listen.

"We're going to the high end of the station," Leeson said, "covering the government buildings. No one expects a serious attack there as the rentable Tau police force is huddled in those structures. All aboard the skimmer—and remember to hold on, these turtles are crazy pilots."

There were muttered groans and curses as we loaded our gear onto the skimmer. This model had been modified for combat. It still had a low railing, but its underbelly was armored by interlocking plates that looked like fish scales to me.

The turtle did his best to make us throw up breakfast, but I think the added weight dampened his efforts. We slewed and wallowed at every banking turn. It was frightening, but not as violent and death-defying as usual.

When we at last cruised into the government district, I was happy to see the streets were empty and quiet. Maybe this mission would be the cakewalk we'd been promised.

As we landed on a flat section of a pyramid-like structure and leapt off the deck, a second skimmer came roaring down near us. Graves himself got off with another platoon. Several more skimmers were following as three units had been assigned to cover this centrally placed building in the district.

The original briefing map had displayed this district as yellow, meaning there was no current combat, but we were bordering enemy forces and had to look sharp. When we touched down, we spread out and moved to cover all the elevators and stairways that led down into the building. Harris took care of that, placing his troops with care.

The Veteran didn't mess with Carlos and me. We were on our own. Leeson walked over, hands on his hips, and surveyed the roof.

"Over there," he said, "west side. Set up your 88 with the best field of fire you can."

His order was extraneous, but I didn't mind. As long as an officer didn't order me to do something stupid, I was happy. I dragged my artillery piece to the edge of the roof and set it up on a corner. I had a great field of fire down two slanting sides of the building.

"Don't you think we're kind of exposed out here on the corner?" Carlos asked me as he towed the ammo after me.

"Yeah," I said, "but you can't do much if you can't see anything. This is a line-of-sight weapon. We have to have a clear field of fire."

"What if they have snipers?"

"We're going to build a bunker up here. I thought you'd be happy out here on this roof. The heavy fighting is kilometers away."

Carlos shaded his eyes and looked out toward the financial district to the west. Smoke trails swirled up toward the big exhaust fans and lurid glowing flames could be seen here and there dotting the streets. Something was going on out there, we could see that much.

"After they take the banks, where do you think they'll come next?" Carlos asked me.

I looked at him in surprise. "Take the banks? Do you think they will?"

Carlos laughed. "I forgot. All you got was Graves' little pep-talk today. That's not the whole story."

His statement concerned me. Carlos was always cynical, but I'd felt that Graves had been holding back. I was also worried that Carlos was referring to Graves' speech as a pep-talk. To my mind, the briefing had laid out a grim scenario.

Carlos knelt and pulled out a portable puff-crete dispenser. It looked like a big caulk gun and worked the same way. You had to be careful though, because if you didn't get the material out cleanly in one go it would harden up and jam the gun. Once it did that, it was almost impossible to reuse.

I got down on my knees and joined him. Soon we were squirting out an instant fortification around the 88. It began to take shape, looking like pink-white paste until it hardened. I kept building it up farther out with a large aperture for firing. It was going to feel weird being perched on the corner of the building and hanging out over thousands of meters of air like I was sitting in a bug's cocoon.

"Listen," Carlos said. "We've lost about half the city over the last three days. I got lucky and was revived early—well, maybe lucky is the wrong word. Anyway, I was ahead of you in line. I got to watch the enemy spread and advance."

For once, I felt no urge to tell Carlos to shut up. He was more serious than usual in his tone as well. I added a reinforced support under the floor of the bunker, attaching it with strands and beads of thick puff-crete and slathering it into place with disposable trowels.

"Just think of what that means," Carlos continued. "This hab is *huge*. Just to march as far as they have without fighting would take days. We haven't been holding them back or forming a front. We've been overrun and pressed back at every engagement. They're advancing like a flood and talk of this being a 'battle' is just wishful thinking."

150

Carlos had never been one to look at the bright side of a situation, but I had to admit he was right. They couldn't have spread so far, so fast, if we'd been doing much of anything to slow them down.

"They have sheer numbers," I said. "I understand that, but what about the city population? How can a few thousand—even a hundred thousand—control millions of civvies?"

"That's just it," Carlos said, "I think they're joining up. I think every neighborhood full of losers they take over is a recruiting ground. The city is rising up. Their ideology—or whatever they're using to get people to fight—is spreading."

I thought about how selfish the Tau were in this place. These aliens only cared about gaining a credit for themselves. I wasn't sure what had gotten them into a fighting spirit—maybe it was a culmination of hopelessness among the countless poor.

"I bet they aren't all joining up," I said. "Most are probably huddling in their houses content to let others fight it out. That sounds like your average Tau. They don't have much community spirit."

Carlos laughed. "Try none at all. The threat of Galactic intervention has always kept this place under control—but that's gone now."

"We don't know that. It's very risky to assume the Battle Fleet won't come back and exact revenge."

Carlos shrugged. "Tell *them* about it."

I looked out of my completed bunker and stared to the west. The smoke clouds seemed a trifle bigger and blacker than they'd been when we'd started. Could the battle be coming closer?

"Break out the goggles," I said. "I want to get a range-reading on the riots."

Carlos dug around in our equipment bags and pulled out the goggles, but he didn't hand them over. Instead, he pulled the strap over his own head and stared through the telescoping lenses, making adjustments.

"Come on, hand them over," I said.

"I'm your spotter, and I'm spotting something right now."

Rather than standing around, I got into my gunner's harness and tried out the swivel controls on the 88. They felt good. I'd trained some with light artillery pieces like this one over the last six months but had yet to use them in combat.

I liked the way the 88 felt. The handholds on the back were like vertical bicycle handlebars. With my gauntlets off they were cool to the touch, and the swivel motion was very smooth. A lot of alien tech was awkward to use. Even the systems they built for use by humanoids. There was always something extra or something missing that made it hard for a human to operate. For example, most seats had a hole for a tail to hang out the back. That was fine if you needed it, but when a human sat in such a chair it felt like your butt was being squeezed into the tail-hole after a while.

The 88 didn't have a tail-hole or a gripping system that was built to be operated by three or four hands at once. It was easy to control and bi-manipulative by design. I could swing the muzzle either up, down, or sideways almost effortlessly. The sights were good, too. I could zoom in and doing so automatically narrowed the projector aperture for longer range precision fire. Zooming out widened the cone of impact, but it was still a pretty tight beam compared to the old shoulder-mounted belcher units I was most accustomed to.

"I think you're going to get to fire that thing after all," Carlos said.

I glanced up at him. He was crouching at my side, intently staring into the goggles and trying not to move at all. I could tell by the way the goggles had telescoped out to nearly a foot in length that whatever he was looking at was pretty far away.

"You checking out the banks?"

"Yes I am—and it looks bad. There are Tau everywhere. I think—I think they just took over the banking buildings. The streets are overrun."

"Crazy," I said, staring at the horizon. Without a visual aid system, all I could see was a pall of smoke. "Why are so many joining in? What's the payoff for them?"

"They must think this is their chance. Only one Tau in a thousand has any real money, you know. They all lust for more. I think they're willing to burn their whole city down for the chance to get it."

"But they have to know that we're going to burn *them* down when they get here. I mean, they might win in the end, but they're going to take horrid losses. What would make them so willing to sacrifice themselves?"

Carlos shook his head and took off the goggles. He looked troubled, and that was unusual for him. In fact, this entire conversation wasn't how discussions normally went with Carlos. He was usually as self-centered as the Tau themselves.

"I don't know," he said. "Did I tell you I fought them in the streets the second day—after you were killed at the umbilical transport hub?"

"No—but it looks like you survived."

"I did. Let me tell you, it wasn't pretty. They came at us near the shopping malls that surround the city's green area— you know, what passes for a park. They swarmed us like lemmings. We burned *so* many down. They might have won except most of them didn't have good weapons. Women, even a few of their young—they were all fighting and dying like animals. But only the Tau. Did you notice that? None of the foreign population has joined in with them. Only the Tau are fighting."

Frowning, I put on the goggles and studied the throngs that marched slowly closer like ants. Carlos was right. There were only Tau in the horde. I noticed another thing. They were all wearing the same colors: maroon and silver. What the hell did that mean?

"Stay on station," I told Carlos. "I'm going to go talk to Natasha."

Carlos grinned and the moment I got out of the gunner's harness he slipped into it and began slewing the gun mount around.

"That's not a toy, legionnaire," I said.

"I know that. Don't you think I know that? I know when I'm manning a real gun. This feels great! I almost hope the squid-faces make it all the way up these streets to us."

I smiled thinly. That sounded more like the Carlos I knew. Whatever twinge of guilt and worry he'd been feeling, it was gone now.

Leaving him at the gun emplacement, I went out onto the roof again to find Natasha. I hoped she'd have answers—she often did.

-19-

As we were stationed on the flat top of a gigantic pyramid-like building, I had to walk a hundred meters or so to our central encampment. I found Natasha there, setting up a large bunker that looked like a bubble of puff-crete on the building's roof. The skimmers had lifted off and left us by this time, and the bunker she was spraying into existence squatted next to the newly outlined air-vehicle landing zone.

After helping her set up the bunker, she deployed a weapons system inside it. I examined her weaponry with a critical eye.

"Anti-air?" I guessed.

"Automated drone turrets," she said without looking up. "They work well for this kind of fortification as long as you can trust their friend-or-foe programming."

"Uh, can we trust it?"

"Of course," she said, a little abruptly. "I edited the scripts myself."

"Must be good then. You got a second to talk?"

She glanced up at me and shook her head. "You never quit, do you?"

"What?"

"Am I the last female on the roof? Or have you already hit on everyone else up here today?"

"What?" I asked again. "No...I mean...I'm not hitting on you. I want to know something."

Natasha turned back to her anti-air drone. She began studiously messing with her turret scripts. That was real work—but I wasn't fooled.

"I've been dead for several days," I pointed out, "not fooling around with women in case you're under some kind of misconception. Did somebody tell you a story?"

She heaved a sigh and faced me. "I guess I'm not being fair. You don't always connect well with women."

I blinked in confusion. To my mind, I was something of an authority on connecting with women.

"What's this about?" I asked, trying to stay on neutral ground.

"Anne Grant."

"The bio? Yeah, she revived me."

"She told me she had a date with you and asked if that was cool with me. I told her it was. I told her she could marry your ass if she wanted to."

I was beginning to catch on. My mind whirled around—twice, I think—then came to a stop.

"Did she say yes?"

Natasha frowned. "Yes to what?"

"To the marriage idea."

Her hand snapped up fast, but I leaned my head back and she missed.

"Look," I said, "I was dead. For three whole days. Can't a man get a break after that?"

She heaved a sigh. "Maybe. But it seems like I cut you breaks all the time. Do you recall we slept together that last night on Earth when this whole vote thing started?"

"Of course, I think of it constantly."

Her lips formed an unnatural pattern. I wasn't sure if she was disgusted or annoyed. "Then why have you barely talked to me since? On the whole flight out here you never brought it up. When we got here, we never went out on the town or anything. You knew I wanted to hit the markets and find some cool tech, but you forgot all about that."

"Huh," I said. "What I remember is going on a crazy gunrunning mission then dying in battle with Tau rebels...nope, no shopping trips were planned or skipped."

"As if you were going to go out with me even if we were having an easy time here."

Truth was, I'd forgotten about her plans in all the excitement. But I knew that wasn't her real problem, anyway. What had her upset was Anne.

"Natasha," I said, deciding to switch the direction of the conversation, "is this situation going to damage our odds for mission success?"

She straightened up in a hurry when I said that. Whatever else she was, she was a good soldier. When she needed to, she could bury her feelings like few others I knew.

"No," she said firmly. "All right then. Forget about my dreams of shopping. Maybe I'm just stressed—it's silly, isn't it? This hab is in the middle of some kind of civil war. I shouldn't be asking you about this at all. Sorry, Specialist McGill."

I forced a smile, even though I knew dropping back away from a first name basis wasn't a good omen. "Great. Here's why I came to you: in your opinion, what's with these crazy rebels?"

She frowned. "You mean why are they fighting? I'm not entirely sure."

"Neither am I. What we know is that they're going completely batshit and the effect is spreading. Could it be drugs? Some kind of secret plan or cult we don't know about? Usually, the Tau are only motivated by selfish profits. What would make them rise up as a single mass and attack us?"

Natasha tapped her face with a finger, puzzling it out. I could tell I'd managed to intrigue her as well as deflect her from asking any more unwelcome questions about Anne Grant.

"That's a damned good question, James."

I dared to let a smile creep back onto my face. I was James again, not that cold-hearted bastard, Specialist McGill.

"You're right," she said thoughtfully. "Why the hell are the Tau acting like lemmings? It just doesn't make sense. After I set this up, I'll do some checking around. Some of the other techs must be working on enemy behavioral models."

"Great," I said. I considered giving her a hug but passed on the idea. I beat a hasty retreat instead. A man has to know when he's been let off easy and not give in to the temptation to go for broke.

Before I even made it back to the little bunker on the corner of the roof that housed Carlos and my 88, the situation changed. An alarm tone sounded in my helmet.

I'd had the visor up, but now snapped it down reflexively. I checked the sky, but found it empty. Natasha's air-defense drone was in slow-scan mode which indicated it hadn't detected a threat. The rest of the troops around me on the roof were doing the same thing I was. We looked at each other, mystified. If the attack wasn't coming via air, where was it coming from?

My helmet crackled and a familiar voice broke into the chatter of confused troops. "This is Graves. Finish those puff-crete bunkers immediately and get to your assigned positions. We're about to have company. The Tau are coming up from the subways and should be visible in the streets soon."

I broke into a run and reached my bunker in ten strides. I put a gauntlet on Carlos' shoulder and pulled him around.

"Get out of my chair, spotter!" I shouted at him.

He rolled out of the harnessed gunner's seat, grumbling. He struggled with the spotter's goggles. "What's the deal?" he asked.

"I have no idea."

I climbed into the harness and strapped in as quickly as I could. Right away I could tell he'd fooled with all my settings. My balls were smashed up against the barrel and my knees were up so high my legs were almost bent double.

"Dammit, Carlos! Did you have to fool with the seat?"

"Sec," he said, slapping a button on the side.

The seat immediately moved, whirring. I was eased back into a reasonable position and grunted with relief.

"I preset the unit for you and me, both," Carlos said.

Frowning at him, I narrowed my eyes. "Why? You're not qualified to shoot this thing. You're a spotter, not a weaponeer."

"That's true," he said. "But remember how you got rank? Your weaponeer died on Steel World and you picked up his gun. I just figured…well."

"Hoping they take out your gunner so you can be a hero, huh?"

He shrugged. "Worked for you."

"I'm feeling the love, here," I said. "Now, give me a range to that subway entrance a block west."

"One-point four," he said after playing with the goggles for a second. "These things are great. They take all the guess work out—holy shit!"

I didn't even ask what he was talking about. I swiveled smoothly, aiming my projector down into the streets.

The Tau were boiling up out of the subway. The street filled with flickering shadows like blurs of somber color.

"Targets sighted, command," I said into my headset. "Do I have permission to fire?"

"How many have you got on your side of the building, McGill?" Graves asked in my ear.

"Looks like all of them, sir."

"Roger that. Same thing on the other side. Take them out before they reach the building. We can't let them get inside the barricades downstairs."

The leading elements of the charge were already roaring forward and hitting the base of the pyramid I sat upon.

I took a deep breath and squeezed the trigger-bars with my gauntlets. The 88 didn't make a loud sound when it fired, but a lot of hot air blasted out of the thing's sides. Carlos was caught by surprise and almost had his goggles blown off his head.

The biggest problem with large-scale plasma weapons when used in an atmosphere was the overproduction of heat. My 88 was no exception to that rule. It seemed to generate almost as much heat from the housing as it did from the muzzle. Like the machineguns of the past, the metal swelled up and the entire thing could malfunction from overuse. As I didn't have any barrels to change out, I had to make sure it didn't get *too* hot.

The meter was tapped into my HUD and displayed inside my visor. The first blaze of plasma only lasted about a second, and by the end of it the temperature was already up into the yellow zone on my internal monitors.

Using the burst as efficiently as I could, I swept the beam in a broad swath across the mob at the base of the building. They were so bunched up I couldn't miss. How many did I kill? I'm not sure. Maybe a thousand—but probably less.

I doubted this crowd had ever seen that level of firepower before, and they reeled back in shock. It had to be a surprise to see twenty ranks ahead of you turn to ash all at once with nothing but a cloud of hot gas and seared individuals at the edge of the kill-zone to clue you in as to what had just happened.

My weapon cycled up to a full charge again, and the temperature fell into the green—but I held my fire.

Graves noticed immediately that I'd stopped firing. "McGill? Are you injured?"

"Negative sir."

"Why aren't you firing your weapon?"

"They're falling back, sir."

And they were. They were stumbling, reeling, and dragging their dead toward the subway entrance.

"Are they dragging wounded?" he asked.

"Uh, yes sir."

"Good, all right. Hold onto that cannon of yours for a second."

I heard him then, up along the rim of the building's roof. He ordered a unit of light troops to the edge. I saw them hustle and kneel there, aiming down into the crowd. Graves was the senior Centurion present, and he had been put in charge of the defending units.

Light weapons began to chatter.

"Snap-rifles?" Carlos asked. He gazed down into the streets. "They're chewing them up."

I felt a little sick. It was one thing to burn down a raging mass of enemy troops who were hell-bent on killing you—it was quite another to shoot retreating civvies in the back.

Slapping the release on my harness, I climbed out of the bunker and walked along the wall to Graves' position.

"There you are," he said. "Do you know what I'm doing, McGill?"

"Killing retreating civvies, sir?"

160

He glanced at me in irritation. "No. I'm wounding them. These troops are aiming low."

I looked up and down the line. It was true, the light troops had their sniper barrels attached and were popping single rounds down, choosing their targets with care.

"An army seeks to wound opponents," Graves told me with the air of one delivering a lecture. "That's preferable to killing them. Each wounded enemy takes another man to care for him."

"The Tau don't have a big history of caring for their fellows," I pointed out.

"True enough. But maybe they'll become demoralized and less wildly excited about charging us."

"I see, sir."

"You don't approve?"

"That's not my place, sir. I'm not in command here."

Graves looked at me. I avoided his eyes and stared down into the streets. The civvies were falling back being driven underground like animals. Hundreds of wounded lay squirming all over the streets.

"That's right, you're not in command," Graves said sharply. "And you never will be if you don't learn a few things."

"Can I ask a question, sir?"

"If you must."

"What's so important about this particular building?"

"It's an armory. A government armory."

Shocked, I turned my full attention to the centurion. "A government armory? Why are we the ones protecting it?"

"You'd think that the government forces would be more interested in doing so, wouldn't you? Well, they're not. They work for pay, and are willing to take a certain degree of risk. But they were unnerved by this crazy crowd. They abandoned the district hours before we got here."

The streets were empty now except for the crawling injured and the smoldering dead.

"We can't let these crazies have real weapons," I said. "They'll be unstoppable."

"Now you understand the true importance of our defensive mission."

"Yes sir, I do."

"Can I ask you a question, McGill?"

"Of course, Centurion."

"The next time I order you to kill a thousand murderous hostiles—civvies or not—will you follow that order instead of fucking around?"

There was sudden vehemence in his statement. He was pissed off, and he had a good point. Our eyes met.

"Yes sir," I said. "Sorry sir."

Graves' attention drifted back toward the streets below which were nearly quiet now. "That was only the first wave," he said. "Their ranks have swollen but their weaponry hasn't. Only one out of twenty of them have a real weapon. They *must* capture this armory."

I nodded grimly. "I understand. They won't get past me, sir."

"Excellent. Back to your post, Specialist."

Our district of the city fell silent for the next few hours. The power went out late, then came back on, then went out again.

I didn't think orbital megahabs were built to operate without power—and I was right. When everything shut down, ominous groaning and grinding sounds began emanating from the roof-vents. I knew these noises were bubbling up from the distant machinery below the streets.

When the generators died the second time, the city streets fell into a strange twilight. The city itself was as black as space, but beams of overly brilliant starlight streamed in from outside the station cutting like cold lasers through the gloom. After a few more hours, the air became stale and the whole place seemed haunted.

By listening to reports from other parts of the city, I came to fully understand how badly this battle was going. It was our side that had cut the power hoping to slow the rioters down— but apparently it wasn't working. The enemy was advancing all over the city. They seemed unstoppable.

Once again, I found myself wondering where Old Silver was. He had to be out there somewhere. Was he working with the Tau openly? I didn't trust that man in any way, shape, or form. He'd known too much about this rebellion from the beginning.

At about midnight Natasha showed up and stuck a tablet in my face. It showed a graphic app depicting Tau attire. You could flick your finger over it and change their dress to anything you wanted, and a caption would appear underneath telling you what it meant.

"Cool vid game," I said. "Did you figure anything out?"

"Try the app," she said, pushing it into my hands. "Make it look like one of the rebels."

I sighed and did as she asked. I toyed with the app, but I soon found myself frustrated.

"It doesn't seem to work," I said. "The maroon and silver—you can't select that."

"That's right," she said. "I don't know why, but apparently no one *ever* chooses that combination. Either that or the app designers don't know what it means."

"Huh," I said, shrugging. "That's weird."

Natasha rolled her eyes. "It's not just *weird*, James. It's part of the answer."

"What answer?"

"The answer to why these people are acting so oddly."

I frowned, chewing that one over. "Are you saying that if we could get these clowns to change their holographic clothing back to normal they'd settle down?"

"I'm not sure, but I'm trying to figure that out."

"We should tell someone about this," said Carlos, leaning his big face in between us.

I pushed him back with my hand. "No you don't. This is Natasha's find. She'll take it to the brass herself and get the credit."

He glared at both of us. "How the hell am I supposed to get rank if you guys won't cut me a break?"

"Do something useful," I suggested.

"I'm going to do just that. I'm gonna take a leak over the side of this building." He stalked off into the night.

"Take the app to Graves," I told Natasha.

"I already did. He said he'd mention it in his next report to the Primus."

"That sounds like bullshit," I said.

"Yeah."

I thought hard for a second then came to a decision. The more I thought about it, the more this tidbit of information

164

seemed critical. Legion Varus was losing this fight, and we needed an edge to change the tide. Understanding the cause of the uncharacteristically violent behavior of the Tau might be just what we needed.

"I'm going to contact Tribune Drusus," I said. "He told me to tell him if something like this ever came up. I'm not sure he really meant that, but he can always give me the finger if he wants to."

"James, he told you that during a different campaign on another planet."

"Yeah, well...I finally got around to it."

Natasha looked nervous. "You're really going to walk right over Adjunct Leeson, Centurion Graves, *and* our new primus?"

"Why not?"

"I'm not sure I want my name on this anymore."

"Why's everyone a chicken when it comes to talking to officers?" I asked.

"Because they can execute us."

"Been there," I said. "It's not that bad."

She laughed and handed me the tablet. "Be my guest, James."

I smiled at her. "Give me a kiss for luck?"

She hesitated, then did it. I wouldn't call it a lingering, passionate kiss, but it was the real deal. I wondered if this particular copy of my body, within which my consciousness currently resided, might get lucky before I got him blown up somehow.

"Damn you," she said almost to herself. Then she left.

Looking at the tablet, I tapped at it again trying to get the configuration right. I couldn't do it. There was no maroon suit—no silver shoes, either.

Sucking in a deep breath, I contacted the Legion commander, Tribune Drusus. I was shocked when he answered my text immediately with a voice channel. I touched a glowing dot on my tapper and heard a familiar sonorous voice in my ear piece.

"McGill? Are you overrun at your position?"

"No sir. Everything's quiet here."

"A social call then? There's a battle going on in two districts. I don't have time—"

"Sir," I said. "I wouldn't contact you to ask you out to dinner—not today, anyway."

"All right then," he said after a moment's hesitation. "What have you got?"

Talking quickly, I told him about Natasha's discovery concerning the Tau holo-clothing. He listened politely but didn't seem impressed.

"I'm failing to see the significance of this discovery interesting though it is," the Tribune told me. "It's only logical to me that the rebels would choose a non-standard set of colors to identify one another on the battlefield."

"I think it's more than that, sir," I said. "The Tau use their appearance to project mood and to infect one another with their thoughts. Every color combination they wear is significant. This one is unknown to us, but Specialist Elkin believes they're spreading the rebellion with these colors, signaling others to join them."

"I didn't say that!" Natasha hissed behind me.

I waved her off and listened to the tribune.

"Hmm," Drusus said. "That's an interesting idea. We're new here, and I do recall that the Tau present emotion, mood, and intent with their colors. They used to do it with physical dress but now use these holographic projections. You're saying that if we changed their projections we could quell these riots?"

"I don't know, sir," I admitted. "But it's got to be worth investigating. We can't kill every civvy on this station."

"You're right about that. They outnumber us by about a hundred thousand to one. All right, hold your position. When your current mission is complete, I'm giving your unit new orders to investigate the matter."

"Uh, thanks sir. We'd be glad to help—but isn't there a tech unit that would be better suited to—?"

"No, there isn't anyone else I can spare. Besides, I think learning the truth of the matter will require a full combat team before you're done."

"How long is our current mission going to last, sir?" I asked.

"I suspect it will all be over by morning."

Drusus closed the channel, and I was left frowning down into the dark streets.

"What'd he say?" Natasha asked.

"We're going to be reassigned. We'll be sleuths after we're relieved from our position up here."

"You've got to be kidding me! You went over Graves' head, and now he'll be slapped with new orders because of it? He's not going to like that."

"Yeah," I agreed, but I barely cared about Graves' feelings. I was more concerned about what we'd been asked to do next. I'd been hoping to pass the matter off to a team of techs—maybe a full unit of them—but apparently Drusus didn't have the resources free for that.

For some reason, I never even questioned Drusus about his declaration that our current assignment would be at an end by morning. I'd simply figured we would be relieved by another contingent of troops by that time. I found out just before dawn that that wasn't what he'd meant at all.

The Tau began boiling up out of the subway again, and an alarm sang in our helmets. I hated to admit it, but I'd nodded off in my harness. Carlos rapped his knuckles on my helmet making a loud knocking noise.

"We're in business again, ace," he said.

I stifled a yawn and sat up, my heart pounding. With bleary eyes, I swung the muzzle of my 88 downward. I twitched it a little to the left as it had drifted and I squeezed the dual triggers.

Smooth, bright death reached down and swept away an unknowable number of Tau. But this time, they didn't fall back. They charged forward climbing over mounds of steaming dead.

Surprised, I rotated the gun on its tracks. The system whirred and clicked. I had to draw a fresh line across the boiling horde of enemies starting farther forward this time.

"You're too far to the right with the muzzle!" Carlos shouted. "You'll burn open street instead of targets!"

He was right. I could see that immediately. But there wasn't time to correct. They were already racing to the base of the building. I struggled to adjust my aim while Carlos shoved a fresh cartridge into the base of the weapon and slapped my shoulder to indicate I was free to fire.

The 88 was an odd weapon. It wasn't like operating something as simple as a heavy machine gun. It could only fire in short bursts before recycling and cooling the plasma chamber. You couldn't hose down everything in sight. You had to preplan your shots and you couldn't afford to miss.

I squeezed the triggers, splashing my beam down on empty puff-crete. Such was the power of the beam that it vaporized a broad swathe of the street's surface, burning about an inch into one of the hardest substances in the known universe.

"Dammit," I said, straining to swing the muzzle back on target. I was partially successful, and Carlos helped by kicking the chassis and nudging me further into line.

The beam finally struck the enemy wave with half the charge expended on nothing. I could tell I was hitting troops as the expanding gases far below on the street changed from dark and thin to roiling gray-white. That was *steam*, I realized. Steam from the bodies of the massed Tau I was annihilating.

"They made it to the barriers," Carlos said, lying on his belly and aiming his extruding goggles down the long sloping side of the building. "There's too many—they'll break in, you'll have to sweep the base of the building."

"Roger that," I said, tilting the muzzle downward until I was staring directly down the side of the building. It felt like I was going to slide off and fall into the middle of them.

Carlos got to his knees quickly and fed me another cartridge. The 88 swallowed that, and the temperature indicators fell from red to orange and down, slowly, into the green.

I'd lined up for my third sweep by this time. It was going to be a difficult one as I'd have to change angles in the middle to go around the corner of the building. But if I could pull it off, I was pretty sure I could repel—

I got no further in thought or action. A blinding light and a crackling feeling of current ran through me.

For an instant, my world was whiteness and seemed to be spinning. Something hot was in my face, and I tried to push

168

away from it but the harness I was in kept me held there like glue.

My eyes began working again a moment later. Although I was dazed, I was able to take stock of the situation. We'd been hit—taken out. I didn't know where the strike had come from, probably from a well-aimed lightning bolt. Someone down there had figured out who was burning hordes of their troops and had aimed very carefully.

Carlos was dead. One of his stick-like goggles was smoking and the other had been blasted back into his head like a spear. As I watched, his body gently rolled over then slid down the side of the building, bouncing and flopping all the long, long way to the throngs in the street.

The 88 itself was damaged. The muzzle had taken the majority of the hit, and I could tell right away it had unleashed its last broad stripe of death.

I shrugged my way out of the harness and crawled out of the bunker. Gaining a little more capacity for cogent thought, I tapped my way into the tactical channel and reported.

"Western corner gun emplacement has been knocked out," I said.

"McGill?" Graves snapped. "Are you still with us?"

I rolled onto my back and stared up at the sky which was made up of fake panels and glimpses of bright, real stars. My HUD said my body was in the green—but I had my doubts.

"Yes sir," I said, half groaning the words. "But I feel like someone has been using my helmet for a church bell."

"Good enough. Join Leeson on the stairway—I sent him down into the building."

I frowned in confusion and hauled myself into a sitting position. Every second, my brain operated a little more smoothly.

"The stairway, sir?"

"The enemy has breached the armory. We've lost the bottom floor."

"Right. On my way."

Struggling to my feet, I grabbed a snap-rifle off a dead sharpshooter—my own gun had been lost when they'd lit up my bunker—and I staggered to the stairs.

169

The scene inside the stairwell wasn't encouraging. Men were shouting, and weapons chattered far below, echoing up the long, long shaft from the ground floor. The enemy was fighting their way upward, and I could tell they weren't in an easygoing mood.

-21-

I checked my snap-rifle with slightly blurred vision. I knew I probably had a concussion of some kind, but I figured the bio people could give me the details whenever they got around to it—if I lived that long.

The weapon I'd picked up was tricked out to be a sniper rifle at the moment. With a longer barrel and a superior scope mounted on top, it had a great deal of range but a much lower rate of fire.

I stepped to the first landing and put my rifle over the edge of the railing. There was a narrow space between the switchbacks on the stairs that allowed me to sight downward twenty floors or so.

Spotting a massed, shimmering movement of maroon, I decided to get into the game early. I hadn't handled a snap-rifle fitted with a scope in a long time, but it still felt like home to me. I popped off shots and put down an attacker with each round. After a dozen or so hits, my helmet crackled.

"Who's up there with the snap-rifle?" Leeson demanded.

"It's McGill, sir," I said.

"Get down here, dammit. I need your heavy weapon on the front line."

"I've lost my 88—and it wouldn't make it down twenty flights of stairs, anyway."

There was a stream of curses. Apparently, Leeson had forgotten in all the excitement that I'd come into this fight with a gun on a tripod.

"All right," he said. "No belcher, huh? Nothing more useless than a weaponeer without a weapon. Just keep popping them as they come up the stairs."

I was happy with those orders as I was still feeling a little woozy and didn't feel like jogging down into the thick of it right now. Firing with steady accuracy, I managed to get about ten more before they wised up and started creeping with their backs close to the walls so I couldn't get a good shot.

There came a moment soon after that when quiet reigned below. I moved around the stairwell sighting from every angle, but I couldn't so much as nail down a silvery shoe.

"Sir?" I said over the platoon chat channel. "I don't think they're still coming up the stairs."

"Keep your positions, everyone. They're up to something. I'm expecting a rush."

As I wasn't doing much, I began slowly walking down the stairway, constantly scanning through my scope for new targets. I didn't see any.

When the Tau finally did make their move, it came as a surprise to all of us. Fortunately, it was less of a surprise for me as I was far above the rest of the troops.

I was about five floors down from the roof when I heard a tremendous crashing sound. Puff-crete split and gouted dust up the stairwell. I barely got my visor closed in time before it powdered me all over like a donut.

"Sir?" I said, hearing nothing but sporadic fire and the cries of the injured. "Adjunct Leeson? What's going on?"

"They brought the floor down. They took it right out from under us. We're on a partially collapsed floor fighting in close quarters. What I can't believe is the number of dead—they brought the ceiling down right on top of themselves!"

I frowned at that. It was one thing to deal with a stand-up fight with a determined enemy, but these guys fought like armed lemmings. They didn't care if a hundred of their troops died as long as they took a few of us with them.

Once again, despite the dust and blood, I was left wondering why these people who were normally anything but self-sacrificing were willing to lay down their lives in droves in order to kill us.

172

The fighting increased in volume as more Tau charged up the stairway. Given fresh targets and a shorter range, I managed to get into a good firing position. I knocked them down as fast as they came into sight.

It wasn't even fair. What amazed me most was how they kept coming. Deciding to create a barrier of bodies, I put them down one at a time on a certain landing about seven floors down. Soon the stairs were slick with blood, and the dead had to be heaved over the side of the railing just to make room for more Tau to climb upward—often on their hands and knees.

How many did I kill? I don't know. A hundred at least. Maybe it was twice that. Maybe more. My magazine was half-empty when it was all over, and a snap-rifle can hold upwards of a thousand tiny slivers of ammo.

"Sir?" I asked, calling down into the quiet. "Adjunct Leeson?"

"Leeson's dead," said a familiar voice. "This is Veteran Harris. I hate to admit it, McGill, but that was some fine shooting. I'm going to recommend to Graves that he bust you back down to the light units. You've missed your calling, son."

"Thanks, Vet."

"Don't get a big head. Just cover us. We're coming back up."

I heard tramping feet on the stairway. About a dozen members of the platoon reached my position. Many were bleeding, and all of them were covered in dust and sweat.

"Did we push them back?" I asked Harris.

"Shit no," he said. "They're just taking a little rest."

I frowned down into the dark, swirling dust.

"Vet? Isn't the armory itself down there—on those middle floors, I mean?"

Harris glanced at me with an annoyed expression. "That might be, McGill. But I'm in charge, and I think our odds of survival and defending the roof are better from up here."

"But…we're supposed to stop them from getting the weapons. Who cares about the roof?"

Harris landed a heavy gauntlet on my shoulder and pushed me back into an alcove for an intense, private chat. The rest of the platoon's survivors glanced at us, but they were content with watching for fresh attackers for the most part. They looked like they wanted nothing to do with this enemy anymore.

"Now look," Harris breathed into my face. He smelled like an armpit, and from the looks of things neither of us was very happy about it. "Don't you go and screw all these soldiers by kicking this up to the centurion—or hell, the primus."

"Wouldn't think of it, Vet. I just thought our orders were to—"

"How many times do I have to tell you, boy? Stop *thinking*. And stop talking, too."

"I'm all over that."

Harris gave me a baleful stare. Then, he heaved a sigh.

"Look McGill, I know you think you're some kind of hero. You've got a complex and should seek professional help. But most of us in this outfit are just trying to make it to the end of the day without dying. Is that okay with you?"

"It seems to me that our odds of survival would improve if the enemy was prevented from arming all of their troops."

Harris chuckled and shook his head. "Don't you know how these things work yet? It doesn't matter if you fight to the death on this funky pyramid or not. What matters is the simple fact that you, I, and all of Legion Varus can't stop ten million crazies. Sometimes the best efforts of an individual, or even thousands of individuals, can't change the outcome of a battle. This mission is hopeless. We're on day four of this rebellion, and things aren't improving—they're getting worse every day."

"I don't see how any of that changes our orders or our objectives," I pointed out stubbornly.

"It changes them because it's hopeless. When a fight is hopeless, there's nothing in my contract that says I have to die over and over again for nothing."

"Actually—" I began, but he cut me off with a chopping motion of his hand.

"Did you hear that?" he asked, looking down over the stair rail.

In truth, I had heard something. It had been a low hum followed by a…a *ripping* sound.

"Upstairs!" shouted Harris. "Everyone, upstairs!"

174

They hastened to obey, but it was too late for a few of them.

Somehow, the enemy had gotten up to the level below us. They'd torn through the supports and collapsed the level. I realized now that the ripping sounds were the firing of their lightning bolt weapons into masonry.

The last eight of us beat a retreat up two floors, almost to the hatch that led out onto the roof. They caught up with us there, and we turned like treed cats. We fought Tau that rushed after us with their bare hands extended and shaped into claws.

I ripped my sniper barrel off, dropped it, and flipped the snap-rifle to full auto. I sprayed the charging mob, and a few of them fired bolts back at me. My eyes stopped working when a hit splashed right into the stairway over my head and the flash blinded me. I didn't take my finger off my weapon, however. I kept it down until the chamber rattled itself dry, showering accelerated tiny bullets into the mass of the enemy I knew was right in front of me.

When my vision came back, another figure hulked near.

"Sargon?" I asked. "I thought you must be dead."

"Can't happen," he said, smiling grimly. "I already died once on this tour, and that's my firm limit."

I looked downward at the stairway opposite our position. A hole had been blown through it. Sargon patted his belcher.

"It occurred to me that the stairway was just a few centimeters of puff-crete. A focused beam right at their feet broke through. They can have a fun time crossing that hole."

Nodding in appreciation, I slapped his shoulder. "I wish I'd thought of that," I said. "I'm sure if I'd had my belcher, I would have."

"No," he said seriously. "No way. You're too damned dumb."

We retreated farther upward and soon found ourselves at the hatchway to the roof. Cautiously, we opened it. As one of the last survivors of my platoon I wasn't sure quite what I'd expected to see when we spilled out onto the roof, but it wasn't what we met up with.

There were reinforcements landing. Legion troops— hundreds of them. There were sane-looking Tau government troops as well. The help had come in skimmers. Each team swooped in and rushed off their skimmers a few seconds after they touched down. Then each of the skimmers zoomed away making room for the next landing vehicle.

Best of all, there were bio people in the mix. I staggered forward with Harris on one flank and Sargon on the other. A pair of bios—both women with concerned faces—rushed to us and began working on wounds we barely knew we had.

I was surprised to see Anne among them. She cupped my face, smiled, and pulled a chunk of masonry out of my cheek that looked like a flint arrowhead.

Smiling back, I sunk to my knees.

"I think I've got a concussion," I said, but I don't think she heard me. Perhaps the landing craft were too loud or my mouth was full of mush—I wasn't sure which it was.

Oh well, I thought, lying on my back and eyeing the stars peeping through vast black polymer sheets that made up the artificial sky above. She'd figure it out. That was her job.

Mine was done.

-22-

Waking up, I half-expected to find myself coming out of the revival machine. But it wasn't my next body's time to live—not yet.

Somehow I'd been transported back to headquarters. I was on the bio deck—a region we called "blue deck" whether it was on a ship or a station like this.

There were tubes running in and out of my arm, my ass, my nose and God knew what else. I'm no medical wizard, but I figured this was a bad sign.

Some kind of alarm must have alerted Anne because she popped into my curtained little tent the minute I woke up.

"Hi Anne," I said, forcing a smile. "Are we having that date tonight?"

She ran her hands and a dozen instruments over me. There was obvious concern on her face.

"We really should have recycled you," she said in a voice like a whisper. "You don't know the pressure I faced."

My smile faded. "Pressure? From who? Why?"

"From my own staff, mostly."

She must have caught the look on my face because she shook her head and tried to explain. "It's not anything personal, James. It's a matter of resources. Your body is like a car. At some point, it's easier to crush you down and make a new McGill than it is to repair you. This body you're running on—well, you crossed that line."

"You're saying I was totaled? I didn't think it was that bad."

"Cranial split—did you know the orbit of your left eye was cracked?"

I frowned, thinking. "It *was* hard to see for a bit."

She shook her head. "A half-dozen puncture wounds from shrapnel, blood loss, broken rib, left lung partially collapsed."

"Yeah," I said. "My side hurt a lot. Still does. But you've got to overlook something like that in combat as long as you can."

Anne sucked in a deep breath and stopped fussing over me. She straightened her back and pursed her lips. "You'll live, but you'll hurt for a while. We had to do partial regrows and flesh-sprays all over the place. Try not to move your face around too much—you'll tear up the new skin."

"Hey," I said, calling after her as she bustled away to the next patient in line. "What about our date?"

Anne tossed me a frosty glance.

"You'd better talk that over with your girlfriend first," she said, then stalked away. I could tell by her walk she was pissed off even if her voice had sounded neutral.

I let my head flop back down onto my pillow. That was a mistake which I regretted immediately. A shower of painful lights went off inside my brain.

Natasha had gotten to Anne. *Damn.* That was the trouble with dating inside your own unit. The ladies were always upset about it no matter what kind of bullshit they fed you about not caring what you did. They never seemed to understand that I just wasn't a one-girl kind of guy. Not yet, anyway. Maybe not ever.

A few hours later, I managed to get to my feet and crawl off blue deck. Anne tried to stop me, but I was done listening to her. The battle was still raging outside, and I didn't want to end it sitting in a bed on plastic sheets.

I found Leeson on the bottom floor forming up the survivors of our unit. Looking around, I didn't see any other officers.

"Sir?" I asked. "Where's Graves? Or Adjunct Toro?"

He gave me a sour look. "They're in the queue to be revived," he said. "But that will take a while. Imperator Turov has decided, in her infinite wisdom, that only officers of units that survived their last post should run their units."

"What? That's crazy."

Leeson chuckled. "You can go tell her that. Her corvette arrived a few hours ago. She's on the top floor of this stack of hamster cages. I'm sure she'll be excited to indulge your every criticism."

I knew damned well Turov would rather see me permed than to talk strategy with me, so I shut up.

Carlos was up and around, and he began following me as usual. As was also his custom, he wasn't keeping quiet.

"This is bullshit," he said for about the seventeenth time since he'd found me. "We're supposed to go out there and fight and die all over again while serving under the biggest chicken officer in the unit?"

"I can't go along with that," I said. "Just because Leeson survived our last engagement doesn't make him a chicken."

"Yeah? Well, maybe you've got a point. He was smarter than you or me. He made it off that roof alive somehow."

"I did too," I said. "After you died in the bunker, Leeson led us into the building. There was a vicious fight, and we barely held the armory until we were relieved by reinforcements from headquarters."

Squinting in disbelief, Carlos peered into my face. He saw the bright scarlet wounds that were healing there. Nu-skin had been sprayed liberally over my cheeks, but anyone who'd seen serious wounding before could recognize the aftermath.

"I'll be damned! James McGill survived a fight—and *I* didn't. Well played, sir. Well played."

I didn't quite know what he thought I'd done so well, but I'm not one to shrink from praise, well-deserved or not.

"Now you know why I wear the extra stripes," I told him.

Carlos' face darkened again. I could tell he'd gone from admiration to wanting to punch me in less than a second. Before it could turn into a full-blown squabble, however, Leeson walked up to us and slammed his hands on our shoulders.

"Gunner and spotter. You guys did good back there," Leeson said sincerely. "You, Ortiz, you took it in the face, but not until you two had cut a few grim lines of death through the enemy. Did you know none of the other gunners did half as well? And McGill—damn, boy! They tell me that after you crawled out of that bunker, you shot down fifty more with a frigging snap-rifle. And you did it while carrying a blood clot the size of my fist inside your brain!"

I don't know which of us looked more surprised, Carlos or me. We weren't used to praise of any kind, and I hadn't known I'd been carrying around a blood clot. I counseled myself to take better care of the bio people next time I had the opportunity. Anne could have had any kind of accident with my person she'd wanted to, and no one would have doubted I needed a fresh grow. I owed her one, seriously.

"Thanks Adjunct," said Carlos, suddenly beaming. He stood straighter and puffed up a bit, like a cobra spreading its hood. "We did rip them up, didn't we James?"

"Yeah," I said uncertainly. "Uh, Adjunct, did you hear anything from Tribune Drusus?"

"Oh yes," he said, laughing tightly. "Why do you think I'm kissing your asses?"

We blinked at him and one another. "Uh, sir? What are my orders, sir?"

"What?" Leeson said, giving me a mocking look of surprise. "McGill is asking *me* for mission orders? I didn't think you bothered with lowly adjuncts."

"Come on, sir," I said. "We're under your command."

Leeson heaved a heavy sigh and eyed us both. His mood had shifted. He wasn't like Graves. Usually, Graves didn't display his emotions outwardly. Leeson was a lot more moody and excitable.

"We've been assigned to head into the streets and poke around with the Tau rebels. Dead or alive, we're to find out what makes them tick. Are you happy? Maybe you want to call some more brass and get us an even better assignment."

Carlos shook his head in disbelief, staring at me and waving his hands in front of himself as if warding off a bad smell. "Oh man, I should have known. McGill, whatever you

180

did, I don't even want to know. Keep your crazy off me. Can you reassign me to a new partner, Adjunct?"

"No. Shut up," Leeson said without even looking at him. "Well, McGill? Are you going to answer me? I asked you a question. Are you happy now?"

"I'll be happy if we can figure out why these people are rebelling," I said, getting a little steamed. "Rather than trying to kill a few million of them, I thought maybe someone could spend some time figuring out how to stop the riots. They shouldn't be acting like this, sir. There has to be a reason."

Adjunct Leeson chuckled and shook his head. "There's no stopping these people. They've had shit all their lives, and now they see us as weak. They mean to take whatever they can get their hands on. It's the have-nots tearing down the haves. The oldest story in the book."

I frowned at him, not quite following his reasoning. "Who's weak? There are only ten thousand of us in the legion, but we're doing our job pretty well."

He shook his head. "I mean the *Empire* is weak," he explained. "Out here on the frontier we're now the sole representatives of law and order. That isn't looking like such a sweet deal anymore, is it?"

I shrugged. "Better than getting our whole race permed," I said.

"They wouldn't have done that. The fleet was already gone."

I had my doubts, but I kept quiet. The Nairb ship had permed the squids in the Zeta Herculis system, and Earth didn't have a defensive space fleet that I knew of. Just one ship could have dropped those hell-burners over Earth instead of the squid planet. I don't know that we could have stopped them.

"You're a bright boy," Leeson told me. "Haven't you been expecting something like this? We've been given the title of 'Enforcers,' remember? Did that sound like some kind of promotion to you? Well, it wasn't. There are a dozen powder keg planets like this one in 921 that are just waiting to blow up. Peace isn't a natural state of affairs on any planet. Don't worry, McGill. As we travel around the stars 'enforcing' things, you'll learn the truth."

I didn't know quite how to respond to his bitter little speech, so I didn't say anything. Carlos looked like he wanted to talk but kept his mouth clamped shut for once.

Leeson walked away from us, counted heads, and engaged the unit-wide chat channel.

"All right people, this is it," he said, waving his arms for attention and cranking up his audio-pickup to an earsplitting level. "We're half-strength, but that's all the revives we're getting today. Walk out the front and load up on the trucks waiting outside. We're heading to the front lines—courtesy of McGill, here."

Carlos fell into step behind me, and we marched to the waiting ground transport. There were three trucks, and they barely held us and our equipment. Carlos and I got into the second one, and I had to hold my belcher unit hugged up against my gut tightly.

"This is crap," Carlos complained. "Ground transport? What the hell? We'll take forever to get across this choked-up city. There must be a turtle flying around out here in something that's better than this."

I looked up, but I didn't see the usual level of air traffic. When I'd first come to Tech World, there had been lights, buzzing vehicles, and throngs of people in every street. Now, there were more debris piles than people and more wrecks than working vehicles.

Ignoring Carlos, who went right on complaining anyway, I worked on my tapper. I messaged Natasha, and she answered right away.

We're looking for answers, I texted her.

I know, she sent back. *I'm in the third truck, and everyone hates me.*

Leeson pushed his way through the crowd and came up close to me, helmet to helmet.

"I'm taking you to the front," he said resentfully. "Anywhere special you want to go, your holiness?"

I felt awkward. As a specialist, I shouldn't really be calling the shots. Maybe this was why Natasha had been so hesitant about walking over the ranks and requesting this assignment.

182

"I know where we could start," I said after thinking it over for a second. "Let's go back to where those first six Tau came from. The ones packing crates of weapons."

"What?" squawked Carlos. "You're taking us back to the shit-river? I don't want to go for another swim, McGill."

"Why the sewers?" Leeson asked.

I shook my head. "Not there. Not exactly. Remember how they came down to where we were on an elevator of some kind? Well, there has to be a building above that location in the sewers. Which building is that? Who works there? I think we should find out."

Leeson stared at me for a second then nodded.

"Good call, McGill. We'll head there. But you'd better hope we find something important. I'm looking for a way to pull the plug on this, and I won't be happy until I do."

"I never doubted you, sir."

He gave me a dark look and waded back through the crowded troops to the driver. The truck lurched and swayed sickeningly. We all stumbled, but no one fell out as the vehicle swerved onto a new course.

I watched the rusting buildings flash by, noticing the streets were empty and silent except for the distant thud and boom of combat. At least the power was back on, and pseudo-sunlight was streaming down again from the fake sky above.

-23-

We rolled and swayed until we reached the coordinates where we'd met up with the Tau smugglers days ago. We were on the street level this time, however, not down in the sewers. It smelled better, and as I climbed out of the back of the second truck in line big drops of condensation splattered my helmet from the distant "sky."

"It's *raining*?" Carlos asked, aiming his face into the air. He was quickly splattered by another drop. "Ew. Doesn't feel quite right. It's warm and kind of...I don't know...thick."

I didn't turn my head up to catch a drop. "You sure that was a raindrop?" I asked him. "Sounds like bird poop."

"No, no. Not that bad. But I wouldn't drink it. There are substances in it besides water. Polymers, maybe. Or some kind of grease."

"Yum," I said, slapping him on the back and laughing. "Thanks for playing taste-tester."

"Yeah, great."

We pressed onward into a tall cubical building that sat at the coordinates we'd been beneath when we'd first gotten our assignment. The interior was nicer than the exterior, and my hopes soared when I saw a sprinkling of Tau civilians. They had normal attire for their kind, shimmering blues and oranges. That was the correct setting for the acquisition of goods and indicated they were nothing more than sedate shoppers.

A beltway of small shops surrounded a central torus which loomed high overhead. In the center were the premium shops—the places only the rich could afford to frequent.

The shoppers we passed along the way hurried to get out of our way without asking our business or offering any details about their own. Doing either would have been considered rude in their culture, so we kept quiet as well and pressed through the throng to the inner doors.

Past the small outer shops was a larger central plaza. We marched through the doors following Natasha whose GPS was capable of pinpointing our former location—and the exit point below where the gunrunners must have met us days ago.

Our tappers were all equipped with GPS systems naturally, but as we weren't on a planet our tappers operated differently. They were built to work when closer to the ground. Even though the orbital city we were located within was directly above a more or less fixed location on the planet and anchored by the umbilical, it wasn't perfectly still. Like a tall building in the city breezes, it swayed and swung. The interior was rolling around to provide gravity via centrifugal force and even local signal repeaters were often mobile in the city, changing locations to better serve the area.

In short, our tappers had a hard time pinpointing our location down to meters, but Natasha had the processing power in her pack to figure it out. It was times like these that having a tech along paid off.

"This is it—as best as I can determine," she said at last. She came to a halt and looked around. The confused expression on her face was mirrored on everyone else's.

"This is *what*?" demanded Leeson, pressing to the front of the group. He'd been hanging back letting us ferret out a possible ambush. "All I see is a fountain."

And that was indeed what we'd found. A simple fountain of puff-crete with a dribble of water still bubbling out of a pyramid-like central obelisk. There weren't any fish in the surrounding circular pool, and no plants, either.

"Should I thrown in a coin and make a wish?" asked Carlos loudly.

"Let's all have a look around," I suggested. "There has to be some kind of way down to the sewers from here. Our Tau clients did it—we all saw them."

Leeson frowned around the chamber we stood in doubtfully. "I don't think so. I think Natasha's lost."

The rest of the group searched everywhere while Leeson looked bored and annoyed. Natasha was running some kind of instrument that resembled a toothbrush over the walls. Carlos spent his time kicking things. He kicked the trash receptacles, a puff-crete bench, and even the fountain itself.

I looked at the fountain and decided to take a different approach. I walked right into it. Clanking sounds turned to splashing, and I was up to my knees after two steps.

"I remember water," I said aloud. "Dribbling and running down from above. When the Tau were slowly lowered into our midst, the platform they were on was wet."

Reaching the central pyramid looking thing with water dribbling out of the top, I fooled with it. Touching the top did the trick—the entire fountain began to drain away.

"Whoa cowboy!" Carlos called after me. He laughed heartily. "You broke it, you big idiot!"

I had to admit that was my first thought too. But after the water had vanished, the bottom of the fountain fell away slowly. I clanked to the edge and almost didn't make it. Within a few seconds the bottom of the fountain was gone, showing a dark hole.

The odors that rushed up to greet everyone from below left no doubt where the revealed shaft led.

"Could someone give me a hand?" I asked, hanging onto the rim of the fountain.

A few strong arms lifted me up and we all gazed down into the darkness together. After a minute or so, the elevator reversed and came back up. The fountain sealed itself and began to fill again with fresh water.

"That's really weird," Carlos said.

"Great," Leeson said, slapping his gauntlets together. "A dead end. We know the Tau came down that shaft, and so they must have come from this shopping mall. But that's all we know. How does that help?"

186

Natasha waved for attention. "There's another secret opening," she said, indicating a blank, curved wall of puff-crete. "I can sense an empty area of space behind this wall, but there's no way in as far as I can see. Help me find it."

In the end, it didn't take long. The builders were cunning, but they'd chosen a rather obvious trigger. The automated lighting systems did the trick. When you passed your hand over it, the lights turned on the way they were supposed to. But if you did it several times in succession, a door yawned open.

"Okay," Leeson said, stepping forward and peering into the dark interior. "I've got to admit, I'm impressed now. Carlos, Kivi, on point. Weapons hot. Get in there and scout this hole."

Grumbling, the two moved forward. Somehow, these two often were picked for "special" duties. They were both complainers and trouble-makers. In Legion Varus, the more irritating you were the more likely your commander was to risk your life.

Kivi was first. She stalked up the steps inside the opening. She crouched at the first bend, and Carlos rushed ahead of her.

I moved forward to follow them, but Leeson held me back. He didn't let Natasha go in, either.

"Wait," he said. "I need you two breathing—for now."

"That's mighty considerate of you, Adjunct," I told him, and I almost meant it.

Natasha released a buzzer, which was a tiny spy-bug the size and shape of a flying beetle. It followed Carlos and Kivi up the switchback stairway and passed them. The stairs led to a chamber above the fountain. It was large, dark, and full of junk.

Natasha linked the buzzer to our tappers so we could all watch its exploratory effort.

"What is that equipment on the far wall?" I asked her.

"I'm not sure," she said, "but I'm dying to check it out."

A bomb went off about twenty seconds later. It was triggered by Kivi as she stepped onto the floor of the chamber above us.

The charge wasn't a big one, but it was shaped and positioned well. Her armor was ruptured, and she lost a foot. Carlos came tumbling back down the stairs dragging her and breathing hard. Ignoring Leeson, I rushed up to greet him and grabbed Kivi's other arm.

The bio people came up from the rear of the group and knelt over Kivi who was white-faced and hissing in pain. They applied the internal choppers—every suit had blades that could sever a man's limbs if necessary—but I could tell it was too late. She'd lost too much blood all in a rush.

Her breath was shallow and came in gasps. She looked at Natasha angrily.

"Should have been *you* up there," she rasped. "This is your bullshit hunt. You and McGill should have eaten this bomb, not me!"

"I'm sorry, Kivi," Natasha said with feeling.

"Bitch," Kivi gasped. Then she stopped talking. She puffed about three more times, but her breaths came with greater pauses between them.

Then, she died.

Leeson sucked in a gulp of air and let it out slowly. "All right. Who's up? Haggerty, get up those stairs."

"Sir, let me," I said.

"You're my weaponeer," Leeson complained.

"Yeah, but Kivi was right. This was my idea. Besides, I have the thickest armor."

Leeson shook his head for a while but finally waved me forward. Before he could say anything else about it, Natasha followed me up the stairs.

We went carefully using Natasha's sniffers and buzzers every step of the way.

"Your bug should have detected that trap," I told Natasha.

"Don't you think I know that?" she asked tightly. "They've got good tech here. The trap was hidden from my sensors."

"Great."

We did things the old-fashioned way when we got to the top. I took out my belcher and used the butt of it to poke and prod every inch of ground ahead of me, wincing as I did so. The explosion had been very tight and focused. If I set it off with my long weapon, I'd probably survive inside my heavy suit.

Just when I'd begun to figure we were in the clear, I found the second bomb. It was to the left of the entrance, cunningly placed where a man might step if he were warily circling away from the steps.

My belcher was wrecked, and the tube jumped in my hands. It shot up right into my chest plate making a bright gouge in the metal.

"McGill!" roared Leeson in my headset. "Status?"

"My weapon is totaled, sir. But I'm fine."

Leeson told me to get my ass back down the stairs, but I assured him there couldn't be more traps—not without endangering the precious objects they were intended to protect.

"I think he's right, sir," Natasha said. "The bombs were placed in open areas of the floor. There isn't much room up here. It's like an attic full of junk. If another bomb goes off, it's sure to break the objects they stored so carefully."

While she argued things out with Leeson, I wandered off down a narrow passage. Natasha moved to follow me, but I cautioned her to stay back with an upraised hand.

"No sense in both of us finding the big one," I said. "Just use your buzzer to find things you want me to pick up for you."

She crouched at the entrance and watched me intently. "Walk softly."

"Ha, funny," I said, thumping along in about a ton of steel. I prodded the items on shelves around me and spoke aloud as I did so. "Okay, so I'm trying to reason this through. These gunrunners had a big stash of cool tech items up here and an elevator down into the sewers. Clearly, this wasn't their first smuggling job, and they didn't stick to guns. So, do you think all this junk is stolen?"

"I can't even identify most of it, but I'm dying to get my hands on something special. James, see that bulbous-looking thing that resembles a snail shell? Near your left hand."

I found it and picked it up. "Looks like a seashell to me."

Natasha's buzzer was my friendly companion hovering near my helmet. I felt a strong urge to smash it—but resisted.

"I'm sensing odd readings from it. Even though it seems inert, I'm getting emanations."

"Like, *explosive* readings?"

"No," she said. "It should be safe to handle. What else do you see?"

I wandered another dozen paces, and found two items of interest. One was a lightning-rod gun like the ones we'd face in the streets many times now. The other was a black box attached to a harness which was dotted with reflective buttons. I picked it up gently and showed it to the buzzer.

"What do you make of this?"

"It's one of their holographic clothing generators. Nothing that special about it. Every Tau on the station has one."

"Hmm," I said, stretching it out in front of me. "I'm noticing something odd."

"What?"

"See here? Isn't that a locking mechanism of some kind on this holo-harness? The buckle too—there's no release."

The buzzer slowly did a scan, moving up and down to give her a close-up view.

"You're right. Bring it to me."

Not wanting to jinx it now that I might have found something useful, I retraced my steps with care. I met Natasha at the entrance and smiled.

"You wanted to come here to find some cool new tech," I told her. "I'm sorry I couldn't score you an unexploded floor-bomb."

"That's okay. I'd just get into trouble blowing up someone who pissed me off."

Laughing, I followed her back down the stairs.

"You wouldn't do that," I said. "Kivi maybe, but not you. You don't hate anyone badly enough to blow them up."

She glanced back at me, and I caught a flash in her eyes. "You're probably right. Not even Anne deserves it."

My mouth opened then closed again. I suddenly got it. She was jealous. She'd been playing the smooth pro so well, I'd forgotten about how she'd warned Anne off and torpedoed my date with her. Weighing my odds carefully, I decided to drop it and pretend I had no idea what she was talking about. That was easy, as it was almost the truth.

We got back to the chamber with the fountain gently pissing out water in the middle of it. The scene would have

190

been tranquil if Kivi wasn't playing the part of a bloody corpse on the floor.

"What did you find, McGill?" Leeson demanded. "And no holding back on me. I didn't send you up there to loot the locals."

I rankled at this. "Loot the locals? These guys are clearly criminals of some kind, and they armed the rebels who are tearing up the city in case you didn't notice, sir."

Leeson shut up and looked over my finds. Natasha drooled over them, particularly the shell-looking thing.

"What is this junk?" Leeson asked.

"This harness is a clothing-generator," Natasha said. "A holographic projection device. This is what passes for clothing for a Tau citizen. The unusual thing about it is that it can be placed upon a person, and they can't remove it. The other item is more mysterious. I don't know what it is."

Leeson shook his head and gave the items back to her. "Junk," he said. "I can't believe we got Kivi killed for that."

"How about this, sir?" I asked, showing him the lighting-rod gun.

"That's more like it," he said. "We never seem to get our hands on one of these while it's still intact. We'll study it and see if we can turn it off remotely. Thanks, McGill."

I cleared my throat as he turned away with the weapon cradled in his arms.

"Sir?" I asked. "I lost my belcher. Could I carry that thing until we get back to headquarters? I've used one before."

He frowned, but gave it up at last. "All right. But if you zap me in the ass with that thing, I'll return the favor when I catch a revive. Do you read me, McGill?"

"Five-by-five, sir."

We left the building then and returned to our trucks. The rain had stopped outside, and Kivi's body had to be crammed onto the floor at our feet. It felt odd, stepping over her and holding onto the handrails.

We couldn't leave her behind, of course. No one even considered letting these aliens paw at her. Hell, they might even sell her for meat if we did. Her equipment, and even her flesh would be reused back at the base.

191

As we rode down the darkening streets, I kept glancing down at Kivi. Intellectually, I knew that she was coming back. I knew there would be the light of life shining from a new version of those dead, staring eyes.

But right now, she looked as dead as a doornail to me.

-24-

"I want to thank you for going in there and grabbing this stuff," Natasha told me huskily as she took the tech gadgets out of my gauntlets and hustled up a flight of stairs to a makeshift laboratory.

Following her, I smiled inwardly. There was nothing like risking your life to bring a girl a present she really wanted. Doing so never failed to transform me into a charming man.

Natasha unloaded her bundles and chased away a few techs who came over to investigate her loot. The lab was really one corner of the tech unit module which she had access to in addition to 3rd Unit's module. There were specialized pieces of equipment here, like computers, sensors, and even a small particle accelerator the legion had picked up for testing various systems. As a lot of alien weaponry used particulate radiation, it was used to test how a piece of equipment would hold up under fire.

"This is a sanctioned exploration ordered by Tribune Drusus," she told the last tech she tried to scoot out of her way. "If I need help, I'll ask for it—thanks." They finally moved off, grumbling and miffed.

While she worked over a device that looked to me like a microwave oven with exposed wires, I loomed close. She didn't object, so I stayed near looking over her shoulder.

"See this?" she asked in breathy excitement. "That's a power lead. I've seen these in diagrams, but this is the first full unit I've had in my hands. You'd be surprised how little the brass cares to respond to a simple request for devices required for intel."

The microwave-oven thing didn't have a door, not exactly. She lowered the holographic clothes-projector into the top of it and slid a lead sheet over it before turning it on and consulting readouts.

"One problem with these is that they're linked to Tau physiology. They don't change appearance due to direct commands. Instead, they read the body output of the owner and interpret his mood. That's how they select what kind of colors to display."

I frowned. "I'd always figured they had some kind of knob you could twiddle."

She shook her head emphatically. "That's what most people think. And to be fair, that's how we'd do it. But these projectors read the mood of the user and adapt to it dynamically."

I frowned as I considered the implications.

"But that means the Tau must be pissed off even before they switch to their rebel-look. It's not something they're doing purposefully."

"We don't know that yet," she said, tinkering. Finally, she exclaimed happily and drew the box back out of the unit. "I've got it."

"You've got what?"

"I've reprogrammed it to register human input. Put it on, will you?"

I twisted up my mouth in concern. "Uh, will it shock me or something?"

"Hopefully not. Come on, get out of that armor. It won't work unless it's against bare skin."

I grinned. "I'll wear it first if you promise to do the same."

It took a minute for her to figure out what I was talking about—then she punched me.

"Get down to your undies, and I'll think about it," she said. "I'm still not happy about Anne."

"Coincidentally, she's not happy about you, either."

I'd meant my comment to be funny, but the second it was out of my mouth I knew it had been the wrong thing to say.

Since I'd already said it, I tried to ignore her glare. I climbed out of my armor and pulled the harness over my head buckling it on. She cinched it up until I made uncomfortable noises. It had been a tight fit to begin with.

"Switching on," she said.

"No last requests?"

"I already said 'no.'"

She flipped a switch, and I lit up like a Christmas tree. It was an odd feeling standing there almost naked but visually being covered head to toe.

"Ha!" I said. "I look like some kind of leprechaun."

"Green and gold," she said, flipping through pages on her tapper. She frowned then she found the right reference.

"Adventurous and experimental," she read. "Is that how you're feeling?"

"Pretty much always."

"Yeah, well—maybe this thing does work."

"Let's experiment with it. Kiss me."

She frowned again. "No, that's not going to be our first experiment. Let's try this."

A jolt of electricity ran through me. It felt like something was vibrating in my teeth and biting my waist at the same time.

Snarling, I laid my hands on the box and jerked on the buckles. "It's shocking the shit out of me!"

"Settle down—I turned it off."

Sure enough, the buzzing ended. I examined my ghostly clothing. The colors had changed to shimmering white with blue details.

"Anger and pain," Natasha read aloud. "Injury displays of this type will bring rental ambulances to a victim quickly."

"How about *you* put this thing on now?" I suggested.

She looked at me and laughed. "Okay, I've had all the fun. One more experiment."

I have to admit I winced a little. Then she came close, stood on her tiptoes, and kissed me passionately. I blinked in surprise but finally engaged with her putting my arms around her waist and pulling her close.

The kiss went on for about fifteen seconds. When it was over and she was trying to pull away, I didn't want to let her go. A few techs wandered back into the lab and twittered at us.

"Success!" Natasha said, turning away and scrolling through her notes. "Orange and gray—arousal and surprise. Notice how the gray is fading? That's because you're not as surprised as you were at first."

"You're a cold one, girl," I grumbled.

She rolled her eyes at me and went back to her instruments. "We've made great progress here. You've been a first-class guinea pig, James."

I eyed her speculatively. "How about you and I spend our last waking hours together? We won't deploy again until morning."

"Nope, not going to happen. I've got a lot of fresh data, and I want to keep toying with it. Go chase someone else."

Taking off the harness, I got back into my armor and shambled away. I felt a little used. I figured that was how she wanted me to feel.

I headed down to blue deck to see if Kivi had come back out of the oven. I told myself I had no plans to hit on her—and I didn't. I'd come down here because seeing her die in my arms had bothered me, and I wanted to see life in her face again— that's all.

When I talked to the bio people, they shook their heads tiredly. "No, she's not up yet. Your unit is low-priority."

This annoyed me, and I went to talk to Anne. "What's this about starving my unit for revives?" I asked her.

She looked over her shoulder and shrugged. "You can't go around pissing everyone off without paying for it eventually."

"What? Graves still isn't revived. Who did he piss off? Normally, a unit commander is put back out in the field after two hours, tops."

Anne avoided my gaze. "You'll have to talk to the Imperator about that."

"Turov? She's really here then? Great. Micromanaging right from the start. If she was in this revival machine right now, I'd drain the bottom pan."

196

Anne gave me a reproachful look. "You shouldn't talk like that, James," she said in a low voice.

"She's leaning on us for petty reasons," I said. "I'm going to talk to her as you suggested."

Anne appeared to be alarmed. "Leave my name out of it—but I wish you luck."

I left her to the grim wet-work of running a revival machine and marched out to the lifts. Leaving my armor behind and taking nothing but a smart uniform and a sidearm, I entered the lift. I selected the highest floor on the list as my destination with a sweep of my finger. A moment later I was shooting up the stack of modules to the one perched at the very top.

Riding the lift up and up, I began to question the wisdom of this move. But the machinery worked too efficiently. Before I could come to my senses, I'd arrived at what we called the brass-level, the command module entrance.

Two bored-looking guards eyed me. I didn't know either one of them. They were both Veterans, but the surprising part to me was that one of them was from Legion Varus and the other was from Legion Germanica.

"State your business, Specialist," said the one on the right. He was from Varus.

"I'm here to see Imperator Turov, Veteran," I told him.

"Do you have orders?"

"I do. My unit has been charged with a special investigation mission by Tribune Drusus. If you could—"

"Drusus *and* Turov?" the Vet asked suspiciously. "You'd have to be a primus at least to get the attention of those two. I smell bullshit, Specialist."

"Vet, this visit would have been performed personally by Centurion Graves, but he's yet to come out of the oven. I have findings I'd like to report to my commander."

The two vets looked at one another uncomfortably. At last, the Legion Varus guy sighed. "Name?"

I gave him my name and unit designation. He disappeared into the airlock that protected the command module and didn't come back for a full minute. During that time, the Germanica Veteran and I eyed one another frostily.

"You ever heard of Adjunct Claver?" I asked.

He laughed. "Old Silver? Everyone's heard of him. He's as slippery as a walking oil slick. Let me guess, he sold you something and it broke. In that case, count those credits as dead and gone, kid."

The veteran's description of Claver matched what I'd heard from everyone who'd come into contact with Old Silver. Within his own legion, his reputation was nearly as bad as it was among Varus people.

The airlock opened again, and the Veteran from my legion waved me forward impatiently. I followed him, and after a lot of pumping of air and popping of rubber seals I found myself standing inside a well-appointed chamber. There were flowers—honest to God *flowers*—in little clusters perched along the walls. I could tell right off they'd been imported from Earth. They looked like orchids. I could only imagine what that extravagance had cost. There were two comfy-looking chairs as well, separated by a small round table of very real-looking hardwood. The deck even had a rug thrown over it which I bet had been woven by hand and transported here from some exotic locale. The rug was like a giant floor tapestry that depicted pallid figures working in a field.

"Wait here," the Veteran said, exiting through a pair of doors.

I overheard the Imperator's voice before it was cut off by the closing doors. Not sure how long I was going to have to wait, I sat in one of the chairs. I was immediately impressed by the way it hugged my butt. This was quality smart-furniture, both self-contouring and weight-balancing.

Staring at the alien rug, I figured out the people depicted in the fields weren't human. But what were they? I suspected they were Tau without their shimmering holographic clothing. I'd heard the poorest of them ran around naked, but I'd never seen such a thing. Only rich Tau lived on the megahab. The poor bastards woven into the rug must have been from the planet's surface.

"Admiring my rug?" asked a female voice.

Startled, I looked up. There was Imperator Turov in all her glory. She wore her twin gold suns like a goddess, and I could tell she loved the rank. The emblems shone on her collar as if there were hidden spotlights aimed right at them.

"Uh...yes sir," I said. I looked around, but the main door hadn't opened. Had she stepped out through a hidden doorway? I hadn't even heard her approach. It occurred to me that this nice waiting room could be something of a trap. If two people were placed here with these comfy chairs and interesting artwork, they may well strike up a conversation. Turov could then pick up information that might otherwise remain hidden.

"The rug is Tau," she said, looking down at it. She touched one of the pallid, toiling figures with the toe of her boot. "They don't live this way down there any longer, of course. The world is covered with structures and open ground is a rare thing. This tapestry is quite old."

I gazed at it and her foot. I wondered what the Tau might think of her using their artwork as a carpet. This piece seemed more appropriately placed on a wall somewhere—preferably in a museum. But I hadn't come here to argue about that.

"Imperator," I began. "I'm here because I've been charged with a mission by my Tribune, and I—"

"I know why you're here," she said, taking the seat beside me. "I set up an experiment, and the results are in. You took the bait and ran with it just as I thought you would."

I had no idea what the hell she was talking about, but I didn't like the sound of it. Turov was a natural-born schemer, and I state this as a member of the same species. The difference was her schemes tended to be overly complex and even more self-serving than mine were.

"May I ask, sir, why you would go to such trouble? You could have just ordered me to walk on up here."

"You're correct. But this way, my purposes have been better served."

Giving my head a confused shake, I pressed onward. "I'm here to report my findings to you. Tribune Drusus ordered my unit to find out why the Tau are going crazy. We've learned several things. Most important is the fact that the holographic projections they're wearing reflect emotions coming from the inside. By that I mean their emotions determine the nature of the clothing projected not the other way around."

"Very interesting," she said dryly. "Perhaps I'll write an academic paper on the subject when we return to Earth."

"Uh...well, there's more. The particular projection that all these alien rebels are currently displaying isn't in any of the guides. We think it means they're off the rails—outside their societal norms."

"Really?" she laughed. "What was your first clue?"

Her attitude was getting to me, but I persisted. "Look, sir, this is important. If we can understand what's making these aliens go crazy, if we can figure out how it spreads, we can stop the riots."

"Whoever said I wanted to do that?" she asked me.

We stared at each other for several long seconds. There was something going on here I didn't understand.

"You indicated you manipulated events to lure me here," I said. "Why?"

Turov pointed up toward the corners of the ceiling. "I have pinhead cameras recording up there. Let me ask you some questions. Did you or did you not break into a secret storeroom in a shopping area and remove certain valuable items?"

"Yes," I said. "I took one of the holographic display units I mentioned earlier. For research."

"And what about the other alien artifact currently on your person?"

I looked at her blankly for a moment then searched my pockets. I dragged out the shell-like thing I'd planned to give to Natasha at some point. "You mean this?"

"Hand that to me," she snapped.

With reluctance I did as she asked. She smiled and toyed with it. "Do you know what this is, James?"

"No, sir."

"I don't believe you. I do not understand this device, but I know it is alien, and not a registered trade product. Therefore, it's illegal to possess it on this planet."

My frown intensified. "How'd you even know I had that object?"

"There are such things as scanners and buzzers. Since my arrival, I've taken great care to watch your movements."

"That's very flattering, sir," I said.

"It's not meant to be. Your criminality has been proven time and again. You're a threat to everything we hold dear, whether you know it or not."

Stunned, I leaned back in my chair. "I'm sorry you feel that way Primus—I mean Imperator."

My misstatement had been an honest one. For years, I'd known her as my Primus. Her recent promotion hadn't sunken into my mind yet. But I could tell she'd taken my words as a personal, purposeful insult. Her easy demeanor, which up until now had appeared to be something similar to the attitude a cat might have toward captured prey it was playing with before devouring, changed into something much worse.

"You represent a rash of mistakes to me," she said in a harsh voice. "I should have made sure when we executed you the first time that you stayed dead. You're irreverent and dangerous to our entire species. Constantly interfering with the plans of others, you've served as an unwitting tool to anyone who bothers to push your so-obvious buttons."

Blinking in confusion, I was beginning to think she'd lost her mind. "Uh…if you say so, sir."

Turov waved the shell-like thing and kept talking. "The interference with the Galactics, the rule-bending, the vote-fixing, the continual disregard for authority—it all ends here."

She quickly drew her sidearm and aimed it at me. I was honestly taken by surprise. I knew Turov didn't like me much, but I didn't think she'd resort to murder in her office.

"Is this petty vengeance, sir?" I asked. "The cameras are rolling—you said so yourself."

"Vengeance? Far from it. Your confession has been recorded."

"Witnesses, sir. You need human witnesses to legally—"

Doors opened silently behind Turov. Two figures stepped out. I'd expected them to be the Veterans I'd met outside, but they weren't. Instead, my eyes widened as I recognized none other than Tribune Drusus, commander of Legion Varus. He looked troubled, but resigned.

The second man was even more surprising. It was none other than Adjunct Claver—Old Silver himself. His expression was easy to read. He was grinning at me—broadly.

"An execution?" I guessed, getting to my feet.

Turov stood smoothly as well, keeping her gun trained on my chest.

"Yes," she said. "Have the dignity to accept this legal verdict without a fuss, James."

I ran my eyes over the officers. There were three of them, and my heart sank to see it. An execution in the field required three officers to make the verdict stick. I recalled this from the first time Turov had attempted to end my existence.

"Looks like you're finally getting your way at last," I told her. "I'll take solace in the fact I'll bleed all over your nice new rug."

As I spoke, I was gratified to see they were all slightly nervous—especially Turov. I guess I had something of a reputation for violence under these circumstances.

The truth was I was pretty much out of ideas. I was in the mode of grasping at straws, and figured that saying anything I could to keep them talking could only increase my odds of finding that proverbial straw.

"I'll take his weapon, sir," Claver said, stepping around me in a broad circle. He darted in and grabbed my gun, and I put my hand reflexively onto his wrist.

"Freeze, Specialist!" Turov shouted.

I eased my hand away again, and Claver took my sidearm. He stepped back to my right side and aimed my own weapon at my head.

"By the authority invested in me by Hegemony and the Galactics," Turov began, "I hereby—"

Indicating Claver with a jerk of my thumb, I sneered. "Doesn't anyone feel like shooting this crazy smuggler instead? He's caused way more trouble than I have. As far as I can tell, he's the one behind the riots. He armed them using illegal credit coins to do it. He—"

"The accused will be silent!" Turov shouted. "Adjunct Claver's actions have been duly noted, be sure of that. He will be dealt with as Galactic Law requires. But this is *your* trial, Specialist McGill, not his. I hereby sentence you to execution for your crimes."

"I'm not guilty, and I'm filing a grievance with the Nairbs!" I shouted.

Turov shook her head, chuckling. "Such hubris. So noted, McGill. If the Nairbs take up your case, you might get a revive and a second execution out of the appeal process."

She took a tighter grip on her pistol, and I knew this was it. I locked eyes with her, but I could tell I wasn't going to intimidate her that way. She meant business. I wondered if I would have the good fortune to catch a revive this time around. My prospects didn't look good, I had to admit.

A pistol went off. I honestly thought I was hit for a second even though, as a man who's been shot dead many times, I should have known the difference.

The Imperator sank down to her knees and flopped onto the alien tapestry on the floor, sprawling limply. There was a perfectly round hole spouting blood in the middle of her forehead.

Tribune Drusus went for his gun, but it was too late. The pistol blazed again, three times. He went down with a gargling sound, flopping over Turov's corpse.

I looked over my shoulder. Old Silver stood there with my own pistol in his hands. The stink of burnt air and blood stung my nostrils.

"She shouldn't have said she was planning to prosecute me as well," he said. "That's when I knew she had to die."

Claver flashed me a grin.

-25-

Two of the highest ranking commanding officers in the system lay dead at my feet. I was in shock, but I watched Claver closely.

"You're in the shit now, McGill," Claver chuckled, keeping the gun trained on me. "Just you and me, two rats swimming in the sewer together."

"I haven't done anything wrong."

"Ha! You think that matters at this point? Give me that device."

It took me a moment to realize he was talking about the shell-like thing Turov had taken from me. I reached down and retrieved the item from Turov's hand. In her other hand was her pistol. She'd never even gotten off a shot.

Claver must have sensed my hesitation. Maybe he figured I was considering a grab for Turov's gun—and he was right. I felt the hot barrel of my own gun as he pressed it into my ear.

"Give me the key," he said, almost in a whisper.

"What do mean 'the key?' Why do you want this thing?"

Claver laughed. "You're even dumber than I thought. You don't even know what you have, do you, boy? Wow, I thought I'd seen luck before...well, let me clue you in. That shell-like thing is what they call a Galactic key. It opens things. Now, hand it over."

I handed the seashell-thing to him. He aimed his gun at me with clear intent to kill. I glared at him and lifted my chin, daring him to do it.

After thinking for a second or two he lifted the gun toward the ceiling and stepped back. "It's your lucky day, McGill. I'm going to leave you alive. You can stay here holding this big bag of crap for me. Talk hard and long when they bust in here. Maybe someone will believe you."

Holding the shell-like thing he'd called a "key" in one hand, he stepped quickly to a door and tapped the lock with the device. The door opened and he stepped through, disappearing as it shut behind him.

I looked after him in confusion. My mind was racing. Here I was with two cooling bodies at my feet and blood everywhere. The Veterans outside weren't going to like this. They'd probably shoot me down as an assassin and ask questions later. Probably that's why Claver had left me alive. He wanted me to slow down any pursuers.

My first instinct was to call for the guards, claim innocence, and show them where Claver had run. But I knew he was harder to catch than a shithouse rat and nearly as nuts. He'd slip away, and I'd be left to face execution all over again.

One of my natural traits is impulsiveness, and I've always been that way. As a kid, I spent all my money on something cool the day after Christmas. As an adult, when I got close to a woman I liked I made a play for her. And when I faced death, I'd always chosen to act rather than to stand around waiting for things to just happen.

In a rush, I scooped up Turov's gun which was still lying in her lax fingers and dashed after Claver through the closing doors.

Half-expecting to be blasted by him the second I entered, I crouched and swept the room while looking over the muzzle of Turov's gun.

The room was *nice*. The outer chamber had been only a taste-treat compared to this. A full bar stood to one side, and a holographic command table glowed in the center. All around were self-contouring chairs and the walls were lined with trophies.

I recognized some of the heads on the walls. Like Drusus' collection, they were all alien species and presumably sentient. First there was a crimson raptor head, proud-looking with skin

205

like an oiled snake. A mantis head was next to that, then a shaggy lump of hair that looked like the rump of a sheepdog, and finally the head of a Tau.

This last surprised me. How could anyone expect to do business with a member of a species if you stuffed their relative's skull with fiber and hung it on the wall?

Below this last trophy was something that caught my eye. There was a panel, and it slid closed as I watched.

"Damn," I said and ran for it. I caught the edge of the panel with my fingers, but it was thick and the motors whined steadily. I had to pull my hands out before I lost my fingertips. It clicked shut, and I was left panting and staring at a blank wall.

I rushed back to the central console. There were a lot of controls there. I tapped at them wildly and ignored most of the responses. The room's lights brightened then dimmed. A gentle sound like that of wind blowing came on and then the room immediately freshened. I realized the chamber had a fragrance-producing air conditioning system built it. Man, these officers had raided the piggy bank for Galactic credits—or had the Imperator taken "gifts" from the locals like Claver? It was hard to say.

A hammering noise began on the door behind me, and I knew what that meant. The Veterans had found the bodies and were demanding entrance into the council chambers.

They'd soon unlock that chamber door, and I had to be gone by then. My actions thus far were only serving to make me look guiltier than ever. They weren't going to make this a calm, smiling arrest. They'd be coming for me with guns drawn.

Why would there be a secret panel in the council room of the command center? I racked my brains for an answer. I could only think of one reason: an emergency exit.

At the command table, I searched for an icon that looked like an escape symbol. I finally found a picture of red flames and touched it.

An alarm sounded, and the door rolled open—but so did the one that led out into the waiting room. Not happy about my prospects of surviving in a firefight with two Veterans, I rushed to the yawning panel and threw myself into the darkness beyond.

I don't know what I'd expected to find back there, but a chute down into an abyss probably wasn't it. Tumbling and sliding, I dropped down a metal slide that never let me get turned around. Headfirst, I launched out of the bottom of the tube and splashed into a pool of dank, oily liquid.

Coughing and sputtering, I broke the surface. I'd lost the pistol on the way down and couldn't see it in the dark water around me.

Treading water, I looked around, gasping. I was in the lower tiers of the megahab. It didn't smell as a bad as the sewer had days before—but it wasn't fresh, either. I figured it was probably some kind of cooling agent.

The sloping walls above me were barely visible in the wan light coming from the top of the shaft I'd fallen down. I could see I was inside a larger tube about ten meters across. It was deep enough to require me to swim, and after a second I realized there was a gentle current. I let the water take me where it would.

After a few seconds of staring and paddling, I heard a clattering sound and a splash. A cold burst of light followed almost immediately.

Plasma grenade. The sights and sounds of such weapons were seared into my memory. I plunged away and stroked hard downstream but didn't completely escape the effects.

Apparently, the guards above had noticed my escape hatch and dropped a gift down the shaft after me. The effects were muffled in water, but still effective. Grabbing up anything it could, the grenade transformed bits of grit and even droplets of the water itself and shot them outward in every direction. My feet were pierced by needles.

I'd been hit by this kind of makeshift shrapnel effect before. The weapon usually wounded rather than killed at a distance, and this case was no exception. I knew that walking was going to hurt for the next few days, but the liquid I was immersed in had saved me from more serious injury. If I'd dived underwater, the concussion would likely have blown out my eardrums at the very least.

Paddling painfully and ignoring the echoing shouts behind me, I soon lost them. The pipe twisted, turned and finally split into three directions.

I cursed and looked around uncertain as to which path I should take. The only light I had now was the glimmer coming from my tapper's backlit screen. It wasn't much, but I could tell the tubes led right, left, and directly upward.

The upward branch had a ladder attached to the wall. I was tired of being down here so I took that direction. My right foot felt like someone had stabbed it about twenty times with a carpet needle all the way through, but it held me up.

Burning in pain, cursing and bleeding, I struggled up the shaft. If I'd known how long it was going to take to climb to the top, I'm pretty sure I would have taken another route. But there was no turning back, so I struggled onward.

When I came up at last to an open grate, I overheard a voice.

"Don't tell me that! There are no valid excuses, only valid actions. Get to my location immediately, or you're fired."

It was Claver talking into his tapper. I had no idea who he was talking to, and I didn't much care. I heaved myself up the final rung of the ladder, and my soaking head popped up over the rim of the open shaft.

Trying to move silently so he wouldn't hear me, I paused to catch my breath. I watched him with one staring eye.

He was alone. We were at the street level about a kilometer from legion headquarters. Claver was checking his tapper and scanning the skies intermittently. I figured he'd called for someone to pick him up and was anxiously awaiting rescue.

Crawling out of the shaft, I almost made it to him. I was about halfway out, looking like a drowned rat after a rainstorm, when he finally turned to see what was creeping and sloshing up behind him.

Sheer surprise saved me, I think. He still had my gun, but it was on his hip in a holster rather than in his hand. I lashed out with one long arm and snagged his ankle. He was as wet as I was, and he slipped when I yanked his foot out from under him.

I'm a big man even without my heavy weaponeer's armor to emphasize the fact. Claver was many things, but he wasn't terribly strong.

Using his body to climb like a ladder, we soon both had a hand on the gun in his holster. I tried to pin his hand so he couldn't draw it while he struggled to pull it loose.

"Son-of-a-bitch!" Claver hissed. "How'd you find me?"

"They say I have a gift, sir," I said, squeezing his wrist.

He must have realized he'd never get his gun out into line with my head, so he pulled the trigger blindly.

The gun flashed and a hot streak ripped down his leg touching my left hip. A strip of my skin three inches long furrowed up and began to bleed. My lips pulled back from my teeth in a grimace of pain.

After that, I slammed his head into the pavement until he stopped moving.

-26-

Many legionnaires in my shoes would have turned themselves in to their superiors. I honestly considered it for about fifteen seconds. The trouble was that my top commander had just done her damnedest to execute me. If she'd had her way, I'd be dead right now—permed.

There was no easy way back into my old world as far as I could see. If there was a route home to being an honorable legionnaire again, it must involve the unconscious officer at my feet, I was sure of that much. He knew more than he was telling anyone. He'd also performed the ultimate act of treason and shot his own commander. If I could get my execution order reversed, I'd be in the clear. But until I did, my own comrades were as likely to shoot me as they were to shoot him—and it was improbable they'd revive either of us to mull over the details.

In my long and storied history with legion Varus, I'd been a fugitive before. I knew the drill. I had to disconnect my tapper from the network so they couldn't pinpoint me.

This turned out to be a difficult task. Legionnaire tappers had been updated since we left Earth and they were harder to switch off than ever. They'd always been like symbiotic parasites, intelligent cancers, and now they were tracing devices we couldn't shut down easily. But I was determined to get the job done anyway.

First, I found something that resembled a rusty nail laying in the gutter. It wasn't a real nail, more of a twisted up spike that had been shorn off one of the buildings that towered around me. Trying not to think about it, I drove the spike point-first into my left forearm. The pain was intense, especially when it encountered stiff resistance and I kept pressing it in.

My skin gave way with relative ease, but my tapper was something like a polymer sheet about five mm thick between the skin and the fatty subcutaneous layer. To get through it, I had to spin the point of the nail like a drill until it punched through at last. The circuitry was resilient, but there were limits. The screen went dark.

Blood bubbled up around the spike and I shook it off like raindrops. I knelt and did the same thing to Claver's tapper. He didn't complain since he was out cold.

I dropped the nail after the grim job was done and grabbed the unconscious form of Claver by the scruff of his neck. Dragging him callously, I made slow painful progress toward the nearest shelter which was a derelict building about forty stories high.

Before I'd gone a hundred meters into the bottom floor, I found it to be a debris field left behind by looters and possibly rebels. I figured out this wasn't going to work. I couldn't drag him far enough or fast enough to hide from the troops that by now were probably scrambling to my last recorded position.

Heaving a sigh, I considered my options. There weren't many. I had a single pistol, an unconscious prisoner, and that was about it.

Or was it? I knelt again and began frisking Claver. Maybe the old bastard...then I found it. I'd almost forgotten in the excitement—the thing called a key. What did it do? How did it work?

I could only experiment. I'd seen evidence that Claver had passed through doors that shouldn't have opened for him. Maybe that's what this key did. Maybe it could open locked doors.

Looking around, I found a doorway in the damaged Tau building. I checked the door first and sure enough it was locked.

The door handle wasn't quite like one from Earth, but it was close enough. Frowning and feeling like an idiot, I tapped the end of the shell on the latch.

I tried the door again and snarled in disappointment. It was still locked.

Baring my teeth, I considered smashing the shell-looking thing on the floor. Claver had wanted this thing badly, Turov had seemed to think it was valuable, but it was a dud for me.

I tapped the door all over with the shell next, hitting the hinges then the door handle again. I tried one end then the other—no dice. Once it seemed to flicker, but that could have been a flash of light from the street.

Spinning around, I realized what it was I'd seen reflected. There was movement behind me. Something had passed behind me—between me and the light from the streets outside.

The source was easy to determine. Claver was no longer lying on the ground, rain-soaked and bloody. In fact, he was nowhere to be seen.

"I've got your damned shell. I'm going to figure out how to use it, or I'm going to break it. Either way, the Legion must almost be here to pick us up."

"You really *are* an idiot," Claver said.

I turned to my left and faced him. He'd gotten close, and I took a cautious step back. There was a chunk of puff-crete in his hand, but he wasn't looking his best. He was hunched and obviously in pain.

Lifting my pistol, I aimed at his chest, but he didn't even seem to notice.

"Why the hell...?" he began, investigating his injured arm in shock. "Did you shoot my tapper?"

"Nope," I said. "I drove a nail through it. Mine too."

Claver flopped back against a wall and groaned while shaking his head. "Your friend—what was his name? I asked him what was wrong with you when we were making that cash delivery to the bank, and he told me you were some kind of backwoods inbred. 'A card-carrying retard'—those were his very words."

"You must be talking about Carlos," I prompted.

212

"Oh yeah, that's the name. Irritating bastard. I thought he was even dumber than you are—but I was wrong. Can you tell me why in God's name you destroyed both our tappers?"

"The Legion techs will trace them. They'd have found us by now and picked us up."

Claver shook his head. "My tapper can't be traced, and I have all the codes. I could have turned your transponder off, too."

"Didn't know that. Maybe if you hadn't run off and tried to shoot me when I caught up we'd be buddies by now."

Claver laughed. "You've got me there. As intellectually challenged as you may be, McGill, you've got to have a certain amount of low animal cunning. You're clearly gifted with physical power and the instincts of a hunter. I can appreciate that."

I gestured with the pistol. "Time to shut up now," I told him, and I lifted the shell. "As far as I can tell, this is the only way we can get out of here. Tell me how to work it—how to make it open doors."

Claver reached out his hand, but I held the shell out of reach. "Tell me."

"It only works on trade items," he said. "Things approved by the Galactics for off-world exports like the modules—we bought them with credits."

I nodded thoughtfully. "Makes sense. I know the Nairbs have the power to turn off our toys. This thing is like that?"

"Yes, but it does more than just turn them off. It can operate them, bypass security, that sort of thing."

"So we have to find something produced off-world. If we do, we can control it, right?"

"Ding!" Claver said, laughing again. He made a gesture over his head, suggesting a light bulb had just lit up inside my dim brain.

"Any ideas, bright boy?" I asked.

He leered. "Why should I help you escape at all?"

"First, there's this gun in my hand," I said, hefting it meaningfully. "Second, there's the skimmer landing back there in the street behind us."

Claver's smile vanished. He followed my gesture and hissed with displeasure.

"They're fast," he said. "I figured you Varus types would take an hour to track down the last blip from our trackers."

"We retards are full of surprises," I told him.

"We don't have to do anything," Claver said, hunkering down in the darkest shadows. "Watch."

Confused, I crouched near him, but I was ready to shoot, run or otherwise react to whatever trick he had in mind for me. We watched the Legion people—a full unit with techs scanning the street for blood and trace evidence. How did Claver think they weren't going to find us? They would be sure to check the buildings. If we ran like flushed rabbits when they came inside, the chase would be on. We weren't in any shape to outrun these guys.

I considered running out on Claver hoping he'd be caught and maybe slow them down, but I didn't get the chance. Another skimmer landed and disgorged a unit on the far side of the building we were in—and then yet another did the same a block away. I could hear them shouting and setting up firing positions.

"They sound like they're expecting us to fight our way out," I said.

Claver snorted. "They aren't preparing to do battle with us, dummy. Look out to the south."

I did, and I understood the true situation immediately. There was a mob coming, a mob that shimmered with a violet hue.

"We're on the front?" I asked.

"Apparently. We have to hold here until the fireworks start."

We didn't have long to wait. The rioters rolled forward. They were strangely quiet up close. Usually when an angry mob approached a line of troops, they shouted and screamed threats. These people marched like a fast-moving army of the dead. They were silent, determined, and vast in number.

Our side fired first. I felt an urge to rush out, pick up a weapon, and join in—but I held my position crouching like the fugitive I was in the dark recesses of an abandoned building.

Scores of Tau went down in the first volley, but they quickly closed the distance, heedless of losses. Weaponeers fired belchers—they didn't seem to have any 88s—and the crowds reeled in shock but soldiered forward. Less than a minute after the first shot, they were in close and a vicious fight broke out on two sides of the building we were hiding in.

A few ran into our shelter and snarled, attacking us on sight. I had to pop shots at them until they fell. Fortunately, the stragglers didn't have anything on them more dangerous than a club.

"Time to go," Claver said. "Before either side wins."

"We can't just run out on our own people."

"Suit yourself!" Claver said, reaching out his hand for the shell. I slapped him away.

"Look," he said. "You can stay here and play hero, but remember those troops will get a revive after this and you won't. Give me the key so at least *I* can get out of here."

I struggled internally, but I had to admit Claver was right. If I went out there and helped, my own troops might be under orders to shoot me down on sight. I had to find a way to clear my name first.

"The key-thing is mine, and don't forget it," I told him at last. "But you can lead the way."

Grumbling, he trotted off into the ruins, and I followed. We crossed a street right behind struggling, screaming legionnaires, slipping past while they were fighting and dying. I felt like a rat, but I didn't know what else to do.

Claver found another grate in the street on the far side of the building, and he pointed at the locking sensor on top. I knew the device as similar mechanisms were all over Earth. They recognized maintenance people with the appropriate identification tags.

"Tap this," he said, looking over his shoulder at the struggle. "Hurry up, they're losing!"

The throng of rioters was like a stormy sea. The flashing lights and shouts were growing quieter as our people died and broke, running for cover. The last knots of resistance were encircled and dragged down. The desperate struggle was only a few hundred meters away. We didn't have long.

"The sewer again?" I asked. "Can't we hijack a skimmer or something?"

Claver pointed at the mob. "We have to disappear immediately."

With reluctance in my heart, I tapped the lock on the sewer grate with my odd little shell. It popped open, rotating and revealing a ladder that led down into the inky, stinking depths.

"You first," I said.

Claver went down. He was spry for a man of his years. I followed him, unhappily sealing the hatch above us with a clang.

When I got near the bottom of the ladder, I half-expected an ambush by Claver, so I let go and let myself drop. I splashed down into a river of filth.

"Damn, boy!" Claver complained. "You splashed me in the face!"

"Now what?" I asked.

Claver led the way. I got the feeling he'd been in these sewers before—maybe lots of times. He followed a twisting path, and soon the pipes became cleaner and the water relatively sweet.

"We're in the runoff pipes—the storm drains. They don't usually get this much use, but Gelt Station has seasons, you know. When the planet's axis tilts relative to the local star, the amount of radiation hitting the station varies. More warmth causes more steam to rise and more condensation to gather on the roof. Weird to think that a space station can be big enough to have its own weather patterns, isn't it?"

Claver liked to talk, but I didn't mind. He knew things. This place was still new to me, and right now I wanted to learn whatever I could from him.

"What's your angle, Claver?" I asked him as we slogged along our backs bent in the dark pipes.

"Angle? Same as anyone's. I want to live as long as possible and extract all the joy I can from life."

"Seems to me you're failing in that department right now," I pointed out.

He paused and glanced back at me. "You've got a point. I wouldn't call this my finest hour. But things are about to

216

change, you watch. If you survive another few days, you'll witness a realignment of the universe—in my favor."

I didn't see how that was possible, but I wanted to keep him talking. "You must know something," I said. "Otherwise, you're as shit-off stupid as they come. You've thrown away your career with Germanica and your life. The legions will never stop hunting for you—you have to know that."

Claver shook his head and pressed onward. "Not so. They have no idea what's coming. Even Hegemony is clueless. They'll be taken completely by surprise when the break-up hits."

"Break-up?" I asked, frowning. "What break-up?"

"I'm talking about the Empire, boy. Not even you can believe it's going to last much longer. Once the Core goes, the fringe can hang on for a little while, flying on inertia, but we can't deny reality forever."

I frowned. I'd known what he was talking about—but I hadn't *wanted* to know. Could this mean rat of a man be right? Was the Empire doomed? The thought of it was terrifying and exhilarating at the same time.

"What do you know?" I asked him. "What's happening in the Core Systems?"

"War," he said seriously. "Civil War. They couldn't hold it together. Silly, in a way. Why destroy something that's worked for countless years over petty squabbles? Who cares which one of their fantastically rich societies gets the next slice of frontier worlds, really? They already have more than we can dream of."

"War?" I asked, echoing the word. It caused me pain inside. I'd known, of course. We all had. The Core Systems were at war with one another. The organization I'd been part of all my life was crumbling somewhere in the center of a billion glowing stars. "What will happen out here on the frontier?"

"*That's* the right question," Claver said, turning around again. His eyes had lit up. "Destruction seeds construction, it always has. New small kingdoms will arise where once there was a single massive Empire. I figure a smart man, an opportunist who's well-connected—this could be his time."

I jabbed my finger at him. "What about serving Earth in this dark time? Your planet needs every smart man she has."

217

His brow furrowed and his lips twisted. "Earth? They'll bumble along trying to maintain the fiction. They'll serve an Empire that's already dead and gone. We're not in a single Empire anymore—can't you see that, fool? Frontier 921 is part of Mogwa faction territory, always has been. They own us. Now that they're independent from the Empire, we serve them. Unfortunately, among the Galactics they're small fry."

His words were sickening me for some reason. I didn't want to believe him. Since my first day of watching net vids and my first day of school, I'd been taught about the good side of the Empire and about the security and certainty it provided for all of us. To know that it was crumbling—that was hard to take.

"Mogwa?" I asked. "Chief Inspector Xlur is one of them, isn't he?"

"Yes, that's right."

"Seems wrong that our fate will be decided by creatures we rarely meet," I said.

"Exactly! Now you've got it! You've grasped just a tiny thread of reality, but I believe it will strengthen and take root even in your dim mind. You'll figure this out, McGill, I have faith in you as I do all common men. We're no longer going to be slaves to a distant Empire. We'll ditch the Mogwa because they'll weaken. They've already withdrawn their Battle Fleet, valuing their territory in the Core Systems a thousand times more than they value our pathetic star systems. But that's the answer, don't you see? We'll rebel. We'll have to. It's only a matter of time, and it's happening right now all over this station."

"Chaos and death," I said. "That's all I see."

"Revolutions are rarely orderly affairs. Who are you, McGill? A soldier, loyal to the Empire down to the last? I would have thought that of all the creatures crawling in the slime of this station you'd be the first to bite your master's hand."

"Oh, I'm a biter all right," I told him. "But don't you think we ought to keep moving?"

"No," he said, gesturing upward toward a closed valve. "We've already arrived."

I looked upward. "This is the way out?"

Claver rolled his eyes at me, saying nothing.

I hesitated. "Why'd you do all this?" I asked him. "The gunrunning, the goons waiting to rob us at the bank. When I didn't let you steal those credits, you left and alerted every thug on the street to waylay us, didn't you? All for a few Imperial coins?"

"Are you going to open that hatch?" Claver asked. "All you have to do is touch the key to it."

"Not until you answer my questions."

"There isn't much time."

"Then you'd better start talking, sir."

He glared at me for a moment, but then gave in. "Yeah, I did it. I set up the whole thing. And yes, I already told you that I believe this is a golden opportunity for a man like me to strike it rich."

"You're standing in a sewer, bleeding," I pointed out. "Your plans have failed."

"A momentary setback," he snapped. "I admit, things haven't gone smoothly. They would have if I'd had more time, but I was forced to act months ahead of schedule."

I almost asked why, but then I realized what he meant. "Legion Varus—we came too early. Germanica wasn't slated to go home for six months, but Turov accelerated the rotation, forcing you to move up your plans."

"Exactly," he said with bitterness. "Now you know one more reason why I shot that woman. Can we get moving now, or do you want a lecture on the birds and the bees?"

I reached up and tapped the valve with the key. It opened. After a rush of hot water ran down over us Claver began climbing out.

"Move fast," he said. "This water is from the cooling jackets. It's mildly radioactive."

His words propelled me, and I was soon standing by his side. I looked around realizing we were in a vast, open area.

There were ships standing nearby—shuttles and skimmers. Claver watched me closely.

"All of these were built off-world," he said. "All of them are therefore controllable by even the lowliest Galactic official. All they have to do is use a key like this one."

Looking down at the shell in my hand, I began to realize the kind of power it wielded. I could control anything built for trade within the Empire. It was like having the pass-codes to operate every spaceship ever built.

-27-

We picked out a quiet, unmanned pinnace that sat far out at the edge of the hangar. The ship was dark as there was no artificial light close enough to illuminate her sleek lines.

Walking up to her, I felt a thrill. I'd been aboard a dozen space-going craft, but I'd never even contemplated stealing one and flying it myself. It was the kind of crazy thing I could see myself doing, but I'd honestly never considered it before.

Claver must have thought he had a dupe on his hands because he didn't stop talking the whole way to the ship's hatch.

"See how the starlight shines out there? There's a barrier field keeping back the vacuum—or rather, it keeps a breathable atmosphere contained."

Starlight shone down on the small ship as we approached her, and I had to admit she was a beauty. Stream-lined so she could fly in space or within a planetary atmosphere, pinnaces served to ferry important people between starships and planets or stations. The big ships like *Minotaur* weren't designed to ever touch the surface of any world. They weren't built to withstand G-forces or endure atmospheric friction. For heavy transportation, they used lifters which were inelegant ships that could enter an atmosphere and leave it again—but couldn't fly to the stars as they had no form of warp drive.

Pinnaces were similar, but lighter, faster and smaller. They were like private jets, the kind of vehicle only the rich and powerful were familiar with.

I tapped the hatch with a thrill of excitement. I remembered that feeling—I'd felt it as a kid while stealing fruit from a government tree.

The hatch opened immediately, like magic. This key was growing on me. I realized it could open doors I'd never thought would budge for the likes of me.

"You like it, don't you?" Claver asked, studying me. "Your first taste of real power. We're not as far apart as you think we are, McGill. I know a kindred spirit when I see one. We're both rule-breakers—old school throw-backs. We don't belong in a universe full of laws, drones, and cameras."

"Or locks either, apparently," I said.

Chuckling, Claver ducked into the hatch and I followed him. I didn't trust the old bastard as far as I could spit—not even half that far.

There was no one aboard. We slid into the cockpit and strapped in. Claver took the controls.

"You're no tech, so I'm assuming you can't even pilot a buzzer."

"I could probably manage that," I said. "But you can fly us out of here. Just where, by the way, are we headed?"

I'd already calculated the answer before I'd asked the question. I was more than certain he'd say he had a hideout down on the surface of the planet. By all reports, it was a hive of villainy and confusion. Where else would a pair of fugitives run? We couldn't drift around in orbit—they'd find us eventually, and they might even shoot us down.

Grinning, Claver pointed through the pinnace's front dome. The blast shields had slid away so he could see where we were going as the small ship powered up and glided toward the bubble-like force field that held back the infinite vacuum of space.

I followed his gesture, and I realized he wasn't pointing at the planet which stretched out, vast and smoke-gray, below us. Startled, I looked at him to see if he was joking. His expression was intent, and I realized he was in earnest.

"We're headed for *Minotaur*?" I demanded incredulously. "How the hell do you expect to get aboard a warship?"

He waggled his finger at my shell. "You've got the key, kid."

The scale of this man's ambition was just beginning to dawn on me. "You're crazy."

"What was your plan?"

"I thought maybe you had a hideout down on the planet. Maybe some smuggler friends you'd paid off or a stash of credit coins that would buy those friends."

"Not a bad guess, actually," he said. "I had those things not long ago. But the riots have gone too far. They're spreading across the planet as well as the station. The brass knows. Did they tell you that part?"

I frowned at him and gazed downward. My commanders hadn't talked about the planet's surface much. They'd been grimly focused on hanging onto the station. The way it looked to me, we were on our last legs up here as well.

"You're saying we've lost this entire world?" I asked. "How could that happen? What the hell did you help unleash?"

For the first time since I'd met him, Claver looked a trifle sheepish. He shrugged. "A man plans and schemes. He does his best. But sometimes, things do get out of hand. A genie is easier to release from a bottle than it is to stuff back in—you know what I mean?"

"No, not exactly. Tell me—"

At this point, a light flashed on the console. A voice spoke.

"This is *Minotaur*. There are no flights scheduled to dock with this vessel. Identify yourself and your intentions."

I looked at Claver helplessly. "What do we say? They'll blow us out of space."

"Don't say a damn thing. Think like a Galactic. Be as arrogant as all hell."

He pointed to the console. "Touch the key to that contact."

I did as he said even as *Minotaur* repeated their order. The voice cut out half way through its little speech.

"Uh—boarding approved," said the voice, sounding surprised and confused. "Are any special accommodations required—sirs?"

"Don't say a damn thing," Claver told me. "Let them sweat. We'll roll in and set down like we own the place—which we do, in a way."

"What's our cover story?"

"We're escorting a Galactic. He's aboard this ship, and this is a snap inspection. Watch them scurry like mice. We'll snip their tails for fun."

Incredulous, I watched events unfold exactly as Claver suggested. After we glided in to land inside *Minotaur's* hangar, he marched off the pinnace with a regal air and scoffed at anyone he met along the way. They all bought his story.

"All personnel are to report to their modules and stay there," he ordered.

The officer who was on hand to greet him hesitated. It was none other than Germanica's Centurion Dubois himself. This was the man who'd handed over Claver to Graves and I for arrest days earlier. I figured Dubois had to recognize me, and I *knew* he recognized Claver. He had to be thinking he was in the middle of one of Claver's infamous schemes.

"This man was Graves' thug, wasn't he?" the Centurion asked, looking at me. "I get it, Claver. You bribed him. Well done. You bought off your own guard and escaped Graves with style. There's a troubling report, however, from Varus. They say—I know this is crazy—but they say you killed the Imperator…?"

"That's a damned lie!" Claver said with a level of conviction I could never have duplicated. "But it doesn't matter anyway. All such petty squabbles have been superseded. I'm escorting a VIP aboard this pinnace."

"Yes," Dubois said. "Dispatch told me about that. I have trouble believing one of their kind is aboard—"

"Centurion Dubois," Claver said. "What you believe is immaterial, but I'll try to help illuminate the situation in two steps."

"That would be appreciated."

"First, there's this," Claver produced a handful of golden coins. They gleamed and shone in the bright lights of the hangar deck.

I recognized them right away—they were illegal credit coins. Galactic credits from the Core Systems.

Dubois' eyes popped, and he stashed the coins as fast as Claver had produced them. Faster, maybe.

"Second, I'll make a statement," Claver said. "A wise man would execute my orders promptly because the only life in this system that truly matters is in jeopardy. Galactic Agents circulate on many worlds. This world happens to be blessed with the presence of an individual of superior rank. I've managed to become her protector and spokesman."

Dubois shook his head. "What a sly operator. Your rep is well-deserved. How do you want to do this?"

"As you may realize, the station will soon be lost to the rebels," Claver began.

Dubois and his subordinates exchanged glances. "You think it's that bad?"

"The Galactic I'm escorting believes this to be the case. What I think doesn't matter."

"Ah, so she wants to save her own skin? I get it. What do we do?"

Claver demanded that a color guard be placed encircling the empty pinnace then had Dubois lead us personally to *Minotaur's* bridge. He requested a vac suit, and one was provided.

I cleared my throat meaningfully. Claver looked at me as if I was an afterthought. He knew I was the only man present that could blow his scheme sky-high. Worse, I still had the Galactic key in my possession. He waved for the men to hand over a vac suit to me as well. We both got into them while the Skrull bridge crew stared with their hindmost eyes.

The crew was, naturally enough, made up of aliens. The Skrull looked like spindly spiders with hard shells and wizened monkey-faces. They were an odd race that hired out as starship crewmen to dozens of worlds. In that way, they were like us. Skilled labor was their trade good just as Earth's had long been mercenary troops.

Once we were suited up, Claver ordered Centurion Dubois to send every man they had to their modules on lock-down. Until that happened, the Galactic wouldn't step out of the ship.

Dubois whistled. "What cowards they can be. I suppose after a thousand years of extended life they get that way. I'll do it, but it's an insult."

"Seal the Skrull crewmen inside the bridge as well," Claver said.

"Oh come now, their species is as harmless as a bunch of housecats!"

The Skrull watched us as closely as they watched their instruments but said nothing. Skrulls rarely spoke to aliens like us. They kept to themselves and performed their hired duties as crewmen. I had no idea what they thought of us. Probably, they figured we were something akin to feral beasts. I got the feeling they were an orderly, peaceful race. In contrast we must have seemed like a species of rabid dogs.

"Your opinions may be correct," Claver said, turning to his broken tapper as if to operate it. "I'll report them to her excellency immediately. Centurion Dubois, I'll need your full name and a designation number to complete my report concerning your refusal—"

Centurion Dubois began to sputter. "Come on, Claver! I'm not *refusing*—look, just tell her it's already done." He turned on his heel and began barking orders. Claver looked on sternly, staying in character.

Soon, the ship emptied. Every Germanica legionnaire was safely tucked away inside a module like a hamster in a cage. Only the group that encircled the empty pinnace remained free and armed.

Claver took care of the color guard next. When he finally made his move, I have to admit the man was ruthless and swift. He walked to the console that managed the vacuum controls. Without a moment's hesitation, he took down the field that kept air inside the hangar deck.

The skrulls eyed him, and a few chittered a comment—but they didn't interfere. They were here to transport crazy humans to battle. What we did to our own kind was our own business.

Down below on the hangar deck, men were sucked out into space, screaming until there was no more air in their lungs. They twirled away into the blackness and soon stopped struggling.

I watched the consoles seeing their eyeballs swell and their blood boil in their veins as the zero pressure environment interacted with their chemistry.

"Was that necessary?" I demanded.

Claver threw up a cautionary hand. "Stop crying over them. They'll get revives eventually. If we die now—we're permed."

"Okay, but why did you pull the whole color-guard nonsense in the first place?"

"Two reasons. First, it makes the entire situation more believable and keeps everyone's focus on the pinnace with the Galactic inside. Secondly, they're bound to have dropped a few weapons onto the deck on their way out."

"Ah," I said, catching on. "That's why you made sure we put on vac suits."

"Right, let's go."

I followed the mad man I'd allied myself with back to the hangar deck, and we indeed found a few working snap-rifles. I stopped him as he went to pick one up.

"Hold it," I said, my pistol placed against his skull.

"I shouldn't have let you walk behind me," he complained.

"That's right."

I took a snap-rifle, and we left the rest where they lay. We headed back toward the modules.

"What's next?" I asked him. "You can't possibly hope to fly *Minotaur* back to Earth."

"Why not?"

"Because I don't think you can talk your way past everyone in Hegemony."

"I suppose you're right. We'll have to fix the situation here."

Frowning, I kept close to him. My newly acquired snap-rifle was loaded, and the safety was off. My finger hovered over the trigger. I thought this might well be the moment where Claver decided his "bodyguard" was more trouble than he was worth.

We moved to a central console outside the stacked modules. I knew these containers were empty for the most part. Only four of them were occupied according to the boards. Three of them held the three units of troops that Germanic had

227

stationed here. The rest were waiting to take the entire legion back home to Earth.

"Uh-oh, a breach. Tap this console with your key, please."

I hesitated. I saw the blinking yellow box on the board. One of the modules had turned off the lock down. Right now, it was probably disgorging troops.

Something had gone wrong. It could have been anything. Maybe the Primus had talked to the people back on the station. Or maybe they'd gotten a report from the men Claver had killed out in the hangar. Possibly the Imperator was back on the scene and had ordered them to arrest us.

It didn't matter what had gone wrong. Something had. The situation was unraveling.

"After all this shit, you're turning into a wimp on me at the last minute?" Claver demanded. "You want to get us permed, McGill?"

Hissing through my teeth with regret, I reached out and tapped the console.

Claver's hands flickered over the console. I didn't know how to operate it, but I knew it was an alien piece of hardware: a control system that the key in my hands had unlocked.

Three of the stacked modules went red. Then they vanished from the stack.

"What...?" I demanded. "What did you do?"

"I let them go. The troops have...disembarked."

I stared at him in disbelief. "You *jettisoned* them? They're your own men, Claver! Your fellow legionnaires! Those loyal men would die following your orders!"

Old Silver shrugged, looking a tiny bit troubled. "You're right," he said, "they would die for a Germanica officer— they're as good as dead right now, in fact, proving their loyalty once again. Look at it this way McGill, it was them or us. The only difference is they would have *permed* us. We couldn't have kept this charade going much longer."

He was right, but I didn't like it. "What are you going to do next?" I growled.

"Next comes the tricky part. I'm going to solve everyone's problems."

-28-

Claver led me to the fire control center. On *Minotaur*, the control systems were oddly laid out. The bureaucracy of the Empire demanded it.

Every species in the Empire had a monopoly on a given trade good. That trade good could be a service or a product. But within their local sphere of influence, such as Frontier 921, that particular product couldn't be duplicated. Some goods and services weren't available in an outlying province—and Frontier 921 was about as outlying as you could get. In that case, a world could trade for goods from outside their home province but at an increased cost.

The Empire's trade and legal systems worked, but they were often cumbersome. In effect, the system dictated that one planet could build ships—but they couldn't fly them. Another planet provided the piloting service. In our province, the pilots were all Skrull. That wasn't the end of it, however. The Skrull were our only locally licensed pilots on any interstellar vehicle, but they weren't warriors of any kind. Even if they'd wanted to be, it would have been illegal for them to participate in actual hostilities. So therefore, even though *Minotaur* had weaponry, the crew that piloted the ship wasn't allowed to operate that weaponry. To do so would have constituted a breach of Galactic Law. If the Nairbs, who were our local legal system experts—sort of like lawyers, accountants and bureaucrats all wrapped into one—determined the Law had been broken, they might penalize the Skrull homeworld. Penalties could be as

229

small as a fine in Galactic Credits all the way up to and including annihilation of the offending species.

Minotaur had a broadside bank of cannons on her armored flank, but the Skrull couldn't legally operate them. Fortunately, humanity was licensed to kill in other star systems, so we could fire the ship's guns. For the sake of convenience and to prevent any misunderstandings, the control system for these weapons wasn't located on the main bridge. It was built into a separate chamber on the decks below. It was to this region of the ship Claver was headed now.

As we got closer to the fire control center, my worries increased.

"Adjunct?" I asked. "You can't be considering firing on the station. If that's your plan, I'm not going along with it. There are millions of people—not to mention your legion and mine—living on that station."

"Relax," he said. "I'm not crazy. I'm not trying to kill everyone in the system just to keep myself alive. That's not the goal, here. Try to remember that you've personally killed more of their citizens than I have."

I winced, knowing his words to be true. My 88 had fried thousands by my best estimates. Those people weren't coming back, either. It had been in self-defense and under orders, but I still felt a little sorry for the Tau.

"What are you planning?" I asked as we reached the big dilating doors that led into the control center.

"Just a sec," he said, standing to one side of the door. "There were crewmen stationed here last time I checked it out."

He tried the lock, but it rejected his biometrics. His handprint and retinal scans apparently weren't in the security system.

I was standing on the opposite side of the big door. We were both hugging the walls like two cops about to burst into a den of thieves.

Claver made a grasping motion, indicating I should toss him the key, but I didn't budge. He made an exasperated sound and waved me to come over to his side. I did so reluctantly.

"Open this damn door, Specialist."

"No way. Not until I know what you intend."

"I told you, I'm going to solve everyone's problems."

I frowned at him. "And just how do you intend to do that?"

"The holographic projectors—the ones every Tau seems to be wearing today—are malfunctioning. The truth is, they've been tampered with. I happen to know where the source of the altered devices is. I'm going to destroy it from orbit."

"Ah-ha!" I said, pointing an accusatory finger at him. "I *knew* you had something to do with the riots. Let me guess, did you sell them defective parts? Or was this all on purpose?"

Claver shrugged. "What difference do those details make? Do you want this madness to stop or not?"

I considered his offer. If his plan worked, the rioters could be stopped. Lives could be saved. Apparently they were passing around devices that had a locked violent demeanor preprogrammed within them. But his story still didn't add up fully for me.

"I don't get it," I said. "I thought the holographic systems only projected the mood of the wearer. How can they change that mood even if they're malfunctioning?"

Claver rolled his eyes. "You really want to hear about this?"

"Yes, I do."

"Think about it," he said. "The Tau projectors have to read a mood to correctly interpret it. They actually take mental and emotional impressions. But what if those devices could *transmit* the mood, not just receive it?"

I stared at him, and my jaw sagged open. "You're somehow involved in this? You built something that influenced their moods? You *should* get permed!"

Claver became angry. "Oh, I get it. You're one of those people who hate entrepreneurs. There's no place for innovation in the Empire!"

"It's not that. You've done something illegal and obviously dangerous."

"I've broken no Galactic Law," he assured me. "The devices are for distribution in this star system only. A purely internal matter."

"So what? You've killed thousands—maybe millions."

231

"No one ever appreciates a great product until it's proven," he grumbled. "Imagine the profits we could have made here! What if these people were feeling down, but with the twiddle of a knob they could make themselves feel happy? Such a product would change lives. It was a goldmine. There are countless millions of Tau, and many of them are rich."

"The projectors don't work, Claver," I pointed out.

"They actually *do* work—a little too well. Okay, let's forget about that. Are you going to open this door and let me end these riots or not?"

I hesitated, then sighed. He had me. Even if he was the root of this disaster, I had to help him stop it.

I touched the key to the lock, and the door slid open. Inside, two surprised noncom techs turned to face us.

"Who are you?" they demanded. "Did you escape the modules?"

"Yes," Claver said, stepping into the control room like he owned the place. "I can't find any other officers aboard. I wanted to make sure this chamber was secure."

They frowned at him and even more so at me. "I'm sorry sir, but you aren't authorized to even be on this deck. We have to ask you to leave."

"Where's your commander?"

"Our Centurion was in the modules when they were released as far as we can tell. We've been communicating with the Skrull. We're maneuvering the ship to catch up with them before they make a disastrous reentry."

"Excellent," Claver said, "but could you tell me why that indicator is flashing red?"

Both the techs turned toward their boards in concern. Claver produced a sidearm from his tunic and shot them both in the back.

I made a choking sound that matched the surprised gasps of the techs as they sank to the deck plates.

"What the hell...?" I demanded, grabbing his wrist. I pushed the muzzle of my snap-rifle into his belly with my other hand.

"Hands off, Specialist," he said in a commanding tone.

"Where did you get that weapon?" I demanded.

He shrugged. "You've been inattentive."

"Drop it."

Reluctantly, he let it go. We'd fought hand-to-hand before, and I could tell he didn't want a repeat performance.

"They had to die," he told me. "Do you really think they were going to let me aim and fire their broadsides without authority?"

"No," I admitted. "But you didn't have to kill them."

Claver shook his head as if I were a grade-A fool. "Loose ends destroy the best of plans. Come now, we have to work fast. These men will be revived eventually."

I held onto him, and the barrel of my snap-rifle continued to prod his guts. "Why didn't you kill me with that hidden weapon?" I asked.

He brightened. "I don't know, but I think I've started to like you. A true rebel. You remind me of my youth."

I laughed. "Right. I think I've been lucky so far—and I always made sure you were walking in front of me."

Claver shrugged and pointed at the controls. "More Tau citizens are turning into rogue rioters every hour."

Heaving a sigh, I let go of him. My every instinct was to fill his gut with pellets—but I didn't do it. If he could stop these riots, he could save the station—and maybe the entire system.

We moved to the control console. It wasn't overly complex, but I didn't know how to operate it. I could tell after a few minutes that Claver was having trouble, too.

"We should have kept those techs alive at gunpoint," I said. "They would've been helpful now."

"I've got it," Claver announced a moment later. "Touch this security module while my hand is on it. Then touch the one over there."

"What's this one?" I said, walking over to the hump of tin-colored metal he'd indicated.

"That's the firing control. The other console lets me aim."

I bared my teeth thoughtfully. I was a weaponeer, but these boards were more like a starship's piloting control system. The controls weren't simple and manual. They were all touch-screen based, and there were numbers displayed everywhere.

Sucking in a breath and baring my teeth, I touched the modules he'd indicated. He made some adjustments, and the ship began making odd noises in response.

My eyes crawled toward the ceiling. Above me, huge automated cannons were traversing, locking onto the newly designated target. The sounds were ominous, like those you might hear in a vast ship below the waterline.

I found a switch on the panel that opened the blast-shields and flipped it. The scene outside was alarming. Two of the cannons were in view—or at least their long barrels were. They thrust out over my viewpoint aiming down toward the planet. They reminded me of factory smokestacks. The shadows they cast were stark in the blaze of the distant sun.

"Dammit McGill," Claver complained as he looked up and saw what I'd done. "We can't fire with the blast-shields open!"

I looked at him, and the barrel of my snap-rifle swiveled so that it aimed directly at him.

"I wanted to make sure you weren't aiming at the station," I said.

"And why would I do that, my paranoid friend?"

"Because you're scared of death," I said. "Everyone who has the power and motive to execute you is on that station."

"You think I'm that selfish?"

"Yes I do, Old Silver. No one lives as long as you have in a legion—not even Legion Germanica—without being very careful."

He stared at me, now and then casting involuntary glances down at the barrel of my weapon. "Is this some kind of threat? Some kind of final card-play you've been planning?"

"I wish it was," I admitted. "But I've been playing this game by ear from the start."

Claver chuckled and turned his attention back to the controls. "I'll close the doors, fire one salvo, and open them again. You'll get a front row seat as the strike lands."

At that moment, I wished I didn't have a gun on him. I wished he was doing this without my knowledge. The fact I was standing there with a rifle in my hand contemplating allowing this lunatic to operate a warship single-handedly was a testament to how desperate I'd become.

"No," I said finally. "Not yet."

"What?" Claver demanded. "They'll overrun the station soon. You saw that street-battle."

"They might win anyway."

"Not without new troops. The legions can keep churning out fresh fighters. If the supply is cut off on the other side, we might win. Every minute you delay is lowering the odds."

"The trouble is," I told him, "I don't trust you. Not at all."

"I can understand that," he admitted. "But you're going to have to in this case, son. We're losing this fight. You can see that, can't you? We've lost ground every day on the station. From the very first day."

"Because of your stupid get-rich-quick scheme!"

"A product, not a scheme. A failed product, that's all it was."

My eyes narrowed as I stared at Old Silver. I could tell he was tense but trying to look nonchalant. He wanted to fire the broadsides, and it was *probably* for the reasons he'd stated. But I couldn't be sure. The guy was too tricky for his own damned good.

"All right," I said finally, expelling a deep breath I'd been holding. "But if these doors go back up and the station is hit, I'm telling you as God is my witness I'm blowing you away. And no one, I mean *no one*, will ever revive your sorry ass."

"I accept your conditions. Hit the damned switch."

I reached out, and I did it. The massive doors rolled shut, and the starlight was cut out.

Seconds later, the broadsides fired. I could feel a concussion wave rolling through the ship. The shock staggered me and almost knocked me off my feet, despite the fact the control room had special dampening systems. Strangely, there wasn't as much of a roar as one might have expected. The barrels were out in space, and much of the energy had been released into the void. The only noise and vibration we felt was due to recoil alone.

I stabbed at the switch. The blast doors rolled back up more slowly than I'd remembered.

Craning my neck, I could see trails of gas following a shower of sixteen projectiles. They'd already hit the atmosphere, propelled by the rail-gun system at incredible speeds that were best measured as a percentage of the speed of light.

The shells were punching their way down through thin layers of gas toward the endless city that sprawled below. It was nighttime down there, and lights twinkled as witless Tau citizens went about their routines without any idea of what was falling from the skies above them. I felt sick, wondering how many would die as collateral damage to stop the cancer Claver had released.

The shells brightened as they dug deeper into the atmosphere. I knew that was their outer shielding, a combination of a projected field and burning ceramics. To prevent disintegration on entry into the atmosphere they were heavily protected.

"Right on target," whispered Claver.

"What have we done?" I asked.

"We've saved a world, that's what. The cancer had to be cut out. Don't blame yourself, boy."

I frowned at him. "Blame myself for what?"

He nodded toward the scene below. The salvo had reached ground and sixteen interlocked white flashes flared. Almost instantly, these impacts were obscured by the expanding clouds of dust and debris. Glowing shockwaves rippled in concentric circles destroying miles of buildings and people.

"I didn't know we were going to hit them that hard!" I said, horrified. "We should have fired just one round!"

"You have to be sure with cancer," Claver said. "Any surgeon will tell you that. When they cut on you, most of what they take out is good, solid flesh. You know that, don't you?"

I didn't look at him or acknowledge him. I was too shocked by what I was seeing below us. I'd never witnessed a Galactic warship's broadsides striking a target before. Hell, I don't know if any human being ever had. The destruction was terrific.

The white flashes had given way to a lurid red glow under the billowing clouds of dust. I saw something, something like a black thick strand coming out of that mess of destruction. As I

236

watched, the strand moved upward, curling and whipping like a snake in slow-motion.

"The umbilical," I said, almost unable to breathe. "That strike—you hit the base of the umbilical!"

That's when he nailed me. I have to admit, Claver's timing was masterful. I'd looked at him not ten seconds before, but I'd spent the subsequent moments staring down in horror as the magnitude of the disaster I'd allowed to occur sank in.

The umbilical had been cut, the station had been set adrift—and I'd let it happen.

My skull exploded in white pain and I sank to my knees.

I knew then I'd made the wrong choice in trusting Old Silver.

-29-

If there's one thing my mama can confirm—should you ever have the chance to ask her—it's that I have a hard head. There have been times in my life she's told me that I should have been stone dead by all rights. Like the day she backed into me with the family tram while I zoomed by on my aircycle, or the time I fell off the fourth story balcony of our apartment and landed headfirst on a pine tree.

On both those occasions, plus a few others, medical types had later tapped, prodded and scanned my cranium to see if I'd suffered a crack. It had never happened.

Unfortunately, I'm not immune to pain. My brain, that lump of gray and white matter that resides within my thick skull, was protesting with the most violent of headaches. But as was usually the case in these situations I stayed conscious throughout the trauma.

As I fell I spun around onto my back. Claver stood over me with a wrench in his hand. It was a wickedly heavy thing built for twisting open hatches and the like. The gleaming end of it had the look of worn steel. The tool had clearly been well-used by a dozen strong men in the past.

Stunned, I lay there with eyelids fluttering as Claver's arms rose up for a second strike. He had the wrench in both hands, and he was going for an all-out homerun this time. His face was screwed up with the effort of it, his teeth bared like those of a killer ape smashing down a rival. I didn't need much brainpower to figure out he was going to bash my face in with his next blow.

My numb fingers squeezed. The snap-rifle in my hand began to chatter. I didn't even know where it was aiming. I barely cared. Just hearing the sound of it was enough for me.

My aim wasn't too good. The recoil from the snap-rifle, although mild, helped out. The gun kicked upward in my weak grip. I barely managed to hang onto the trigger, to keep it hammering out tiny rounds.

The first shower of pellets splattered the ceiling of the fire control room. Dozens of orange sparks flashed up there before the recoil slewed my aim farther upward. I drew a line across Claver's belly, stitching him with at least ten projectiles. They ripped upward through his body and a few stabbed right up into his skull.

Snap-rifles fire a lot of rounds quickly, but each bullet is small, about the size of a BB. At the speed the rounds were traveling, it didn't much matter. They tore right through the man's unprotected body and blew bigger holes out of the back of him than they made going in.

Claver never landed his second blow with the wrench. Instead, he sprawled out on the deck beside me.

It took several long minutes of groaning before I could get to my feet. There was blood in my hair and more of it ran down my back. If a bio had been around to witness the situation, they might well have recommended I start over again with a fresh body—and the way I felt at that moment I might have agreed with them.

But in the end, I managed to get to my knees and then my feet. Swaying, I took the opportunity to look at Old Silver.

He was a mess. His eyes were bulging in shock, showing all the whites like boiled eggs with blue yolks. There was blood and fragments of bone everywhere.

"I hope you stay dead," I told the corpse. Then I looked down at the planet below us.

The destruction I saw down there made me want to puke. I scanned the billowing clouds of dust, rubbing my head absently as I did so. It looked as if a meteor strike had landed—a big one.

Gathering my wits and my strength, I staggered out of there and headed for the modules. Claver had only ejected the three occupied units. Maybe there were more people aboard.

I could have contacted the Skrull—but what good would that do? They were hired hands here. They had no stake in this battle. If everyone in this system killed one another, they barely cared as long as we didn't molest them. In fact, they *couldn't* interfere or even disobey an order from a legitimate source without incurring the wrath of the Galactics.

Unfortunately, I wasn't a legitimate authority. I was an enlisted man. I was mere cargo as far as they were concerned. That meant I couldn't control this ship, not even with the Galactic key. I could control individual subsystems, but I couldn't fly the ship itself. The Skrull would only listen to an officer.

Limping around the modules, I found no one. I cursed and raved. Claver had been thorough, and his Germanica victims had been obedient. They'd all sealed themselves in their modules and been promptly ejected into space.

I took stock of what resources I had left. There wasn't much. I could commandeer a pinnace and fly back to the station—but that didn't look like a very good idea right now. The station might well be doomed and spiraling in a decaying orbit. At the very least, it was full of deadly rioters and even more deadly legionnaires, all of whom had to know by now I was to be killed on sight.

The broadsides were still under my command, I realized. But who was I going to blast next? I barely understood their operation much less how to precisely target them. Besides which, I had no intention of causing even more misery and pain today.

I turned my thoughts back to the modules. I took a quick look at the non-standard units. There was the tech module, a combination of laboratory and workshop. The armory was reasonably well-equipped with thousands of weapons I had no need of.

Then I came across a bio module. Here, as on every ship, it was called "blue deck". I stepped inside and had a look around. Soon, I had a flesh-printer in my hands and was running the wand over the back of my head. Pain-relievers, fresh skin cells and a trickle of stimulants made me feel better almost immediately.

My eyes drifted to the locked sub-chamber. There was a revival unit in there, I thought. There had to be.

I shut off the flesh printer and walked to the door. It was locked, but a touch of the key solved that.

Inside the room, I regarded the dormant revival machine. I hated these things. To this day, I didn't see how bio people could handle working with them all day, every day. They were slimy, disturbing—and they smelled pretty bad, too.

Due to an unusually colorful past in Legion Varus, I was able to operate this strange piece of equipment. I needed more people. I couldn't run this ship alone. Accordingly, I tapped the priority list and stabbed the go-button. The machine would decide who I needed first, and I trusted its judgment. Whoever was on the top of that list was the best person I had available to me.

The revival machine gurgled and sloshed inside. The thought that it was working to grow a new human being was freaky, but I was beyond feeling such emotions.

My mind drifted to the Tau below. Sure, they were an overpopulated, irritating species, but I didn't think they deserved to be slaughtered wholesale for all that.

Before the revival machine finally signaled it was finished, I'd found the stimulant cabinet and partaken of the ampules inside. I had a faint smile on my face and my aching head was a distant worry.

The revival unit's maw fell open with a wet sound. I sighed and got out the spatula-like tool.

Feet. Bare feet. It was giving birth to a woman by the look of it. She was small and shapely. I got the tongue of the shovel-like tool under her butt and pulled, but she didn't come out right away. I had to tug at her feet, grunting with effort.

She finally flew out with a popping sound and a gush of thick fluids. Wrinkling my nose, I struggled to get her onto a gurney without accidentally injuring her.

I assumed she was an officer, possibly a Germanic bio. When she was functional, she'd have a lot of questions for me.

I didn't want to even contemplate what answers I was going to provide her.

The woman was attractive and seemed way too young to be an officer. I had her on the table, and she tried to speak, but couldn't. I checked the readings, squinting at them.

"Atrial fibrillation?" I read aloud. No one answered. No one was there to tell me what to do. "A bad grow right off? Crap."

I considered grabbing her and shoving her into the recycling slot. She was barely conscious, and she wouldn't remember this short lifetime. But I couldn't do it for some reason. There was something familiar about this woman. I couldn't put my finger on it, but it was there.

Unlimbering the defib equipment, I shocked her repeatedly. After the fourth try, she came awake, puking and gasping. I checked the reading.

"All clear," I said, smiling. I'd done it despite the fact my body was operating on stims and sporting a serious head-injury. I felt mildly proud.

The woman rolled away from me then, curling up in a ball on the gurney. Then I knew the truth.

She had a distinctive set of hips. Her shapely posterior that was more than a little familiar. I'd stared at her for years. Of course, I'd never seen her without clothing, but a man like me knows a shape that stands out.

"Turov?" I asked.

She coughed and weakly struggled to sit up.

"McGill?" she asked. "I'm going to kill you. Over and over again."

"Yes sir," I said. "You probably are. Did you know your hair is a different color?"

"I dye it, you idiot."

"Oh, right. But you're also a lot younger than the last time I saw you. Haven't you backed up your body over the last couple of—decades?"

She glared at me with red eyes. "I haven't died for a long time in the service of the legions."

I nodded slowly. "Yeah, but you look like you just joined up."

242

"Are you high or something?" she asked.

I thought about the pain meds. I'd partaken liberally. I smiled a small smile. "A little, yeah."

She produced a sound of disgust. "Give me some damned clothes."

Smart-cloth soon covered her body. Like a wrapper closing and cinching, flaps slid over her breasts and thighs. I was sorry to see them go.

"It's going to be hard on you as an Imperator," I pointed out. "You look like a kid. In fact, you've got to be younger than I am now."

Glaring, she twisted up her lips. "Why the hell did you revive *me*?"

My mouth opened, and I almost told her I'd hit the priority-revive button. But some part of my brain was still operating. I knew you never told a girl that chance had brought you together. She had to be special.

"I needed help," I said. "I couldn't think of any one better than you for the job."

She narrowed her eyes at me disbelievingly then they slid down to the snap-rifle I still had on a strap over my back. There was blood on my hands and my face and—everywhere. Her eyes widened and she bit her lip.

"You're sure this isn't some kind of odd fantasy of yours?" she asked. "Did you revive me for a chance to make me suffer? I hadn't thought you were that kind of a man."

She sounded confident enough, but there was a new note of worry in her voice. She'd finally picked up on the fact that there was no one around except me and her.

It was true, I realized as I thought about it. I could murder her right now. After stuffing her body into the recycling chute, no one would be the wiser.

"I'm not a fiend," I said. "I needed a ranking officer to help me handle this emergency. I immediately thought of you."

"What emergency?"

"Uh...what's the last thing you remember?"

"I was in the lobby outside my office—and that rodent Claver shot me."

"Right, well...a lot has happened since then. Can you walk?"

"Certainly," she said, batting away my helping hand.

She got down off the gurney and almost did a facer right there. I was ready for it, and managed to grab onto her before she hit the floor.

"Get off!" she shouted.

I ignored her complaints and stood her up like a doll. I supported her elbow as she took her first steps despite her protests. Soon, she had the hang of walking again.

"I can tell it's been a while since you went through a revive," I said.

"This isn't going to get you out of execution if that's your plan," she told me. "Anyone could have revived me."

"Well...maybe not," I said.

"What's that supposed to mean? Give me a headset, now!"

"Just give me a few minutes to show you the situation."

Turov eyed me. "So...I am your prisoner? You won't get any pleasure out of this, McGill. I assure you of that."

The revival machine began to churn and slosh, creating fresh life. I could only guess who it had chosen to be second off the line. That process would take a few minutes, so I thought now was as good a time as any to reeducate the Imperator.

I could tell she wasn't going to believe anything I said, so I figured the only thing I could do was *show* her the situation. I took her to the fire control room. As we walked down the echoing, empty passages, I wondered why the machine had chosen to revive Imperator Turov. I guessed that it had decided such a high-ranking individual deserved special treatment. Probably, back on the station the bio people had been too busy churning out combat troops and throwing them at the front lines to bother with wasting time on the brass. They hadn't had time to pamper the officers. They'd needed fighting troops to stop the enemy advance.

By the time I managed to get Turov to the fire control center, she'd figured out she was on *Minotaur* and that there was something massively wrong with that.

244

"Why is this place empty?" Turov demanded. "You can't have killed *everybody*."

I didn't bother to answer her question.

"Where's the staff?" she demanded. "Where are the Germanica Legionnaires? What have you done, you crazy fuck-up?"

I gestured toward Claver's body, which was still sprawled on the floor and staring. Right then, I decided to take a few liberties with the truth.

"Sir, this situation is admittedly hard to explain, but I've been chasing your murderer for about a day now. I caught up with him here and found him raving about stopping the attack on the station."

Explaining quickly, I told her about Claver's claims that the hologram projection equipment the Tau civvies wore had been tampered with—and that he'd done it himself. Then I explained Claver's belief that it was the root of all the riots, and the production of such systems had to be stopped.

By the time I got this far, she'd wandered to the viewports and gazed outside. Horror materialized on her pretty face.

"You've destroyed the planet!"

"Not at all, sir," I said. "First of all, Claver did it. Secondly, only one small section of the planet has been damaged. He only got off one shot with the broadsides before I killed him."

Turov looked at me, then Claver. "He struck you?"

"Yes. I've got new skin itching and growing right over the hair on my scalp."

"Incredible," she said. "This is an unbelievable diplomatic breach. I thank you for stopping him, and I now understand why you revived me."

"You do?"

"Yes, of course, McGill. I may look like I'm nineteen, but I'm not naïve."

Nineteen? I thought in shock. Could she really be that young? Looking at her, I knew that she could. Thirty-nine in the mind and nineteen in the flesh. That was going to be confusing for everyone.

"You're hoping to curry favor with me," she continued. "You killed my killer and apparently stopped this same madman from destroying an entire world. I'm now in the strange position of being in your debt. Perhaps millions of Tau are as well. But I'm not sure about one thing."

"Uh..." I said, not certain which of her leaps of logic she might be questioning.

"Why won't you let me communicate with the station?"

"Oh...that," I said. Then I showed her the station, which had drifted almost out of view and explained that the broadsides had disconnected the umbilical.

Her eyes widened to an improbable size.

"I don't believe it," she said. She looked at me, and her shock was infectious. "He's killed them *all*! That must be why I wasn't revived on the station. They might all be dead already if there is a hull breach. Think of it, Germanica and Varus wiped out together—all at once. Earth has never lost two of her legions in a single campaign, James. Not since Roman times."

"The Battle of Teutoburg Forest," I said thoughtfully.

"Yes. I'm surprised you know of it. I'm glad Varus still teaches her lore to enlisted men."

"Let's call the station and learn the truth," I suggested. I gave her a headset, and she pulled it over her head.

She hesitated before opening the channel. She looked at me for a moment, and I could see in her eyes that she felt lost. I knew that she didn't want to verify that we might well be the last living human beings in this star system—or that we soon would be.

Her face was so full of youth and relative innocence that I found myself feeling differently toward her. I knew it was just my mind responding to what it was seeing rather than what I knew her to be. But I couldn't help it.

Standing before me, Imperator Turov was a fine-looking, frightened young lady. I wanted to hold her in my arms and comfort her.

I told myself I must be completely nuts, but that's how I felt.

-30-

Could it be that a younger version of a person was really a *different* person? More like a relative to the original rather than a direct copy?

That was what I was wondering about as I watched Imperator Turov attempting to communicate with our legions on the station that drifted nearby. There was no response, and her eyes began to redden. What was that expression? I'd never seen it on Turov's face before. Was she actually going to break down and cry?

Partly, her emotional state had to be related to her recent revival. It had been a very long time for her, and that must be affecting her thinking. I'd been there many times myself. Nothing makes a man reconsider his place in the universe more than dying and being reconstructed from slime.

It was more than that in Turov's case. Her new body was too young for her to be the same person she'd been before she died. People underwent vast changes as they aged. Those changes weren't all due to the slow rerouting of our neural pathways—what we called memories and experiences. Our brains aged just like the rest of our bodies did. Our hair turned gray and our organs wore out. Our sleep-patterns changed—and the way our minds worked changed as well.

Younger people had more musculature. They were much better at healing and scored very differently on IQ tests. Their brains worked faster but were also more chaotic, impulsive and emotional.

I could see these realities playing out on Turov's face. She wasn't the same bitter woman she'd been the last time I'd seen her. She was battling with youth, uncertainty, and surging hormones.

For me, whenever I died I lost less than a year of time, so I was pretty much the same guy I'd been for years. I'd gotten a little wiser maybe, but not much. Perhaps that was why people kept telling me to "grow up", but I never seemed to do so.

Imperator Turov had frozen herself in time. Today she'd returned as she had been in her youth. Everyone thought they wanted to be young again, but it wasn't going to be easy for her, I could tell already.

Struggling to drop these thoughts and worry about our current situation, I waited for her to give up attempting to communicate with Legion Varus, then Germanica.

She put the headset aside and stared at it. "I think they're all dead," she said.

"What? The station has lost some atmosphere, but it can't be that bad yet."

She shook her head. "The rioters—they were attacking hard before I was killed. They might have overwhelmed the legion. They outnumber us thousands to one."

I stared out into space, shocked. How could they *all* be dead? The battle must have been going worse than I'd believed. I felt bad about having run out of there chasing Claver.

"Some of the civilian Tau are still alive at least," she continued. "I heard some traffic but nothing intelligible on our command channels. Possibly we've lost our communications stations, and there are still knots of troops fighting aboard the station."

We both gazed out the viewport.

"What are we going to do, sir?" I asked her.

"I'll contact the Skrull. We'll get *Minotaur* moving and circle the station to assess the situation. Stay on the open channels."

"Good idea, sir," I said. "But I request permission to return to the revival unit. It's processing another birth and I need to be on hand to keep the person alive."

"Oh—of course. Do that immediately. You're sure you're qualified?"

"Not at all, sir. But I've done it before and we haven't got anyone else."

I turned to go, but she called me back.

"James?"

"Imperator?"

She reached out a small, smooth hand and squeezed my arm. "Thank you. I'm going to formally drop the charges against you."

"Uh...that would be appreciated, sir."

I rushed out, knowing that the revival unit was probably spitting out its next victim any minute. I gave my head a little shake as I trotted down echoing passages.

The look in her eyes—she'd been thinking about *kissing* me. Call me a fool, call me crazy, but I'd seen that look before. Plenty of times.

Reaching the revival unit, I was in for a new shock. There had already been a birth, a male who'd fallen out of the maw and turned blue on the floor.

I scramble forward and tried to bring him back—but I'm not a bio. I'm a front-line fighter. I failed.

Cursing and breathing through clenched teeth, I carried the body over to the chute. I knew I should recycle him—but I couldn't do it. I didn't even know the man's name. Here he was, dead in my arms, and I'd caused it because I hadn't been here when he'd needed my help.

I felt pain in my chest, a pang of guilt. To steel my resolve, I reminded myself that millions had died today and the dying wasn't over with yet.

I let the body slump on the floor, pushing it out of the way with the toe of my boot. There was just too much crap going on today, and I refused to shove him into a wood-chipper. I'd heard the recycle machine buzz in the past, doing its grizzly work, and I just couldn't take that right now. I was on my last nerve.

"This shitty job isn't *my* shitty job," I said aloud to nobody. I walked to the console, determined. I flipped through the touchscreen interface, scrolling through to the bio specialists.

249

To hell with letting this machine decide who popped out next, I was going to make the choice.

So many dead! I could scarcely believe it. Never in all my years with Varus had there been such a disaster. I knew that there were two legions worth of names on that list, and that was too grim to contemplate. Just reviving them all would take weeks.

Flipping through the names of various bio people, I automatically selected Legion Varus troops over Germanica. Germanica had given me the gift of Old Silver, so screw them. I figured they could wait their turn in a very long line.

There was a name that stood out to me, one which made me pause immediately. Anne Grant.

I almost selected her name, but stopped. She would hate me for this. *Thousands* of revives? Work without rest for long days? Why do that to her? I decided to let the poor girl rest.

I kept scrolling with a new goal in mind. I found another name, one I hadn't had the pleasure of dealing with for a long time. Centurion Thompson.

Long ago, back on my first campaign on Steel World, she and I had not gotten along. She was a bio and an officer. She'd done everything she could to perm me, and I'd hung on to life despite her best efforts. Smiling, I tapped her name and confirmed.

Who deserved to be set up as a slave to this machine other than my least-favorite high-ranking bio? I couldn't think of a better candidate.

Then I charged the tanks and rushed back to find Galina—I mean, the Imperator. She was still standing on the deck of the fire control room. The view out of the front portals had changed. No longer were we staring down at the planet. Instead, we had turned and were gazing at the station.

The massive structure looked like it was operating normally, but then I saw escaping gas near the bottom. It looked like a jet of steam flowing out into space.

"What's that?" I asked her.

Turov stared without turning around. "At first, I thought the lower tip of the station was touching the atmosphere. But I don't think that's the case. She's venting. Overheating. Now that she's drifting, she's getting too much sun."

"I assume you got into contact with the Skrull?"

"Yes. They've been monitoring the station, but not 'interfering'—as they put it. How could a spacefaring crew watch such an ongoing disaster so callously, silently waiting for millions to die without bothering to lift a finger?"

I didn't answer her. We both knew the truth. The Empire made such insane levels of caution a necessity for all frontier civilizations. We had to work the harsh calculus every day. Breaking a Galactic Law, no matter how good the cause, could result in disaster for one's entire species. It was the kind of situation that revealed the worst side of the Empire.

"I'm reviving a bio now," I told her. "And I've got an idea. I recall Claver saying he'd ejected several modules—modules full of Germanica's troops."

She turned to me. "Yes. The Skrull reported that. What a psychopath. To commit his own people to such a death—"

"Right," I said. "But what if their orbits haven't decayed yet? Maybe we could retrieve a module or two and save them."

She brightened. "Excellent thinking, Specialist." She contacted the Skrull and soon the ship swung around in space. We were skimming over the clouds, and a tiny, box-like object grew in perspective.

Turov looked at her tapper, listening to the Skrull at the same time.

"Just one left," she said to me. "The others—it's too late. Their orbits decayed almost immediately."

Just one module. A hundred Germanica legionnaires. I hated to be choosy at a moment like this, but I really hoped the troops aboard this one didn't recognize me. They might tell Turov a different story about my interactions with Claver. I hadn't been one hundred percent forthcoming about my involvement with him.

"Gotta go check the revival machine again—if you don't mind, sir."

"Of course. Go."

Trotting down the passages again, I made it back to the machine before the maw opened this time. Curling my lips and

251

wrinkling my nose, I endured a shower of fluids when the maw finally sagged open.

The body of a woman slipped out. She was thin and had a pinched face, but she came out kicking. She coughed and panted. There was a wild look in her eye.

"You're all right," I told her, helping her onto a table.

"Get off me," she managed to say, slapping at my hands weakly.

I smiled. This one wouldn't need a defib or some other procedure I was even more hazy on. She was in fighting shape fresh out of the oven.

"Centurion Thompson," I said. "I hereby declare you a good grow."

She looked around, dazed but ornery. "What's this? James McGill? What the hell are you doing in a revival room? Where are the bio people?"

"I'm it, sir," I said. "Sorry to disappoint."

"I don't understand," she said, looking around with squinting eyes. "This isn't even the right module. Are we on the station?"

"No sir," I said. "We're on *Minotaur*. We've lost contact with the station. We fear the legion—they might have wiped."

Her gaze became distant, unfocussed. I knew that look. She was reliving the circumstances of her death.

"I remember now. I thought it must have been a dream. They flooded right in coming out of underground tunnels and air shafts. While we struggled with them, more surged down the streets and right into the front door. I watched the monitors. The troops killed thousands upon thousands—but they kept coming."

"It's best not to think about that too much right now," I said. "Just think of it as a dream."

Her eyes came back to me, but they looked through me. She was still seeing that other place, that other time.

"They crawled up the walls," she said. "They ripped men apart barehanded. I was working on blue deck—they came in and killed us all in the end. They had guns—our guns. They were stripping the dead as they came, and we couldn't stop them. McGill you have to—"

252

Her voice had been rising and her eyes widening. Her breathing had increased to a hyperventilating pant.

I slapped her lightly on the cheek. She recoiled and snarled at me. "I'll have you up on charges!"

"Sir," I said in a reasonable tone. "You're going into memory-shock."

"I wasn't," she snapped. "I'm fine. Get me some clothes."

I did as she asked, and she climbed down to the floor while toweling herself off. About one second later, she hit the deck with her butt. I grabbed her elbow, but wasn't fast enough.

"You let me fall," she said blearily.

Frowning, I flashed a meter into her eyes. The dilation was on the high side, but the machine didn't register any brain damage.

"How long has it been since you've been revived, Centurion Thompson?" I asked her.

"I—I don't know. Years."

Nodding, I helped her to her feet. "Try to pull it together, sir. You're just experiencing what every trooper feels when they come back to life after a bad death. It's all normal to us. Routine. Shake it off, sir."

She tried. I almost felt sorry for her despite our bad past. She put her elbows on the table and slumped over it.

"Can you get me some water?" she asked.

I did as she asked and tapped at the revival machine. Time was wasting. I selected a senior bio off the list. A noncom Centurion Thompson was sure to know and be able to work with. She was going to need an assistant.

"I'd forgotten," she said, sipping her water. "I'd forgotten how much this sucks. You asked me how long it had been since I'd been revived."

"Yes sir, I did."

She turned and looked at me. Her teeth were bared and her finger was up in an accusatory gesture.

"Have you forgotten? It was you. The last time I was revived, it was after *you* murdered me."

I felt a little jolt of embarrassment. That had been years ago. I hadn't figured—I did the best to hide my dismay and shrugged.

253

"Water under the bridge, sir. That unhappy misunderstanding is all in the past now."

"Maybe for you it is," she said. "Why the hell did you pick me to revive, anyway?"

"I wanted the best, sir. I'm a heavy infantryman who takes lives wholesale rather than saving them. I'm not qualified to operate this system, and I wanted someone I knew could do the job."

Thompson blinked at me. "But I haven't done grunt work in one of these chambers—never mind…" She seemed to get a grip on herself then. Often, people were like sobering drunks or sleepwalkers during their first moments in a new body. But she was pulling it together rapidly, I could see that.

She stood straight and squared her shoulders. She was dressed now, and except for the fact her hair was wet and sticky, she looked almost normal.

"All right, Specialist," she said. "I must thank you for your confidence in me. I won't let Legion Varus down. Now, if you don't mind getting the hell out of my chambers, I've got work to do."

I gave her a small tight smile and left. Out in the hallway, I allowed my expression to spread and widen. I grinned to myself, certain that there was one officer on this ship who was going to earn her pay today.

"McGill?" a voice squawked in my earpiece. It was Turov, but her voice was higher pitched than it had been days ago, so I almost didn't recognize her.

"Go ahead, Imperator."

"Get down to the hangar. Move everything you can out of the way. The module is coming in hot."

I frowned. "I don't understand, sir."

"I'm telling you this isn't going to be a picture-perfect docking, Specialist. The module is tumbling, and we don't have time to make this pretty. We're going to suck it into the hangar and hope someone survives."

"Sir, I can't recommend this course of action," I said as I began hustling down the tubes and passages toward the hangar. "Maybe we should just let the module burn up and revive the troops when we can."

"I'd do that," she said, "but we need every gun we can get." Her voice shifted again, sounding less professional. "There are ships coming toward us from the station now, McGill. They aren't responding to any kind of challenge, and the Skrull say they're on a collision course."

My mind raced almost as fast as my feet. I was regretting the fact I'd taken off my armor to work in the bio lab, and there was no time to put it back on now. Turov had to be nuts to try this.

"But sir...they could be boarding parties. We can't let them get onto *Minotaur*."

"They're coming directly toward us, and they're already in too close now to use the broadsides. We've got some PD armament, but I'll be damned if I can get it working up here. I don't have the codes—we don't have any defenses, James."

"Understood. What do you want me to do in the hangar?"

"I'm going to drop the field so the hangar will evacuate. You'll be dealing with hard vacuum. Do you copy that?"

"Yes sir," I said, turning the last corner and slapping down my visor. I was wearing a light vac suit and little else. Her timing was impeccable.

"Get in there," she said, "move aside every small ship you can—I'm hoping not to do too much damage when the module slams into the hangar."

"Right..." I said, my heart sinking. All I could think of was how insane her orders were. If the module slammed right into the deck, I'd be killed and anything it touched would be damaged.

"You have four minutes, McGill. Run faster."

"Plenty of time, sir. Don't worry about a thing."

-31-

The module we'd caught up with was indeed spinning, but it was doing so at a fairly sedate pace. I'd say it made a full revolution about once a minute.

My task in the hangar was, naturally, impossible. But I did it anyway. The element that allowed me to actually accomplish anything was the Galactic key. I'd placed that device in my pocket right after gunning down Claver, and I hadn't used it since.

This seemed like the perfect opportunity to work a little magic. I ran from ship to ship, entered the hatch after slapping the vessel with the Galactic key and set the vessels onto a scatter-pattern autopilot protocol.

I'm no pilot, but these pinnaces and tugs weren't designed to be flown by wizards. They were standard issue small spacecraft, manufactured within Frontier 921 and designed to be operated by any humanoid that wanted to buy one. Most of them accepted voice commands, and with the help of the Galactic key, I was able to get my orders across quickly.

After setting up two of the small ships and seeing them scoot out into space to save themselves, I headed for a third—but I knew I wasn't going to make it. There just wasn't any time left.

The module loomed outside the ship. It was coming closer at a relatively sedate pace, but an object that big could crush a man even if it was moving at a dead crawl.

I pulled a U-turn and headed back to the airlock. I almost made it, a testament to my long legs and my uncommonly strong instinct for personal survival.

What I didn't figure on was Turov's last-second action. She dropped the containment field and the air escaped into space. I was sucked backward, and I in my urgency to fling myself flat I slammed onto my face onto the deck plates so hard my visor cracked. I barely managed to hang onto the Galactic key and secure it, and I was very happy I'd remembered to pressurize my suit before coming in here.

The module sailed right over me, blocking out everything for several long seconds. It was like having a house thrown at you. I tried to keep low, but I was still sliding toward open space myself, being sucked out with the atmosphere.

Somehow, I escaped being crushed. The module didn't fare as well as I did, first plowing into a pinnace and causing a silent orange bloom of flame. The module came to a stop when it hit the back wall of the hangar, cracking open and spraying out gas everywhere like a cube-shaped teakettle.

"Turov!" I shouted. "The module is inside, but ruptured. Activate the field again!"

She did it, but it was too late for me. I was already past the barrier and twirling out into open space.

"What's your status, McGill?"

"The air release propelled me outside *Minotaur*," I reported. "Can you affect a rescue?"

"Negative. I'm going down to help the troops. I need some effectives before the invaders reach us."

"Roger that."

"You're on your own, McGill. Sorry about that."

"No problem, sir. I understand."

The connection closed. For several long seconds, I figured I'd bought myself yet another death. I was in a gentle spin, heading toward the huge disk of the planet below.

Some men might have opened up their suits right then and there figuring that would be better than cooking to death an hour later on reentry. But I didn't want to give up. For one thing, I might not get a revive for a long time—maybe never. If the small complement of troops aboard *Minotaur* couldn't repel the invaders, all would be lost.

The first thing I had to do was get my spin under control. I used my snap-rifle, which was still slung across my back. I set the rifle for single-shot mode and popped off rounds in the direction of my spin until I almost had myself steady.

Using every trick of my null-G training I could remember, I managed to get myself turned around and began popping off shots toward the planet to slow myself down.

Fortunately, the kick on a snap-rifle was pretty strong. I was able to use the released energy to counter my motion and reverse it. My biggest worry was that the Skrull would decide to—

"Dammit!" I shouted inside my helmet.

Minotaur's engines flared blue. They were trying to run, and by doing so, they were leaving me behind.

I relaxed, resigning myself to my fate, but silvery flickers of movement nearby caught my attention. Between my position and the surface of the planet, slipping up out of the darkness like ghosts, were the small shuttles and pinnaces of the enemy. They were all utility ships—tugs and the like. None of them were armed. But they were in pursuit, and they were infinitely more nimble than *Minotaur*.

Knowing this was my last and only hope, I turned my snap-rifle toward open space and began firing bursts. I propelled myself downward, closing with the line of tiny ships. They loomed large and—

Crunch. I'd collided with something. It was like being run over by a whale. I'd been struck and was clinging to what appeared to be a claw-arm, unsecured and swinging around in open space.

Dazed, I barely had the wits to hang on. My gauntlets closed and I clung to the ship, but I never could have kept my grip if I hadn't been half-wrapped around the claw-arm's boom.

When I could breathe again, I cursed and fumbled, finding safety straps and wires to attach to myself. It couldn't be too long before—

A sickening lurch began and didn't end. The universe spun, and I fought a powerful urge to vomit. When I had that under control, I saw the blinding glare of engines blooming. The tug that I'd hitched a ride upon had spun around and begun to decelerate.

That could only mean one thing. I braced myself as best I could, but nothing could completely deaden the next impact.

The tug plowed into *Minotaur* at low speed—but it was enough. The claw arm I was clinging to swung forward under power now, pinching the hull tightly. A half-dozen of its brothers did the same all around me.

We'd boarded *Minotaur*, and I was the first invader to touch the hull.

Crawling carefully, I wormed my way over the claw-arm and the ship. The nose of the tug had buried itself into a soft spot in the bigger ship's hull. *Minotaur* was only armored on its prow, around the broadsides. The tug had been rammed into its stern.

Inside the ship, I was sure that unfriendly invaders were disgorging onto the decks. This made me angry for some reason. I was getting pretty tired of all these crazy Tau, and now that they'd seen fit to leave their station behind and carry their warlike behavior onto what I considered my turf, well, let's just say that my patience had run out.

Instead of crawling onto *Minotaur's* hull, I scuttled out toward the tug's engines. The tug was no warship. It had no armor, no defenses—I wasn't even sure if the crew could see me with external cameras or if they would care much if they could.

But they ought to have cared. I tapped the rearmost hatch with the Galactic key, forcing it to open. Both ends of the airlock now yawned open breaking every safety code in the book.

Gas rushed out, and I was nearly blown back out into open space. I'd been expecting this and managed to hang on.

Within three short seconds, the ship depressurized. Bodies spun past me and shot out into space as if fired from a hose. They spun and squirmed and died. It was all over quickly.

Crawling into the aft airlock, I prodded the bodies I found inside. Two of them had suits on which were probably stolen from the original crewmen. They were alive, but confused.

Before they could gather the presence of mind to take a gun off one of their asphyxiated comrades, they died in a hail of snap-rifle shots.

My magazine finally rattled dry after the second man stopped moving. I dropped it and crawled around until I found one of those lightning-rod guns they were so fond of. I checked the gauges on the side. As far as I could tell, it had a full charge.

Smiling grimly, I forced my way over a dozen stiffening corpses and into the airless passageway beyond the nose of the tug.

I was back on *Minotaur*, armed, and ready for more.

-32-

Minotaur had never been constructed to repel invaders from small ships. That sort of action was probably unthinkable to the designers of any Imperial warship. The Empire had no peers, after all. There was no external enemy, thus no threat to guard against. Warships were designed to deliver troops, threaten helpless planetary populations, or possibly participate in a major battle as part of a massive armada with another Core System rival.

This lack of defenses had always puzzled me, but I thought I understood it now. The designers from the Core Systems never viewed populations such as those in Frontier 921 as any kind of credible threat. They were worried about one another. Therefore, their ships were built to line up in vast formations, broadsides all pointing at an equally impressive host of enemy ships from a rival space fleet.

From the beginning, as far as I could tell, the alliance between the Core Systems had been a tenuous one. They'd never possessed anything like brotherly love for one another. They'd cooperated because it made them rich.

Why was it all falling apart? I'm not sure any human knew the truth. Maybe a man who lived on the edge and worked with aliens every day—a man like Claver—he might know more than most. It was almost a pity that I'd never get a chance to ask him about it. Almost.

My first mission once aboard *Minotaur* was to get to the hangar deck. Monitoring tactical traffic on my tapper, I knew we had operating legionnaires there and they were in a tight battle. I didn't contact them, not wanting to pinpoint myself to the enemy with an active signal. I was alone and could easily be taken out by a roving band of invaders. There was no guarantee I'd get the drop on them a second time.

I only fired my newly acquired weapon twice on the way to the hangar deck. The first time was to burn down a Tau sentry in a passageway. I almost felt bad as his head burned away. I could only imagine the effort he'd undertaken to get this far— all the way out into space and breaching the hull of a huge Imperial warship—only to get clocked by me from behind by one of the rebel side's own weapons.

The second time I used it was to blow open the hatch the sentry had been guarding. I'd deduced that now wasn't the time for subtleties. This ship could be won or lost in the span of the next few minutes, and if I was going to influence that outcome, I had to get back into the game immediately.

The hatch went down with a clang, which was significant. If I'd heard nothing, the hangar would have still been depressurized. But it was full of gas—and troops.

A pitched battle was going on when I stepped into the smoking opening. One group consisted of Germanica legionnaires. They were crawling out of cracks in their module which was resting upside-down against the back bulkhead of the hangar. Under the module was a crushed pinnace.

Two enemy tugs had penetrated the field and disgorged troops. Shimmering with a lavender haze, they were better-armed than most of the mobs I'd faced. They also outnumbered the human troops by at least two to one.

Outgunned and pinned down by enemy fire, the Germanica troops weren't giving up. They crawled out of their cracked-open module on their bellies releasing sprays of suppressing fire and seeking cover. They were better-trained and disciplined, but many of them were injured when they entered the fight. They'd suffered broken ribs and the like, and they snarled in pain as they wormed their way out of their module.

From my position, I had only one advantage that I could identify—I was behind the enemy lines. They were arranged in a half-circle, peppering the emerging legionnaires with fire, and I was at one end of that crescent. All I could see was the backs of Tau rebels, working their weapons to deadly effect. Some of them were armed as I was, but most weren't. They had snap-rifles and laser carbines—weapons doubtlessly stolen from our own troops.

Another man might have hesitated, but it just wasn't in me. There's something about watching humans dying to aliens that flips my switch. I went prone to present the smallest possible target and hosed them with my lightning-gun.

A dozen or so went down, hit in the back with a withering streak of energy. I had no idea how to use my new-found gun, so I went wild with it. I slashed them with a continuous beam until the survivors turned and saw me.

They went mad. Howling, they charged toward me firing as they came. Projectiles spanged and sparked everywhere as simultaneously my weapon gave out. I'd probably fried it by unleashing such a long, continuous beam.

I ran in a crouch and retreated into the passage behind me. About three seconds later, they reached the opening and fired a hail of tiny bullets from chattering snap-rifles after me.

Fortunately, I was around the first bend by that time. Unfortunately, so many bullets chased me that some ricocheted and caught up. Three splinters of metal pierced my light vac suit and stung, punching tiny holes in my flesh. I wasn't sure if they were actual rounds or just shrapnel from the walls themselves, but it hardly mattered. My right leg wasn't in great shape anymore, and blood was running down from my kidneys to my boots.

I turned at bay, and shook my lighting rod. I ran my eyes over it, but didn't see a heat gauge or a power meter—at least not one that I could read. In truth, I didn't know what was wrong with it.

"Damn," I said. Realizing I could never outrun them, I scuttled back the way I'd come. I drew my knife and decided to try to take the first one that rounded the corner in the passage. With luck—extreme luck—I might be able to grab up his weapon and be back in the fight.

My plan, vague and desperate as it was, didn't work out at all. I was too slow on my feet. The enemy rounded the corner

263

before I could reach knife-range, and there were two of them rather than one.

Reflexively, I squeezed the trigger on the lighting gun. To my surprise it emitted a brief blaze of energy. Apparently, there'd been one last gasp of juice in the thing after all.

The two enemies were seared and fell before they could return fire with their snap-rifles. I hobbled closer—and listened.

Silence reigned.

Frowning and distrustful, I dropped the lightning-gun and picked up a snap-rifle. I felt more comfortable with a weapon I knew how to operate.

When I finally summoned up the balls to look around the corner, I came face-to-face with another man armed just as I was.

We almost blasted each other. It was close. But after a brief muscle spasm on each side, we eased off our triggers and grinned.

"Germanica?" I asked the recruit that faced me.

"Yeah. Varus?"

"That's right. What's going on back in the hangar?"

"We've cleaned them out. They got hit from behind somehow, and we were able to get out of that wreck and take up good firing positions. We swept them pretty fast. They're rank amateurs."

I nodded, noticing the kid was full of himself. That's how most Germanica people talked. They were all tough as nails and twice as sharp.

"There are more invaders on this ship," I told him. "I need to talk to your commander—and we need to find the Imperator."

"The Imperator?" the kid asked, frowning. "You're telling me she's aboard this ship?"

"I revived her myself," I said and the other guy's frown told me he wasn't sure if he believed me or not.

"Whatever," he said. "This way, Varus."

I followed him, dragging my leg. He passed back a nu-skin patch which I gratefully applied. That stopped the bleeding at least and relieved a little of the pain.

264

I met up with a Germanica Centurion in the mess that had been the hangar deck.

"This is unprecedented," she kept saying. "How many did we lose?"

"Sixty-one, sir," a veteran told her. "Most from the initial impact. Half the rest are wounded."

"Are we still out of communication with dispatch? How about headquarters direct?"

"Nothing, sir."

"Unacceptable," said the Centurion. She was at least in the thick of it. She helped drag wounded back into the module where they'd set up a medical triage unit even as she complained about how unbelievable her predicament was.

For my own part, I was relieved to see her face. I didn't know her. There was no way she could rat me out to the Imperator, or anyone else, for having colluded with Claver.

"Sir?" I asked.

The Centurion eyed me like dead meat. "Varus? What do you want here?"

"I'm the one who engineered your retrieval, sir."

"Really?" she asked, turning around and putting her hands on her hips.

She was a tall one with narrow hips and even narrower eyes. She was older than most centurions were in Varus, but that didn't mean she was a softie. I got the feeling she'd seen her share of combat rather than playing it safe.

"I'm Centurion Leeza," she said. She had one of those foreign accents that sounded faintly British. "By Hegemony's rules of conduct I'm declaring you a battlefield asset, and I'm commandeering you as an asset. Do you have a problem with that, Specialist?"

"No sir," I said. "Not as long as my own officers aren't around."

"Excellent. Name?"

"Specialist James McGill, sir."

"McGill... Where have I heard that name before?"

I shrugged. "Not sure. Maybe the Imperator mentioned me."

My reference to the Imperator created the instant effect I'd hoped for. She forgot all about asking me to tell my story.

"You've seen the Imperator? She's alive?"

"Yes sir, and still in command of this ship as far as I know. I last saw her on the fire control deck."

Leeza frowned. "Why hasn't she contacted me yet? There's nothing on my tapper—nothing on local tactical chat, either."

My heart sank. Turov had never stayed quiet for long. If she was silent, she was most likely dead. For some strange reason, I didn't like that idea.

"I suggest we go check on her, sir," I said.

Leeza looked around and spied the recruit standing next to me. "Take Chisholm, here. Report back to me when you have news of her status."

"Roger that."

We left in a hurry. I was still limping, but it wasn't as bad now as it had been. I took a few seconds to raid the medical kits of the two surviving Germanica bio people who gave me what I needed to keep moving.

We passed up two firefights but got caught up in a third one as we approached the tactical control room. This was because the combat was going on right outside the door of the facility itself.

A freakish-looking combat suit stalked the hallways. It was so big I thought it was a drone at first, but then I saw real eyes inside that slitted visor.

Servos whined as the suit turned at the waist and claw-like grippers pinched closed, grabbing a Tau by the waist. The alien struggled and shot his weapon bravely into the monster's face, but the rounds only splattered, turning into orange sparks on the heavy titanium armor.

The pinchers closed, snipping the Tau in half. Hanging together by a thread of spine, the alien slipped down in a messy heap onto the floor when the pinchers opened again. Around the metal suit's splayed feet were the crumpled forms of several other Tau, all similarly dispatched.

The monster turned, sighting us next. It took a clanking step forward.

The recruit I'd come with lost his nerve. He backed away, lifting his weapon and cursing repetitively. I knocked the barrel of his weapon down.

"Identify yourself, please!" I shouted at the suit.

It took two more clanking steps toward us. The recruit at my side shrank with every stride. Finally the head popped off, and a grinning young lady beamed down at us in amusement. It was none other than Galina Turov.

"Nice to see you again, McGill," she said. "I found this thing in the weaponry closet. Pretty neat, isn't it? I think all our legions should buy them. Tech World is a great market for hardware like this."

"Sir," I said, "Centurion Leeza of Germanica sent me to find you. May I ask why you haven't been communicating with the rest of the ship's defenders?"

"Couldn't," she said. "It's hard to hear in this thing. The motors whine and roar. Besides, I couldn't reach my tapper with my arm inside the actuator."

"I see. What are your orders, sir?"

She grinned. "Let's kill all the Tau then plan our next move."

"Yes sir."

The next half-hour troubled me somewhat. I began to understand Turov's personality—the darker side. She liked to fight as long as the enemy couldn't touch her.

I thought maybe a lighting gun could take her out, suit or no. But despite following along in her stomping wake as we mopped up enemy resistance across the ship, we didn't run into any more lightning-guns to test my theory.

-33-

Hours later, after the ship had been cleared of invaders, I returned to the fire control center. There was Galina Turov, standing with her right hip canted at a provocative angle while she worked the boards. I felt a surge of relief that the battle was over, and that she had survived it.

How odd... I began to ponder why the hell I cared whether this woman had survived or not. Staring for a full minute, I thought it over. She was standing with her back to me, unaware of my scrutiny.

As far as I was concerned, Turov had been a devil from the first day I'd met her. I should *want* to see her dead. The thought of finding Turov's corpse—young and lovely or older and snarling—should have brought a smile to my face. After all, hadn't she sent goons to harass me in my own house? Men who'd actually *killed* me in the end?

But as my gaze lingered on her form, I found I didn't want her to die. The only answer I had for my mood was it must have been a natural response to her youth and beauty. Men like me—we're suckers for a pretty woman. We're just wired to want to give them a break.

I felt sympathy for every cop who'd ever let a girl slide—but then I sternly reminded myself she wasn't just guilty of dodging speeding tickets. This woman had been a conniving, cast-iron witch.

"Are you going to report, or stare, Specialist?" Turov asked me suddenly without turning around.

I jumped and stepped fully into the room. There were cameras on me—there had to be. Damn.

"Sorry sir," I said, deciding to cover by completely ignoring the situation. "Yes, I'm here to report—and to check up on your status."

Why the hell had I said that?

She turned around slowly. Her head cocked to one side questioningly. I found the gesture eerie and entrancing at the same time. She was like some kind of vicious animated doll. I knew an evil spirit was hidden in that package. I could only imagine her charm had helped propel her up the ranks early-on and that, as she got older, ruthless ambition had finished the job.

She had pinned her golden suns on her lapels by this time. Two suns—the rank insignia of an Imperator. I knew I should feel overawed and stand at attention—but I couldn't muster that sort of reaction. I was tired, and she looked all wrong in the role of high-level brass. She looked more like she'd just graduated high school. Revivals like this one could be very confusing.

Her eyes studied me thoughtfully. "I understand," she said after a moment, sighing, "and I forgive you."

She turned back to her console, and I stepped forward cautiously. I understood that I'd been forgiven—but for what exactly, I wasn't sure. It could have been for my lack of respect or simply for being caught staring at her butt. Then again, it could have been something else entirely. As a man who often needed forgiveness, I certainly wasn't going to blow it this time.

"Thank you, sir," I said in a neutral voice.

"You still haven't given me your report."

Relieved, I did as she asked. I avoided looking at her by staring out into open space as I spoke. I found it was easier to convince myself I was talking to an Imperator if I didn't actually have to look at her.

I told her the ship was clear of invaders. But, as far as we could tell, Gelt Station was entirely in enemy hands. At least it wasn't sinking into the atmosphere—not yet, anyway. Number-wise aboard *Minotaur,* we were nearly up to a full strength unit due to Centurion Thompson's relentless efforts.

"Pitiful," she said when I'd finished.

I didn't argue. She was right. Two Earth legions had been essentially wiped out, and we were down to a handful of troops struggling to survive aboard *Minotaur.* We were cockroaches—hard to stamp out but, for the most part, harmless.

"I screwed up, you know," she said suddenly.

I glanced at her which was a mistake. She looked sad. Was her lower lip trembling? I couldn't believe it. This woman was normally made of steel! I could tell she had a better grip on her mind than she'd had when she'd first been revived, but she still wasn't in the clear.

"A bad death, that's all it was," I said, echoing the words of my commanders since I'd joined Varus. "We all have them, and we all have to learn to shake them off."

She sucked in a breath through clenched teeth. I thought she might cry or something, so I tried to stare down at the planet below. There was plenty to see. The impact of *Minotaur's* broadsides hadn't fully dissipated yet. There were storms and dust clouds spreading over a quarter of the planet. I could only imagine the number of deaths that had been caused by that single salvo Claver had launched.

"Normally," she said in a stronger voice, "your advice would be sound. But this occasion is very unusual. Have you looked at me, Specialist?"

My eyes widened. For me, that wasn't a safe question when I was around Turov. Never had been. Rather than replying, I bided my time. Sure enough, she started talking again and the awkward moment slipped away.

"I'm—I'm a kid!" she said. "I was a fool."

A small fist hammered on the console.

"Oh—that. Yeah, you're looking a little on the young side, sir.'"

"It will ruin me," she said bitterly. "Don't you see? Normally, when a Legionnaire dies it's a shock. But you can get over that shock. People treat you the same way as they did in your previous incarnation—but how can that happen now?

How am I to command, to climb higher, if I look like I should have a curfew every night?"

I shrugged. "Look on the bright side, Imperator. You've got your youth back. Doesn't everyone want to go back in time at some point?"

"Yes, of course. That's why I didn't update. I got notices, you know. If you last long enough—more than five years or so—the bio people start to send you requests to update your body records. In some cases, they can compel you to do so. But not me. I had too much rank. I slipped by them and ignored their wisdom."

"Why'd you do it—if you don't mind my asking, sir?"

"Selfish reasons. Fantasies. Who doesn't want to freeze their body at that perfect moment in their lives? I was vain. I wanted my youth back some day. I fantasized about it now and then."

I was kind of surprised she was confiding in me about all this but not *too* surprised. I'd found that people were often their most honest and philosophical after a solid death experience. Turov's had been extreme. I figured she was correct, too. It would take years to regain the respect she'd once commanded. Those Hegemony pukes back on Earth could be vicious. They probably already disliked her—hell, I couldn't blame them for that.

But worse, Hegemony people rarely died. They weren't like frontline legionnaires. At least people in Varus had some understanding and sympathy for the side effects of revivals. None of that would translate well back on Earth where Tribunes and Imperators had bellies that pushed against their desks and receding hairlines to match.

"You're getting it now, aren't you?" she said, reading my expression.

"Yes sir, I do see your problem. But it's just a setback, that's all."

She shook her head. "Combined with this disaster?" she asked, waving a hand toward the portal where the planet's atmosphere still roiled. "I'll be lucky if I'm a centurion a year from now."

I wondered if she could be right, but I didn't say anything.

"I can't believe it, McGill," she said. "You're actually a good listener. Of all the hidden traits I might have suspected you of having—that must be one of the last."

"Uh…thanks."

"I'm not trying to insult you," she said, putting out a hand to touch my arm.

It was a natural gesture, but her touch felt like a shock to me. I wasn't used to being gently touched by an officer. And especially not by one that resembled a cheerleader.

She withdrew her hand, but I could feel her touch there afterward as if it was burning my skin.

"What's the plan, sir?" I asked, trying to change the subject.

"We'll build up. We'll wait. The rebels have very little armament. The station is stable, so I think we have some time."

I frowned. "Time for what?"

"To revive our legions and retake the station—what else?"

I blinked but managed to nod. I'd been thinking more along the lines of flying home to Earth where we could revive all our people in a day. I almost suggested it—but held my tongue. I could tell she wasn't in any mood for more suggestions from enlisted types today.

The more I thought about it, the more I understood her line of reasoning. She *couldn't* go back to Earth—not now. At this point she was a monumental loser, a close equivalent to the original Tribune Varus of Rome himself. He'd managed to lose the province of Germany and three legions all at once, barely beating Turov's new record. In fact, maybe Earth would christen their next legion of misfits "Turov."

That thought brought a smile to my face. Unfortunately the Imperator noticed it quickly.

"What's funny?" she asked me.

"Uh…nothing really. I was just thinking of the commissary."

"The what?" she asked, frowning.

I was proud of my quick dodge. I'd been thinking of the commissary—but only at a very low level. The best misdirection contains an element of truth. After all, I was a little hungry.

"Claver didn't eject all the modules," I explained. "That means there's a commissary full of food and drink nearby. It also means there's almost no one aboard to share it with."

"Drink…" she said, as if the thought had never occurred to her before. She opened a channel to Centurion Leeza. She ordered that a watch be posted here at the fire control center then she turned back to me. There was an odd look in her eyes.

"Come with me, Specialist."

What could I do? It was a direct order from a high-ranking officer. I followed her down the passages until we came to the commissary in question. It was, in fact, the officer's pub that we stopped in. She took a seat and slapped the bar.

"I need something strong," she said. "What does a weaponeer drink when he wants to get drunk immediately?"

I grimaced. "Sir, I'm not sure that's a good—"

She slammed her small hand down on the bar again. "Shut up, McGill. You talk all the time. I want you to play bartender."

Shrugging, I dug into the cabinets.

"Wow, I'm impressed," I said a moment later. "These Germanica friggers do like the good stuff."

I poured her a glassful of eighteen year old single malt scotch and left it on the bar between us. She looked at the brown liquid dubiously.

"Can you at least give me an ice cube?" she asked.

"Sure."

I gave her three, and after she let them melt a bit, she took a swig. The results were comical, but she managed not to spit it out on the floor.

"My taste buds," she said, "they're operating fully again now that I'm young. This stuff tastes like gasoline."

"Over six hundred Hegemony credits a bottle," I said, pouring myself a glass and clinking it into hers. "That's expensive gas."

Galina laughed and drank her drink. She drank too fast—and I let her. When a soldier has just finished a hard battle, they want a drink at that moment like no other point in their lifetime.

I found some chips and peanuts under the bar that weren't too stale. We ate them, but it was already too late to slow down the booze. We were getting drunk.

"Galina," I said, staring at her with glassy eyes.

"What?" she asked, laughing.

"Why did you send goons to my place back on Earth?"

She rolled her eyes and looked a little embarrassed. "Oh—that. Can we talk about something else?"

"Sure, as soon as you tell me the truth."

I figured this was going to be my one and only chance to get some honesty out of this woman. She was pretty loaded, and her defenses were down.

She shook her head. "I did it because you posted that note telling people to vote against joining Hegemony."

"Yeah, I get that," I said. "But was that the whole story? You sent them just for petty revenge?"

"Noooo," she said. "Not at all. I'm not that kind of person. I wanted to discredit you."

I chewed that one over fuzzily. I tried eating more peanuts, but I was still baffled. "I don't understand. Arresting me was supposed to make people distrust my word?"

She gave me a smile that was almost shy. "I *know* you, James," she said. "I knew what you would do. You performed perfectly."

Frowning, I thought that one over. "You knew I'd kill those men?"

"The odds were good you'd resist arrest. That makes you look guilty."

"I see," I said, irritated. "It didn't work. The vote went my way."

Galina nodded. "Yes. You won that one."

Her admission made it easier to forgive her—that, and the booze. We shared two more shots, and soon we were both laughing about it.

What happened next was predictable but unplanned—at least, it wasn't planned by me. I wasn't so sure about Turov. She was a woman who got what she wanted any way she could.

274

We ended up emptying the bottle and making love on top of a pool table. The balls had all been sucked down into the table, stowed for flight so they didn't get in the way. The whole time we were doing it, I was thinking to myself something along the lines of *this is crazy! You're crazy, McGill!*

But it didn't matter. We did it anyway, and we were just lucky no one came in and caught us.

Afterward, I found myself stretched out on my back with her draped over me and snoring. I could feel her small tight breasts against my belly. I wondered if anyone was going to notice a large sweat-stain on their pool table in the morning. The thought made me chuckle, causing Imperator Turov's cheek to bounce on my ribs.

Not wanting to disturb her, I lightly wound my fingers in her hair. It felt silky and nice.

I had the time to contemplate who'd taken advantage of whom. There were a number of mitigating factors to consider. First off, she was an officer while I was enlisted. Technically, that meant *she* was in the wrong.

There were countless extenuating circumstances, however. I was a big guy who was physically older than she was. I'd plied her with strong drink which her young body had no resistance against—that was wrong even if she'd ordered me to do it.

I decided in the end there was plenty of guilt to go around between the both of us. In my honest opinion, I figured even a council of Nairbs would've declared the situation to be a tie.

-34-

When I woke up, Galina was gone. Instead my eyes focused upon a very pissed-off looking Centurion Leeza.

Her face loomed into mine. I'd thought before that she was too tall and had narrow eyes like a ferret, and her newfound rage hadn't improved things. She was as sour and sneering as an officer could get.

"Get off that table, Specialist!" she roared.

I rolled off with a groan. An empty bottle went over the edge with me, making a splintery crash.

"Varus trash!" she shouted. She made my legion's name sound like an expletive. "This is just what you're famous for. Disorder, slovenly behavior, drunkenness—"

I didn't really listen to the rest, but the list was a long one. I got to my feet. Behind the Centurion were several of her grinning noncoms. They were obviously enjoying the situation.

"Sorry sir," I said. "Tough battle. I'll be going back to my unit now."

"Unit?" she scoffed. "What unit? You're alone on this ship, Varus—except for that crazy bio and a few of her sidekicks. She revived my unit to full strength first."

I nodded, unsurprised. It was standard operating procedure after heavy losses to revive entire units together instead of spreading the service around. What good would it do to have a dozen solo centurions standing around? Better to have a cohesive force that knew one another and had trained together.

276

"Can I be dismissed, sir?" I asked, tugging and patting my uniform into place until it started to grab and latch onto my shoulders.

Smart clothing generally attempted to cover a person up, but if you pushed it away repeatedly, it was intelligent enough to give up and stop trying. Later, you had to coax it into covering your body fully again. That's what I was attempting to do now.

"No," she said, putting one hip up on the corner of the pool table and swinging her leg like a cat lashing its tail. "I want you to tell me how a man like you—an obvious moron—managed to take out a shipload of invaders almost singlehandedly."

I smiled a fraction. "There was nothing 'almost' about it, sir. I fried them all."

"How?"

"They're not too bright, these rioters. They're untrained and their brains are only operating on half-power anyway if you ask me. All I did was flank them and unload."

She nodded and heaved a sigh. "This is Germanica's officers' mess—you know that, right?"

"Yes sir."

"Why would you put me in this position? I owe you a great deal—without your aid both our legions might have been permed. Immediately after your heroic effort, you have to go and do something like this. Something that would get any of my men flogged. How am I supposed to handle this situation?"

I knew she was telling the truth about the flogging. Just as they'd done so long ago back in Roman times, our legions still flogged men for things like breaking into the officers' liquor. If a soldier was beaten so badly a coat of sprayed-on skin wouldn't fix him, well hell, they could always run him through the revival machine again to freshen him up.

"You could let me off with a warning this time, sir," I suggested hopefully.

Leeza shook her head and her troops chuckled. She tossed them an annoyed glance over her shoulder, and they quieted immediately.

"I will," she said, "if you tell me why you broke in here in the first place."

We stared at one another for a full second after that. My head swam with words I couldn't afford to let out of my mouth. I could have told her the truth—that a very youthful version of our Imperator had ordered me down here, fed me booze until we were both out of control, and then proceeded to strip me down on the pool table. But somehow, I knew that wasn't the way to go.

For a full second I didn't know what the hell to say, but fortunately God has gifted me with a quick wit and a quick tongue—at least when I'm faced with the kind of dilemma where I need to come up with a good story or be flogged.

"After the battle, I really needed a drink, Centurion," I said. "As far as I knew, this was the only place on the ship I could get one."

Leeza heaved another sigh and nodded. "At least you've been honest. Everyone was wiped out aboard this ship, is that right? Everyone except for you and the Imperator? Then you began reviving bio people."

I nodded warily. Could this woman know the truth about Turov and me? Was she having a little fun right now? Was all this being recorded and posted on the Germanica legion laugh-boards even as we spoke?

"Dismissed, Specialist," Leeza said suddenly. "But don't pull this crap again. I won't stand for more petty crimes, not even from you."

I was halfway to the door by the time she finished her sentence. "Won't happen again, Centurion," I said over my shoulder, "and thank you, sir."

One of her veterans, who'd been looming behind her this whole time, flipped me off on the way out. I touched my hand to my brow and gave him a very informal salute in return. There never had been any love lost between our two legions.

Not knowing where else to go—and not wanting to meet up with Galina again right now—I headed to the bio module.

Blue deck was even busier and steamier than it had been the night before. The first thing I saw was a muzzle in my face when I entered. Germanica had posted guards. I thought it was a wise move.

278

"State your business—" began the guard, but he broke off. "Oh, it's you, Varus. What do you want?"

The trooper lowered his gun. I was surprised he'd recognized me. I guess I'd made quite an impression by coming to their rescue while they were pinned down in that module.

"Where's Centurion Thompson?" I asked.

He pointed with the butt of his snap-rifle. I followed the gesture and saw the bio was indeed nearby, sprawled out in a chair. Her hair was matted with blood, sweat, and that unidentifiable goo that drips from the lower regions of revival machines.

"She worked all night and passed out. They finished getting Leeza's unit together and started on yours. Your people are operating the machine now."

I walked past the man and peered into the revival chamber. There was Anne Grant working the machine with two orderlies. I smiled, but she didn't even look back at me.

Reviving Centurion Thompson had been a good move, I thought to myself. She wasn't Germanica so after she'd finished a full unit of their troops she'd started on one of ours. Which unit? Why, mine of course. Why not? They already had an active weaponeer who knew the score. That was a good start. The revival machine might have made the same choice if they'd left it up to the AI.

"Anne?" I asked, coming up behind her.

She glanced at me and smiled thinly. She looked tired but determined. I sympathized with her plight. Bio people got the worst of it after the battle was over, and generally, their little slice of hell lasted longer than the battle itself.

"McGill! Can you give me a hand?"

I stepped in even though my stomach was jumping from too much alcohol and too little food. I knew she needed the help, and by now I'd helped to revive enough fresh troops to qualify as an orderly myself.

A few minutes later, I had a chance to check the roster on the machine's console. "Sargon is up next?"

"Yes. All the bio people in the unit are already back in the game. We're working on front line people next, then the officers and auxiliaries."

"Can I make a request?"

She immediately frowned. For some reason, the bio specialists were very finicky about their technology. They didn't want us to know anything about it, and they certainly didn't want their decisions second-guessed by an amateur.

Anne heaved a deep breath. "What?"

"Bring Natasha out next."

Her face darkened, and I realized immediately I'd made a grave error.

"No, no, no," I said, throwing my hands up in a cautioning gesture. "I think our unit needs her. She was working on a system to turn off these rioters."

Still frowning, she crossed her arms. She made a small gesture indicating I should continue speaking. I explained the holographic clothing, the tampered boxes, and the rest of it.

"So," I finished, "that's what Claver was up to."

"You're blaming everything on him? All of this? You're claiming that he went so far as to blast the crap out of this planet to stop the spread of the infected holo machines?"

"Pretty much, yeah. He was in the midst of a dozen scams, trying to get rich. When Turov ordered Legion Varus to replace Germanica, his timetables were screwed up. He had to rush everything to go home. His schemes came apart. Unfortunately, he just about took the planet down with him."

Anne stared at me distrustfully. "That's a longer story than usual," she said.

"Oh, come on. I didn't make all this up."

"Who can back up your story?"

"Natasha can, that's who."

Sighing, she tapped at the revival unit's control screen until Natasha's name came up. She selected it and engaged the unit.

"I hope you're happy," she said.

"I'm miserable. Hey, you've got enough people working in here. How about you and I get some breakfast?"

"No," she said in a quiet voice, not looking at me.

280

Behind her, the two orderlies exchanged glances. They gave each other a nod. I frowned at them then returned my attention to Anne. I had to wonder why everyone in the unit acted like I was always up to something with the ladies. Sure, I'd had more than my fair share of entanglements, but lots of people did. I guess my rep had come because my affairs tended to be a little more high-profile than the norm.

"Come on," I said to Anne. "When's the last time you ate?"

"I haven't yet. Not since she brought me back," she said, jabbing a thumb at the lanky, sprawled figure of Centurion Thompson.

"If she wakes up and complains about you leaving your post, just blame me," I suggested. "She'll believe any story that points a finger in my direction."

Chuckling, Anne finally gave in and accompanied me out the door. Behind us, I noticed one of the orderlies slapping money into the other one's hand. I'd won someone a bet.

We walked together to the wardroom. Fortunately Centurion Leeza had moved on, and we avoided the closed pub in any case. We were after food, not booze.

We ate ravenously, barely talking until we'd stuffed ourselves with real eggs, toast, hash browns and coffee.

"Wow," I said, leaning back and sighing in satisfaction. "That's almost enough to turn me into a smuggler like these Germanica snots."

Anne frowned at me. "They aren't all like that. Like Claver, I mean."

"No? I could tell you a story or two—but I won't. Let's just say they like to live well while on deployment. We get remanufactured pork and beans while they eat and drink the real stuff."

"It *is* good," she admitted.

She shifted uncomfortably in her chair and didn't look at me for a moment. I could tell she wanted to say something, so I stayed quiet and sipped my coffee.

When she got done staring at her plate, she finally spoke. "James? Could I ask you something real for once?"

"Sure."

"Do you ever get serious? About women, I mean?"

281

"Uh…sure I do. Especially when they're about to kill me."

Anne nodded as if confirming a suspicion. She got up and took her tray to the recycler.

"Did I say something wrong?" I called after her.

She gave me a tired smile. "No, not at all. Thanks for the company. I'm going to check in on blue deck then hit a bunk, if you don't mind."

We parted ways, and I drank another cup of coffee before heading out. I found a bunk for myself and stretched out on it. This was easy to do as the ship and most of the unit modules were as empty as tombs.

Despite the caffeine in my blood, I could hardly hold my eyes open. My head found a musty pillow, and I was snoring like a baby two minutes later.

* * *

Someone woke me up hours later. This time, it was Natasha. Unlike the other women aboard, she actually seemed to be happy to see me.

"James," she said. "I heard what you did. I can't believe it. You've given us all a second chance!"

"Yeah?"

"Are you still asleep?"

In truth my mind was fuzzy. Last night's booze hadn't completely exited my bloodstream and neither had thoughts of Galina Turov. By the stars, I swear that woman knew things most girls her physical age hadn't dreamed of yet. I had to remind myself that for all I knew she was actually seventy years old. It was a strange thought.

"Are you listening to me?" Natasha demanded suddenly.

"What? Yeah, sure I am. Keep talking."

She gave me a quizzical look then let it go. "You've given us a chance to recover. It's a thin one, but we've got to take it before they arrive."

Natasha had my full attention after I'd absorbed that sentence. I didn't ask who "they" were. There was only one "they" that mattered.

"When do they get here?"

"Technically they're already in-system, but they're cruising toward us slowly. I think they're watching us, and they must want to see how we're going to react to the situation."

She was talking about the Nairbs. She had to be. Physically the Nairbs were green bags of protoplasm that resembled seals, but they acted more like entrenched government accountants.

"Did they bring planet-busters this time?" I asked bitterly. More than a year back, I'd watched them erase a civilization. Sure, the alien squids living in the Zeta Herculis system had been vicious bastards, but what species deserved annihilation for the crime of wanting independence from the Empire? To my mind, they'd been in the right. But no one wanted to hear my opinion.

"I hope not," she said. "Their ship is certainly big enough for bombs. It's a stellar cruiser with an unusual configuration."

"Why come here if not to dispense justice upon a helpless population?" I demanded.

She was thoughtful. "What they love most is holding a trial and declaring guilt or innocence. If they find wrong-doing here—you're right, they'll eradicate someone eventually."

The more I thought about it the more irritated I became. The Nairbs didn't have to get involved in this. Local affairs were not their problem. That said, I was certain there were plenty of Galactic trade goods and aliens on the station which elevated this to the level of an interstellar crisis. Probably one of the aliens had reported the situation and brought it to the Nairbs attention.

"They gave us the job of local enforcement," I complained, struggling with my boots. "They should stay out of Frontier 921 and let us handle it. We'll do what has to be done."

Natasha shook her head and patted my shoulder. I was standing now, stretching and yawning.

"We can't control that, James," she said. "What we can do is affect the situation at hand."

"How?"

"Gelt Station is sinking, James," she said. "And Turov is thinking we should let it go all the way down."

I frowned. "But there are millions of people on that station. Most of them aren't involved with the rebels. They—"

"Turov has made the call. I went back down to blue deck when I heard that Graves was coming out of the oven. Those bio people hear a lot of things, you know. Turov talked to Graves about one minute after he was off the table. He listened and agreed. What a cold fish that man is."

She gave a little shudder, and I splashed water in my face at a stainless steel sink. Damn, I needed a shower.

"You're saying Graves seconded the motion?" I asked. "To let all the Tau civvies die?"

"Not just that. He came off that table so calmly, so matter-of-fact. He was like a man who's awakened after dozing off on the family sofa while watching vids. He swung his legs off the table, took Turov's words in, and concurred with her judgment. Then he thanked the bio people and left. It was like there wasn't any fear in him—no questions about who he was. Nothing."

I looked at her, and saw she was a little haunted. All bio people looked that way, but techs like Natasha only did when they got close to the reality of the process. I didn't have time to worry about that kind of thing, however. There were bigger issues at stake.

"Come with me," I said, "we've got to talk some sense into people."

"Who? Graves?"

"Yeah, him first."

"Then Turov," she said. "That's what you're thinking, isn't it?"

I glanced at her. She had an odd look on her face. What did that mean? I pushed the thought from my mind. I wasn't good at reading women, and this wasn't the time to learn how to do it.

"Right," I said. "We've got to lay out a plan, tell them about it, and convince them it can be done."

"What plan?"

"I'll tell you on the way up there."

I explained, and Natasha became alarmed. She argued with me all the way up. She finished her objections outside Graves' quarters, still whispering reasons why it couldn't work. But in the end, she went along with my plan.

That's why I liked her. She was always willing to take a chance.

-35-

Graves was neatly dressed, showered, and fed when we called on him. Somehow, he looked a lot better than I did even though he'd been as dead as space itself an hour ago.

Natasha and I exchanged glances, and I forced a smile. Graves didn't reciprocate.

"Sir?" I asked, getting his full attention.

"What is it, McGill?"

"We need to talk to you, sir."

He looked at me expressionlessly. After a moment, he gestured for us to sit in collapsible chairs in front of his desk. We did so.

"Talk," he said.

"Sir, it's come to our attention that the Nairbs are in the system and that—"

"Stop," he said, looking up. We had his full attention. His eyes slid from one of us to the other. "McGill, you're not getting away with this. Not again."

"Um...getting away with what exactly, sir?"

"Interfering in Galactic business. Shooting Nairbs and the like."

"I've never shot a Nairb, sir. The incident you're thinking of involved a Galactic."

He closed his eyes in pain. "I was covering. You weren't supposed to ever mention that event again, McGill."

I glanced over at Natasha. Her eyes drifted around the room then they landed on Graves.

"I already knew about the event in question, sir," she said quietly.

Graves began rubbing his forehead with his fingers. "How is it, McGill, that I can die and return to life without a qualm, but I can't have a conversation with you that lasts more than thirty seconds without getting a headache?"

"My mama always said I was gifted in that department, sir."

"She was right. Now, tell me what you're talking about."

"Is it true, sir, that the Tau station is sinking? That it will burn up in the upper atmosphere soon?"

"Of course it is. You should know what's destined to happen. After all, you blew up the umbilical personally, didn't you?"

I felt a jolt of alarm at his statement. "Uh...Claver did that, sir."

"Right... He came up here, took out three units of Germanica troops, and then polished off the staff at the tactical fire control console. You caught up when it was too late and shot him to death—from a prone position no less, according to the bio-people I had examine the scene just now."

I squirmed in my seat. It suddenly felt too small to hold my butt. "He was a clever operator. You said so yourself."

Graves continued to stare. "Clever enough to take out the guards, hack the control system, and fire *Minotaur's* broadsides? Then nearly finish you with an improvised weapon?"

"Apparently so, sir."

His lips twisted up into a grimace. I could tell he didn't believe me. He knew there were some falsehoods in my story. Hell, it was full of holes. What was probably saving me so far was that he wasn't sure exactly what *had* happened.

I'm not the kind of guy who worries about a possible disaster before it hits me, but I knew this could turn into a bad one. I'd really hoped people wouldn't figure how deeply I'd been involved in all that grim business with Claver. Dammit, why did Graves have to be so on the ball?

Absently, my hand crept to the pocket where I kept the shell-like thing Claver had called a "Galactic key". It was still

287

there fortunately. I figured if it came down to it, I would use it again to escape custody.

"Sir," I said, getting an idea. "What if I said Natasha and I might be able to fix this whole mess?"

I got a cold stare in response. "Go on."

"Claver said the boxes were hacked—I'm talking about the holographic projectors all these Tau wear. That *he* was the man who'd hacked them and set them loose. We've had the chance to look at one of these boxes and dissect it. Natasha here has a good handle on how the problem could be fixed."

Beside me, Natasha had begun to squirm. She was staring at me, and I knew I was overselling the deal. So far she was staying quiet, and I hoped she could keep up the facade.

"Are you serious, McGill?" Graves asked me.

"Absolutely, sir. We're talking about stopping the riots and saving millions of lives. That's worth a shot, isn't it? What's the worst that could happen?"

Graves huffed. "We could all be permed. All of Earth could be permed. I can think of plenty of other results as well that would be less dramatic but still unpleasant."

"I'm sure you can, sir," I said. "All I'm asking for is a chance to fix things. You know the Nairbs are watching. They're just hanging out there in space judging our actions. If we can turn this around now—"

Graves lifted a hand. "We don't know that's a Nairb ship. It's interstellar, but it's not of any known design."

I frowned. "Could it be from the Core Systems then?"

"Maybe," Graves said. "The point is the vessel isn't communicating with anyone or doing much of anything. That sounds like a Nairb or Galactic ship. They like to sit aloof, judging us in secret. But we can't be sure."

"Well then, let's give them a show, Centurion," I suggested.

Graves heaved a deep breath. "Personally, I think it *is* a Nairb ship. In my opinion, they're staying quiet and filling out a score card on us. Remember that we're Enforcers now and very new to the job. They're probably trying to figure out whether they should fire on us or not over this mess. But that works in your favor, McGill, because we can't afford to wait to end this."

Graves sat back in his creaking chair and stared at the ceiling for a few seconds.

"All right," he said at last. "I'm convinced it's worth a try, God help us all. How many troops do you need to make your attempt?"

My jaw sagged in surprise. I could hardly believe my good fortune. "We only need one squad, sir. Preferably a squad of heavies. Just enough to cover us while we test out the system."

"Test out...?" Natasha said, breaking into the conversation. "Test out what?"

"Your equipment," I said firmly. "We'll see if we can broadcast a signal that will infect their holographic boxes. It will spread exponentially in their massed crowds. Claver's software did it—so can yours."

Natasha's eyes were big when they met mine, and she gave me a tiny shake of her head.

I smiled and nodded as if she was affirming my every word.

"There's just one thing, McGill," Graves said.

"Sir?"

"You've convinced me, but I'm not in charge. You'll still have to convince Imperator Turov."

I chewed that one over. "I think I can, sir."

Graves frowned. I figured he'd expected me to groan and complain while trying to get him to let me perform this mission on the sly. But I hadn't gone that way, and he didn't know why.

"McGill, just remember—she's not a kid," he told me seriously. "Not even if she looks like one."

"I would never make that mistake, sir," I lied.

Out in the hallway, Natasha let me have it.

"James!" she hissed. "I don't have *anything*! You know that! I'll need a week or two, at least, to figure out how to do this."

I pulled the Galactic key out of my pocket and handed it to her.

"What's this? A seashell?"

289

"A tech present," I said. "The best one any girl ever got."

I explained the device and what it could do. Natasha was floored.

"The possibilities…" she said in a dreamy tone.

"Yeah, maybe later," I told her. "For now, we need a tech miracle using this tech tool. The holographic systems are trade goods, aren't they?"

"Yes, they aren't native to this system. The locals really love them, though. There must be a rich world out there somewhere that sells these things."

"There are billions of credits involved. That's what Claver was up to. He was trying to duplicate the product and make his own, cheaper."

Natasha gasped. "That's illegal! They're patented products, traded in good faith."

"Right, sure. But he figured the Empire was crumbling and a businessman like him might make a quick billion credits off a scheme like this. With no Battlefleet in the sector, who was going to stop him?"

She looked troubled by the idea. She examined the shell-like object carefully. "I need to take this to my workshop and test it. I don't know if what you promised Graves can actually be done."

"It's got to work—either that or all those people aboard that station are going to die."

We looked at each other, and she shook her head. "I'll go to my lab and give it a try. Wish me luck."

Natasha kissed me on the cheek and left. I turned toward the lift which went up to the top of the stack. Turov had left the tactical fire control room and moved back to the penthouse module. I rode the lift upward, wondering if she would have a posse of legion regulars waiting to execute me.

What had possessed me to sleep with the Imperator? I asked myself that, and I didn't have a ready answer. If I ever sat down with a psychologist and told him all my stories— well, I don't think the prognosis would be good.

Turov didn't have guards waiting outside her office this time. I suppose there weren't enough troops around to warrant it. There was, however, another visitor. It was none other than Centurion Leeza.

When I tapped at the open door, the two women officers looked at me. They both stiffened, and I got the feeling no one was happy to see me.

Standing at attention, I saluted. "Specialist McGill, requesting a moment of your time, Imperator."

Centurion Leeza cleared her throat. "I should be getting back to my unit anyway," she said.

"I'm expecting a report on our defensives by 1400, Centurion," Turov snapped.

"Yes, Imperator."

Centurion Leeza gave me an odd look then slipped by and disappeared. I stepped into the room.

Galina Turov seemed to be much more like an Imperator today. She was still incredibly young-looking, but there was something different in her eyes and her manner. I knew right off that the shock of her death had faded, and her old self was reasserting dominance.

I'd seen this pattern before. When you first died, or if it had been a long time or a particularly nasty and disturbing experience, people tended to be in a fog of introspection after they returned. They might do or say things they regretted later. Bio people had told me there were neurological reasons for this as well as psychological ones. The truth was, a regrown brain had been copied and burned in with fresh neural pathways—but it was *still* a new brain. Sometimes, it took a while for people to get back to normal.

Finally, Turov looked up at me. "James McGill," she said. "What are we going to do with you?"

My mind came up with a few choice retorts, but I held them back. If anyone was going to mention what had happened between us last night, it wasn't going to be me.

"I've come to ask your permission to engage in a critical operation, sir," I said.

"Really? I thought it was something else. Something more personal."

I glanced at her. I couldn't help it. She looked amused, but there was also a bit of underlying tension. She was definitely

291

thinking about our night together on the pool table. I wasn't sure what that meant. I'd been hoping she would have shrugged it off by now. No such luck, I could tell.

"Perhaps we could discuss that another time, sir," I said. "I'm here to try to save millions of lives."

"Oh that," she said. "Graves sent me a text on the topic. Some business about you sneaking onto the station with a magic box. It's not going to happen."

"Why not, sir?"

"Because we haven't got the tech—and it hardly matters if we do."

"I don't follow you."

"Think about it. If you turned every mind back to peaceful thoughts on that station, it would still go down in flames days from now. Once that orbit decays enough, the lower edge will dip into the atmosphere. At that point, she'll start to burn up. There aren't enough ships in the system to apply sufficient thrust to pull her back up again."

I frowned. "But sir, we don't *know* that."

"Yes, we do. I've looked into it. I've talked to their engineers on the ground as well. Would you believe that they insisted on charging me for a consultation? Here we are, trying to help them save their own station, and they won't give me advice on the topic for free. They're an unbelievably ungrateful species."

"Yes…well…if they don't have the engines, how did they get the station up here in the first place? Doesn't it have engines or stabilizers of its own?"

"To a degree, yes. But they depended on the umbilical for support and to hold the megahab stationary. The main engines were one-shot systems designed to carry mass into orbit. They were long ago cannibalized for more mass to build the station itself. Most of the rest of it was transported here from asteroids and the like and built in space, piece by piece."

"Still, I think it's worth the effort. If we could use *Minotaur* and their own shuttles—we could save thousands, if not millions."

"Very noble of you, McGill. I'm impressed. But—"

"Look," I said, stepping closer. "I don't need much. Just approval and one squad. We'll fly out there in a pinnace and give it a shot. If the rebels don't respond," I shrugged. "I guess we did our best."

Turov thought about it for a few moments then shook her head. "No."

"Why not?" I demanded in what was possibly a more strident tone than she'd expected.

She frowned at me sternly but then softened and answered. "The Nairbs are here watching everything we do. They're passing judgment. I can feel it. I don't want to be blamed somehow for what's happening to the station. We could lose our status as local Enforcers for the Empire."

"Screw the Nairbs," I said. "If that's even who's operating that ship."

Galina appeared to be startled. Then she frowned. "That's your answer to everything, isn't it? Just screw it."

It took me a second to get her point. I rolled my eyes. This pissed her off.

"I understand it all now," she snapped, standing up and beginning to pace.

I watched her the way a man watches a beautifully sleek and deadly snake.

"This is why you can't have sex with your subordinates," she continued as if talking to herself. "I'd only understood it as a rule before—but it's more than that, its wisdom from long ago. You, McGill, are a textbook case. You no longer respect my authority because we've been intimate."

"Sorry sir," I said, "but you're dead wrong in regard to my motivations. I just don't understand why you won't allow me to risk my life to save so many. You can always revive me if I fail."

"Your gesture is a noble one, but the answer is still no. You're dismissed, Specialist."

I paused. I was getting mad, and that was a bad thing. I tried to stop it, but I couldn't. Words began to come out of my mouth.

"She suspects, you know," I said quickly.

Turov turned and stared at me. "Who suspects what?"

293

"Leeza. She gave me a little knowing smirk on the way out. Wait a minute—you *told* her, didn't you?"

Turov's face turned red. "I told her nothing! And neither will you."

I threw up my hands. "I'm just saying I think she suspects. She caught me on the pool table after you left me there. You must not have been gone for long, and—"

"Shut up," she snapped, stepping close and glaring up into my face. "How can you cause me such trouble? I don't understand it. Many men have opposed me, McGill. They're nowhere to be found today. They have no rank, no power. They aren't even in the service anymore."

We glared at one another for a few seconds.

"I'm not trying to start anything," I told her, softening my tone. "All I want is a chance to fix what's happened here. No matter who caused all this devastation, I'm sure it was someone from Earth who killed all those people."

"I see. You feel morally superior, and thus you're willing to threaten me. I see."

She reached down suddenly and began to stab and swipe at her console. A face appeared in response. It was a bio—one of the people running the revival unit.

"Imperator?" the face asked. The bio was startled, but trying to hide her concern.

"I have an emergency revival order," Turov said.

"All right, sir. We'll queue that up immediately. Can you give me the name?"

"You do not understand," Turov said. "I do not want you to queue it up. You will replace the current revival project with a new one—now."

"I—I don't understand, sir."

"Dump whatever is in the machine, damn you. Abort it. Recycle the current grow you're working on and start fresh. Do so now."

"Ah—yes sir."

I felt a little sick. She'd just ordered the bio to kill a half-grown human. I gritted my teeth but kept quiet. I wasn't quite sure what she was up to. At first, I'd assumed she was ordering a firing squad to come up to her office and finish me forever.

Now that that idea seemed wrong I had no idea what was on her mind.

"Imperator?" the bio asked a moment later. "It's...it's done."

"All right," Turov said, looking straight at me again. "Now, I want you to cue up Adjunct Claver from Germanica. Do it now."

"Isn't he—?"

"Do I have to replace you, Specialist?" Turov asked, raising her voice.

"No sir. The change-order has been input and confirmed. I'll contact you when the processing finishes."

"Don't bother. I'm on my way down to your station."

She disconnected, and she eyed me with a mixture of contempt and triumph.

I had to admit at that moment that the old Turov was behind those eyes. Galina, the young lost girl I'd enjoyed the night before, was gone.

Turov had a plan, and even though I didn't have a clue what her plan was, I knew it wasn't a nice one.

"Claver?" I asked, stunned. "Why the hell would you bring *him* back? Isn't he best left permed?"

"Because you can't do this without him," she said. "Who would be better to reprogram these crazy Tau than the man who scrambled their minds in the first place?"

I thought about it, and I realized that she was correct. I also realized something else. Claver was going to point a finger right at me when he came back to life. Every sin we'd done together was going to be heaped upon *my* head. By the time he got done talking, I'd have destroyed the umbilical single-handedly, caused cancer, and personally bioengineered six new species of houseflies in the bargain.

Further, I now understood why she was doing it this way. I had a handle on her, to her way of thinking—a threat over her head. Now, she was going to have one over me.

"I understand, Imperator," I said.

"Do you...? Yes, I see that you do. Keep that in mind the next time you dare to contemplate threatening me."

I heaved a small, internal sigh. Imperator Turov was back. The new version was as cute as a button—but also as mean as a half-stomped rattlesnake.

-36-

When Claver showed up at Natasha's workshop about an hour later, I eyed him with vast distrust. He returned my expression—except possibly with more malice.

It was weird to see Old Silver with only a touch of gray in his hair. He'd lost ten years at least. I was mildly surprised to note he hadn't been as vain as Turov in this regard. He hadn't kept himself in cold storage as a permanent twenty-year-old. If I had to guess, I figured he was about thirty-eight years old physically. It was a far cry from fifty-something, but respectable.

Behind him were his hands, clasped in manacles. Behind them stood two MPs who had ugly mugs and even uglier shock-sticks in their hands.

Turov stepped forward, slipping past the men with lithe grace. "McGill, this is your guide. Make use of him. He's been informed of his status, and I hope he won't give you more difficulty than his existence is worth."

There was an obvious underlying threat in her words. I could tell that Turov, possibly more than any of us, hated Claver.

When she'd left, I gave him a smirk. "You've got to be careful what you say around that lady," I advised him. "I don't think she likes you."

"McGill," he said, "I don't like you, either. But I'm frankly amazed to be alive at all, so I guess I should shake your hand and put all our differences behind us."

Frowning, I approached him. Natasha watched this, shifting uneasily. She didn't trust him at all, but I thought that was silly. The man was tricky, but he wasn't a magician.

When I got close, he made an effort to pull his hands around from behind his back, grunting and straining. He smiled a little sheepishly.

"Sorry," he said. "I forgot about these things. Have the guards remove them, will you? I can't do much work with them on, and I certainly can't shake your hand."

I smiled, stepped forward and reached behind his back. I clasped a hand firmly and gave it an awkward shake.

"No problem at all. See? We can still shake hands. And don't worry about helping out. We need your wisdom for this job, not your hands. Just tell Natasha all about how you built the hacked holo-boxes and we'll get along fine."

As fast as his expression had changed before, it changed again. He jerked his hand away from mine and snarled at me. "Why should I help you? You murdered me. You murdered *everyone*—millions of innocents down there on the planet alone!"

My smile tightened, but stayed fixedly on my face. "Now, now," I said, "you don't want to be like that. We should start over. You've got a fresh grow and I've got the upper hand for the time being. Work with it, Claver. Don't get all emotional on me now."

Claver tilted his head and stared at me quizzically for a second.

"I'm beginning to catch on," he said. "You're a small-time schemer, aren't you? You're *not* an idiot—at least, not completely. You play the fool so very well McGill, I was sucked in. I have to admit it: I was played. Wow. I stand impressed and mortified at the same time. Do you know that—"

Before Claver could get on my nerves any further, I interrupted him. "Enough chatter. Let's get to business. Natasha, show him what you've got."

I wasn't a tech, but I've had a little training. Natasha had built a box with a transceiver in it rather than a simple projection device. It was designed to transmit a signal to other

298

boxes of its own kind. The trouble was we didn't have the protocols. We could simulate input and transmit it to another box that was listening for mood input, but we couldn't figure out exactly how to get the other boxes to accept it.

Rather than bending my brain over the tech jargon, I watched Claver instead. I didn't stare right at him, but I made sure his every move was noted in my mind. Thinking back, I'd seen Harris do the same thing countless times. He would position himself to watch a trooper carefully. When the man made his move, thinking himself unobserved, Harris would pounce.

Claver could see that he didn't have any leverage, so he sullenly cooperated. His eyes wandered while he answered Natasha's questions, looking around the room curiously. At last, they landed upon the shell-shaped key, which was tucked most of the way under a computer scroll on the desk.

Natasha had used the key to open up a holobox and to get it to accept new programming. Now that he'd spotted it, Claver sidled closer to it, turning his back. His plan was so obvious that I decided to have a little fun.

Long before he managed to reach the key under the computer scroll, I'd gotten over there and removed it. Standing with the item behind my back, I pretended to be absorbed by Natasha's monologue about holographic projectors.

"I've learned so much," she said. "These devices are ingenious! Simultaneously sophisticated and simplistic, I've been fascinated by their internal design. Patching a transmitter in here to override the receptors in other units almost feels like a crime."

"Uh-huh," said Claver, backing up a step and fondling the computer scroll behind his back. I could tell he was going for the key which was no longer there. It was all I could do to suppress a grin.

Claver kept playing it up, smiling and saying polite things. Finally, I figured I'd had enough.

"What are you rustling with back there?" I demanded harshly, stepping forward.

Claver looked innocent. "What? I'm working, do you mind?"

I peered over his shoulder and the guards loomed close.

"He's got something!" I shouted. "Right there! Guards!"

They'd been bored up until now, but they didn't hesitate to relieve the tedium once I'd given them an opening. Shock sticks came out, and were raised high crackling with lavender-green power. They came down onto Claver, and he slumped to the deck, twitching.

"Here it is," I said loudly, holding up the Galactic Key in front of his eyes. "He was after this. Good thing he's clumsy. Those manacles are foreign-made. He might have released himself with this thing."

Claver was beyond speech, too stunned by dual touches of the shock-sticks to respond. His eyes, however, tracked the key in my grasp. I was sure he couldn't believe he'd missed grabbing it or that I'd spotted him. That was just fine by me. He'd killed countless people with his scheme. Having a little fun was the least I could do to avenge the dead.

The guards hauled him rudely to his feet. They were glaring at Claver, and I was smiling.

Only Natasha was frowning at me. She knew me too well.

"James, stop fooling around and fix him. I need his help."

"All right, all right," I said. I threw a cup of water into his face and gave him a light slap on the cheek.

"I didn't say you should beat on him!" Natasha complained.

"He's fine. Tough as nails. A few kilovolts are nothing a Germanica man can't bounce back from."

When Claver could stand on his feet unaided, he glowered at us all.

"I'm done," he said. "You and the Tau can all burn up for all I care."

"You'll die if you don't cooperate," I told him. "The Imperator will execute you without a qualm."

"Don't you think I know that, fool?" he asked me. Some of his bravado had returned in the form of a gleam in his eye. "I'm not really Claver. I'm a copy. You don't think I would take all these risks without knowing I couldn't be taken out, do you?"

"What are you talking about?"

300

"That's your problem, McGill," he said. "You think outside the box—but only an inch or so. Me—hell, I don't even know where the box is, boy."

I frowned at him not understanding and not at all liking that I wasn't getting it.

Claver made his move then. He reached backward and grabbed the sidearm of the guard on his left—it was an insane move as his hands were still locked behind him.

He squeezed the trigger and cut a smoking line across the man's leg. The second guard whipped out his pistol and burned Claver down.

He flipped around onto his back and lay there, gasping.

I put my hands on my knees and bent lower, staring into his face.

"You pretty much killed yourself," I said. "Who's the fool now? Turov won't revive you a second time."

Claver struggled to speak. The smell of burnt flesh tickled my nose, but I didn't pull back. I wanted to hear what he had to say.

He managed to lick his lips and wet them with fresh blood. "I'm not Claver," he said. "Not the real one. Pray you don't meet me again, McGill."

That was it. He died on the spot.

Natasha had her arms crossed and her face twisted up into a frown. "You couldn't have kept him alive for five more minutes?"

I looked at her. "I didn't grab a gun, he did! He was trying to get himself free before, and I stopped him. Why doesn't someone else keep their eyes on the ball?"

The two guards looked sheepish. The one with the burnt leg was limping badly, and I ordered him to head for blue deck for a spray of skin cells.

When we were alone, Natasha sighed. "I think I can do this alone," she said. "He didn't give me the exact protocols—but he gave me several ideas as to how to find them. I'll program a loop trying every frequency until I find it. Then I'll do a combinatory sequence—we'll find it by brute force if we have to. After all, I'm ninety percent of the way there."

"Good," I said. "What do you think he meant about being a copy?"

Natasha looked at me in surprise. "You didn't get that? He means he's been duplicated. He's been revived elsewhere."

I frowned. "How could he know that?"

She shrugged. "Probably his mind was stored on another system somewhere. Wherever the data has been residing, it's been updating since his last revive. That's why he remembered being revived elsewhere, but not dying. Our system picked up the most recent copy of his mind and rebuilt him here."

The idea horrified me. "What we had here was a clone, then? An illegal copy? That's a Galactic Offense!"

Natasha shrugged. "Don't act outraged. You've performed a few Galactic crimes yourself. And remember that I might have a clone, too, out in the Zeta Herculis system. She's probably frozen or fried by now—but we might never know the truth."

For some reason, this kind of talk disturbed me. I guess I'd believed that I was the one and only true James McGill. That when I died and returned, it was more like I'd dreamed one life and awakened in another. But to accept that there were multiple copies of Claver running around—that dashed my universe to pieces.

"I've got to stop thinking about it," I said, sitting down and rubbing my temples.

Fortunately, a call came in from Imperator Turov that drove away everything else I'd been worrying about.

"McGill," she said, "report to me immediately."

"Sorry sir," I said, wincing.

"For what?"

"Sorry about Claver. We couldn't stop him from killing himself."

"I don't care about that. The ship that's been lurking around the system has made contact. I need you here immediately."

I got to my feet and headed to the door. It opened, and I took long strides toward the lift.

"On my way to the command module, sir," I said into my headset.

"No—come to tactical command. That's where I am."

I frowned. I hadn't even checked my tapper to locate her, but now that I did I saw she was indeed in tactical control.

"What's going on, Imperator?" I asked. "What do the Nairbs want?"

"It's not the Nairbs, James," she said. "It's not the Galactics, either. I need your help because you've talked to these people before. Get to my position. Turov out."

Alarmed, I clanked quickly toward tactical control. If the ship wasn't from the Empire, who could it be? What could Turov possibly mean by saying I'd talked to them before?

An answer formed in my mind that I didn't like—but which I felt in my heart had to be correct.

I picked up the pace, running full speed through the passages. Engaging my exoskeleton, I could barely control the pounding metal legs.

I crashed past a pair of light troopers, dashing them into the walls and shouting I was sorry—but I didn't slow down.

If I was right, there was no time to lose.

-37-

When I reached tactical control, Turov was waiting for me. The screen on the aft wall showed the situation clearly—she didn't have to say a word.

A looming figure filled the screen. It was alien and bulky. There was an indescribable aura of menace about the being. Something about the way its thick dark tentacles drifted and rasped the deck around it was menacing.

The being was a cephalopod—better known to the troops of legion Varus as a "space squid". I'd believed them all to be wiped out. A year back, I'd witnessed hell-burners falling on their ocean-covered world. The life there had been removed leaving it ready for what the Galactics called a "reseeding."

Every commanding officer we'd managed to revive thus far was present in fire control. Turov, Graves and even Leeson were there. No wonder they'd called for me. Except possibly for Turov herself, I couldn't think of three less capable diplomats. They were fighters—killers—but they hardly knew how to schmooze.

I looked at Turov, and her dark eyes returned my gaze steadily. I could tell she was scared but hiding it well. She looked too young to wear such a calculated expression.

"Specialist McGill," she said officiously. She waved toward the creature on her wall. "Meet Ambassador Glide—at least, that's how our translation systems have interpreted the meaning of his name."

"Your Excellency," I said, nodding to the image on the wall.

Turov flashed me a tiny smile. I knew that she was happy I'd responded diplomatically.

"Let me explain the situation," she said. "The Cephalopod warship in this system has come to visit us unannounced. Due to past associations and possible misunderstandings, they feel that they're technically at war with the Galactic Empire."

My eyes were as big around as boiled eggs by this time. The squid vessel was a warship? That meant the planet the Nairbs had burned away had to be a colony, not a homeworld. Further, the presence of a warship indicated they had to have another basis of operations in the area.

My mind jumped to conclusions. What if when we'd met up with the squids we'd made a terrible miscalculation? We'd assumed they were a single-planet species. In Frontier 921, multi-world civilizations were very rare. In fact, to the best of my knowledge, Earth with her lone small colony outpost on Zeta Herculis was the only level 2 civilization in the region.

Could all of that have been a mistake? Looking at the squid which so far had remained silent, I could see he was indeed in a ship built for his kind. There was a sloshing tank of water under his body, buoying him up. Cephalopods were amphibious but more at home in water than on land.

"It was only one of their colonies…" I said aloud.

Graves and Turov looked alarmed while Leeson squinted his eyes at me suspiciously.

"Specialist," Turov said loudly. "Let me explain why you're here. The Ambassador demanded to meet everyone who'd witnessed the events that occurred at Zeta Herculis, and refuses to believe only Graves here was aware of the details—"

The squid lifted a single thick tentacle and spoke. "Wait."

We all looked at him.

"Let the large being speak," the squid said. "I wish to follow its thought processes by sifting through its output directly."

Turov cast me a worried look. I was pretty sure she was already regretting giving me an invitation to her party.

"Very well," she said. "Explain yourself, McGill."

"I was just theorizing aloud," I said. "My apologies. I shouldn't have interrupted."

"You *have* interrupted," said the squid, "but that's immaterial as the proceedings thus far have been fruitless. Complete your statement, being."

"Uh...well, I was going to say that it all makes sense to me now. If you squids had one large spaceship back in the Zeta Herculis system, we should have known you might have more of them. Since you were capable of travel between local planets at speed, you might well have been capable of traveling between the stars as well."

"I see," the squid said. "Therefore, you have surmised that my race populates at least two worlds—and perhaps several."

"That now seems logical, sir."

The squid turned an accusatory pair of bulging eyes toward my officers. "Was this the nature of your miscalculation?" he demanded. "Has your underling put his appendage on the crux of the issue? Did simple incompetence drive you to believe you could strike with impunity against our kingdom?"

Turov stepped forward. "We ordered no strike against your people," she said firmly. "That was the Nairbs and Chief Inspector Xlur. They are direct representatives of the Empire."

"How then might your role in this matter be classified?" the squid demanded.

I had to speak up. Sometimes the urge just bubbles inside me. Ask anyone who's told me to shut up more than once—the list of such individuals is long and distinguished.

"We're mercenaries, Ambassador," I said.

The squid turned back toward me and lifted a tentacle higher. "That term—Ambassador—I've been unable to translate it until now. I'm not an Ambassador."

I had a few more choice names for him, but I managed to hold my tongue like the others who were staring nervously.

"If you're not an Ambassador, what are you?" Turov asked bluntly.

"I'm a Conqueror. It's my function to coordinate the enslavement of all beings that I meet."

Slavers, I thought. That figured. The first time I'd met up with the squids they'd had a ship full of altered humans. They'd treated them like slaves, too.

"Your fear is visible," the alien said, studying us. "This fact cools my flesh. There is no pleasure in subjugating beings that do not understand their peril."

"There is no need for violence," Turov said. "However, you should know that this ship is capable of defending herself."

The Cephalopod made a slashing gesture with his uplifted tentacle. "Nonsense. If you had effective weapons, you would have used them to destroy us upon detecting our entrance into this system. Instead, you've shown weakness at every turn. The orbital habitat nearby teems with life, but you do not control it. Instead, it has attacked your ship. This is clear evidence of pathetic weakness."

"We haven't struck the station because we value it. We wish to regain control of it—not destroy it."

"Ah!" boomed Glide. "You admit that you do not control the habitat? Excellent. Weakness, yet again. You've demonstrated it at every turn. I can scarcely believe such abject beings held back the full fury of the Cephalopods during our previous encounter."

"Listen, squid," I said. "We're quite capable of defending ourselves, but we should get one thing straight—we didn't bomb your world at Zeta Herculis. The Nairbs ran that ship, and they did it without asking our opinion of the action. Inspector Xlur must have ordered the attack."

"How do you know this?" the squid asked.

"I was there. I looked out the window as our ship rolled over. I watched the hell-burners drop—nine of them."

"Interesting. Your account matches perfectly with recordings transmitted from the colonists during their final moments. Let us assume for a moment that I believe you witnessed the genocide personally. What I find inexplicable is your repeated implicit claim that you're beings apart from the Galactics and their fading Empire. You've called yourself mercenaries. You've said you didn't order the strike. Neutrality? Rebellion? Do these terms describe your political status in regard to the Galactics?"

307

We all looked at Turov. I'd said enough—even I knew that.

She cleared her throat. "Yes," she said. "We're independent. We have dealings with the Empire, but our worlds aren't to be blamed for their actions."

I stared at her thinking over her words. She'd lied, of course. We were an active part of the Empire. Hell, we'd recently taken on the role of local Enforcers. By all rights we were obligated to repel this squid ship and protect the local population, but Turov wasn't interested in sticking her neck out. She rarely was.

"You place me in a difficult position," the squid said. "I'd hoped my decisions would be clarified by this communication, but instead you have muddied the waters further."

"We should take this opportunity to talk," Turov said. "We have no love for the Empire. We stand apart from it. You can gain much from our cooperation—from our gathered data."

Turov's words surprised me. She was selling out. Maybe she knew more about the situation than I did—but I doubted that.

As far as I could tell she was playing it safe. I had to agree with her move. After all, Earth was quite possibly at risk in this situation. Battle Fleet 921 was gone, called back to the Core Systems. On the other hand, the squids were here with a warship. Maybe it was their only one—or maybe they had a thousand more.

"I will consider your words, being," Conqueror Glide said. "Do not provoke us. Do not approach this ship. We will not allow it."

"I'm glad you haven't yet forced us to destroy your vessel," Turov said. "That would be unfortunate. Please answer a question, Glide. How many star systems are populated by your species?"

The squid's tentacles churned briefly. "We swim on many worlds. More than do your legged beasts—but not so many as are controlled by the Galactics."

Turov accepted this answer even though it was pretty vague. The squid had placed his Kingdom at somewhere between three and a million star systems in size.

"We invite you to talk to us again at a later date," Turov said.

"If it is convenient for us, we shall do so," said the squid, and the screen went dark.

Immediately the three officers let out a collective sigh and separated, shaking their heads.

"I told you we shouldn't have brought McGill to the party," Leeson said. "We were almost squid-meat."

"Adjunct Leeson," Turov said. "You're dismissed."

Leeson looked at her in surprise then at me. He left, shaking his head and muttering.

Graves studied the ship on a projected display of the system. "They're lingering in far orbit. Too bad *Minotaur* isn't a real battlecruiser. We could take them out quickly if we were geared for space-superiority. But *Minotaur* is more about troop-support than anything else. God only knows what kind of armament they have."

Turov turned to me. "McGill, you were undiplomatic as usual, but you did give the squid what it wanted to hear. Your description of the bombing convinced it you were a witness."

"Yeah," I said. "I hope that bought us some time. What's the plan, Imperator?"

She took the question very seriously. I could tell she'd been doing some hard thinking. Turov had always been a rank-climber, but this was different. This time it wasn't about glory—it was about survival for all of us.

"The truth is," she said thoughtfully, "Earth has been playing it by ear out here on the frontier, day by day, for better than a century. We've always lived at the sufferance of aliens even before the Galactics made contact—whether we knew it or not."

She walked to the console and worked the controls. The image of the squid ship Graves had been studying vanished. He threw her an annoyed glance, but she didn't notice. Probably she didn't care.

A vast swirl of stars appeared. There were many pinpoints of light and they all seemed to blend into a pinwheel shape.

"This is our galaxy," she said. "The Empire possesses most of the star systems partly because the center is so thick with stars. But there still exists a lot of unexplored territory past Earth, which is half-way out from the center to the edge. About a quarter of all the star systems in the Galaxy are outside the Empire's reach. Due to the realities of the central, older stars, many of these outlying systems are believed to be inhabited. We've clearly encountered a new hostile entity—what did the squid call his political body?"

"A kingdom, sir," I said.

"Right. A kingdom. Earth therefore is caught between an Empire of vast size, and a kingdom of unknown proportions. Let us assume for argument's sake they have colonized a hundred stars."

She used a stylus to light up an oval of stars past Earth's position farther out toward the rim of the galaxy. They lit up in red.

"Here we are with two lonely stars." She moved her fingers, and Sol lit up along with Zeta Herculis in green. Then she touched a contact and a massive number of stars glowed blue. The whole center of the Galaxy was blue—millions of stars.

"See?" she asked. "The Cephalopods are absurdly small in comparison to the Empire, but it doesn't matter as we are absurdly small in comparison to them. Encountering a new political entity full of hostile aliens has to be about the worst thing I can conceive of happening—especially when our own protectors are conspicuously absent. For all we know, our position is hopeless."

Graves was studying her map with interest. "Do you think it's that bad?"

"We have to assume that it is," she said.

I stepped closer. I didn't like what I saw. Our worlds consisted of a tiny pair of dots—like two discolored sand grains on a vast beach.

"We're like an egg placed between two boulders," Turov said, echoing my thoughts. "If these two behemoths start a fight, we'll be crushed in the first years of the conflict."

"The squids do seem to have a lot of guts," Graves said thoughtfully. "They clearly knew about the Empire when we first met them, which means they have scouts or at least active probes."

"I agree they must have had some idea what they were going up against—and yet they hit our ship *Corvus* anyway," Turov said thoughtfully. "To me, that alone indicates their kingdom is large enough to contemplate a border skirmish with the Empire."

"For them it was a question of either fighting, or submitting," Graves said. "Apparently, they thought they could stand against the Empire. I now believe they know what they're doing better than we do. We didn't know how greatly the Empire has weakened along the frontier—not until Inspector Xlur admitted it and made us local Enforcers. The squids *must* have spies, perhaps drones crawl among us even now. We have nothing."

"That's not entirely true," Turov said. "Hegemony knows more than they let on. What matters now, however, is that we make the wisest choice we can make at this critical juncture."

Graves turned to face her. "Imperator Turov, to that end I would like to formally request that you revive Tribune Drusus next. We need his insight."

"Insight? The last time he drew breath he was shot down like a dog by Claver. He didn't see that one coming."

"Maybe not. But he's a thinker. He's been on the frontier for more years than any of us."

Turov chewed that one over. She turned to me. "What do you think, James?"

Startled, I gave my head a shake. "I just want to do my job. Let me take a squad over there on a pinnace to stop the slaughter among the Tau. I can at least do that much. Maybe they can help us."

Turov snorted. "The Tau? Help? They'll try to collect a fee for allowing you to dock your pinnace. Or perhaps they'll sue us for violating licensing agreements with your altered holographic devices."

"Nevertheless, sir, I request that you let me go on the mission."

She looked at me for a moment then nodded. "Go. If the station is under some semblance of control, maybe the squids will think we're still dangerous."

I hurried out of the room before she could change her mind.

-38-

Natasha had a working model of her holographic reprograming device less than an hour later. Taking a squad of heavies—including Kivi and Carlos—we boarded a pinnace and flew toward the station.

We glided through space warily, watching for some kind of attack. I couldn't see the squid ship. It was far out in space lurking in a long, elliptical orbit around the planet.

"The station looks darker than it did last time I saw it from space," Natasha noted.

"You're right," I said. "A lot of the external power systems must have shut down. I hope the life support systems are still functioning."

"I studied the station's schematics before we left Earth. The life support units will be the last systems to shut down."

I thought about those giant machines, the ones down in the region known as the Vents. They were pretty low in the station's superstructure.

"If the bottom of the station begins to overheat—won't the life support modules shut down?" I asked.

Natasha looked at me worriedly and licked her lips. Then, she shook her head. "It's worse than that. If the bottom rim of the station touches the atmosphere, the pressure will tear the whole thing apart. It will be like dipping a spider web into a river—too much pressure and too much friction. The whole thing will start to come unraveled."

I nodded my head. "I get the picture. Well, we have to move fast, that's all."

Time crawled, and so did our pinnace. I thought the best approach would have been to rush in, engines flaring, do a spin at the last second, and land while blasting our engines hard and fast. Why give them the chance to see us coming and react to our move? Unfortunately, I wasn't the pilot.

We landed a few minutes later on the outer skin of the station. Clangs and thumps heralded our arrival. I heard the hiss of escaping gasses.

"That's it," I told my team. "Magnetize your boots and check your power readings. We're walking the rest of the way in. Remember, Natasha is our queen bee on this mission. If she's in trouble, throw your life away to save her or there's no point to any of this."

"Easy for you to say, McGill," Kivi complained.

I glanced at her but didn't respond. I figured she was still a little peeved at me for events that had occurred long ago. Mentally, I shrugged. She could hate me if she wanted to as long as she followed orders.

We unloaded, grunting and struggling to climb out of the airlock and clank out onto the hull. Open space yawned to my left and to my right the blue-white-gray arc of the planet stretched wide. It felt like I was going to fall off and never stop falling. It didn't help to know that we were very close to doing just that.

After our navigational systems got their bearings, they led us to a maintenance hatch. We tried to open it, but it wouldn't budge.

"McGill?" Natasha said. "I think it's been welded shut—from the inside."

"Great."

I came over to her and knelt awkwardly. Carlos and I both applied our exoskeletons and strained on the wheel-like door handle.

"On three!" I shouted. Both of us roared, grunting and straining. Our boots slipped, and we braced them against nearby struts. About twenty seconds passed—and then we heard a terrible screeching grind.

"That's it!" Carlos shouted. "We did it!"

I lifted the circular door handle up into space. It came free in my hands and floated there. "We sure did," I said, tossing the wheel away. "We broke it clean off."

Everyone groaned and complained. I went to look for another hatch. We soon found one, about two hundred meters higher up on the hull of the station. It was welded shut, as well.

"We're screwed," Carlos complained, bumping along behind me. "We're totally screwed. Ridiculous, that's what we are. Absolutely absurd. The Tau shitheads who did this are probably inside watching on security cams and having themselves a belly laugh."

"I doubt it," I said. "They don't seem to be big on humor. Especially not when they're wearing their rebel colors. Stand clear—I've got an idea."

Carlos threw himself backwards with comic frantic motions. "Everyone run! McGill's up to something! We're all gonna die—again!"

I chuckled, unlimbering something I'd brought along in my kit. It was a short-barreled weapon with a tip of fused metal.

"Is that one of those lightning things? The ones the Tau brought—"

Carlos broke off because instead of answering him I unleashed a bolt of energy with the weapon, scorching the second hatch we'd failed to open. The blow-back wasn't that bad, but the jolt of current that came up from the hull into my boots and into my toes hurt.

"Shit!" screeched Carlos, hopping from foot to foot. "You buzzed me! You crazy mother—!"

I gave a little hop, allowing myself to float above the surface of the hull and squeezed the trigger again. The weapon blazed into life. This time, I held it down until the power bar registered empty and the blazing arc of blue-white electricity died to a few sparks.

"You bastard," Carlos said, clumping up close to me. He had to crank back his head to look up at me. "My feet feel like they're numb and my teeth hurt."

I pointed toward the smoking hole below me. The center of the hatch had been burned clean through.

"Stop complaining and stick your arm in there. You should be able to blow the hinges."

Grumbling, he did as I asked. Meanwhile, Natasha threw me a line and I reeled myself back in.

"You could have fried us with that stunt," she complained. "Or at least yourself."

"Yeah," I said. "But we don't have much time. If we can't get into the station, we're as good as dead anyway."

A few minutes later we had the smoldering hatch pried open. We wriggled into an airlock and then the passages beyond. Fortunately, there wasn't any resistance.

After following a labyrinth of tunnels, we found our way out onto the deserted streets. The first sign of enemy activity we saw came from a large gang that roved along at street level smashing air car windows and tipping over anything they could. They seemed to be having a good time.

The second they caught sight of us, however, their demeanor changed. They froze as one and turned in our direction. I'd seen this behavior before. They were going to charge us.

"Turn it on, Natasha," I said.

"It *is* on," she hissed back.

"Well, it's not frigging working!" Carlos shouted unnecessarily.

"It might take some time—" I began, but Carlos already had his rifle out and up.

I smashed it down. "Hold your fire! That's an order!"

"Are you crazy? We'll all be permed!"

"No we won't," I said with a confidence I didn't feel. "Natasha is relaying our data. We'll catch a revive on *Minotaur* if—"

That was all the time the gang of around three hundred rebels gave me. They charged us in a silent wave. They'd seen something unlike themselves, homed in on it, and decided as a single mass mind to make their move.

"Behind us!" screeched Kivi.

I turned in her direction. Another mass of rebels—bigger than the first group—had come around the corner. Maybe

316

that's what the first group had been waiting for, I'll never know.

All of them charged us from two sides. With a greedy, careless thirst for blood, they were so eager to reach us they knocked one another down and trampled their own comrades.

I'd seen this behavior before. Their very disregard for their own safety made them more dangerous. Fortunately, I didn't see any advanced weaponry on them. These were average citizens converted into raving lunatics by Claver's digital virus.

"All right," I shouted as they came in close. "Force-blades out. If they get in melee range—you can take them out."

"So very considerate of you, McGill!" Carlos said bitterly.

We braced ourselves, putting our backs together in a circle. Our force-blades shimmered and extended in deadly lines from our arms. I made sure Natasha and her device were in the center. The box she'd been babying since we'd left *Minotaur* buzzed and glowed—but judging by the enemy approach, it wasn't doing much.

"Hold them!" I shouted. "Hold the line!"

The wave of bodies lashed us like a torrent of water. Even inside my armor, I was rocked backward. Rebels launched themselves overhead, diving over the bodies of their comrades as I cut them down.

I made an effort to stop those that were trying to climb over us to the center. I couldn't afford to have them take out Natasha. That wasn't as easy as it sounded because bodies were piling up fast and the latest group to arrive climbed over the fallen, up and up to where they almost slid over our helmets into the circle.

Maybe they *knew*, I thought. *How could they know?*

The line broke a moment later. I don't know who failed me—it didn't matter. Someone tripped or slid on blood and entrails. They went down, and there was a hole in the circle.

I stabbed and slashed, shortening down my blades to a half-meter and thickening them up. I tried to shuffle toward the breach, to close it, but I could barely move. There were so many squirming bodies all around me, living and dead, I was locked into place.

317

"They're on me, James!" I heard Natasha say in despair. "They've got a hold on the box!"

My heart sank. We were all going to die, crushed down by a thousand raving lunatics. What a way to go.

Then, something changed. I don't quite know how I knew it—but the sensation was undeniable.

"They're slowing down," Carlos said. "They're running out of gas. You guys are going to pay!"

"Don't!" shouted. "If they try to get away, let them!"

Hansen was down. So was Gorman. As team leader, my helmet had automatically presented me with printed names around the bottom rim of my faceplate, which was now starred from impacts. Seven names were red, indicating they'd been pulled down and killed. The rest were still green, including Natasha's.

"They're crawling away!" Kivi said. "Let's kill them before they regroup!"

"No!" I roared. "Let them go. That's an order."

Soon, the fight was over. We were left with a mound of bodies ten feet high. We had to climb out of there on our hands and knees with dead people shifting under us and sliding away under the weight of our banged-up armor.

When at last we could see the artificial sky again, we gazed in dull amazement.

The rebels were standing nearby—but they looked different. They weren't maroon and silver anymore. They were slate-gray. Like living granite statues sculpted into the shape of humanoids, they were everywhere, standing around in confusion.

"People of Tau Ceti," I said loudly, projecting my voice through a microphone in my suit. "Listen to me, you've been freed!"

They looked from one to another aghast and dazed.

"We need your help," I said. "You must walk among your own kind. Sneak upon them. Hug your loved ones. Free them as we freed you. Your projectors will pass on the cure, and you will all be saved."

They ignored me and backed away. They dripped with gore from their fallen comrades. They gazed in fear and disbelief from one to another.

"They're freaked out," Carlos said. "Too scared to help."

"Maybe it will work anyway," Natasha said. "The virus I put into their holo-suits will infect anyone they come into contact with—but it will take time."

"That's not good enough," I said, wading through corpses toward the retreating citizens. "You have to work with us," I shouted after them. "Stop!"

The man nearest me paused and studied me. "What do you offer us in return, Earth man?" he asked.

I shook my head and snorted in disbelief. "Life!" I shouted. "Liberty! You'll get your city back."

He shook his head. "Get someone else. If I help, I'll die. No one will aid you without benefit."

"You'll die anyway," I told him. "The only way you'll live is if you cooperate!"

He shook his head and turned to go. "You don't understand us. I would help if I thought others would—but I know they won't. It is not our way. I'll look for a way down to the surface."

I stood there, aghast. The plan had worked. The solution was in my grasp—but these people were too damned greedy and selfish to do anything for their fellows.

Watching them walk away, I had to question my efforts today. Maybe they weren't worth the effort after all.

"That's so typical," Carlos complained as the citizens of Tau wandered away to find somewhere to hide.

I looked at him and narrowed my eyes. "Give me your Imperial coins, Carlos," I said.

He appeared startled. "What? What are you talking about—?"

I grabbed him, and a force-blade extended in my hand. "Give them to me—all of them. I know you've got them. People told me."

Carlos' eyes went to Kivi. "Damn you girl," he said.

319

I grinned. I'd had no idea whether Carlos had stolen any of the credits or not, but I'd figured it was a pretty good chance he had. Now, my suspicions had been confirmed.

"It serves you right," Kivi said. "But I didn't tell him shit."

I looked at her. "Yours too. They'll just get you permed in the end. Hand them over."

Grumbling, the two of them gave me about a hundred coins. I had a suspicion that wasn't all of them, but I figured it would probably be enough.

"A thousand Imperial credits for each of you paid in cold hard cash!" I shouted at the retreating Tau. "Get back here!"

The effect was dramatic. Not just a few of them stopped—they all did. Even the women, the elderly and the injured stopped. They did a collective U-turn and crept back in my direction cautiously.

I held up an Imperial credit piece which was as golden and lustrous as their illusory clothing was drab.

"Here it is!" I boomed. "One coin now and another when this crisis is over. Give your IDs to Natasha. Your claims will be made good."

We got nearly a hundred recruits. I ran out of coins and was unable to convert any more of them into evangelists.

There was one thing that was good about the natural avarice of the Tau as a people. They were industrious and reliable—as long as they were paid.

"It's like the biggest union shop in the galaxy," Carlos laughed as they lined up and took their coins.

"It's not enough," Natasha said.

I looked at her. "Why not?"

She shrugged. "A hundred people trying to convert a few others? They'll do it—but just enough to get paid. Then they'll hole up again. They won't risk themselves once the money runs out. And we don't have enough coins to bribe everyone on the station."

Nodding, I thought that one over for a second. The answer seemed obvious. I walked forward and waved my arms. Turning on my external speakers, I used my booming amplified voice to cut through their chatter.

More than anything, I was surprised by their lack of concern over the mound of dead that lay just a few feet away in the street. Seeing their own kind heaped up in mass death alarmed them—but it didn't sicken them or make them mourn as it would have a human population. These people were truly alien in their thinking.

"I have a further proposition," I shouted. "For every ten Tau you convert and turn into new supporters, you'll get an additional coin."

There was a whispering of excitement around me.

"No limits?" demanded the first guy I'd recruited. "There are millions here. Surely, you can't have that many coins."

He was suspicious, and rightfully so. I'd pretty much wiped out my supply of coins already.

"There *is* a limit," I said, doing some quick calculations in my head. "Tell your people they will have to work for you. You will share in their profits. They'll get half the amount— and the man below him will get half that, a quarter of the original bounty."

The man I'd talked to glared. "That's less than a credit after ten people in the chain."

"Yes," I said. "But what do you care? You'll get *their* credits! Thousands and thousands of people will be paying up the line into your pockets!"

The light of greed returned. I wasn't just offering them a fee now, I was offering to make them rich off the backs of others who toiled underneath them for less.

"Who will pay this debt when it is accrued?" several of them demanded.

"I'll give you a name, a rich business man by the name of Adjunct Claver. Perhaps you've heard of him."

They looked from one to the next quizzically, but one man had heard of Claver's exploits.

"It's true," he said. "I heard that man stole millions of credits from the central banks."

"Then get out there!" I roared. "What are you waiting for? If you don't think I have enough money, you should be working fast to get your share before I run out!"

That was it. They split up and rushed in every direction. There was new energy in their step as they raced down every street hurrying to do my bidding.

"How will you pay them all?" Natasha said, coming to stand by me.

I shrugged. "There are a lot of credits in their banks. And I bet if we shake down some of these Germanica pukes, they'll jingle with looted coins."

Carlos walked up shaking his head. "Don't be fooled," he told Natasha. "He has no intention of paying any of them. That's McGill in a nutshell. He sets up a pyramid scheme, gets these poor losers running around in circles thinking they'll get rich—then stiffs the lot of them."

Laughing, I had to agree with him. Carlos knew me too well.

"Does it matter?" I asked them. "They'll get their station back. They'll live to start again. I came here to save their greedy asses, and they can damn well help out with the job."

"I thought the station was probably doomed," Carlos said.

"I believe in these people," I said firmly. "They built this place, and there's a serious profit to be made if they can repair it. Let's see if they're up to the task of helping themselves. It's all up to them now."

No one argued about that. When the last of the gray figures vanished from the streets heading to meet the rebels wherever they could find them, we turned around and headed for the pinnace again. We'd done what we could, whether it worked or not.

-39-

Nothing spreads like a digital virus. By the time we boarded the pinnace and cast off, the Tau we had liberated had infected over three thousand of their comrades within hours. The next generation spread the effect much further. The rival projectors had no immunity to Natasha's virus, and it was overwriting Claver's original scripting like wildfire.

"They'll retake Gelt Station within a few days," she said. "And at that point, they'll want payment."

I waved her words away. "Then Claver had better have a lot of cash saved up," I said. "That's all I have to say. He's going to need it when they track him down."

Carlos produced a nasty laugh. "That's good. That's really good, McGill. If anyone needs a good screwing, it's that guy. Speaking of which, what's this I heard about you and our lovely Imperator Turov?"

I froze. Then the smile on my face slowly melted. If there was anything on this world Carlos was good for, it was exposing a man's weakness. He could kick you when you were up—or down. This time, his foot had landed hard upon my backside.

Knowing I shouldn't do it, I glanced around to see who had heard his comment. Only Natasha and Kivi were staring at me. No one else seemed to have noticed—but of course, they were the people who mattered.

I gave Carlos a death stare. He grinned in return.

"So it's *true*?" he asked, giving a little war-whoop of amusement. "I was just fishing, I swear it. I had no idea. Sure, I'd heard about you going to drink with her, and you waking up on the pool table—what a laugh. You must have been drunk out of your ever-loving mind. Did you shit yourself, too? That would cap it all off—"

I punched him. Here we were, two men who'd just fought to the death, back to back, standing against an overwhelming horde of insane Tau—but it didn't matter. I wanted to kill him and close his fat mouth permanently.

Carlos wasn't as big as I was, but he'd always been able to take a punch. He was one of those guys who are hard to take out. I think his skull must be about an inch thick.

Snarling, he punched me back, and it was on. Most of those around us had no idea what was wrong, but they'd seen us get into it before. They backed up to give us what room they could on the crowded pinnace.

Rage was on my side. I pinned him after about thirty seconds. Our sides heaving, he spat out a tooth and gave me a bloody scowl.

"Was she *that* good?" he demanded. "Is all this just to defend her honor? Have you forgotten everything she's done? What's happened to you, man?"

The fight drained out of me then. I got up, sighing, and went to sit apart from the others. I wasn't defending Turov. I was embarrassed, that's all.

In a way, I couldn't blame Carlos for gossiping in public. I'd slept with the woman, not him. Legion Varus was a pretty tight-knit group. We had plenty of secrets as far as outsiders were concerned, but inside the legion itself everyone heard about everything eventually. If I hadn't wanted people to know about it, if I hadn't wanted people to have a good laugh—then I shouldn't have done it.

The rest of the trip back to *Minotaur* I didn't talk to the others. I'd been humiliated. Turov was something of a demon in our group. Instead of lying with her being seen as an accomplishment, the others saw my transgressions as something low and degrading. I wasn't used to that, and I hadn't reacted well.

When we docked up and exited the ship, I was the last one to climb out of the airlock.

Kivi was waiting for me when I got out onto the hangar deck. Our eyes met. I expected her to laugh out loud or to scold me, but she didn't do either.

"What happened, James?" she asked. "Did she make you do it?"

I blinked in surprise. "Uh...not exactly."

"I know she has a lot of baggage to hang over your head. She sentenced you to be permed, for God's sake. I know about that part by the way—we all do. Did you romance her to get her to drop the sentence?"

I shook my head. "I don't know what happened," I admitted. "We fought hard, lived through a battle, and afterward we felt like having a drink while the revival machine pumped out fresh troops."

She stared at me for several long seconds. Then her face darkened. "So, you're telling me you really *are* some kind of man-whore?"

"Come on, Kivi," I said. "You've died, haven't you?"

"Of course I have."

"That's right, and I've watched you do it plenty of times. Sometimes we live, sometimes we die and come back. Either way, it rattles our minds. Haven't you come out of a tough fight and felt like celebrating? Sometimes sex is just a way of dealing with a bad situation."

Kivi sucked in a deep breath and sighed. "Okay," she said. "I know what you're talking about. I know that feeling. It's just that...*Turov*? How could you? She's such a witch. She's so *mean*. I can't visualize you doing this act—even if she did come back all young and cute again. That part is totally unfair, by the way. She should never have come back young again. It's wrong."

I didn't quite know what to say, so I said nothing and started walking again. Kivi fell into step beside me.

"So..." she said. "If it wasn't some kind of sexual payoff—how did you convince her to let you off the hook? She had you convicted and ready to be permed."

"I saved her," I said. "I revived her first, and then we fought hard together. I think she liked that."

Kivi punched my arm. I didn't feel it, but my armor rattled.

"Don't be fooled," Kivi warned me. "Just because she had a weak moment with you—that means nothing. Her personality is poison. She'll turn right back into the snake she's always been."

I knew she was probably right, and I nodded. But part of me hoped Kivi was wrong. Experiences *did* change people. Physically, Turov wasn't the same person she'd been before she'd died. So many years of aging had been lost, and an old mind in a young body wasn't entirely old anymore. I knew youth had to be battling against experience within her. If I'd been a psychologist, it might have been an interesting experiment to watch play out.

After talking with Kivi, I felt better. At least there was one person who didn't hate me for what I'd done.

Graves demanded my report after I reached 3rd Unit's module. I gave it pridefully. I described the battle in the streets and reported the deaths I'd recorded on my tapper.

"Sir," I concluded, "I think the mission has to be considered a success. Installing the virus took longer than we expected, and we had to do it while in very close proximity with active hostiles. However, I managed to improvise and get the locals to spread it from here on. Now all we've got to do is wait."

Graves nodded thoughtfully. "Too bad it didn't come sooner. Events have progressed, and I don't think there's any way to turn back now. Unfortunate."

I frowned. "What are you talking about, sir?"

"Never mind. Why don't you head up to see the Imperator? She specifically requested that you report to her in person." Graves looked at me, deadpan. Was there a hint of amusement in his eyes? I felt a hot rush of embarrassment.

"Uh...okay, sir. Thank you."

"Dismissed, McGill."

He turned away, giving his head a shake. I left his office feeling uncertain what he was thinking. He'd hinted that my mission hadn't concluded quickly enough. I hoped that didn't have anything to do with the fact the station was still sinking into the atmosphere. Had we made a herculean effort only to find we were a day late?

Trying to push such thoughts out of my head, I hurried to the lift and rode up to Imperator Turov's office. I was greeted at the door by an armed MP—a Veteran. He looked at me and my sidearm with displeasure.

"I think I should hold onto that for you, Specialist," the MP said.

I frowned and put my hand over my gun. "I don't think so. Not this time."

Another voice interrupted our discussion which was about to become heated.

"Let him have it, Sullivan," Imperator Turov said. She'd come out of her door to see what was going on.

I couldn't get over how young-sounding she was now. She turned and vanished back into her office, and I followed. I resisted an urge to grin at the MP. I'd gotten myself into enough trouble lately.

The door swished shut behind me. I looked around, but didn't see any armed men ready to jump me. I tried to relax, but failed.

"You wanted to see me, sir?"

"Yes, Specialist," she said. "Could you come over here and help me?"

"Help you with what, sir…?"

I trailed off, as the answer to my question was immediately obvious. She was opening her uniform.

My jaw hung low as more skin was revealed with each passing second.

"Sir…?" I asked. "I'm not sure this is an appropriate time—"

"Shut up and pull this over my head. Or do I have to do everything myself?"

I heaved a sigh. She turned around and kept stripping down. I felt my pulse rate increase.

"This isn't really fair, sir," I said.

She looked over her bare shoulder and laughed. "Are you kidding me? Are you trying to tell me you're an innocent? I'm not pulling rank. I'm not ordering you to do this. I'm just feeling....I don't know, *different*, since my revival. I haven't felt this kind of hormonal rush in years."

"No, I didn't mean that. I mean it's not fair to display yourself so brazenly in front of a man. We can't always do the right thing when we're faced with this kind of temptation."

She stared at me with a mix of confusion and growing irritation.

"What is this crap?" She demanded, mostly naked now. "You go around screwing everything that moves, McGill, and now suddenly you're a boy scout?"

"Well, it's not like that. People...people already suspect, sir. They know about what happened the other night between us."

"Ah," she said, stepping out of her shoes. She strutted toward me around her desk.

My heart began to pound. She was buck-naked and looking great. Her steps were like those of a dancer—lithe and graceful.

"I get it," she said, touching my cheek with a single finger. "Your friends are making fun of you. They're calling you names like boy-toy, is that it?"

"Hardly, sir."

"Stop calling me sir, dammit!"

"Yes sir—uh, Galina. You see? Right there—this is kind of weird. You're a high level officer. I'm just one step above a grunt."

"What? Are you bargaining for rank already? Forget it. You're not getting such perks that easily."

I rolled my eyes. "This isn't—"

She kissed me then, full on the mouth. She pressed herself up against me, and I almost grabbed her.

"Get out of that damned armor," she hissed at me. "I can only touch your face."

I realized I had the power to walk out on her. I didn't have to put up with this. I could turn around, hit the door, and step outside. Maybe the MP would see his commander naked, and maybe he wouldn't, but either way I'd escape and I doubted Imperator Galina Turov would ever try tackling me again. Oh, she might crap on me and give me a hard time—what else was new? But she wouldn't risk a second humiliation.

Scorning her would come with a price, of course. She'd be pissed—probably for life. But I was considering it seriously. I swear it. I really was.

Then she did something dirty. She popped off my gauntlet and placed my hand on her bare skin. I lost it then. Her flesh was warm and smooth and urgent.

What was I thinking as we stripped off my armor together and got busy on her desk? I don't know. I don't think men have complex thoughts at moments like these. If they do think, they probably aren't enjoying themselves as much as they should be.

Imperator Turov and I didn't hold back. If anything, our second time was more intense than the first had been. Our passion was brief, but thorough. I had to wonder afterward if Turov had developed a thing for me over the years. Maybe it was only now, in her new, young body, that she had the self-confidence to demand my attentions. Whatever her motivations were, her seduction had definitely worked.

Leaning back in a chair, I sighed heavily and pulled my armor back on. While I did so, Galina watched me with predatory eyes. I could tell the smirk on her face was one of satisfaction.

I didn't much care what kind of fantasies of domination and triumph were going on inside her little head. I'd had a good time, and I figured that since everyone in the legion knew about us, it didn't make much difference anyhow.

"Sir?" I asked as I completed snapping up my kit. She was dressed now, too. That was a shame, but I couldn't have everything.

"What is it, Specialist?"

"I heard something odd from Graves. He indicated the success of my mission had come too late—that it was too bad I hadn't managed to cure the Tau earlier. Do you know what he's talking about?"

"No. But the recovery of systems has been unexpectedly good. The station is rising again, slowly. I underestimated what they could do to help themselves. The Tau themselves are

329

repairing their station with uncharacteristic energy. I'm surprised by that—there's no budget for the repairs, after all. They're working together as if they expect a huge payoff. Mysterious."

I frowned, thinking of my pyramid scheme. Could it have gone that far? I squirmed in my seat. "What was Graves talking about then?" I asked.

Her eyes dipped down to her desk then raised back up to meet mine. "We were contacted again, James. By the Cephalopods. While you were on the station, fighting—I had to make a hard decision, and I made it."

Frowning, I leaned forward. "Could you be more clear, sir?"

"They delivered an ultimatum to us about two hours ago."

"What kind of ultimatum, sir?"

"They demanded payment for their losses at Zeta Herculis. They said they would hold humanity personally responsible if we didn't agree. It was an unfortunate situation, and I have to admit at the time I didn't think your scheme was going to work. You have to understand that, James."

Our eyes met, and she stared at me with cold concern. I frowned. I wasn't getting it yet, but what I *was* getting I didn't like at all.

"What did you do?" I demanded.

"That's not an appropriate tone, James—"

"Come on," I said. "Not appropriate? You just jumped my bones right here on this desk—"

"Threatening my reputation won't gain you anything," she said dangerously.

I laughed incredulously. "Just tell me what you did—what was the nature of this ultimatum?"

"The Cephalopods are an intransigent race. They demanded material restitution for their losses on their colony world. Keep in mind, the Nairbs did burn their entire colony down to the bedrock."

"Yeah," I said, "but what did you give them?"

"The station."

330

We stared at one another. My sweat and hers was mingling and cooling on our bodies, and I could still smell her hair in my nostrils, but I felt cold nonetheless.

"You gave them the *station*? Are they going to haul it off to their homeworld or what?"

She shook her head slowly. "They're looting it. They're docking up now I would expect. They'll board with their slavers and their regular troops. They'll round up the people they want as captives and take whatever else they can find before it sinks down into the atmosphere and burns up."

"I thought you said the repairs were working."

"They are," she said, shrugging. "But I expect that attacking and pillaging the structure will disrupt that process."

"Are you totally insane?"

"James," she said sternly. "I understand you're feeling emotional about this topic as you just fought to save the Tau, but try to see it from my perspective. The Cephalopods may well have the power to wipe out Earth. Battle Fleet 921 might come back next year and wipe them out in return—but then again, it might take decades. I can't risk our species to save a few million Tau."

I nodded slowly. I did see her way of thinking—at least partially.

"You figured I would fail," I said. "And that the Tau were as good as dead and bat-shit crazy. Is that it? You might as well get some mileage out of them. Maybe they'll even kill a few squids for good measure. Damn, what a way to serve and protect."

"Rudely put—but essentially, you're correct."

For several seconds, I sat there staring into space. Turov kept on talking about something, but I didn't hear her. Finally, after those seconds passed, I stood up.

Galina's eyes widened involuntarily. My movement had been purposeful, and I was armed and wearing battle armor again. I realized then what she must have understood in that moment—that I could tear her apart with my gauntlets if I wanted to.

But I didn't attack her. I was upset, but taking it out on her wasn't going to change anything.

331

"Sir," I said loudly. "Am I dismissed?"

She looked at me for a second and nodded. "Dismissed, Specialist."

I left her then, clanking on my way out. The MP outside looked up at me and gave me a smirk. I wanted to bash him one—but I held myself back. I was on a new mission now, and nothing was going to get in my way.

Nothing.

-40-

I didn't think I could manage my plan without help, so I headed down to 3rd Unit's module and stepped into the common room. Everyone looked up when I appeared in the doorway. A few of them shouted greetings, but most were quiet. A few got up and left immediately—not a good sign.

Spotting Natasha, I walked toward her. She avoided my eyes and got up, packing away a pile of equipment.

"Is that your buzzer control system?" I asked her.

She glanced at me, and then looked at the deck. "I've got to go."

"Uh..." I said, looking around.

Grins met me, mixed with a few frowns. Some people snickered. I began to suspect the worst.

Natasha tried to slip past me, but I reached out and clasped her wrist. Women hate that, but this was an emergency.

"Let go of me, James," she said, still not looking at me.

"Listen for one second—Turov has sold them out. She's letting everyone on the station die."

Natasha finally looked at me. "What?"

I quickly explained what I was talking about. She seemed conflicted.

"There's nothing we can do," she said. "I'm leaving."

"Look," I told her quietly. "I have a plan. It might work. But I need your help. I need my friends."

"I'm not doing anything for you."

333

I looked over her shoulder at what she was holding. It *was* her buzzer equipment.

"You've been spying on me, haven't you?" I asked.

"It doesn't matter."

"Well, apparently it does to you. Let's forget about whatever it was you saw with your spy-bugs. People are about to be permed—millions of them. They might be annoying aliens, but I don't think they deserve to be enslaved and slaughtered wholesale."

Natasha let out her breath until she looked deflated. She sat down quickly. "Just tell me what you want to do, James."

I told her, and she didn't look any happier.

"Are you *crazy?*" she demanded in a harsh whisper.

"I get that a lot."

"We can't take over the ship!"

"We won't have to—at least, I hope not."

"James, there are four full units revived now. Not just a few people will stand in your way, hundreds will. There's the Germanica Unit, too. They're back to full strength."

"Yeah, well…I know about them."

"That's not all. Turov had them revive both the Tribunes— Drusus and Armel."

"Really? That does change things. Wait for me here, and work on those calculations."

"You think you can just order me around?" she demanded. "You didn't even ask if I would help or not."

"Well? Will you?"

"We could get permed."

"People are getting permed back on the station right now."

"They aren't *people* James—not exactly."

I frowned at her. "Look, the Tau are a lot friendlier than the squids. If Claver hadn't set them off with his holo-box virus, they would still be peacefully selling everyone their gizmos. Instead we abused them thoroughly, and now we're letting the squids have a turn."

Natasha winced, knowing I was right. "All right," she said. "I'll see what I can cook up."

"Thanks," I said. "I can't promise you won't regret it, but it's the right thing to do."

I slid the key across the table, and she took it quickly. She stood up and headed for her workshop. She looked like a condemned woman heading up the steps to the guillotine.

Heading in the opposite direction, I caught up with Carlos in the rec room.

"Oh, no," he said, catching sight of me. "Just forget it. Don't even start with me."

"What are you talking about?"

"I don't know, and I don't want to know. Whatever you just pulled on Natasha, save it. I don't want to hear a word."

Frowning, I approached him anyway. He was standing in the null-grav zone ready to exercise with nothing on but a skin-tight smart-cloth suit.

"Mind if I join you?" I asked.

"I sure as hell do mind."

I shed my outer gear and joined him anyway. There were a few others in the room as we drifted and dragged ourselves along the ceiling using rings bolted there for the purpose, but they were out of earshot and making too much noise to listen.

"Carlos, I need your help."

"No you don't. You need a psychiatrist."

I gave him the short version concerning the Tau and their predicament. Oddly enough, the story struck him as funny.

"You're kidding me?" he asked. "These heartless bastards have been sold to the squids as *slaves*? That's irony at its best."

"No it isn't," I said, becoming annoyed. "Well, yeah, maybe it is. But it's not just ironic. It's tragic. These are people we came here to protect. Now, we've sold them out to the squids."

"Better them than us, brother."

I could tell I was going to have to take an entirely different approach to get Carlos to help me. Pulling on his heartstrings was hopeless.

"Let's try to take the long view," I said. "What do you think the squids will do next?"

"I don't know. Maybe they'll fart around in this system plundering it long enough to get the attention of the Galactics. Then, hopefully, the Core Systems will send back our fleet and rip off a few trillion of their tentacles. It'll be calamari time!"

"Yeah," I said, "that might be how it goes. What do you think the Galactics will do when they see how their new enforcers wimped out?"

Carlos frowned. "Um...they aren't going to like that."

"No. The Nairbs will have a special crime on their books for it—you know they will."

"Yeah. It will all be our fault somehow. They left us in charge."

I was nodding. He was following along and I thought I might almost have him in the bag.

We'd warmed up on the rings and now glided into the sparring pit. This amounted to a spherical cage. Once the door slammed shut, we began to wrestle. This is harder than it sounds in null-G. We went into one spinning, grunting clinch after another, but neither of us could pin the other.

"Let's try another hypothetical," I said, straining. "What if the Galactics *don't* come back? How will it play out then?"

Carlos disengaged and I let him. He looked even less happy.

"That will really suck," he said. "The squids are ruthless. They'll come for Earth after a while and take us out. We'll be the next slave race on their menu. They already like to catch and breed our kind—it would be a natural for them."

"Exactly," I said, and the more I thought about it, the more I realized I was talking myself into action as much as I was talking him into it.

"We're damned if we do and damned if we don't," Carlos said, doing a flip and floating down to the floor.

"No," I said. "We're damned if we don't do anything no matter whether the Galactics come back or not."

He climbed out of the sparring cage, and I followed him.

Carlos looked at me. "What do you want to do, then? Besides screw our coldhearted Imperator?"

I let his comment slide with difficulty. "We've got to knock out the squids."

He shook his head and snorted. "Just like that?"

"Yes."

Seeing I was serious, he floated closer and lowered his voice. "Just go to Turov. Butter her up, if you know what I mean. Get her to see reason. We'll hit the squids just as they unload into the station. That's got to be the moment."

"I tried that already," I said. "She wasn't listening."

Carlos smirked. "So it's true, then? I heard it from the MPs, but I didn't believe it."

"What?" I asked, my heart sinking.

"They said you and Turov had another little meeting. Right there in her office? You are insatiable—like a goat, I mean."

I launched myself at him, and we locked arms. We went into a spin. Others watched, laughing. It had to be a comical scene.

"Let go or we'll land bad," Carlos said, gritting his teeth.

"No," I said. "Fifty-fifty, you'll be on the bottom. I'll take my chances."

We struggled in a clinch, and crashed into a wall. Unfortunately, it was my back and skull that took the brunt of the impact.

"All right," Carlos said, drifting away and breathing hard. "I'll help. But first, you've got to tell me about Turov. What's the deal between you two? Is this becoming a habit? I don't know if I can take that."

"What do you mean, take it?" I asked, rubbing the back of my head. Blood wet my finger.

"Making love to a lady more than once changes everything," Carlos told me. "That officially makes this an *affair* not just a random event, McGill."

"The second time makes it an affair, huh? At what point does she turn into an actual girlfriend?"

"I don't know...tenth time, I guess."

I shook my head. "I bow to the expert. You know it all, don't you Carlos?"

This made him angry. A lot of things make Carlos angry, but any reference to his relative lack of success with women always did the trick.

"If you can't beat them, then screw them, is that it?" Carlos demanded. "That's your policy isn't it, McGill? And don't lie to me—everyone knows what you've been doing with Turov. *Everyone*."

337

"Is my policy such a bad one?" I asked. "Sort of like 'make love, not war.'"

"Yeah, sure... You disgust me."

"Only because you aren't as good at the game as I am."

Throwing his hands up, Carlos traveled hand-over hand to the exit and left the chamber. He slammed the door on the way out. I was just as happy to see him go. How could someone be selfish and judgmental at the same time? I didn't get that. I was plenty selfish too, I'd be the first to admit that. But at least I didn't go around giving everyone else I met a lecture on how to behave.

Cursing, I remembered I had to have his help. I dragged myself over the rattling rings to the exit and followed him.

"I talked, and you promised to help if I did," I said when I caught up to him.

"I know. I'm heading for the armory, aren't I?"

"This isn't going to be like that. Get on a light suit—with a good seal."

He eyed me, shaking his head. "I don't like this plan already. Why can't we just go in with our guns hot?"

"Because we don't want to be fried for it afterward, that's why."

He grumbled, but he listened. We got into light suits and wore nothing but air tanks and helmets. No sidearms—no weapons at all.

Natasha met us out in the hallway. "Graves might be getting suspicious," she told me. "He's ordering a full roll call at 1700."

"We'll have to move fast. What have you got?"

She handed each of us a grenade. They weren't shrapnel grenades. They were silvery canisters about the size and shape of a beer can.

"You pull the ring on the top and toss them close. Not much range. No odor, no visible smoke trail."

I eyed the canister dubiously. It didn't look pro.

"You sure this will work?"

"Are you sure you want to do this at all?" she asked in return. "Because this is your idea, and I'm willing to bail out right now."

"What about cameras and their tappers?"

"They'll be blanked out. That's the best I could do."

I sighed. "No way you could record some kind of fake squid attack?"

"No," she snorted. "Not unless you give me a studio and a week to work it up. Besides, who would believe the squids did this?"

"No one," I admitted. "Well, that's it. Let's roll, people. Black it out, Natasha."

She licked her lips and studied a tiny screen. "You sure you want to do this, James? Really sure?"

"Oh yeah," Carlos said. "He's sure. If it's dangerous, insane and just plain wrong—McGill's your man."

Natasha reached up and activated a script. Moments later the lights in the passageway went dark, and I started to run.

We burst in on the tactical ops people two seconds after we'd rolled the canisters in. They were mostly unconscious, but one of them stared at me from on his knees, grabbing the console with both hands like a drowning man. Then he toppled onto the floor and sprawled onto his back, out cold.

"I thought you said this stuff was instantaneous!" I complained. "That guy saw me, I'm sure he did."

"I did the best I could," Natasha said.

"Not good enough."

"Let's call the whole thing off," Carlos suggested.

I stood there in the room. Wisps of vapor drifted toward the vents overhead. The gas the small canisters had released wasn't as invisible as Natasha had said it would be, either. For a sick second I wondered what would happen if it filled *Minotaur* and knocked people out all over the ship. Anything seemed possible at this moment.

"No," I said firmly. "Natasha, try to delete their minds one minute back. Carlos, help me with the controls."

I pulled out the Galactic key and approached the console.

"James, fooling with their memory backups is dangerous. We could purge months, or even years. Besides, that won't help unless we kill them. You know that, don't you?"

"Yeah," I said. "Just do it."

Carlos made a sound of pain and worry, but he didn't say anything. That had to be some kind of a first for him.

I approached the console and punched in the coordinates that Natasha had worked out. Outside, the huge cylindrical barrels of *Minotaur's* broadsides began to move, swiveling and locking onto their new target—the squid ship.

-41-

You'd think that after all I'd been through with the squids, launching a surprise attack on their ship would be an easy thing to do—but it wasn't.

I'm not totally stupid. I knew I was pretty much starting an interstellar war. But I took solace in the fact that the squids had started this whole thing—or maybe that the Galactics had. Either way, it wasn't Earth men who had launched the first attack. Squids had been abusing our colonists on Zeta Herculis for decades. They'd also attacked the Galactics and taken out *Corvus* back in the middle of our last campaign.

In turn, it was the Galactics that had melted their colony world to component organic molecules. None of those actions had been initiated by my people—but we were making our first move, right now.

As soon as the broadsides had swung around and locked, I hit the ignition touch area on the console. The firing process began, but rather than a roaring sound, an alarm rang. The console lit up with warning lights and flashing orange failure messages.

"What's wrong?" I shouted.

"You have to close the blast shields over the windows first, or we'll be killed in the back-blast."

"Right," I said, slamming a physical switch home. The shields began to roll swiftly over the windows, blocking my view of the planet and the station.

"Let's get out of here," I said. "The guns will fire the second the shields are down."

We ran like we'd never run before. We were three ghosts in sleek suits, and we made it a hundred meters or so before the broadsides boomed.

I was tossed onto the deck by the reverberation. One second the floor had been two meters under my feet then it seemed to buck up and slam into my face. I climbed to my feet painfully.

Carlos hooked a hand under my armpit and hauled me up. "No napping now, McGill," he grunted, propelling me forward.

On my feet and staggering, I broke into a shambling run again. The plan at this point was relatively simple. We'd take the back passages to our unit module and stretch out on our bunks. The vid-blockers Natasha had set up would expire, and we'd appear as innocent as the day was long.

The plan almost worked, too. Sure, there were klaxons going off, and Natasha was summoned to join the tech brigade investigating what kind of malfunction had occurred, but for about three minutes, Carlos and I actually got to lie there in our bunks.

We fought to control our breathing and contrived to shape our faces into a semblance of innocence.

"McGill?" Carlos whispered down to me.

"What?"

"Hey, you owe me. Right? You know that, don't you?"

"Yeah, I guess I do."

"Good, here's what I want you to do."

I rolled my eyes. Apparently, he'd already worked out what form of repayment he wanted on our newly established debt.

"First," he said, "when this all goes tits-up—which I totally know it's going to do—leave me out of the story, okay?"

I thought about it, and shrugged. "Sure thing," I said. "I did this whole thing solo. They can perm me, but I won't budge from that story."

"Good man. Secondly—"

"For crying out loud, isn't that good enough?" I demanded.

"Hold on, the second thing is easy! Just tell me how it was with Turov. I mean, is she as hot as she looks? Is she a screamer?"

I rolled my eyes. "She brings the house down, Carlos. Every time."

"Ha! I knew it."

"You happy now?'

"Actually, there is one more—"

I never heard what his third demand was because at that moment the door tore apart.

If you've never been in a quiet room when the door is literally torn off the hinges, you can't know just how shocking it can be. One second, we were talking quietly in our bunks, pretending innocence. The metal door squealed and crumpled being pulled outward like tinfoil.

There in the doorway stood a nightmare that was worse than any squid that had ever lived. It was a battle suit—a monstrosity of metal claws and whining servos. Worse, I knew the face behind the visor, the being who was driving the metal terror. I'd seen her in this battle suit before, and I knew what it could do.

Imperator Turov was young and pretty, but her face was twisted into such a state of rage that I barely recognized her. Shouldering her way inside the small chamber, she dented up the framing bulkhead, and dropped the hatch itself which was still clenched in one gripper.

"Imperator?" I shouted, jumping to my feet and standing at attention.

Carlos followed my cue and did the same thing. He looked like he was about to pee himself, and I probably wore the same expression.

"McGill..." she said, rotating the battle suit's upper body back and forth. "McGill and Ortiz. Is that it? Where are the others? You don't have the brains to do this by yourselves."

"Sorry sir?" I said. "Has something gone wrong?"

She hissed at me. She honest-to-God let loose a hiss of displeasure.

"Are you going to bullshit me, NOW?" she demanded. "Are you honestly going to give that a try at this point?"

343

The volume of her external microphone had been cranked up punishingly high, and I winced as her words washed over me. They had a slightly muffled sound to them as she was inside an enclosed environment.

I faced the machine resolutely. Standing a hair taller than me in her suit, she looked down with predatory anger. The suit's balancing tail-section swerved and twisted in reaction to her every motion.

Carlos, up until this point, had said nothing. "Sir," he said at last, "whatever McGill has done, sir, I wasn't involved. I apologize for sharing a room with him, but I don't think it would be fair to—"

He broke off as Turov had thrust a gripper in his direction. It flexed and snapped closed. Blood shot out as if a balloon full of red liquid had popped. Carlos' head had been snipped off. Just like that. I stared dumbly at the floor where his eyes stared back. Those eyes were flung wide and possibly appeared even more surprised than I was.

Turov bent over the head and spoke to it. "If you can still hear me, Ortiz," she said. "I accept your apology."

I thought about attacking her then, but I knew it was hopeless. In fact, such a move might provoke a second beheading. I stood at attention and averted my eyes from the mess on the floor.

Turov turned her attention back to me. The servos in her suit whined as she leaned the suit's jaws close to my face.

"Why did you do it, McGill? Why did you blast the squid ship to atoms?"

Despite everything, I felt a rush of relief. After all, I'd never actually witnessed the broadside salvo striking the squid ship and taking it out. Now I knew that, even if I died today for the final time, it had not all been in vain.

I looked at her, square in the eye.

"Because we're already at war with the squids, Imperator," I said. "There's no point in denying it. Did you really think they'd be satisfied with looting Tech World? No way. Giving them an easy victory would only cause them to report back that we're weak and ripe for an attack. More of their ships would come. At that point, Earth would be faced with war anyway. This way, we struck the first blow."

"Such decisions aren't yours to make, McGill! You're only a frigging *specialist!*"

"You're right about that, sir," I said. "I know I went beyond the bounds."

Turov began to pace around me in a tight circle. The heavy metal feet of her machine crumped close to mine threatening to crush my bones and pop my toes.

"I don't even understand *how* you did it," she fumed. "How could you have convinced the broadside crew to fire their weapons? They aren't even your friends."

I glanced at her realizing she had that part of the story wrong.

"I guess my arguments persuaded everyone except for you, sir," I said.

"That's the conclusion I came to—as incredible as it seems. The crewmen said they'd been knocked out or some such nonsense, but I know how this ship operates. They *had* to operate the controls personally. The system is linked to their biometrics."

I nodded thoughtfully. "What did they say when you pointed this out, sir?"

"They tried to bullshit me, so I killed them both."

She reached out a gripper and snapped it several times in front of my face. A tiny splatter of blood and gore flew. I thought I saw dark strands of hair there—they probably belonged to Carlos, but I could be looking at the remains of the gunnery crew. It was hard to say.

"What are your orders, sir?" I asked, returning my eyes to front and center.

Turov circled around me one more time.

"I have to think," she said at last, "and it is difficult to think clearly with you standing here in front of me. You distract me, McGill. You always have."

I wasn't sure how to take that, and I opened my mouth to make a polite reply—but then she took radical action.

There was a sudden movement followed by a loud snapping sound. I was never sure afterward if the last sound I heard had been my spine breaking or the clacking together of the pinchers as they closed shut after passing through my neck and striking one another.

The results were the same either way. I collapsed onto the deck in two pieces—and died.

* * *

How many times have I died in the service of Legion Varus and mankind in general? I don't know—I think I've lost count. Or maybe I don't want to remember. Just thinking about it makes me feel a little sick.

This time around I became aware again beginning with a sharp pain. The pain was in my ribs, on my right side. The pain repeated itself.

When you first regain consciousness after a death, it's like waking from a dream. Your mind isn't all there instantly. So it was today as what my senses were telling me *couldn't* be happening.

Someone was stomping on my chest. Crashing their foot down onto my ribs like they were trying to kill a rat.

My hearing came into tune next. There was someone else here—a female. She was talking, egging on the rat-stomper.

"Do it, Carlos. Put him back into the wood-chipper thing!"

Kivi. That voice had to be Kivi's. I'd recognize her accent anywhere.

"Kivi?" I called weakly. I put my hands up to stop the stomping, but it shifted toward my face.

"I'm going to do his throat," Carlos said. "I'm going to! He deserves it. Let the next version of him apologize."

"If you kill him fast enough," said Kivi, and her voice dripping venom, "he'll never remember any of this."

My strength was returning. Following an instinct, I shifted my hands up to cover my throat. If they crushed my larynx— well, it would be all over. I'd suffocate.

I had just enough in me to grab that bare foot and twist it when it came down the next time. Carlos cursed and crashed to the deck. I followed up my foot-twist with a kick. It landed but wasn't enough to put him out. He crawled away.

Struggling to one elbow and wiping goo from my eyes, I took a quick, wild look around.

Kivi was crouching over me. She had a blade in her hand—a scalpel. My eyes flicked around the room. There was one more body here besides Carlos. It had to be Anne Grant.

That made me angry. I reached for Kivi's wrist, and got a long cut drawn down my arm as a reward.

"What's wrong with you?" I demanded, sitting up.

She took a combat stance. I waited for her next attack. I thought I could defend myself from the ground if I had to, but if she attacked when I stood up and was off-balance—well, that glittering blade would be rammed into my guts.

Carlos climbed back to his feet. I realized we were all three naked. We'd been revived and left without clothing or gear. I quickly began to figure out the sequence of events even though it was difficult to get my brand new brain functioning.

"Let me guess," I said. "They revived us and strapped us down as we came out. One of you broke free and killed Anne. Are you two proud of that?"

"I am," said Kivi with more than the usual level of snarl in her tone. She'd always had a short fuse and an emotional take on life. She could be your best friend and your worst enemy—maybe both at the same time.

"What did Anne ever do to you?" I demanded.

"She brought me back to life to stand trial, that's what."

I squinted at her then looked at Carlos. "Trial?"

"That's it, buddy. We're all dead. We're all as good as permed thanks to your insanely stupid plan. I want you to think about that before we kill you right now for revenge. I want you to own it."

I got up slowly—and Kivi lunged. She knew she didn't want me on my feet. Fortunately, I'd expected her to do that. I rolled back and threw a big, size-thirteen foot into her face stopping her dead in her tracks.

Another cut appeared along my calf, but Kivi was down and the scalpel clattered on the deck. Carlos dove for it, and I landed on top of him. I put a knee into his kidney and pinned him, wresting the blade free.

Kivi was up and circling, eyes wild, looking for another weapon. I kept Carlos pinned. My blood ran down from my arm and my leg, splattering all over his back.

"I should kill both of you clowns, right here, right now," I said, my sides heaving.

"Do it!" Carlos said from the floor. "It won't make any difference. We're all screwed."

"Then maybe we should be figuring a way out of our situation rather than fighting amongst ourselves. Turov is probably recording this and sipping a martini right now. Maybe this was her plan all along. Let's keep going—wouldn't want to disappoint."

Kivi frowned and looked around at the walls, which might very well have cameras. They were everywhere these days, and the low-res models were no bigger than a needle.

"Let him up," Kivi said, gesturing toward Carlos.

"You promise not to try killing me?" I asked Carlos.

"Sure," he said. "Why not? If you can get us out of this, McGill, I'll clean your kit for a year. And Kivi—well, she'll warm your bed for a year, no charge. Won't you, girl?"

She kicked him, and I didn't interfere. He deserved it. He always did.

I got up off Carlos' back and he struggled to his feet.

"You're bleeding bad," Kivi said to me.

"*Now* you care?" I asked incredulously. I found a skin-printer and ran the wand over my injuries.

"Do you really have a plan?" Kivi asked. Her eyes were desperate.

So odd, I thought. She'd been hell-bent on cutting me a minute ago. I took a second to reflect on just how dying all the time could twist a person's mind. We were effectively immortal—but that only made us fear the process of death more because we knew what it was really like. At the same time, we'd become callous about the lives of others and terrified of getting ourselves permed. Now that perma-death was a very real possibility—even a *probability*—all semblance of civilized behavior had been stripped away.

348

"People," I said, "we have to pull it together. Where's Natasha? Did they catch her too?"

Kivi slapped me. "Always thinking about your women! All of them except for me, that is. I wasn't even involved in your scheme and Turov didn't believe me. She came into my room and murdered me. She clipped off my arms and legs first. My head was the last to go."

I thought I saw a single tear welling up in her left eye. That was unusual and significant. Turov must have made it traumatic if Kivi was even close to crying.

"Forget all that," I said. "Forget about Turov. I'm asking about Natasha because she's the only one that can help us."

"Then we're screwed, big guy," Carlos said. "She was arrested too. I don't know what they charged her with, but I can guess."

The revival machine burbled then. We all looked at it. Kivi's lip curled.

"Who do you think...?" she asked.

We approached the machine, and I worked open the jaws. There were feet in there—female feet. I pulled Natasha out and revived her as gently as I could.

"Good," said Kivi. "She deserves to join us. I'm the only one who shouldn't be here."

"Kivi," I said, nursing Natasha who was groggy and feeble, "I'll tell Turov that. I'm not sure she'll believe me, but I'll tell her at the trial."

"There's going to be a trial?" Natasha asked weakly.

I felt a wave of regret. Sure, I'd blown away the squid ship and saved the Tau and their station, but my friends and I had paid a grim price and it was about to get worse.

When the hatch finally rattled, I stood close to the door. Carlos moved like a spider poising himself behind the door, but I waved him away. That wasn't going to work.

Sure enough, three heavies in full armor strode in. They plucked Carlos out of his hiding place like he was bug on the wall. They gave us clothes at least, but no weapons. We had nothing but thin cloth.

We were marched down a long passageway. I hadn't remembered the passage being this long before. As we passed a viewport, I glanced outside.

Tech World was gone. Instead, stars glided by. I knew the image was projected, not actual. We were in warp, and the viewport was only reporting to our eyes what we would have seen if mere vision could have penetrated an Alcubierre warp-bubble—which it couldn't.

When we got to the command module, Kivi, Natasha and Carlos were left manacled in the waiting area. At least they had comfortable seats.

I was ushered into the next room. As the ringleader, I guessed I was going to stand trial first.

-42-

Imperator Turov gave me a little smile as I entered her office. I could tell she was looking forward to the trial. I reflected that maybe she was happy about the situation. After all, she'd been trying to get me permed legitimately almost since we'd first met. What a cold witch she was! We'd had two bouts of passion recently, but none of that seemed to be impinging on her now.

Tribune Drusus was there, but he didn't look at me. Tribune Armel arrived a moment later. He had a drink in his hand, and somehow I knew it wasn't iced tea.

"Here he is," Armel said with an odd smile. "The famous James McGill. The man who embodies Legion Varus with his roguish charm."

"Shut up, Armel," Turov said in a mild tone of voice. "This is a trial. I demand decorum."

"Right you are, sir," he said, finding a chair and sinking into it. He took a long slurping drink from his glass and eyed everyone expectantly.

"Let us begin," Turov said seriously. She took a seat as well.

For my part, I stood at attention facing the three of them. I stared over their heads, studying the wall. My face was as expressionless as I could make it.

"Specialist James McGill," Turov said slowly. "Where did we go wrong with you?"

I wasn't sure if I was expected to answer, but I did anyway. If man can't talk when he's on trial for his life, well, there's no justice in the universe.

"Legion Varus wanted me, sir," I said. "They saw my psych profiles. It's all there. No one should be surprised."

Drusus leaned forward. "It's one thing to see a number on a chart, McGill, and another to have one of your enlisted men mutiny and start an interstellar war."

As nothing had been asked, I made no reply.

Armel shook his head suddenly and gave a bray of laughter. He was mildly drunk, I could see that now. He rattled his glass and the ice cubes chased one another around in a swirling circle.

"You should give this man a medal!" he said exuberantly. "He's right—he's the poster-child for your entire outfit, Drusus."

"Give it a rest, Armel," Drusus retorted. "If it wasn't for Varus, you'd have been out of a job by now. Earth would be toast. You know that."

"Ha! Fantasies! Hegemony gives you shit-work and tells you how important you are. Haven't you ever considered the idea that anyone could do these 'critical' missions? That they're left to your misfits precisely because no one else wants to experience whatever meat-grinder planet you'll been assigned to next?"

Drusus' face darkened and he began to stand, but Turov waved him back down. She'd been smugly watching the interchange up until this point, but now she seemed to have grown tired of the show.

"That's enough," she said. "We've talked for nearly two hours, gentlemen. The time has come to make a decision. What is to be done with the defendant? You've had plenty of time to come to a conclusion. How do you vote?"

This statement caught me by surprise. I flicked my eyes downward and scanned each face. Drusus and Armel were looking at each other, Drusus was angry while Armel was amused. Turov, for her part, was staring right at me. That look—it made me uncomfortable.

Tribune Armel was all smiles. "Guilty!" he said, leaning forward and swilling down the last of his drink. "Perm him— you really should have done it ages ago, my fellow officers. I can't comprehend why you didn't take appropriate action after previous abuses. Now is a fresh opportunity to correct your past errors."

Armel's vote wasn't really a surprise to me. My eyes slid to meet those of Drusus. He was my best hope.

Tribune Drusus heaved a sigh. "I've been hoping for years it wouldn't come down to something like this," he said. "But I'm afraid I have to agree with my colleague this time. James, you've gone too far. We can't allow people to take policy into their own hands. Surely you can see that?"

I didn't know what to say. I liked Drusus, and I could see that his decision pained him. Maybe he liked me just a little as well.

"I put you in a bad spot, sir," I said. "I know that. But I believed then as I believe now that we're going to have to fight the squids sooner or later. They're bullies, sir. To show weakness to their kind will only invite further attacks. Regardless of how you people judge me, history will tell the truth."

"A philosopher!" shouted Armel suddenly. "A prognosticator! A seer of the future! Drusus, really, you shouldn't have hidden this gem for so long. So good of you to share him with us at last."

Drusus cast Armel a venomous glance.

I found Armel's behavior annoying but also baffling. The Tribune wasn't acting his age. He had to know that the situation was a serious one. Maybe getting loaded, taunting Drusus and perming me was his way of coping with the magnitude of what was occurring in this star system.

All eyes now fell upon the Imperator. As the commanding officer in the system, she could veto the execution—or go along with the verdict and order me permed.

"Gentlemen," she said, standing up, "please leave me with the accused for a moment, will you?"

This caused a general look of surprise from the Tribunes.

353

"Imperator?" Drusus asked. "Are you sure that's a good idea? The accused has been known to turn violent under similar circumstances."

Turov touched her sidearm confidently. "I think I'll be fine. Do you really think he could kill me?"

"Frankly...yes," Drusus said.

Turov frowned. "Get out."

They hesitated, but only for a second.

On his way past me to the door, Armel gave me a wink and suggestive twitch of the lips, as if he suspected I might well be kissing Turov in his absence. I wanted to punch him or at least flip him off, but I did neither. I was in enough trouble as it was. And besides, I had to admit that if romance was what Turov had in mind, she was going to have her way with me today.

When the two of us were alone, the Imperator immediately came to the point. She opened her top desk drawer and lifted the Galactic key in her hand. The iridescent shell-shaped object was placed on her desk where the screen glowed around it. Usually, desk computers would helpfully identify and connect with any technological gizmo you put on them, but not this time. The desk glowed, but only a question mark in a bubble appeared beside it.

"What is this, James?"

I eyed the invaluable object. My expression indicated vague interest on my part.

"That is a trick cigarette lighter, sir," I said. "It's difficult to operate with a human hand, but if you give it to me I'll show you how."

She blew air through her lips and rolled her eyes. "I will do no such thing. You will explain this artifact and how it functions. I want to know what role it played in your scheme."

For the first time since my current body had been born, my lips curved up into a smile. It wasn't a broad grin—but it was definitely a smile.

"What's it worth to you, sir? As a condemned man..."

"You aren't condemned yet. But as your every word is annoying me further, you're getting closer to that goal."

We stared at one another for several seconds, at an impasse.

"Fine," she snapped, reaching out with a finger toward her desktop. "I will summon Natasha Elkin. She will be slaughtered here on my carpet. I will then revive her and ask her about the artifact again. If she doesn't answer to my satisfaction, I'll repeat the process until we make planetfall over Earth."

I frowned. "Why don't you try that with me, sir?"

"Because I don't think it would work. At least, not as quickly as it will with Specialist Elkin."

I sighed. "All right," I said. "But you have to leave the others out of this. They weren't responsible—I was. Hell, Kivi didn't even know what we were up to."

"Really?" she said thoughtfully. "Then I made a miscalculation in her case. I didn't think you could pull off something so elaborate without the help of all your comrades."

"It wasn't all that elaborate."

"Yes, it was. You essentially took command of our weapons systems and managed to hit a target of your choosing. Not only did you hit it, you destroyed it."

"I'm a weaponeer, sir. Legion Varus has trained me well."

She nudged the key on her desktop. "What does it do?"

"Are you voting to perm me or not?"

"That depends entirely on your answer."

Chewing that over for a few seconds, I pondered my options. There weren't many. I could try to jump her, but she was on the far side of a big desk. All she had to do was pull out her sidearm and fire a single shot. Even a representative of Hegemony brass should be capable of doing that much.

"First, I want some assurances," I said. "I want my friends let off the hook—not just me."

"Fine—if this item is worth anything."

"It is, don't worry."

"So what is it, damn you? How did you pull off all these tricks?"

"No trickery was involved," I said. "The magic was all technological. This item is what's known as a Galactic key."

I went on for a few minutes to explain the key's purpose and operation. As I spoke, Turov's eyes widened.

355

"I don't believe it," she said, picking up the object and turning it slowly in her hands. "This explains so much... I must admit I'm in your debt for having brought it to me."

I frowned. "It's mine, sir."

"No it isn't. This item belongs to me now. You will also maintain full secrecy as to the nature of it—even its existence. In return, I'll stay your sentence and pardon your friends. Further, as your entire scheme was my idea originally, I'll promote you to candidacy for Veteran as a reward for having executed my plans flawlessly."

My eyes squinted into two narrow lines. "What? *Your* idea, sir?"

"That's right. You followed my orders. You succeeded in a clandestine mission. You aren't authorized to talk about it further with any other persons. Are these conditions clear?"

My face twisted up in disgust, but I quickly saw the advantages of her offer.

"I accept your terms, sir," I said. "And I hope you're happy with the way I executed your brilliant plan."

Turov was barely listening to me. She had the shell-like key in her hands, and she was turning it this way and that, gazing at it from every angle as if it were made of the purest diamond.

"Yes," she said. "I'm happy with you, James. Very happy indeed."

-43-

Graves chuckled. "You lucked out, McGill. Do you have any idea what kind of spot you put the Imperator in? She *had* to say it was her idea. How would this have looked back at Hegemony otherwise? What if they heard that some specialist managed to start a war while she was in command? What do you think the brass would have to say about that?"

"Nothing good I'm sure, sir."

"That's right. Her new pretty ass would be in a sling, and her recent promotion would be history. This way, she can make it look like the squids attacked the station and she decided to fire on them. A reasonable course of action a commander might have been forced to take—but not our Turov. She doesn't like to get into something she doesn't know how to win."

I thought about it, and I had to agree with Graves. At first I'd thought maybe she was sweet on me—but I'd since rejected that possibility. She hadn't vetoed my execution for my sake. She'd done it to save her own skin.

I couldn't help but compare her behavior now with the way she'd acted when she'd first been reborn. When I'd first helped her out of the revival she'd been all young and smooth-skinned to start with. But Natasha had been right, within a few days the Imperator had returned to her old ways. She was still young-looking on the outside, but in her heart there lurked the scheming rank-climber she'd become later in life.

"There's another thing," Graves said. "She wanted the video of her blaming you for everything at that trial. She's keeping that vid just in case."

"In case of what, sir?" I heard myself asking.

"Insurance. If the Nairbs eventually show up and want to know what the hell happened out here, she'll show them the vid file. You'll have the starring role. The renegade McGill was caught and executed. Case closed."

I nodded. "And since we all look pretty much the same to them, we should get away with it. I mean—they wouldn't have to actually execute me. The Nairbs won't know the difference."

"Yeah, sure," Graves said with amusement. "You'll be fine when that day comes."

I frowned as I didn't think he was being sincere. Great. Now I knew of another way for me to die in the future.

Graves cleared his throat and rattled a computer scroll. He smoothed it out flat and put his sidearm on one edge to hold it down.

"These new computer scrolls the Tau sold us are thinner, but they won't lie flat," he complained.

"I wonder if they're knock-offs," I said. "I suspect a lot of their goods are illegal copies."

He looked at me sharply then shook his head. "Forget you ever had that thought, Specialist."

"Consider it forgotten, sir."

"Good… Ah," said Graves suddenly, shaking his computer scroll flat again. "I see one more thing." Working his tapper, he summoned Veteran Harris.

"What now, Centurion?" I asked.

Graves waved for me to be quiet. I felt uncomfortable as Veteran Harris responded to the call and entered the room. Harris looked me over with disdain, while I avoided his gaze.

"Is this man bothering you, sir?" Harris demanded.

"I'm not a school girl in a city park," Graves laughed. "But yes, McGill always bothers me."

"I feel the same way," Harris said.

"Then I'm going to make you happy. Veteran Harris, I hold here a warrant for McGill's arrest, signed by Tribune Armel himself."

Harris' eyes lit up. *What a bastard,* I thought.

"What are the charges, sir?" Harris asked eagerly.

"Sedition. Acts unbecoming. Assaulting superiors from another legion. There's quite a list, here."

"I knew it!" Harris said, staring at me like a dog watching a hamburger. "I knew you'd blow it! Germanica doesn't put up with your kind of crap. They're fancy-boys, every last one of them—but they play it by the rules, you have to give them that."

"That might be the first and only time I've ever heard you praise Germanica," Graves remarked.

"A man has to give credit where credit is due."

"Well said. Veteran Harris, place Specialist James McGill under arrest."

Warily, Harris approached me and snatched away my sidearm. I thought about fighting with him, I really did. But something told me I had a better way to play my cards. If I went to the Imperator, maybe she could get me out of this. After all, we had a deal.

Harris was grinning at me like a kid on Christmas morning.

"All right," Graves said, heaving a weary sigh. "Specialist McGill has now been placed under arrest."

He lifted his tapper and began recording. He took vid of me standing there with Harris at my side pointing a gun at me.

"I'm performing an inquiry," Graves said. "McGill, did you cause the death of Germanica troops during our short stay on Tech World?"

"Uh—probably, sir."

"I'll take that as a confession. Did you disobey the direct orders of higher ranked Germanica legionnaires?"

"Sir, I worked with those people. I saved their sorry butts. If it wasn't for me, they'd all be permed."

Graves waved away my words as if they stank. "Yes or no will do."

I sighed. "Yes, I suppose I did that."

"And lastly, did you collaborate with one Adjunct Claver of Germanica to perform treasonous acts?"

Bristling, I shook my head. "That doesn't make any sense, sir. First, they claim I disobeyed the orders of one of their officers then they say I'm in trouble for obeying the orders of another?"

"Just answer the question, McGill," Graves asked in a bored voice.

"Yeah, sure," I said. "I followed Claver's orders. You sent me on the mission yourself!"

Graves glanced at me in irritation. He worked on his tapper, editing the recording. The absurd questioning was beginning to get to me. I began to feel a burning sensation around my neck.

"I'm cutting out that last sentence," Graves said. "Please keep your remarks to the point. Last question: did you or did you not assault and personally murder Adjunct Claver?"

My jaw clenched, but I managed to answer evenly. "Yes," I said. "I did kill that weaseling bastard. They should be glad I did it, too. He created the entire disaster on the megahab and caused the deaths of over a million of civilian."

"Well said," Graves muttered. "All right then, based on the evidence and your confessions, I find you guilty. I sentence you to imprisonment without appeal for an indefinite period. The manacles, Veteran Harris."

Harris' hands shook as he handed over the manacles. I put them on after he pointed his gun into my face.

"Excellent," Graves said. "Hold those a little higher will you, McGill?"

I did as he asked, but I didn't know why I was cooperating any longer. This was bullshit.

"Sir," I said. "I've done plenty that was off-script on this mission."

Harris and Graves shared a dirty laugh over that.

"You're a master of the art of understatement," Graves said.

"But sir, I don't think this punishment is just. How can you lock me up and leave me to rot? I'd rather be permed."

Harris perked up and he lifted his gun meaningfully. "Maybe we should listen to his plea, Centurion."

Graves looked at his tapper. "Hold on."

"Sir?"

He waved a finger to silence me, still staring at his tapper.

I heaved a sigh and stood there, baffled.

"One full minute has passed," Graves announced at last, lowering his arm. "All right. Release him, Harris."

"What?" demanded Harris.

"Did you not hear me pronounce the sentence?" Graves asked calmly. "I said I'd sentenced McGill to imprisonment for an undetermined amount of time. I've decided since then that his sentence is complete, and I've released him."

"One minute?" asked Harris, aghast.

Graves motioned for Harris to get on with releasing me, and I lifted the manacles toward him helpfully. Harris grumbled curses, but he unlocked my wrists.

"Thank you, Veteran," I said. "I'm sure I learned my lesson today."

Harris rolled his eyes. Graves dismissed him, but he had me stay behind.

"Now, to our last order of business," Graves said. "You've been promoted to candidacy for the rank of Veteran by the Imperator. Are you aware of that?"

"I am."

Graves nodded and eyed me in speculation. "I never would have thought you'd be so good at horse-trading. I can only imagine what you held over her head to get this perk on top of everything else."

He grinned at me briefly, while I pretended not to get his implication. Without letting on, I found I was pleased by Graves' assumptions. If people thought I'd promised to keep my mouth shut about Turov's transgressions with an enlisted man in trade for rank—well, that was better than having them know the truth. No one needed to know about the Galactic key.

"Harris isn't going to like this," Graves said. "In fact, I wouldn't give you the best odds of passing the trials. But, you've got the Imperator behind you—what can I do? I'll sign it."

Frowning, I nodded as if I understood—but I didn't. Not really. What I did know was that getting to the rank of Veteran in Legion Varus wasn't completely straightforward. The commanders announced new candidates for the rank of Veteran, but that alone didn't guarantee the promotion. Each candidate had to prove himself to the other Veterans in the

361

cohort first. The exact nature of the process was somewhat arcane and shrouded in secrecy. What I did know was that a lot of it depended on a man's popularity with the other Veterans. Unfortunately, the Veteran I knew best downright hated me.

"You have the right to turn down this promotion to candidacy," Graves said, looking at me expectantly.

For an honest second, I considered exercising my option of refusal. But then I felt a spark of anger. Harris had been so greedy to see me dead or imprisoned, and I knew there was hardly anything I could do that would piss him off more than gaining the rank of Veteran.

"I accept the promotion, sir," I said formally.

Graves shrugged. "Your funeral. Dismissed, Specialist."

Wondering about the nature of my future, I left his office and returned to my quarters.

* * *

We arrived on Earth several days later. Our mission had radically altered over the course of the campaign, and it had been decided that leaving Tech World early was the best option.

Going home solved many of our problems. Both legions Varus and Germanica had suffered crippling losses. Worse, due to the loss of all but one of our revival units, we weren't able to rebuild our strength. By going home, we could regrow every trooper within a few days. Hegemony could then decide if they wanted to send us back or utilize our skills in some other capacity.

When *Minotaur* came out of its warp bubble and glided close to Earth, I gazed through a viewport thoughtfully. I wondered how long I would have here at home before I was shipped off to war again.

For the first time, I had another thought in the back of my mind. What if the war followed me to here? What if Earth was the next battleground?

The thought was disturbing because I didn't think we could beat the squids if they launched a full-out attack—not yet. Maybe not ever.

* * *

A month later, I was back at home in my shed. Things had improved around the homestead. Even though I was only a Veteran candidate, my pay had increased. I'd also collected my higher active-duty pay, and for once I had a good deal of cash on my hands.

Spending a few credits on extras, I bought a real environmental control unit. It was one of the new models that gently conditioned the air to whatever temperature, humidity, or even barometric pressure you wanted inside your home. It even had settable oxygen levels—and I found I liked mine just a little bit on the high side. It was an alien device, naturally, but it worked like a charm. Fall was setting in, with the cool breath of winter coming in on the wind behind it. I knew that even if it snowed I'd always be comfortable in my place.

Natasha showed up one night in November. It was cold outside, but warm and perfect in my shed. She came in when I invited her and marveled at the change.

"This is so different from the last time I visited here," she said.

"Yeah, I even cleaned all the bloodstains off the walls."

She gave me a wry face. "Don't spoil it."

"Sorry."

She looked down at her hands for a second which were fidgeting with one another. Still looking down, she began to speak. "James...James, I came to tell you I'm sorry."

This surprised me. *Really* surprised me. Of all the stuff I was expecting this girl to throw into my face, an apology had to be dead last on a very long list.

My mouth opened a tiny fraction, but I clamped it shut again. Under no circumstances was I going to screw this up.

She looked at me, and I looked back at her with a blank poker face. I honestly didn't know what else to do.

363

She looked down again, and I was off the hook. "I've been studying these cases—ones like yours, I mean. I've read up on them. Sexual predators come in all shapes and sizes, James. I know that now. I didn't understand before."

I wanted to say something. I wanted to choke or even laugh out loud. But I didn't, and I was proud of my self-control.

"Turov was your superior. You were taken advantage of. That's how I understand it, and I want you to accept my apology for getting angry with you about sleeping with her."

"Okay…" I said. I felt I had to say something.

She gave me a little kiss then grabbed me by the chin. "But don't go back to her. Not if you want to ever be with me again. I hate that woman. She's a monster. Do you understand me?"

I nodded. "Yeah…look, Natasha…"

"What?"

What was I going to say next? That I'd been as guilty of any transgressions as Turov had? That blaming it all on the officer was bullshit in my book?

I couldn't do it. Instead I hugged her, and I poured her a glass of wine. It was perfectly chilled, due to the precision-engineering of my new alien-made fridge. The old one had never recovered after taking a bullet months ago.

Sitting with Natasha again, I handed her the wine and we chatted about light things for a time. Finally, the subject of the squids came up. The topic never seemed to be far from anyone's mind these days.

"Do you think they'll come *here*, James?" she asked me almost in a whisper. "They might, you know. They know what we did."

"Are you sure? We blew their ship up in a single salvo."

She shook her head. "I'm a tech, remember? We went over all the radio signals while we were stabilizing the megahab. They got off a packet of data with a powerful transmitter. They sent it on a tight beam toward the rim of the Galaxy. Somewhere out past the edge of the frontier."

I frowned. "You think it was an SOS?"

"What else could it have been?"

"Hegemony knows about that, right?"

She pursed her lips at me. "Of course."

364

"I'm just asking because I haven't heard anything on the net."

"They're not talking about it on the online reports, naturally. There's no benefit to causing a panic."

A panic. The words rang in my mind. Natasha was right—if the people of Earth knew the real score—that unknown worlds full of Cephalopods were out there and enraged with us... If they knew that Battle Fleet 921 was gone and not scheduled to return... Yes, they'd panic all right.

"Did we do the right thing, James?" Natasha asked me in a small voice.

I looked down at her. I could tell she was freaking out. It was true we'd taken it upon ourselves to blast the squids. Sure, Turov was taking the credit and was now doing a talk-show circuit—her new looks were helping her there. But it had been Natasha, Carlos and I who'd pulled the trigger on this new war.

"Absolutely," I said, putting my arm around her and pulling her close. "We didn't have any choice, really. They were bullying Earth, and we punched them in the face. They'll think twice before they come after us again."

Natasha seemed happier, but I wasn't sure she bought my bullshit. Hell, I didn't even buy all of it.

We sipped our wine until the bottle was empty and fell asleep together on my couch. Alien air pumps wheezed and thrummed softly. Somehow, it was a comforting sound.

The End

More Books by B. V. Larson:

UNDYING MERCENARIES
Steel World
Dust World
Tech World

STAR FORCE SERIES
Swarm
Extinction
Rebellion
Conquest
Battle Station
Empire
Annihilation
Storm Assault
The Dead Sun
Outcast

OTHER SF BOOKS
Technomancer
The Bone Triangle
Z-World
Velocity

Visit BVLarson.com for more information.

52471323R00205

Made in the USA
Lexington, KY
14 September 2019